FLYING THE MOUNTAIN ROUTE

The dragons stormed out of the clouds like gulls.

Jael stared into the moonlit night in astonishment. Dragons! Dreadful winged shapes, sparks of red flame flickering about them. Jael could scarcely believe it. Dragons were something from fairy tales and primal dreams, from lies fabricated by boastful riggers. But . . . *there were dragons* in the sky right now.

They grew in the moonlight: rugged creatures breathing fire into the air. One swooped close to her spaceship, startling her. Its eyes shone ghostly green.

She shivered, wishing she had flown another way.

Are you afraid? she heard. *Shall we be kind, and kill you quickly . . . ?*

Jael gaped. *Then it's true! You dragons . . . are real!*

The dragon made a noise that might have been a sigh or a snarl. *Of course! Now duel, rigger!* It climbed high above her; then, dropping one wing, it dived. It bore down upon her in the moonlight, its massive shape growing large, larger . . .

Jael screamed.

BOOKS BY JEFFREY A. CARVER

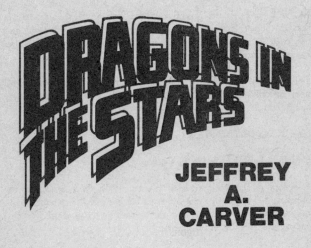

DRAGONS IN THE STARS

JEFFREY A. CARVER

A TOM DOHERTY ASSOCIATES BOOK
NEW YORK

This is a work of fiction. All the characters and events portrayed in this book are fictitious, and any resemblance to real people or events is purely coincidental.

DRAGONS IN THE STARS

Copyright © 1992 by Jeffrey A. Carver

A portion of this work appeared in substantially different form as the novelette "Though All the Mountains Lie Between," first published in the *Science Fiction Times*, and the anthology *Dragons of Darkness*, copyright © 1980 by Jeffrey Carver.

A Tor Book
Published by Tom Doherty Associates, Inc.
175 Fifth Avenue
New York, N.Y. 10010

TOR® is a registered trademark by Tom Doherty Associates, Inc.

Cover art by Jael

ISBN: 0-812-53303-8

First edition: April 1992

Printed in the United States of America

0 9 8 7 6 5 4 3 2 1

For Chuck—
one of the good dragons

and

For Crystal—
a true dream rigger

In the annals of starship rigging, it is said that the story began in a realm far from the paths of human thought. . . .

PROLOGUE
THE WORDS

SKYTOUCH?

There was no answer to the dragon's whisper. The crystalline dracona lay broken at his feet, but a tingle in the dragon's mind told him she was not gone, not yet.

"Skytouch," he hissed again, venting smoke from his massive nostrils. Those who had knocked her from the sky lay torn in pieces, just beyond the ridge. He had answered her cry in time to avenge her, but not in time to save her.

"Highwing," whispered a voice to his left. "Stay your grief! You must listen!"

He swung his massive head in anger. "Iffling! Are you here to view the dead? Leave us in peace!"

"Highwing," answered the shimmering being, "your quarrel is not me. Will you not accept my help?"

Highwing blew fire over the iffling's head. The creature floated out of the way, unperturbed. "If you want to help, then show me who encouraged those . . . *un-garkkondoh* . . . to do this."

"They were followers of one whom we do not name,"

whispered the iffling. "They meant to instill fear. You must not let them succeed. You must listen."

Highwing ignored the meddlesome being. What did its words matter? His mate lay dying, victim of a senseless, savage attack. She had come from the Dream Mountain to sing the memories of the realm; but some, it seemed, no longer approved of such stories, though the telling of them was an almost sacred function of the draconae. Those ungarkkondoh had deserved far worse than the death he had given them in punishment. But it was he who would suffer now. *Skytouch, why did I not stay with you?*

"Listen to her!" urged the iffling. "Listen while you can!"

Highwing did not answer. As he gazed down at her broken crystal wings, beautiful even in the fading twilight, his eyes filled with memories of Skytouch under a noonday sun: wings of gossamer crystal riding the wind, eyes ablaze, her flightsong gladdening the air. Now her eyes were nearly extinguished. Listen to her? He reached out in thought. *Skytouch?*

Her left eye glimmered faintly. He tilted his head, narrowed his gaze to peer into the interior of her eye. Deep within its facets a fire still burned, though faintly. *Skytouch,* he whispered with his mind. *Can you hear me?*

There was a golden flash in the center of his vision, and an image danced in his eye: the two of them on wing, riding midday thermals. He sensed laughter, through the pain. But he could not return her laughter, not now. *I wish I could take you back there,* he thought. *Or to the Dream Mountain.* To the draconae, to the other females.

L-i-s-t-e-n . . .

He was astonished to hear her voice in his mind. *Skytouch—*
L-i-s-t-e-n . . . t-o . . . t-h-e . . . W-o-r-d-s.

His gaze penetrated deeper into the dying coals of her eyes, into the pain, sharing it. Listen to the Words? Now?

Her mind-voice strained to be heard. *Y-o-u . . . Y-O-U . . . m-u-s-t . . . r-e-m-e-m-b-e-r . . .* And before he could do more than quiver in surprise, another memory grew bright in his thoughts.

* * *

It was a bowl-shaped dell. The fledglings crouched, listening to the elder dracona sing of events past, and of events yet to unfold. The fledglings stirred impatiently as the elder's shining eyes turned to a tiny, jeweled glass dracona named Skytouch. "Daughter, speak the Words of the future."

The young female rose, tinkling. Gazing into the sky, she sang in a crystalline voice:

> *From beyond life*
> *will come one*
> *From beyond hope*
> *will come one*
> *Without friend*
> *will come one*
> *And the realm shall tremble.*

> *Innocent of our ways*
> *will come one*
> *Challenging darkness*
> *will come one*
> *Speaking her name*
> *will come one*
> *And the realm shall tremble.*

> *From that one*
> *comes a beginning*
> *From that one*
> *comes an ending*
> *From that one*
> *all paths diverge*
> *And surely the realm shall tremble.*

The vision darkened, Skytouch's strength ebbing.

Highwing rumbled in wonder. He remembered the time. It was his first sight, as a youngling, of Skytouch. There had been more words than that, words of warning, of admonition. Prophecies of demons entering the realm, of innocence challenging darkness. Of deeds that might come to pass. Of the need for wisdom, the need to discern what is or is not garkkondoh. Words of little meaning to him then, or now.

He blinked slowly, so as not to break the weakening bond with his mate. There was little light left in her now. Why had Skytouch wanted him to see that memory? He was no dracona.

She seemed, even in the growing darkness of her thoughts, to be aware of his question. *Y-o-u . . .*

Skytouch?

. . . m-u-s-t . . . r-e-m-e-m-b-e-r . . .

He breathed smoke. *Yes. For you. But why?*

Her fires were failing rapidly. But a spark flickered in her eye and one more image appeared in his thoughts. He recognized himself, flying high in a night sky. There was danger in the image: someone there, someone not of the realm. He imagined that he felt the mountains trembling. *Speak not of this, but hold it close to your heart*, he seemed to hear her say.

What is it? he whispered. But the image was fading. *Skytouch? Wait!*

Be wise, son of Strongwing. Be wise . . .

He seemed to hear her last words chiming on the air. The connection was cold. Her eyes were dark now, the last spark gone. She had fled to the Final Dream Mountain. The glass shards of the vessel that had held her in life were now empty. *Skytouch*, he whispered, *call to me and I shall hear you wherever I may be, though all of the mountains lie between us.*

There was no answer.

He raised his head. Even the iffling was gone.

Highwing tipped back his head and roared into the night sky. He lit the sky with a thundering flame. What had she been trying to convey? What duty? He would not learn it here, not now.

Wings unfurled, he leaped into the air in fury and grief. Her death would be repaid—not now, perhaps, but one day. He would keep her thoughts in his heart, though he didn't understand them. He would ponder them and learn. One day he would understand.

For now, bewildered and alone, he could only beat his way into the cold stinging wind, high into the deepening night sky.

Part One

RIGGER

. . . In those early days, long before the founding of the RiggerGuild, starship riggers lived with constant insecurity. Often enough, they found themselves controlled by shrewd masters—sometimes subtly, sometimes not— but controlled nonetheless; and in those days, riggers were rarely successful in supporting one another against abusive masters. But if they suffered oppression in the normal world, they found freedom in the net, in the dreams by which they steered their ships, which their masters, however powerful, could never share. The lucky rigger found a way to carry that freedom out of the net, to the other side of life. . . .

Jona' Jon'
—*Gazing into Yesteryear:*
A Brief History of Starflight

Chapter 1
GASTON'S LANDING

JAEL PAUSED at the edge of the spaceport lobby, heart pounding. She was late for the afternoon spacing call, and she could see from where she stood that today her name would go to the bottom of a very long list. The spaceport was crowded, noisy, clotted with people competing for space, for time, for service—shippers, stewards, unrated crew, normal-space pilots, riggers. Loud voices echoed across the room, voices of the stewards calling riggers for possible assignment. The calls seemed to float over the lounge area where the riggers congregated—riggers for hire, too many of them—all hoping that the stewards would come to them, match them with ship masters, ask them to fly.

Jael drew a breath, and almost turned away, but forced herself to remain. She was ready—more than ready—for an assignment. She had the schooling and the space-trial credentials, and she looked presentable: a slender, dark-haired young woman, not beautiful maybe, but neatly groomed, in a tunic suit, grey edged with scarlet. Did she have the stomach for the disappointment that was almost sure to come? She surveyed the lobby, considering. Her eyes widened as she glimpsed a young rigger of her acquaintance, Toni Gilen, threading her way across the lobby toward a steward. Jael shook her head and strode in. Toni was one of the shyest riggers Jael knew; if Toni could be assertive, surely Jael could be.

She felt no particular hope; she felt only the need that drew her here. It was the same feeling that drove all riggers: the almost irresistible need to shape, to explore, to live the fantastic realities of a realm that nonriggers could never touch or master, but could only dream of. And she sensed the ubiquitous conflicting emotion, almost palpable in the air. It was fear: fear of failure, fear of the shippers whom the riggers hoped to serve. She felt the need and fear combine like a thrill in her gut, her groin, her spine; but beneath it all, somewhere, remained the hope that today might be the day she would contract to fly.

She walked past the waiting area, toward the registry window, her feet moving quickly on the tile floor.

"Hi there, Jaelie!" she heard, and despite herself, she turned. A hawk-nosed young man was laughing from within the railing that set off the rigger lounge. "Gonna show us how to cheat the odds today?" Jael opened her mouth to reply, but the young man was already strutting away, grinning.

Burning with anger, Jael stalked on. Riggers, she thought bitterly. They were such misfits, most of them. Self-centered, insecure, social incompetents. Walking raw nerves, in a world none of them was suited for. Was she like them? She hoped not. And yet, these were the people who navigated spaceships through the slippery mists of the Flux; it was their unique gifts of vision that made travel among the stars possible. Jael was proud to be a rigger. But she was not always proud of the company she had to keep.

She approached the registration window nervously. She was always aware of her youth and her relative inexperience, but among the spaceport officials and shipowners, she felt even tinier and more vulnerable than she really was. A raggedly bearded unrated crewman brushed by her and winked, grinning lewdly. She ignored the gesture, or tried to. She hated this place and those who worked here, always ready to prey on the weak and the uncertain. But if she wanted to return to space, she had to do it from here. And more than anything in the world, she wanted to return to space. To the net. To the vision. To the freedom.

A young man was ahead of her at the registration window, talking in a croak, a rasping whisper. Jael waited, fidgeting, until he left and it was her turn at the window. A middle-aged woman with bluish hair spoke without looking up. "ID?"

Jael touched her bracelet to the dull-surfaced eye of the reader. "Jael LeBrae."

"Didn't ask your name, honey. It's right here in front of me." The woman turned, touched something on her console. "Jael LeBrae," she said, reading the output. "Available for single Class Three or multiple Class Five. Is that correct?"

"Yes."

The woman looked up, pursing her lips. "You the daughter of Willie LeBrae?" Her eyes bored into Jael's.

"Yes." The familiar tightness took hold in her throat. Was the woman going to ask about her father? She didn't want to talk about it, about him.

"I see. Well, nothing right now. Do you want to wait?"

Jael hesitated, struggling not to resent the indifference in the woman's voice. "Are you expecting anything?" she asked finally.

The woman looked at her in surprise. "Why, how would I know, honey? We hear about them when they come in. If you want to wait, you can wait. Is that what you want to do?"

Jael stared at her without answering. Could she stand it? It was the one way, the only way. "Yes," she whispered.

"Fine. Now, make way for others, won't you?"

Jael walked away from the window and joined the other riggers in the lounge. As she glanced back, she saw that there was no one in line behind her.

There were no empty seats in the quiet area, so she stood near the wall watching some of the riggers playing board and tank games, until a bench space opened up. As she slid into the empty seat, the young man to her right moved a few inches farther away. Jael tried not to let her resentment show. She was tired of being blamed for her father, for people and events over which she had no control.

But there were ways of dealing with emotional discomfort, and Jael used one of them now. She sat perfectly still, her back and neck erect, balanced. Closing her eyes halfway, she slowly erased the visual input from her consciousness. She let her inner mind see, without her eyes.

She was aware, with her inner eye, of the expressions borne on the faces of the riggers waiting in this place. Boredom. Nervous tension. Desire. Inward-turned senses. Outward eagerness that belied the darker feelings roiling within. She smelled the aura of hot fear and desire that marked a roomful of riggers, the way musky body scents marked the dens of animals. These riggers came from dens all over the continent to this spaceport: to wait in this lounge, to hope, to need and dread the chance to take a starship into space.

But Jael didn't want to think about them now, didn't want to think about the competition. She had better things to dwell upon: memories that gave her a shiver as her thoughts fled from the here and now. As they fled into the past, to the time of her first flight, not so very long ago—a training flight, the first of four . . .

She had been working with other riggers, but it had been different then—not the bitter competition she faced now. Riggers depended upon one another in guiding their ships through the currents, through the reefs and shoals of flight. It was by navigating the Flux—an other-dimensional realm of mystery and imagination—that starships physically passed among the stars. And in steering their ships, riggers had to work together, not just cooperatively as would the crew of any ship, but as artists meshed in psychic union. Joined by shared intuition and inner vision, melded in working unity, they steered their vessels. In the schools it was difficult and challenging, flying simulations from the libraries, navigating any of a thousand actual and imagined courses. In space it was doubly challenging, because it was real, and life was at stake—and in the conquest of the challenge, it was infinitely more rewarding than any simulation.

On that first flight and those that followed, Jael had left it all behind: the fears and needs, the problems of life back on the world, the family, the business, the reputation. All that disappeared when she entered the rigger's net and wove together the threads of real space, of the Flux, of her imagination . . . and crafted of it a world so cunningly real that the spaceship slipped through it as surely as it passed through the vacuum and weightlessness of normal-space. On that first flight, she and her crewmates had carried the ship through a magical undersea realm of tropical waters, warm and crystalline blue. And where were those crewmates, her fellow students, now? All gone, off among the stars . . .

"Listen up, people, I have some new openings here!"

For an instant, she wasn't sure whether the voice had come from her memory or from the outside. She widened her eyes, brought them into focus. A shop steward was standing in the center of the lobby, job slate in hand. He was calling out positions to be filled.

Jael shook herself to alertness and listened.

". . . a two-rigger crew to make a fast run up through Aeregia Minor, with calls at Parvis III and Chaening's Outpost. We need a four-rigger crew for assignment with a passenger-carrying line; you'll have to go through the complete screening and testing on that one. And we have two seats for single-rigger jobs, one freight and one courier." The steward paused and looked around at the attentive, brooding faces. "Don't crowd, and don't apply if you're not qualified," he concluded, then turned and disappeared into the office.

Jael rose, along with at least half the riggers in the room. There was some crowding and jockeying for position at the half dozen ID readers, then she was in line. The woman ahead of her glanced back skeptically, but shrugged and said nothing. Frowning, Jael remained intentionally oblivious to any other glances, until her turn came to slide her ID bracelet into the reader niche. She drummed her fingers, waiting.

The screen blinked and displayed:

We're sorry. We cannot consider your application for any presently available position.

Jael stared at the words. For three months now, since her last flight, she had received nothing but rejections. It would have been one thing to lose out on positions if she'd been unqualified, but she was consistently being denied even the chance to prove herself.

"Hey, are you going to stand there all day?" complained a voice behind her. Turning, Jael focused her frown upon the voice's owner. "What'd you expect, anyway?" the complaining woman muttered sarcastically. "Why don't you try the other side? That's where you belong, isn't it?"

I don't know—what *did* I expect? Jael thought, turning away. Fair treatment? I don't know why. She returned to her seat with as much dignity as she could muster. A young man she recognized from rigger school kept looking in her direction; she did not return the gaze. But the anger kept bubbling back up. *Why don't you try the other side?* The thought made her tremble. The other side of the spaceport lobby was where the unregulated shippers hired riggers—riggers so untamable or unfit for society, or so desperate, that they would fly with virtually no legal protection, not even the minimal restrictions imposed on the registered shippers. It was there that her father had hired his crews. It was there that the family name had been turned from a name of pride to a name of derision. *Never*, she vowed.

But other words echoed in her mind, words she had heard someone mutter behind her back more than once: *"Who the hell wants to hire a daughter of Willie LeBrae?"* She hadn't responded to the comment; she never did. But that didn't stop it from hurting.

And that was the worst of it, really. Her fellow riggers, if anyone, ought to understand, ought to sympathize. Most of them knew the pain of rejection well enough. But it was as though they only knew how to cut deeper, how to make a wound hurt even more. There were those, of course, who just sat there, lost in their own worlds, neither harming nor helping. They barely stirred even to answer the calls; they were hardly going to rise to anyone's defense. And then there were her schoolmates—those whose trust she had gained anyway—but they were scattered like dust now, among the stars.

Jael *was* going to fly again, to join her friends out there; of that she was determined. Sooner or later they would have to give her a berth.

If she had to wait here forever.

The next few hours felt like forever. There was only one other call, and that for a single passenger-rated rigger, for which she was unqualified. She got up and went to the lunch counter and bought a cup of leek chowder, the only thing they sold that was any good; and she stood at the edge of the lounge, spooning chowder into her mouth, tasting the thick pasty sauce and the chunks of spud-vine and leek. By the time she'd scraped the little bowl clean and licked off the spoon, she'd decided that enough was enough for one day.

With a last tentative gaze over the lounge—as though one more call might come, as though waiting just a few moments more might make the difference—she trudged toward the door. And with a final dark glance across the lobby toward the unregulated area, she strode out into the late afternoon sun. A tremendous oppression seemed to lift from her shoulders as she left the spaceport building—not the weight of her unfulfilled dream, because that never lifted, but the weight of the enduring and the silent frustration. It was a burden she was willing to bear, because she had to for the sake of her dream; but it felt good to put it down for a while.

The road home to the multidorm wound up through the hills. It was a fine, crisp day—a good day for walking, for shouting at the wind, for sighing under the consoling caress of the sun.

"Jael!" The voice was behind her.

She paused and turned, blinking, only half-focusing. Her mind was still in the sky.

A figure was striding up the hill toward her. "Jael, how are you?" It was a dark-haired young man with striking silver eyebrows, waving a hand, trying to get her attention. "Ho, Jael! Are you in there? Anybody home?"

Slowly her inner concentration melted away. "Dap—hi!" she said, smiling slowly. "I didn't expect to see *you*. When did you get in?" Dap was her cousin, also a rigger—and one of the few people still based here on Gaston's Landing whose presence could bring a smile to her lips. Last she'd heard, he'd been out on a long flight.

"I just got in a few days ago," Dap said, falling in alongside her. "You walking up to the rigger hall?" He pointed up the road.

Jael nodded, resuming her stride. "A few days? I haven't seen you."

Dap shrugged. "I've been lying low since I got back. Wanted to be by myself for a while." As they walked together, he broke into a grin. "How have you been? It was really some flight, Jael. I didn't want to wreck the memory by coming in here right away and facing all that." He waved back toward the spaceport.

"That's great," Jael said softly, and felt a twinge of guilt. This was her cousin, and she wanted to share his excitement, but just now it was rather hard.

"You look a little down in the mouth there," Dap said. "What's the matter?"

"What isn't?" she growled, and instantly regretted her tone.

Dap chuckled. If anyone else had laughed, she would have wanted to murder him. With Dap, she was willing to forgive. "You think it's funny?" she said finally.

He nudged her with an elbow. "Naw. You know I don't think that. But are things really so bad?"

She shrugged and kept walking. "I can't get work. That's pretty bad, isn't it?"

"I know what you mean," Dap said. "But we all have trouble with that at some time or other. When you only have a few qualifying flights under your belt, it's tough to break in."

"It's not that. I've had two paying flights. It's not just breaking in."

Her cousin looked puzzled. "Then what—"

"It's that they *won't* give it to me. They don't *want* me. They're keeping me out."

Dap frowned. "You mean, because of your father's—?"

"Of course! What am I supposed to do? Change my name? Move to another planet? How can I do that if they won't let me fly?" She blinked back a tear, and had to steel herself to keep from crying. She couldn't help what people thought, but she didn't have to let herself be affected by it. And she didn't mean to wreck Dap's day too.

Dap grunted. They walked up the road, their feet crunching on the loose gravel. After a while, the movement began to dispel her gloom, and she asked, "So how was it? Your flight, I mean?"

A smile tugged suddenly at the corner of Dap's mouth. "Beautiful. Just beautiful." He turned suddenly. "Would you like to share it with me?"

She was startled. "What do you mean?"

"Dreamlink, Jael. There's a machine at my dad's friend's cottage. We could go there right now, and instead of my telling you about it . . ." Dap grinned and caught her hand. "It might lift you a little, Jael, to relive it with me. Taste it, feel it, smell it, see it. Jael, it was wonderful!"

Jael tensed with desire and fear. She felt Dap's hand release hers as she looked at him, looked into his intense, earnest eyes, dark under those silvery brows. "Well, I . . . I don't know."

"Jael, have you ever been in the dreamlink? It's as close to rigging as you can come without being—"

"Yes, I know." She blinked her gaze away, embarrassed. "But it's awfully . . . personal, Dap. I mean, it's not like we're . . . I mean, we're cousins. We're not—" She'd heard how some riggers used the dreamlink during their off time. It made a very interesting enhancement for lovers. Or so she had been told.

"Hey—hey! Jael, it's not like that." Dap laughed gently and touched her arm. "Jael, don't worry—it's not sexual, if that's what you're thinking of." Now he looked embarrassed. "Or anything like that. I mean, sure it can be, but it doesn't have to be. It's just a way of sharing thoughts and memories and feelings and . . ." He hesitated, and shrugged.

She trembled, avoiding his eyes. This was Dap she was

talking to, her cousin, her friend. What was she afraid of? Didn't she want the chance of feeling what he'd felt as he took wing between the stars? "I—" She felt her mind churning, her feelings turning over and over. Perhaps she should; at least it would give her a taste of what she'd been yearning for. At least it would be with a friend.

"Jael," he said, "we'll be looking right into one another, and our souls will link—"

"Okay," she sighed, interrupting him. She nodded and murmured huskily, "Okay, let's go."

Chapter 2
THE DREAMLINK

THEY DROVE in a groundcar from the rigger hall, gliding along the roadway. They passed around the far side of the hills, into a gorgeous pink sunset—with two of Gaston's Landing's three moons just hanging there, slim crescents shining in the reddish glowing sky. They drove to Dap's father's friend's cottage, where the dreamlink machine was located.

Jael felt a rush of nervousness as they got out to walk up a short path to the retreat. It was a real house, not a multidorm. Dap touched her arm, smiling reassuringly. The gesture helped her to overcome her doubts; she drew a breath and accompanied him to the front door. Dap fumbled in his pocket and fished out a slim metal wafer and slid it into a slot in the edge of the door. "The Donovons don't believe in ID bracelets—you have to use a key," he murmured. The door clicked and swung inward on hinges. Jael followed him in.

She peered around the front room as Dap secured the door. The house was small but elegantly designed, with a curving wooden staircase and soft-textured beige and white walls. Jael strolled around, touching the wall surfaces and banisters with a certain fascination. Perhaps it was a consequence of living in the rigger halls too long; it startled her to encounter luxury.

"Back here, Jael."

She followed Dap into a small sitting room, in the center of which was a silver-hemisphered device standing waist high. Dap passed his hand over the device, and it came on, producing a golden light. She'd never actually seen a dreamlink machine before, but she knew what it was: a specialized type of synaptic augmentor. It should be no big deal, compared to a rigger-net. As she approached it, she felt a soft inner glow pass through her. It seemed to match the light that the hemisphere produced. The feeling stayed with her as she crossed the room to where Dap was moving a pair of seats into the fringe of the glowing field. "We'll let it coalesce for a few minutes. Would you like something to drink?" he asked. "Some sparkly?"

Jael nodded. She sat and tried to relax while Dap disappeared into the kitchen; she smiled, drumming her fingers, and murmured thanks when he returned with two slender glasses of carbonated water. She inhaled a faint scent of juniper and lime; it tickled her nose and throat as she sipped it. Dap took the other seat and clinked glasses with her.

"What do we do now? What's going to happen?" she asked, thinking, this is your cousin, good old Dap—why are you worried?—he knows what he's doing.

Dap leaned forward and winked teasingly. She wondered if he was amused by her naivete, or perhaps being just the slightest bit flirtatious. She blushed and took another sip of sparkly. "You'll know what to do," Dap said. "If you can handle the net, you'll have no trouble with this." He settled back into his seat looking relaxed and eager, and Jael thought, I'm worrying about nothing after all. Nothing. The field was growing in intensity, very slowly, a pleasant glow surrounding her mind.

Dap began to talk, just idle conversation about this and that, riggers and family—his, fortunately, not hers (they were actually second cousins, and she knew his parents and sister only slightly)—and all the while, she felt the glow sinking deeper into her mind, warming her, almost a physical sensation that tingled at the edges of the iciness that lingered inside her. She shivered as Dap suddenly shifted tracks and described his last flight—a three star-system hop, fast and exciting—played in the net as skipping-stone islands across a broad, sun-spanked sea. His eyes sought hers as he spoke, laughing. "Jael, it was just the two of us, Deira and me. The owner was going to come, but canceled out at the last minute. No owner, just the two of us, captaining ourselves, and crafting this vision!"

As he spoke, Jael began to see a glimmer of the vision Dap had held during the flight—just a glimpse at the edge of her own vision, dancing like spots before her eyes as his memories were spun out in a tapestry of words and expression. His words tugged at her as he spoke of the intimacy he had experienced in the teamwork with Deira, as they'd piloted their star freighter through the Flux. "Jael, that was the best part about the trip," he said, his eyes still seeking hers, holding them just a little longer than she wished them held, his thoughts reaching out to hers. "But it was fleeting." And his voice turned a little wistful. "She's already gone out on another flight, this time on a long haul with three others. I miss her already." Did his voice catch, just a little? He kept talking. "But the experience . . ." And sparks of excitement seemed to radiate from his voice as he spoke again of the flight itself. "Imagine an absolutely clear, deep sea and an enormous, beautiful sky and a series of islands laid out like jewels on the sea . . ."

Something in Jael knotted up as he went on, causing her to choke silently. She tried to contain it; she didn't want to let her envy show. But as the warmth of the field worked its way slowly through the remaining iciness inside her, she felt certain feelings of resistance giving way, and she realized that there was no need to hide her feelings from her friend. That was what the dreamlink was all about—wasn't it?—tugging loose feelings, sharing them. As she looked at Dap, she felt a gentle release of something within, and she no longer only heard his words . . .

Dap's vision of space . . . the space *he* had flown . . . blos-

somed open directly in her mind. The glowing blue sea, and
the space freighter leaping over and through that image of a
sea like a magnificent dolphin, plunging through the clear
waters and the air alike, plunging through—or rather,
around—the light-years of normal-space distance as a dolphin
plunged through the sea. And she glimpsed the woman Dap
had rigged with, Deira, and his attraction and growing intimacy with her. She felt his exultation, the feeling of release
and freedom that came from steering a ship through the
Flux. She'd felt that herself, those few times she'd flown, but
never with the kind of intimacy that Dap was showing her
in this memory.

Jael shivered with envy, and with nervousness, because she
sensed in Dap a sly querying interest toward her now. But
he had assured her that his interest was only friendly, that
he would never push her into anything she didn't want. She
could trust him, she had to trust at least someone in this
world, and what was she so afraid of, anyway?

*Deira and I . . . we shared this vision, and more. Can you see,
Jael? Can you feel it?*

As she sensed Dap's thoughts, feelings stirred in her heart
that she could no longer control. Yes, she felt it, and she
did not want to know such envy, but she couldn't help it.
Before she knew what was happening, thoughts and images
began to gush up out of her own mind like water from a
fountain. They spilled out into the image of space, into the
dreamlink . . .

First came memories of her own training flights, dancing
down the lanes of nearby space, among some of the cluster-
mate stars of the sun of Gaston's Landing. It was sheer joy,
like swimming for the first time, stroking and panting and
dancing across the sea of stars. It was demanding to find the
way and keep the vision steady—oh yes! But every light-year
passed was a triumph, and she and Mara and Joizee-Bob
(wherever they were now—how she missed them!) had
threaded the passage so well on their last flight that they'd
arrived ahead of schedule, wishing that they could turn
around and fly it again. Such a release of feelings she had in
the net! Such cooperation!

And those memories mingled with hopes of flights to come, flights that would vault the distances of much greater space, with new crewmates or maybe some of the old, flights that so far were nothing but hopes . . . hopes, and frustration, and pain . . .

She quickly tried to divert her thoughts from that, but the direction was inevitable; she could not control it. Before she could even catch her breath, she was showering Dap with other visions. Visions of the past . . .

Visions of pain.

Glimpses of her frightened half-brother Levin, steeling himself against the abuse of their uncaring father, so frightened that he was unable to reach out even to his sister, rejecting even her sympathy. Glimpses of Levin striding out of the house and out of sight down the road in dwindling daylight; of Jael herself gazing at her father's closed door, unable to gain his attention, suffering and wanting and needing . . . but her father was too busy with the machinations of his business, too busy with his consorts . . .

Jael, what is this? Dap whispered.

Images of Jael, years later, this year, arming herself with a self-esteem she didn't feel, and reporting to the rigger hall. But it wasn't like the rigger school, where she'd known classmates she liked and trusted, where at least some people hadn't known yet of her father. Instead, the images were of her rigging on the only two paying flights she'd gotten in the year since her graduation, before word of who she was had spread finally to the last corners of the shipping community. They were solitary flights, because she was fearful of seeking out companions, ashamed to let her fellow riggers know of her deep loneliness and need . . .

Jael, I had no idea! It . . . it doesn't have to be that way!

The anguish welled up in her. *Doesn't it? What was I supposed to do? Can't you see that no one would fly with me? No one, no one . . .*

But Jael, you have to assert your rights. You can't just . . . I don't know . . . hide from it!

Oh no? How about this? She couldn't prevent it from spilling out now in a great rush: all the years of loneliness and failed hope, glimpses of her inner self that she had never meant to let anyone see. It was all pouring into the dream-link now, thundering onto Dap like a waterfall: her anger toward her father for ruining her dreams—not by forbidding them, but by failing to care, failing to make her dreams his own—by destroying the honor of the name LeBrae through his greed and dishonesty in the spacing business. And there was anger not just toward her father, but toward her brother as well—for his unwillingness to stand, and to *live*. And anger toward herself—for not cutting them both loose and making her own way in the world—for being a failure, not just as a rigger, but as a person.

In the dizzying energy of the dreamlink, she could sense that the link between Dap and herself was straining, like a fabric being pulled, stretched, torn. What was she doing? The openness of mind and soul was the dreamlink's strength, and its danger. Leaking back to her through the link was Dap's surprise, and dismay, his astonishment that anyone could feel, or could release such staggering need.

Just fantasies, she lied to him, but the lie crumpled in an instant. *I can't help it, I didn't want you to—* And her coherent thoughts broke off as her embarrassment became a trembling glow, reddening the images of the link.

Jael, he whispered, *I didn't expect—how could I know? How could you be keeping all of this inside?*

And Dap's thoughts blurred into a hiss of static as he struggled to absorb what she'd shown him. For a few moments, no words came back to her through the dreamlink, no comprehensible thoughts. Dap seemed so appalled by her need. He seemed to want to pull away. She sensed his . . . what? Revulsion?

Jael, I knew it was hard for you, but . . . how can you . . . how could anyone . . . live with this? And his thoughts lost all clarity and spun away.

Dap! You promised me understanding! *Wait—please don't—!*

But it was too late; the bond was severed, torn by Dap's horror. What else could he possibly feel? *Dap!* But he was already doing what any sane person would do. Without a sound he closed himself off from the dreamlink. Without physically moving, he faded like a ghost from the glow that had become the world around Jael, the glow that was now only a suffocating shield around her, protecting only her own hurt and self-loathing. She sensed that Dap could no longer even look at her; she sensed him rising from his seat and turning away, leaving the room. And she cried mutely in pain.

She made herself her own last audience; she let her pain dance in the field like threads of fire, tightening around her like a noose, choking her. There was no one here to help her escape from her pain—there never had been, not in Dap, nor in her father before—they forgot their promises and closed the door on her, one just like the other. She wanted to kill someone, she wanted to kill them both, she would kill herself with this hatred if she didn't do something to—

—control it—

—bottle it—

—which she did, gathering it in from the burning glow of the dreamlink and wrapping it tightly around her finger and corking it back inside where it belonged. And then, when she knew she was safe and still sane, she rose and turned off the dreamlink augmentor. The glow died, leaving the room cold and silent and sterile. There was nothing here that could hurt her now.

Except what lived within her.

Unwilling to cry, unable to answer Dap's croaking harshness—"Wait, Jael! I'll take you home—" from the hallway, she strode out of the room and out of the house and began the long trek on foot back to her room, through the gathering evening darkness.

Chapter 3
CONTRACT TO FLY

WHEN SHE arrived the next morning at the spaceport lobby where the riggers mobbed and brooded, she saw, to her relief, no sign of Dap. He'd caught up with her last night, followed her in the car to make sure she got home safely; but she'd been too angry to get in or speak with him. She'd been embarrassed, humiliated, shamed. She couldn't believe that his concern was sincere, not after the way he'd left her like that in the dreamlink.

She would put Dap behind her, as she had put all of the others behind her. Regardless of what anyone here at the spaceport thought, she meant to rig on a starship. She would not be kept from it by Dap or by her fellow riggers or by what anyone thought of her father. They could discriminate if they wanted to, but they couldn't stop her.

Her determination kept her going through that day. But the presence of the other riggers in the halls was a drain on her spirit—not so much any one individual as the sheer numbers, the weight of all the riggers competing with her for work. She found herself glancing across the lobby from time to time, watching the activities of the unregulated shippers.

Once in a while, a rigger drifted over that way from the lounge, but most of the riggers who worked for the unregulateds stayed away from their peers on this side of the lobby. There was a clear, if unofficial, class distinction between the two groups of riggers. Those who worked for the unregulateds were more poorly trained and paid, more exploited, more likely to fly substandard equipment, more likely not to return from space. And in those riggers, there was often a certain look in the eyes, an appearance of resignation, weariness, and defeat.

Never will I do that, she had vowed. And as she watched, thinking of the riggers who had worked for, and been worn out by her father, she silently renewed that vow. And yet . . . she knew that for many unfortunate riggers, it was the only way to make it into space. On this planet, at least, there were too many riggers and not enough registered ships. And when one had the dream . . . when one was driven by the need, by the compulsion . . . it was a matter either of taking whatever means there was to get into space, or of withdrawing into a self-absorption that made them unfit for any work at all—except maybe the selling of their dreams and visions to the commercial dreamtapers, and what a squandering of talent that was. But so too was it a waste to be used up and discarded by shippers who valued one's talents only for a brief and inexpensive career. No, she wouldn't give in to that temptation. Not yet, anyway.

She left the spaceport feeling discouraged, but not beaten. Not quite. She went to the rigger hall library and spent a couple of hours alone, running simulations of local star routes. For a time, she managed to keep her spirits up.

By the next morning her courage seemed to have evaporated. She opened her eyes and stared up at the blank ceiling, without the slightest trace of hope. She spent most of the day in her room—withdrawn, trying to muster the will to return to the spaceport, but unable to find the determination. When she shook herself out of her mood, finally, late that afternoon, she vowed that she would, she must return for the spacing calls the following morning.

That simple declaration gave her the focus she needed to

begin gathering her inner strength again. It took just one day to get an assignment, she reminded herself—one right day, one right convergence of events. It was a matter of persisting until the stewards could no longer deny her without due cause. And because she had the credentials and she had good performance reports on the flights she had made, there was no due cause, no just reason for denying her work. There was only prejudice because of her father—because more than one shipper here claimed that Willie LeBrae had cheated them out of business. But prejudice could be overcome. Had to be overcome. With persistence. With strength.

She was reminded of just what kind of strength it would take when the following day she arrived well in advance of the morning call, and watched the stewards pass her over in favor of three riggers her own grade who had come in after her. It took another hour, but eventually her anger reached the boiling point. She approached one of the stewards. "I want to know why you won't give me a chance," she said, in a voice that to her, anyway, seemed loud.

The steward looked surprised by her question. He glanced around the rigger lounge, where several people had looked up. A thin smile cracked his features. "Well, now." He rubbed his fingernails across the front of his blue shirt. "You must really want to fly, I guess."

"Yes. And you know it." Jael glared at him, until his smile became waxen and twisted by self-consciousness. "I don't care what you think of my father's company, either," she said. "I had nothing to do with it. Nothing."

The steward looked down for a moment, his lips moving in silent thought. His eyebrows went up. "You think we're not being fair—because of your father?"

You know damn well, she thought bitterly. But she said nothing; she just kept the steward fixed in her scowling gaze.

"What do you expect me to do?" The steward cast a deliberate glance across the lobby, toward the unregulated quarter, as if to suggest, Why don't you go over there?

"You can give me work!" Jael snapped, ignoring his intimation. She was suddenly aware of an increasing number of people looking in her direction, but she no longer cared. "On *this* side," she said, a little more softly. "I've earned it."

The steward's eyes narrowed.

"My ratings are good enough."

He shrugged. "Maybe."

"You know they're good enough." She was pushing her luck, she knew. But what did she have to lose?

"I'll see what I can do," he muttered, and turned away.

She started to call after him. But the steward had already dismissed her. She returned to the lounge and took a seat in silence. Almost, she made the room go away by retreating to her inner mind, but something told her not to let it go that easily; even as she called to mind happier images, she kept one eye on the steward's corner. She would not let him think that she had quit, or forgotten.

The next three hours passed slowly indeed.

"LeBrae." Poke. *"Jael."* Poke.

Her eyes flew open. She was being nudged awake in her chair by the young rigger she'd seen the other day, Toni Gilen. "What? What is it?" she murmured.

"Over there." Toni was pointing in the direction of the registration area. "They asked me to come get you."

"Who did?" Jael asked. But she already saw who Toni was pointing at. Beyond the lounge area, the steward she'd talked to was standing beside a large, bearded man dressed in a black tunic-length vesta robe over loose black pants. They were discussing something, and glancing in her direction. "They want to see me?" she asked Toni.

The younger rigger's eyes widened, and she took a seat without saying anything more.

Very well, then, Jael thought. They want to see me. She straightened her clothes and strode toward the two men.

"Is this the one?" the large man asked the steward as she approached.

The steward's lips curled into a self-satisfied smile. "This is Miss LeBrae."

"LeBrae?" said the other man. He nodded, as though in

thought. "What's your first name, Miss?" he asked, in a gravelly voice.

"Jael. Jael LeBrae," she said. "Qualified for Class Three single and Class Five multiple." Her voice trembled slightly, and she struggled to keep it steady.

The shipper pursed his lips. "Would you be interested in flying a Class Three single, Jael?"

Her heart thumped, and she almost squawked, *Yes!* But caution made her swallow the urge, and she stammered, "Could you tell me . . . please . . . the particulars on your ship?" She glanced at the steward, who was supposed to act as the provider of such information.

The steward's gaze was guarded, but his voice was needle-sharp. "I thought you were anxious to fly."

"I'll tell you everything you want to know," the shipper boomed, interrupting. "My name is Captain Deuteronomous Mogurn, and I'm flying a freighter, *Cassandra*. She's out in docking bay 27 right now, ready to go as soon as she's crewed."

"And your cargo?" the steward intoned, fulfilling his role sarcastically.

"Artifact goods of substantial value," Mogurn said with a wink. It wasn't clear whether the wink was meant for Jael or for the steward. But the cargo description was as much as he was required to give, and no more. No specifics were required to be given the rigger, though there was no reason to expect secrecy, either.

Jael blinked, considering his answer. "And . . . your registry information?"

The two men exchanged glances. Then Mogurn slowly smiled. "Perhaps we should step over here to discuss that," he said, gesturing away from the rigger area.

Jael froze, and for the space of perhaps three seconds, she was aware of nothing except the pounding of her heart. What did that mean? Unregistered? Registry stewards were not supposed to engage in solicitation for unregistered shipping. Was someone being paid off here? *What are you doing to me?* The two stood waiting for her response, their expressions betraying nothing. She tried to find her voice, and at last managed, "Why can't we talk about it here?"

For an instant, the two men seemed taken aback. Then the steward's smile widened slightly, and he answered, "Well, Miss LeBrae, what we're offering you is something a little different. And you have to discuss it over there—if you want to go to space, that is."

I told you, she whispered to herself, then realized that she hadn't spoken the words aloud. She cleared her throat. "I don't want to fly unregulated. I said that before."

"This isn't, perhaps, what you think it is," Captain Mogurn said in a dry voice. "Won't you even hear us out?"

As she looked back at him, she couldn't tell whether she should dismiss him out of hand or not. Perhaps it wouldn't hurt to hear what he was offering; after all, no one could force her to fly. "Okay," she mumbled reluctantly, and followed the shipper a short distance away from the rigger lounge. The steward bowed, and somewhat to her relief, left them.

Mogurn led her to a quiet corner, then turned, and for a moment seemed to examine her critically, looking her up and down. Jael felt her face growing warm under the scrutiny; she was aware, more than ever, of her slight stature, of her youth. After a moment he said, "Do you mind telling me, Jael, why you wish to go into space?"

The question took her by surprise. She'd expected to be asked about her record, her skills—but not this, not so bluntly. How could she explain a burning desperation to fly—to see space again, to witness the landscapes of the Flux? Her voice caught a little, as she tried to answer. "I suppose it's really . . . the only thing that interests me."

"The chance to see all those worlds?"

"Yes . . . I guess. But mostly it's the flying. It's what I'm good at. I don't . . ." She hesitated.

"Don't what, Jael?"

She groped for words. "I . . . don't know what I'd do if I couldn't rig." And at once she regretted her forthrightness. She didn't even know this man!

Mogurn chuckled softly. "You wouldn't turn inward like

a vegetable, would you, like some of your . . . peers?" His thick eyebrows quivered, and she couldn't tell if he was laughing at her, or at all riggers who couldn't live without their chosen work.

She shrugged indignantly.

"Well," Mogurn said, his tone changing to one of accommodation, "would it surprise you to know that I understand how you feel? That I know what it's like to want, even to *need* to do something? That something like that got *me* into space in the first place?" He stroked the front of his vesta robe, scowling. A slight twitch had appeared in the corner of his left eye, and he rubbed at it for a moment with his fingertips. "This is all a long-winded way of saying, maybe you shouldn't lump all shippers in the same category. There are some unregistereds who are better than some of your fully registered shippers."

"Well—"

"There are shippers here, I imagine, that someone like you should never come near. Registered shippers. People who would use you and throw you out like an old dog when you were no longer useful to them." Mogurn's eyes, which were blue-grey and more than a little bloodshot, squinted at her. "Stay away from those people, Jael! No good can come of dealing with them!"

She blinked, unable to answer. Of course there were shippers like that. Her own father had been one of them. Was Mogurn claiming to be different?

"But don't throw the good out with the bad," Mogurn continued, gazing across the lobby. He stood beside her now, as though standing *with* her. He glanced back over toward the rigger area. "It's not always so great over on that side, either."

"What do you mean?"

His breath hissed out heavily; he was a very solidly built man, but he seemed slightly asthmatic. She wondered how old he was. Fifty, maybe? Sixty? "Don't you know?" he asked. "I think you do." And he paused, as though to make the point. "Regulated, unregulated—there's no guarantee you'll be treated fairly either way. Wouldn't you agree?"

Jael flushed and nodded ever so slightly. "I guess that's sometimes true."

"Of course. We both know it. And *the regulators* know it. And yet they maintain this fiction that the only safe way for a rigger to work is within their cozy little system—where they have control!" Mogurn seemed to realize that he was speaking too loudly; he cleared his throat and readjusted the shoulders of his vesta.

Jael could not answer. She'd been thrown off balance by his assertion, but how could she deny it? The registry made a pretense of fairly apportioning jobs, but it was only a pretense, and no one resented it more than she.

"May I ask you something?"

Startled, she tried to focus on Mogurn's words; she kept drifting off into her thoughts. "What?"

He rubbed his cheek. "How old are you, Jael?"

"Why? What does that matter? I'm sixteen, local. That's about eighteen, standard."

"Yes. Well, I just wanted to point out that you cannot expect to fly all of your life. Most riggers have to stop by the time they're twenty-four or twenty-five, unless they're exceptional." He paused. "Perhaps you are exceptional. But . . ."

She closed her eyes. She knew what he was going to say.

When she looked again, he was gesturing toward the lounge full of riggers waiting, passing time, and she thought of all the boredom and frustration there, and knew he had pointed at the truth: most of those riggers would end their careers in frustration, rarely flying; and with each passing year, many of them would slowly lose that curious, intangible inner vision that had made them riggers in the first place. "You might not have that much time left, Jael," Mogurn said in a soft growl. "And I'm offering you a chance."

She trembled, two powerful desires conflicting in her mind. Never, she had promised herself. Never would she fly with an unregulated shipper. But what if her choice was that, or never to fly at all? Which was worse? Was she being ruled even now by her father—by her reaction to him? Was she wrong to assume that all unregulateds were like him?

"And," Mogurn continued, "I'm offering even more. I'm

offering something that can help you become one of those exceptional ones."

She turned. "What do you mean?"

His eyebrows arched. "I have a method, Jael. It is both a training device and a reward. Riggers on many other worlds compete for it—a way to enhance their skill, to improve the odds. You've been at an unfair disadvantage here—but I can help you, if you fly my *Cassandra*. And that is a promise that I'll wager none of these others"—and he jerked his head toward the registry area—"can offer."

Jael drew a sharp breath, her suspicion conflicting with her curiosity . . . with her desire, flaming in her heart. "I . . . don't know." A way to improve her chances in the future? She at least ought to consider it. Shouldn't she? "Can't you tell me more about what it is?"

Mogurn sighed impatiently. "Can I tell you what love is, Jael? Or life? You have to experience it, to know. And now you must display some courage, and the will to fly!"

Jael looked away from him, stalling.

"Don't be undecided too long, Miss LeBrae," Mogurn warned. "I subscribe to a shipper's code of ethics. But I need a rigger for my ship, and soon. If you are not interested in flying, I must seek another. I have little time, and I have given you much of it already." Mogurn's eyes seemed to bore into hers.

A hundred thoughts flew through her mind: all of her vows, her hopes and doubts and fears, and her determination to fly. She gazed at the rigger lounge and saw the steward who had brought her to Mogurn. He saw her, as well, and his eyebrows went up as he turned away, as though saying, There will never be a job for you here, not on this side. And she felt a renewed rage and frustration, and for a moment, she felt utterly incapable of decision. Then her determination burned through again, and she drew a slow breath. *Which is more important—some self-defeating vow, or flying?* She remembered her father standing over her, saying, "Never pity yourself, Jael! Seize the moment!" She never thought she would take her father's advice, but as she looked back up at Mogurn, she heard herself saying, "I want to know more about your ship before I say yes or no. Do you have the specs and service records for me to see?"

A smile twitched at the corner of Mogurn's mouth, and he nodded. "Of course. If you'd like to come with me, you can review everything." And Jael swallowed and drew herself to her full height and followed him across the lobby.

Chapter 4
DEPARTURE

SHE MET Dap on her way out. She was just tucking her flight contract into her tunic pocket when she saw him approach.

"Jael, wait! Please," he said, falling into step beside her. "Can I talk to you—please?"

She paused in midstride and looked at him, frowning. She no longer felt angry, exactly, just distant. "About what?" She started walking again, more purposefully than she had walked in a long time.

"Well, I don't . . . I just . . . just want to apologize," he stammered. "Jael, I know I was rude the other night. I don't blame you for being mad."

"Good," she sighed.

"But I wish . . . I wish you hadn't walked off like that! I could have explained why I was . . . anyway, I'm really sorry."

"Yes. So you said before," she answered, not meeting his gaze.

"I guess you don't believe me, but at least let me try to explain!"

"I believe you," she lied. "I'm very sorry, Dap, but I've just signed onto a ship and I have to get ready to leave. Maybe I'll see you when I get back."

That stopped him in his tracks. She barely glanced back at him as he hurried to catch up again. "You got a job? That's wonderful! I'm really happy for you. Jael, who is it with?"

That stopped *her*. She sighed to herself and turned. "Do you really care?"

"Yes, of course I do!"

"I'm flying with a shipper named Deuteronomous Mogurn, and his ship is *Cassandra*." She had a feeling of unreality as she heard herself saying the words.

Dap's brow furrowed. "Mogurn? I don't know the name. But *Cassandra*. Isn't that an unregist—"

She stepped away angrily. "I know what it is. You don't have to tell me—"

"Wait—I didn't mean—*Jael!*" He finally grabbed her arm and physically brought her to a halt. "Jael, you aren't flying an unregistered ship, are you? After everything you said?"

"Yes I am and would you please let go of my arm?"

He stared at her, dumbfounded. "But . . . why?" His grip loosened.

She pulled her arm free and straightened up. "Because I want to fly and it has been made clear that that is my only avenue at this spaceport. Is that reason enough?"

"But . . . you don't have to . . . you could tell them—"

"What, Dap? What? I just accepted the job and gave my word that I would be aboard in three hours. All right?" She started to walk away again, but something in his expression made her pause and look back at him.

He nodded and said softly, "I guess I understand. If I had to, I suppose I might do the same." His eyes seemed to lose their focus as he gazed out over the hills. He shook his head, then focused back on Jael. "But I really hope . . ."

She waited. She didn't know why she was standing there listening to him, but she waited. "Hope what?" she said finally.

"That . . . you've chosen well. That you'll be . . . very careful." He swallowed, then fumbled in his pocket. "Here, I'd like to give you something." He brought out a thin gold chain, with a small, luminous stone on it. "This was from Deira, to me. She said it was to help me remember our time in the net together. Well . . ." he cleared his throat nervously—Jael had never seen him so fidgety before—"I'd like you to have it as a keepsake. Sort of a good luck charm. And a way of saying, I hope it works out all right for you . . . out there." He held the chain out to her, his gaze wide and earnest.

She hesitated, then opened her palm and slowly closed it around the cool metal chain, the stone. For a moment, she almost forgave him for the other night, but the weight of her anger was too great, and her fear over what she was about to do too strong. She could find no words to say any of that, so instead she said, "Okay. Thanks. And now, I really have to go."

"Good trip, Jael."

She sighed and nodded. Then she turned and strode, then ran, up the hill toward the multidorm and her quarters.

She set her bag on the ground and looked up at the starship. It was a modest-sized floater: silver-grey, shaped like a flared, flattened teardrop. It drooped like a guppy's belly in the middle and was festooned with a variety of protrusions for maneuvering units and flux-field and rigger-net projectors. The name *Cassandra* was painted in black just above the bulge of the flux-field reactors, but the letters were well worn by the elements of space and atmosphere, as were the identifying numerals amidships. It looked like a sturdy enough vessel, though one could hardly tell much by external appearances. Still, the service log had seemed acceptable, more carefully annotated than she had expected from an unregulated shipper; and the owner was flying with her, as captain, which provided some incentive for good maintenance. Perhaps her worries about substandard equipment, at least, were unjustified. The spaceport service crew had just driven away as she had walked up. She would check over the rigger controls herself before departure.

Jael strode to the base of the ship where it nested in the docking cradles. The outer door of the entry lock was open, at the top of a short ramp. She stepped into the airlock and searched the door panel for the communication switch. "Jael LeBrae. Request permission to come aboard."

There was a short silence. Then a staticky voice answered, "Come on up to the bridge, Jael. Top level. Seal the lock when you come."

She touched the appropriate switches and stepped into the ship. The outer hatch, then inner hatch, hissed closed. She glanced around at the power deck; the ladder up was in a pool of light, spilling down from deck two. She slung her bag strap over her shoulder and climbed. The next level was a second engineering deck. She located and climbed one more ladder, and stepped off into a tight, ring-shaped hallway. It took only a moment to figure out the layout. In the center of the ring was the commons area; several other doors around the outer circumference of the hall were living quarters. Around the circle to her right was the entrance to the bridge.

Mogurn emerged from the bridge and greeted her. "Put your bag in the first cabin, then come join me on the bridge. We're checking out for flight." He turned and disappeared again.

Jael pressed the entry plate on the next door beyond the bridge. When the door paled, she walked through it into the cabin. It was small and spare: a bunk, a fold-down chair, and a tiny lavatory. All perfectly standard, perfectly Spartan. She stepped back out into the hallway, opaqued the door, and hurried to the bridge.

It was dimly lit, but filled with illuminated displays. Mogurn was seated at the front, his back to her; he was inspecting a thicket of instruments, mostly normal-space gear and remotes from the rigger-nets. There were two Seiki-model rigger-stations, one flanking either side of the bridge: couches recessed into tight, horizontal alcoves. That was where she would do her flying. Two rigger-stations, one rigger. The second station was a backup, or possibly where a co-rigger would fly, if there were one. It was hard to tell at a glance; the variety in ship and rigger-station design was almost endless. Some setups were complex, like tall-masted ships of the sea, requiring several riggers working in perfect harmony;

others were compact and without frills, perfect for single riggers. She fleetingly wondered if Mogurn might be cutting corners, using only one rigger where two were optimal. Such a thing was not unheard of, especially among unreg—but never mind that, she thought. What sensible owner would endanger a valuable ship and cargo in order to save one rigger's salary?

"Go ahead and familiarize yourself with the setup," Mogurn said, glancing up into a small mirror. "I'll be through here in a few minutes."

Jael nodded and began looking over the instrumentation near the starboard rigger-station, which was marked as the primary station. She could inspect a station in her sleep if she had to, which was a good thing, because suddenly it was hitting home that she was about to depart for deep space with a man she scarcely knew, and whose credentials were marginal at best. She had flown solo before, yes, but never in such an unprotected fashion. Not that she was concerned for her own personal safety; there were implicit guarantees, even with men like Mogurn.

There had been a time when a female rigger might not have dared to board a ship like this, to be isolated with a man of unknown character for days or weeks at a time. But over many decades of starship rigging, the loss of too many ships had proven one thing: the fragile balance of sensitivity, imagination, and control that enabled a rigger to steer through the Flux was easily destroyed. Whatever the treatment of unemployed riggers planetside, the well-being of a rigger in flight was considered sacrosanct. Even the unlicensed shippers acknowledged that fact. Even Jael's own father had recognized it.

These reassurances flickered through her mind as she ran through her checklist on the rigger-station. It was important to make herself ready for flight, as well as her station. The worries of the world, of the rigger halls and the spaceports, had to be purged from her thoughts. The sooner her head was clear, the smoother and safer the flight would be.

"We're bound for Lexis on the first leg," Mogurn remarked, without turning. "Bypassing the mountain route, of course."

"Ah," Jael said, searching her memories for what she'd learned in training about that route. Oh, yes . . .

"No point in getting into any trouble with . . . unnecessary hazards . . . on that mountain route, is there?" Mogurn added.

"I guess not," Jael murmured. There were legends about the route from decades of rigging, but perhaps no more than with any of a hundred other unusual regions, each replete with legends. What was it here? Dragons, as she recalled. Nothing to worry her.

"No. No point in getting into trouble," Mogurn said. He was still busy at the nose of the bridge, and for a few moments, neither of them spoke. Jael continued her checkout. Then he asked, "You do know the route, don't you?"

Jael paused. She had never flown to Lexis, but she knew the essentials of the route, the library hypno-briefings on the various currents of the Flux. She said as much to Mogurn.

He turned in his seat and gazed at her. "Well, I've been that way many times. So even if you're the rigger and I'm not, I trust you'll accept some guidance in the matter of navigation."

She blinked. "Of course," she said, shrugging.

"Good." Mogurn turned back to his panels. "Just so you know. The mountains are dangerous. I'll expect you to keep me informed."

As if she wouldn't do that anyway, she thought, checking the last of the instruments on the outside of the station. She leaned in to peer at the actual flight readouts. "All right if I—"

"Go ahead. It's part of your checklist isn't it?"

"Yes." She slid into the alcove, reclining on her back on the couch. Squirming into a comfortable position, she allowed the nape of her neck to touch the neural contacts in the neckrest, and she waited for the tingle which confirmed that she was in contact with the dormant net control. She focused her eyes on the instruments over her head and began bringing power to the control system. After a few moments, she closed her eyes and allowed the tingle of the system to spread into her limbs and into her mind.

She felt herself surrounded by darkness. She reached into the sensory net with imaginary hands and tested it, probing at its limits to see how it felt. The net was still confined within the spacecraft hull—it would be extended fully only after they were in space—but its form was sufficient for testing. She stretched the arms of her imagination against the darkness, and her inner eye sketched out lines of perspective against that darkness, lines that gave shape to the nonspace surrounding her. As she explored the field with her mind, her physical body remained motionless on the couch. Once she was satisfied that the field was responding adequately to her thoughts, she withdrew from the net, withdrew back into her physical body.

She opened her eyes. The monitors overhead gave a reading of the field strengths she had used in this simple check, and the trial efficiencies of the field. She pursed her lips and nodded. It was well within acceptable limits.

There was a movement beside her, and she realized that Mogurn was standing beside the rigger-station. He bent down and peered in. His eyes shifted back and forth, scrutinizing her. What was he doing—looking for flaws, for signs of weakness? His eyes, close up, looked bloodshot and rheumy. "Everything okay?" he asked.

"Seems to be," she said, running her fingers over the monitor faces. It made her uncomfortable to be stared at. There was no reason why he shouldn't observe her, of course; he had a right to know if his ship was in capable hands.

"Good. We'll be lifting soon. You have anything you need to do before I call for the tow?" Mogurn asked.

"May I have a minute in my cabin?"

Mogurn straighted up. "Of course. I'll make the call now. It'll take them a few minutes to get to us, I imagine."

As she slipped out of the rigger-station, he was leaning back in his command seat, watching her. She could not read his expression, but she was aware of his gaze on her back as she walked off the bridge.

In her cabin, she spent a few minutes stowing the contents

of her duffel and poking around in the drawers and compartments. She paused to gaze at herself in the tiny wall mirror. Her face looked a little drawn, she thought, and her flyaway brown hair needed brushing. But her hazel eyes were clear and determined; or at least, they seemed that way when she frowned at herself and thought, *You're committed now. It doesn't matter whether you were smart or not. Just do the job and do it right, and it'll be okay in the end.* She tried to smile. The expression looked foolish to her.

Enough. Time to make ready for space.

"Jael, is your station set?" Mogurn asked, from the nose of the bridge.

"Set," she answered, looking up at the monitors one more time. There was really nothing for her to do at this point but enjoy the ride and keep a watch on the systems for later.

"Tow *Juliette*, this is *Cassandra*. At your convenience," Mogurn said.

She couldn't see him from where she lay in the rigger-station, but in the monitor, she could see the tow ship as it approached Mogurn's ship from overhead. It looked like a thin four-legged spider dropping down on an invisible silk thread. Soon it blocked the overhead view as it settled atop *Cassandra* and latched with a barely perceptible bump. Then Jael felt a vibration under her couch as the landing dock freed the ship. A moment later, a weight pressed lightly upon her as they lifted free of the ground and began to climb. In one monitor she could see the ground falling away; in another, she could see the globes at the ends of the spider's legs glowing red, then orange. Those were the Circadie space inductors that would propel them into orbit and take them well away from the planetary mass of Gaston's Landing, far enough away to begin the rest of the voyage under their own power.

A few moments after liftoff, the ship's gravity fields came up on internal power, and the feeling of weight on her chest subsided. The monitors confirmed, however, that the true acceleration was increasing. The curvature of the planet became visible as the sky turned black, and Jael wished her homeworld a silent farewell.

Minutes later, the planet was visible as an enormous ball in space, shrinking as they left their orbit behind. Jael felt exhilaration rising in her breast as the ship and its tow accelerated across the emptiness of the planetary system, the stars brightly beckoning before them. It was a good feeling, a true rigger feeling, the almost primal joy of bursting the bonds of planetary life, of expanding outward, stretching, reaching. And as she watched it all happen in her monitors, she began to trace the Flux indicators, the signs that would tell her when it was safe to submerge the ship for the *real* journey. And she began to imagine the coming entry into the Flux, to prepare in her own mind for what was to come.

Chapter 5
CAPTAIN MOGURN

"YOU'RE ON your own, *Cassandra*. Have a good flight."

"We are clear, *Juliette*. Thank you."

Jael was aware of Mogurn's voice on the communicator; and she was aware of the tow's space inductors changing color as it altered course and broke away; and she was aware of the tow dwindling and disappearing into the night, just as the planet had. But mostly she was aware of the dormant field tingling around her as she prepared for Mogurn's okay. Her mind was filled with an expectation of images, of landscapes.

"Jael, are you ready?" came Mogurn's voice directly in her ear-com.

"On your signal."

"Are you familiarized with the course?"

She frowned at the monitor where she'd been reviewing the navigational library information. "As clear as I can be without actually taking us in there."

There was a movement nearby, and she realized that Mogurn had walked back to peer directly down into her rigger-station. She shifted her eyes in his direction, but only for a moment. It was more important to keep an even keel mentally than to respond directly to his presence. She sensed Mogurn returning to his seat at the front. "Very well," she heard. "Set course for Lexis. At your discretion, rigger."

Her eyes closed and she felt her own lips tracing a smile. The sensory net sprang to life around her, filled her with energy. She relaxed as her bodily senses darkened. Her inner senses threaded their way into the net and reached outward, stretching into space. Altering the shape of the net with unspoken commands, she sank her fingernails into the fabric of space itself, and without fanfare, drew the spaceship into the realm that would carry it to the stars. It was the energy of the flux-pile that did the work, of course, but she guided the flow of the energy. Silently, swiftly, like a swimmer upending herself and stroking downward into the depths of a sea, she left behind the cold emptiness of normal-space, and swam down through the shifting multidimensional layers of spacetime, down into the currents of the Flux. And she towed the starship along behind her.

What she saw next was a synthesis of her own intuition and the reality of the spacetime topography that she had just entered. She and the starship were floating in a sea of turquoise mist, translucent and cool. It was an undersea color, but the mist was airy and swirling, and it shifted like cirriform clouds touched by a high jetstream. Jael extended her arms like wings—strong limbs that were at once imaginary and real—and she stroked the mists as they passed her by, until she began to sense the wind direction and currents. She stretched her wings a bit wider and felt them bite into the current, and she executed a slow bank to her left and caught sight of what looked like a lemon-lime sunset in the distance. That, she knew instantly and intuitively, was where she wanted to go.

That knowledge was all she needed. She caught the wind, and she and the starship took flight upon the streams of space.

Jael, how are you doing in there? Mogurn's voice reached her through the net, through the ghostly presence of the com-signal.

I feel good. It's going well. She had been flying for a couple of hours already. The mists had given way to a clear tangerine sky. Smudges of charcoal cloudiness in the sky indicated distant presences, perhaps the analogs of stars or nebulas in the adjoining regions of normal-space. She had turned the starship into an image of a broad-winged airplane, and she was steering a course well clear of all such disturbances.

It's time you came out for a while. I don't want you getting fatigued. Are you in a clear stretch? Can you leave the net?

Jael considered. *Pretty clear. I guess so.* She felt reluctant to leave it behind. But she knew that his instructions were probably wise. It would not do to push too far, especially since the flight was just beginning. Still . . .

Do so, then. Set your stabilizers. Mogurn's voice was calm but unequivocal.

Doing so now, she sighed. It took only a moment to adjust the net's stabilizers. Like a sea-anchor, they would keep the ship drifting quietly and safely during her absence. She pulled her imaginary arms back to her sides and withdrew from the net.

With a blink, she focused on the monitors overhead. Her physical senses returned to her gradually, as she became aware of light entering her eyes and the weight of her body pressing down on the couch. She drew a deep breath and exhaled slowly. Only after she felt that she had really returned to her body did she climb out of the rigger-station.

The bridge seemed like a small chamber of arcane technology after the free open spaces of the net. Mogurn rose from his seat at the nose and turned to face her. "The readings look smooth and stable. That tells me that you are flying skillfully," he said. "But we must not overdo it. Besides, I have something for you now—a sort of reward for work well done." He smiled broadly.

A reward for work well done? she thought. Work well done was its own reward. Then she remembered his promise, back at the spaceport. Something about a learning method.

"But perhaps you'd like to eat first," Mogurn said. He pursed his lips. "Yes. We will eat first. And then you will experience . . . the *pallisp*. You will enjoy it, I think. And as for what it will do for your rigging ability . . ." He shrugged, and his smile widened.

Pallisp? She opened her mouth to ask, "What is . . ."

But Mogurn wasn't listening. He gestured toward the exit and followed her off the bridge and to the commons in the center of the ship's circle. "What would you like, Jael?" he asked, gesturing toward the auto-food panels. "Are you hungry? How about . . . oh, some nicely crisped carrot-fish?" Before Jael could answer, he nodded to himself and touched several buttons. The smell of frying fish filled the commons.

Jael shrugged. Fish was all right with her, she supposed. While Mogurn fussed with the settings, she sat at the round table in the center of the room and watched. He drew a glass of what looked like a straw-colored ale and turned. "This is nonalcoholic. Would you like some, Jael?"

"Yes, please," she said, wondering if any other response would have made any difference.

Mogurn drew a second glass and placed it in front of her. A minute later, the food panel whispered open, and he pulled out two steaming dinner plates. "Here we are. I think you'll like this."

Jael waited until Mogurn had taken a bite from his own plate before she tentatively lifted a fork and tried a bite of the fish. It looked more like crisped cheese; it tasted like a flavorless vegetable with a breadlike texture. But, she thought, it was no worse than what they served at the rigger halls. And it was food.

Mogurn ate quickly and without conversation. He hummed softly to himself, reaching up occasionally to stroke the back of his neck. When he looked in Jael's direction, he didn't seem to see her; it was as though he were looking at something beyond her, beyond the walls of the room. That was all right; she was happy enough to be silent with her own thoughts. Mogurn, hardly to her surprise, seemed a rather self-absorbed person. She doubted that he would be very good company even if he spoke.

She was only halfway through her meal when Mogurn

rose, leaving his dishes and utensils on the table. He pointed to a black panel and said, "The dirty things go in there. When you're finished tidying up, come to my cabin. It's the second door after yours." In response to her surprised expression, he added, "Don't be long, please." And then he turned, his robe swirling, and left the commons.

Jael stared after him and scowled at what was left of her dinner, which now seemed unappetizing. She started to formulate a reply—that she was employed as a rigger, not as a housekeeper—but cut the thought short. It would do no good to be angry about it. She had to live with Mogurn for the rest of the trip, and she hadn't expected him to be perfect. Perhaps she ought to count her blessings and enjoy the aspect of the flight which was her reason for being here—the rigging, the dreamlike freedom of the net. The thought calmed her enough to take a few more bites, before she decided that she was no longer hungry. She drank some of the ale, then carried everything from the table to the disposal panel. A soft whine told her that the processing unit had accepted her offering and was tidying up.

She stood, looking around the room, wishing that she could simply return to the net and continue flying. But she remembered Mogurn's instructions. Don't be long. Very well, then. She would go to the captain's cabin, and she would see what this "pallisp" business was all about.

The corridor was virtually silent, only the whisper of the air circulator breaking the stillness. She found Mogurn's cabin door—the ship was so small that it was only a few steps to any compartment—and stood before it for several moments, thinking. Then she pressed the signal plate. The door paled and she stepped into Mogurn's cabin.

It was larger than hers, and expensively appointed. A crystal tapestry adorned one wall; it gleamed and twinkled before her eyes, fragments of colored light dancing within it. Beneath the tapestry was a bench-seat. Across the room from the door, Mogurn sat in a velour-covered chair, smoking. He did not look directly at her, but she sensed nevertheless that he was watching her. He exhaled a plume of sharp-scented smoke and waved his long, tubular smoking pipe. "You have come, Jael. Sit." He gestured toward the bench-seat.

Jael obeyed. She looked at him uneasily. For a moment, he made no move to shift from his apparently comfortable position; then he turned his head to gaze at her. "Have you found the course clear and easy to visualize, so far?" he asked.

She inclined her head slightly. "So far."

"And have you sighted the mountains along the route?"

She shook her head. "No mountains yet. I sense some change coming in the landscape. But it's too far away to tell yet."

"Yes, well . . ." he drew a breath of smoke and exhaled. The smoke eddied up around the ceiling before it was drawn away, gradually, by the ventilators. "That would be the mountains, I expect. You may not see them as mountains, precisely, but that is how it has most often been described to me."

She nodded. She was familiar with the navigational charts. There ought to be no problem.

"You will find danger in those mountains," Mogurn warned, and for a moment his eyes glinted with some unspoken tension. "The way around them to Lexis is longer. But it is safer, and therefore to be preferred."

"Yes," she answered. "As we spoke of before."

Mogurn smiled. "Quite so. As I spoke of before." He glanced at his pipe and set it aside. "And now." He rose and stood before her, and in his hand was a small gleaming cylinder with a dull grey sphere attached to one end. His eyes searched hers briefly. "You've gotten us off to a good start on this trip, Jael. So I especially want you to enjoy this first experience with the pallisp." He glanced down at the instrument in his hand.

She followed his glance with suspicion. Drawing back a little, she pressed her lips together. "What is that?"

"This is the pallisp, Jael." He tilted his head. "It will not harm you." He rubbed at the tic that had reappeared in the corner of his left eye.

"Maybe not," she said doubtfully. "But I don't want to just use it without knowing what it is. You said it was a learning device, a learning *method*."

"Yes, Jael. Precisely. It is a synaptic enhancement device, specially designed for riggers. It triggers relaxation reflexes in the mind. You should find it restful, and pleasurable. Isn't that all right?" Mogurn peered at her wonderingly, and perhaps impatiently.

Jael shrugged. "I guess so. But what's that have to do with learning?"

Mogurn pursed his lips. "A fair question. The relaxation is only the outward sensation. If you're like most individuals who use it, it will gradually sharpen those very sensitivities that serve you so well in the net. Over time, this pallisp will make you a better rigger, Jael."

She wondered fleetingly why, if it was so good, she had never heard of the pallisp before. It was possible, of course, that a device common on another world simply had not been introduced to Gaston's Landing, which if truth be told was little more than a backwater colony. But if that was the case . . .

She had no more time to think about it, because Mogurn was extending the pallisp toward her right shoulder. She felt a small wave of pleasurable radiation from it, and pulled away. "Wait!" she protested.

"What is it now?" he demanded.

She struggled to put words to her fear. "Are you sure this isn't . . . harmful?"

Mogurn sighed as he shook his head. "I told you. No."

Jael frowned. She wanted to trust him, but . . . how could she be sure?

"This is to make you a better rigger, Jael. That's in both of our interests, isn't it? Now, may we begin? Bend your head down and pull your hair away from the back of your neck."

Taking a deep breath, she did as she was told. Mogurn stood close to her and touched the ball of the pallisp to the back of her neck. She shivered with a sensation of warmth, though the touch of the ball was cool. The ball came to rest against the hollow at the base of her skull. The warmth blossomed, flowed first into her brain, then outward into her body, into her limbs. A glow seemed to appear inside her mind, a glow of friendliness and comfort.

It was like the dreamlink, but far better. The golden light that swelled into her awareness was like nothing she had ever felt, but it was like a feeling she had often imagined—a feeling not only of warmth, but of companionship and love—all of the feelings of love that she had ever dreamed of but never felt in reality, emerging from that light and spilling through her in a caressing stream. Unlike the dreamlink, this did not ask her to open herself, did not invite vulnerability. Unlike the dreamlink, this was purest pleasure and fulfillment. It was like floating in a warm, pulsing amniotic sea. It was like being safe again in the womb. . . .

Chapter 6
THE PALLISP

SHE SHIVERED as the warmth ebbed away. Don't stop! she wanted to cry. But it was already disappearing; the glow was fading. She felt as though she had just been to Heaven, and she wanted to go back! Blinking, she wondered how long the feeling had lasted; it seemed only moments, but it was like a dream fleeing, intangible. She might have been under the pallisp for hours.

"Are you awake, Jael?"

Drawing a breath, she raised her head and focused. Mogurn was standing in front of her, nodding in apparent satisfaction. He slipped the silver-and-grey pallisp into a pocket inside his vesta. "Um," Jael muttered, suppressing an urge to reach out and seize the pallisp from him. Whatever that instrument was, it was wonderful. Wonderful!

"I told you it would be interesting, Jael. Would you agree with me?"

Slowly, drawing her awareness back in, centering herself, she nodded. Interesting, she thought. Indeed it was.

"Would you like more?"

She peered up into his face and could not read what she

saw there. His eyes seemed to focus on her with a greater intensity, a greater curiosity, than she remembered. "I . . ." She faltered without finishing her answer.

"This will become a regular reward for you, for work well done." Mogurn returned to his chair and rested his head back, observing her as she stretched, coming back to full alertness.

"What does it do?" she asked, choosing to let her puzzlement show, rather than her desire for more. "It must stimulate—somehow, I guess—the pleasure center of the brain?" She sounded like an idiot, she knew. But it was not an idiotic question.

"Something like that, Jael. The important thing is that it will help you to release your own greater potential when it comes to flying." He lifted a bushy, half-grey eyebrow. "It's not dangerous, if you're still worried about that. I told you that before." He pursed his lips and let out a deep sigh. "And now, I require your help. Would you come here, please?"

Jael rose unsteadily and approached.

Mogurn shifted restfully. "I'm going to ask you to help me with my own synaptic augmentor. My reward for work well done." His thumb and forefinger stroked away a smile that had come to his lips. His gaze sharpened. "But first you must have your instructions. While I am under the augmentor, you may sleep—after first double-checking our position. You are not to fly, however, unless extraordinary conditions demand it. I will tell you when your next shift begins. Until then you will maintain stability in the Flux, and no more. Is that clear?"

Jael nodded uneasily. She acknowledged, but did not understand his unusual request. Ordinarily, a rigger would determine her own flight routine. Still, she didn't suppose it mattered. She closed her eyes for a moment, remembering the blissful warmth of the pallisp, and she sighed softly. Opening her eyes she saw, hanging from the padded arm of Mogurn's chair, a small holotronic unit with what looked like a headpiece attached to a thin fiber-op cable.

Mogurn's eyes followed hers, and he nodded. Reaching for the headpiece, he said, "I must ask you to help me adjust this." He donned the headpiece, showing her how to adjust the slender contact arms to the proper points on his temples and the back of his neck. "Yes. Now, you must set the controls on the unit. Two hours at intensity four. You must observe the power fluctuation for a moment to make the adjustment. Do you see it?"

When she had followed his instructions, she stepped back warily. Mogurn no longer seemed to notice her presence. He sighed deeply, his eyelids fluttered, and a broad smile came over his features and grew to a grin. His eyes did not close, but appeared to focus on nothing at all. "Are you . . . is that all right?" But Jael realized, when he did not answer, that there would *be* no answer—not, at least, until the unit switched itself off, two hours from now. And what was Mogurn experiencing under the influence of the synaptic augmentor? Was it like the pallisp? She backed away a few steps and watched him. His hands began to twitch, as though he were in a deep dream-state; they began to take on a life of their own, making squeezing and stroking motions. Jael began to feel embarrassed.

She backed toward the door, fascinated but repelled. Was this what she looked like under the pallisp? She remembered only peacefulness and warmth and light. Whatever this augmentor was designed to do, it looked more powerful than the pallisp, and more dangerous. It looked like nothing she would care to experience.

She crept into the corridor with a feeling of relief. The door turned opaque behind her, leaving Mogurn to his solitude—leaving her alone with the starship, perhaps the only conscious human being between here and the distant star system of Lexis. With a shiver, she circled around the hallway, exploring what little she had not yet seen of the deck: one other empty cabin, and one storage compartment. There was not much else to look at. But she did have another duty to perform.

As she entered the bridge, she could not help remembering the glow of the pallisp. She wished it could have lasted just a little longer; it was so comforting, so reassuring, so restorative. Just a little more. . . . She exhaled deliberately and walked forward to the rigger-station. A glance at the readouts told her that nothing had changed much in the net; a glance at the instruments in the nose of the bridge confirmed that all systems were functioning normally.

Should she enter the net? Mogurn had said not to fly, but he'd also said to make sure that all was well. That, in her mind, meant taking a firsthand look. Besides, she wasn't ready to sleep yet.

Slipping into the station, she entered the net. Her senses darkened and reached out of the ship, into the glowing realm of the Flux. It looked exactly as she had left it: tangerine sky and gently sighing breezes bearing the ship like a stately, royal barge toward the horizon. Toward whatever lay beyond. She extended her vision, trying to discern what that might be. Was her sensitivity any sharper now? She couldn't tell. Were there mountains ahead? She felt a presence of something strong and substantial, perhaps mountains. It felt like a living presence. Sometimes the landscape of the Flux was like that; it was as though it were itself alive. Soon they would be close and she would see.

But now it was time to readjust the stabilizers, to close the net and retire. She sighed as she withdrew, as her eyes blinked open, as she studied the hard cold presence of monitors overhead. There were times when she wished she could stay in the net forever. With a frown, she climbed out and took one last look around the bridge, and went to her cabin.

Sleep did not come quickly, or easily. Her thoughts danced between memories of the net and of the pallisp, and feelings of hope and excitement fluttered helplessly against her uneasiness about Mogurn, against the recurring image of the man twitching and sighing under his synaptic augmentor.

At last she drifted off, carried on the winds of sleep and dream.

She awoke to the sound of Mogurn's voice on the intercom, summoning her to breakfast. They ate in silence, Jael trying to wake up fully for the flying that lay ahead, and half wanting to remain in the somnolence that still enveloped her. But Mogurn, once done with his own breakfast, rose and hurried her to the bridge.

To her relief, he sent her directly into the net, with the same cautions as before. She was on her own to fly. It was

Jael and the sparkling net. Jael and the endless currents of the Flux. She reveled in the freedom.

The imagery changed, with a little coaxing from her half-conscious thoughts. An orangish sky turned into an autumn forest in full color, leaves and needles of gold and crimson and russet, rustling in the wind and dancing against the sun. Jael and her ship were a great flying creature, diving and swooping over the forest with whispering speed.

She flew for several hours, threading her way along a twisting wooded valley, along a thin gleaming river, along the twists and turns of spatial dimension that, paradoxically, so shortened the distance between the star systems. She flew with a confidence that her path was straight, figuratively speaking, and true. In time, she found herself remembering the sensations of the pallisp, and while it did not particularly affect her flying, she found herself eagerly awaiting her next exposure to those sensations.

When the time came to leave the net, she did so with a feeling of accomplishment and pride. And, as she'd hoped, Mogurn ushered her into his cabin, and there she bent her head—this time with greater anticipation than nervousness—and received the softly glowing warmth of the pallisp.

And afterward, with the glow still warm in her heart, she gratefully assisted Mogurn with his own synaptic augmentor. She slept then, and awoke eager and ready to fly once more.

The fourth time she emerged from the pallisp, she did so with what she recognized for the first time as a deep reluctance, a feeling of almost physical attachment to the sensations. It required an effort of will to leave it, and not ask for more. Still, she shook off the feeling and flew her next shift with greater determination, and a greater than ever desire to return to drink again of the pallisp. Almost, she asked Mogurn if they might skip their meal so that she could have the pallisp sooner; but Mogurn's stolid expression, and her own sudden sense of fear and shame, caused her to remain silent and to wait impatiently.

It wasn't until the next day that it dawned on her that she now wanted the pallisp even more than she wanted to fly. She began to wonder if she was perhaps in danger of growing dependent upon the artificial feelings of warmth and companionship that the pallisp gave her, feelings that she craved, but couldn't find elsewhere. She said nothing of her worries to Mogurn, but as she flew over a seemingly endless series of scarlet and umber mesas and canyons, she decided that she would forbear from the pallisp today—just for today—to ensure that she did not actually become addicted to it.

Mogurn's eyes glinted as she said haltingly, over lunch, "I'd like to . . . just rest for a while. I'd like . . . not to use the pallisp this time."

Mogurn studied her, without betraying his thoughts. "Of course, Jael. I wouldn't force you to do anything you don't want to. But if you change your mind, well, the next chance will be—"

"I'm not going to change my mind," she interrupted, wondering, even as she said it, whether it was true.

"Very well, then. Come help me in a few minutes. And then you may relax as you wish." Mogurn rose, and his expression seemed to flicker between irritation and a faintly amused smile.

"Yes," Jael said to the empty room after he'd gone.

"Yes," she repeated a moment later, when she realized that she really did, in fact, want the pallisp.

No. Not this time. She drew herself a cup of fully caffeinated coffee and sipped it slowly, savoring the rush that the caffeine sent to her brain.

When the time came, she went into Mogurn's cabin and, trembling a little, adjusted his synaptic augmentor before retiring to her own cabin. It was only moments later, when genuine crushing despair set in, that she knew she should not have denied herself her reward. The world seemed to close in upon her. Lacking the warmth of the pallisp, she felt only the ponderous weight of her friendlessness, the emptiness of knowing that she might never again fly with a registered shipper, and the haunting chill of the suspicions she harbored in the back of her mind about Mogurn's character. She felt a terrible weight of oppression. And edging around the corners of her consciousness was the fear that she had been tricked terribly, that she had, in these past few days, succumbed to a force that would never release her—the force of the pallisp.

She wanted it badly now; her heart ached for it.

She sat in her cabin, dreaming of the pallisp, of the golden warmth of it; and she shivered in the air that suddenly seemed cold, and she began to cry a little, but only for a few moments. Taking a deep breath, she blew her nose and began pacing the tiny floor of her cabin. She toyed with a book-cube, then put it aside, and she put on her music necklace and paced some more, with symphonic music swelling in her bones. Nothing helped. She thought of going to Mogurn and begging him for the pallisp, but to do that she would have had to interrupt his own pleasures, and that she dared not do.

Finally she left her cabin and went to the bridge. She took the seat up front and tried to find some comfort in the flickering presence of the instruments. But what she really wanted was to go back into the net. She knew she wasn't supposed to while Mogurn was under his wire . . . except to check on the stability of the net and the Flux.

So, go check.

But I shouldn't, really.

But you know you will, in the end.

And, in the end, she did. She took her place in the riggerstation and let her senses expand outward, beyond the ship. They were drifting smoothly, she found, with no sign of instability. She remained in the net, comforted by the scenery—a warm buttery sun shining down on the placid waters of a smooth-flowing river. She felt comforted for a little while—until she began to remember what she had missed in the pallisp . . .

And then she began reflecting upon other things: Dap's heartlessness in the dreamlink, two nights before her departure; and her father, and how he had once been a decent man, or so she'd heard, until his changing fortunes in shipping had changed him as well.

The net began to rumble.

This pattern of thought was not a good one for flying. The sun slid out of sight behind a dark thundercloud. The river's surface began to swirl and eddy and roil. Alarmed, she tried to readjust her thoughts, to keep them focused. Rigging required a delicate balance: the currents and patterns of the Flux were objectively real, but it was her imagination, her thoughts and emotions transmuted through the net, that colored in the detail. And the detail was no less real, coming as it did from her mind. When a rigger's thoughts became disturbed, danger to the ship was always a possibility. And if her sensitivities were growing keener as a result of the pallisp, so too was the danger from imagining the wrong things.

She knew she ought to set the stabilizers and withdraw until she had her thoughts under control again. But she worried about what might happen if she left the ship in this condition. And she worried about what Mogurn would say. And so she flew a little longer to see if she could straighten it out, and straighten herself out. And after a time, she managed to calm herself, and she stayed with the river image, but found smoother waters and set a steady course upon them. And though the bright warm sun did not return, the threatening storm clouds thinned into a grey canopy which reflected her feeling of melancholy, but also seemed to offer safety and stability.

At that point she readjusted the stabilizers and withdrew. As she came back to her own senses, she realized how tired she was, physically as well as emotionally. She climbed out of the rigger-station and stretched.

"Jael!"

She jumped, startled. Turning, she found herself facing a grim Deuteronomous Mogurn. "You have been rigging," he accused, his voice harsh but controlled. His eyes were lined with blood vessels. He looked furious. She wondered how long she had been in the net; she had not expected him to be awake this soon. "What were my instructions about rigging while I was not here?" he demanded.

Jael glanced down guiltily. "You said . . . only to check on instabilities." She felt cornered, she had to defend herself. "And I . . . when I was in there, some instabilities came up, and I . . . had to deal with them."

Mogurn stroked his chin warily. "I see." He studied the external instruments for a moment. "Perhaps so. But you were in there a long time. And the readings do not look that good. They do not look that good, Jael." He stared back at her, and she could see that he was not convinced. "Are you certain you did not just decide to stay in the net for a while because you missed something else?"

Nervously, she shrugged. What's so wrong with flying the ship? she wondered. And what have you done to me, anyway, you liar? She thought of what she might have missed; she thought more than longingly of it.

Mogurn seemed to be reading her thoughts. "Did you miss the pallisp, Jael? Was that it?"

She frowned, not wanting to answer. Finally, she nodded unhappily.

"I see." Mogurn nodded, rubbing his temple. "I'm not incapable of understanding that. I'm not an insensitive man, Jael. Would you like the pallisp now?"

She tried not to look at him, but she couldn't help it. "Yes," she whispered. And as she said it, the smile that flickered across his face gave her a shiver of fear. But it didn't change her mind.

Together they left the bridge. Instead of going to the commons to eat, Mogurn ushered her toward his cabin. He told her to sit, to bend her head forward.

Jael obeyed gratefully. And in the instant that the cool sphere touched the base of her head, she knew that she had indeed been trapped; she was already enslaved to this device.

But then the warm glow of the pallisp spread through her, and she no longer cared at all.

Chapter 7
BETRAYED

When she came out of the glow this time, she felt a wave of dizziness. It took her head a few moments to clear, and when it did, she saw puffs of smoke and realized that Mogurn was sitting with his pipe, watching her. She felt a sudden rush of anger toward him, but instead of letting it show, she just smiled thinly.

The memory of the pallisp lingered in her mind, but she recalled even more vividly her last thought before the instrument had robbed her of consciousness: the thought that she had, in that moment, given up her freedom to the pallisp. And Mogurn was the master of the pallisp. She gazed at him, her stomach knotted, and she wondered if she ought to hate him for it.

"Are you feeling better now, Jael?" Mogurn inquired.

She took a breath, let it out slowly, and nodded. She was careful to keep her feelings hidden. "I think I would like to sleep now," she said. Her voice was ragged.

"Indeed. And you may. But first let me explain something to you." Mogurn puffed his pipe, and the smoke rose in a living cloud that curled toward her, stinging her nostrils. "I have just shown you compassion because I know that you acted out of . . . let us say, *ignorance* . . . when you rigged without my permission. You did it because you missed your pallisp, and you did not know how to act without it."

Jael started to nod and caught herself. Admit nothing, she thought.

"But you must know this: I will not tolerate disobedience. If it happens again, you must forfeit the pallisp—not just for one time, but perhaps altogether." He puffed his pipe, his rheumy eyes not leaving her. She tried not to flinch. "I take this sort of thing very seriously. Very seriously indeed. I trust you will, too." Puff. Puff. "If we understand one another, perhaps we can forge a working arrangement that will last." Puff.

She remained motionless. When she finally couldn't stand his stare anymore, she nodded slowly.

His heavy-lidded eyes closed and opened. "I'm pleased you understand. And now Jael . . . if you would help me . . ." He coughed suddenly on a lungful of smoke. He laid his pipe aside, frowned, and sat back. He lifted his headset over his grey-streaked hair.

Frightened, Jael rose. "But weren't you just under this a little while ago?"

"Don't question my orders!" he snapped. She stepped backward, alarmed by his tone, but he smiled woodenly and beckoned her forward again. "And now, Jael, please do me the honors. One hour will be sufficient." He closed his eyes.

She knelt and made the adjustments. Sighing, she rose and looked down at his inert form, at his fingers twitching—and she felt a rush of loathing. She also felt an appalling weariness and confusion. Mogurn had, after all, given her the chance to fly which everyone else had denied her. And the pallisp—whatever it was or did—brought her a pleasure she had never known before. Was that so bad?

She was hardly sure any longer. She was hardly sure of anything except that this flight was turning into something far different from what she had dreamed.

Mogurn was sighing and murmuring to himself, his eyes seeing nothing. Jael walked toward the door, intending to leave him to his peace, if that was what his present condition could be called. But instead of leaving, she found herself peering around Mogurn's compartment, which she had not really looked at closely since the first time she'd come in. Then she'd been so taken with the crystal tapestry, and absorbed in her own anxieties, that she'd not noticed much else. But now she peered about, surreptitiously and a little guiltily, feeling like a trespasser.

The cabin was decorated with some expensive-looking oddments of art, mostly sculpture, and in his half-open wardrobe she noted the sheen of silken, satiny cloth. She turned toward the door again, and was startled to realize that the wall to the left of the door was a full-sized holo-screen, with controls on a panel in the corner. With a hasty glance back at Mogurn's unmoving figure, she thumbed through the holo-selection. She stopped, flushing, when she realized that at least half the titles sounded like pornography. Serves you right for prying, she thought. But as she turned once more to leave, she noticed two other items framed on the wall. She stepped over for a closer look. One was a series of holo-prints: a young dark-skinned woman with a haunted gaze, a humanoid Denedrite with intense red eyes and a pointed nose, and an incredibly pale young man with an expression as desperate and defeated-looking as that of the woman's. Jael sensed at once that all three were riggers. What else could they be? Mogurn's former riggers? What had become of them? she wondered with a shiver. She looked at the other item. It was a legal document, bearing the seal of the planetary government of Eridani Prime—a long-settled and powerful world. She scanned the text.

And suddenly had trouble breathing.

The paper was a certificate of indictment against one Deuteronomous Mogurn, in federal planetary court of Eridani Prime. The indictment listed six counts of smuggling, three counts of receipt of stolen property, and two counts of possession of illegal goods. The specifics were listed, and at the bottom of the list, under the heading of illegal goods, one word caught her eye: *pallisp*.

She blinked, staring at that word, a feeling of despair rising in her. "Damn you . . ." she whispered.

She'd never heard of a pallisp before this trip—but it was illegal on one of the most important worlds in the known galaxy. And what about the rest of this? Mogurn had been brought up on all of these charges. Or had he? Squinting at the bottom of the sheet, she saw a date and time: his scheduled hearing. Beside the date was scrawled a single exclamation: *Hah!* Trembling, she turned to look back at Mogurn, twitching and pawing himself: the man whose ship she was flying; the man who had framed his own certificate of indictment, apparently as a badge of honor. Had he escaped from that world before he could be brought to trial? It certainly helped explain his unregistered status at Gaston's Landing—not that anyone there was likely to notice, or care about, an outstanding warrant.

It could also explain Mogurn's reluctance to discuss his cargo. She'd let the question pass because he had the right to confidentiality. But now she wondered, what hadn't he wanted her to know?

Heart pounding, she crept out of the cabin. Mogurn was still inert, his head rolled to one side, his eyes closed. Leaning against the wall outside, panting, she let the door turn opaque behind her. Then she staggered into the commons room and sat and listened to the thundering of her heart and prayed, *Dear God—if there is a God—tell me what I've done!*

All she heard was the rushing and pounding of blood in her veins.

After a time, she rose and went out into the hall and stood by the ladder that led down to the engineering decks. Would it also take her to the cargo holds? She might be able to see for herself what the ship was carrying—if she had the nerve.

She stood by the open hatch, staring down into the gloom. At last she sighed painfully and turned away. She went to her cabin and locked the door, and there she brooded, huddling on her bunk in near darkness. And after a long time, she felt her eyelids growing heavy, and eventually she curled into a tight ball and slept a sleep of exhaustion.

* * *

She confronted Mogurn at breakfast, though not immediately. She pushed some pieces of cut-up griddle cake around on her plate for a while, then said, "What is our cargo, anyway?" After waiting a moment for an answer, she realized that she had spoken too softly to be heard. Mogurn was scratching his beard, muttering to himself as he pored over a datapad at his elbow. Jael had no idea what he was studying. She chewed a syrup-dampened bite. She started to repeat her question, then hesitated, and instead blurted, "I saw the certificate on your wall." She looked down again and stabbed another square of griddle-cake.

When she raised her eyes, Mogurn was gazing at her. She realized that he was squinting in puzzlement. She cleared her throat and started to say, "The . . . court thing—"

"What did you say?" he asked, cutting her off. "Something about my wall?"

Jael's face burned, her stomach knotted. "Your certificate," she said. "I saw it."

"My what?"

"Your—" Her throat constricted and she tried one more time, taking a deep breath. "You were indicted. You were in trouble for smuggling. And for—" Her throat tightened again, but she saw the sudden flash of understanding, and the glint of amusement in his eyes, and she was suddenly determined to speak her mind. For the pallisp, she thought. For the damn pallisp. "For possession of stolen goods," she said.

Mogurn cocked his head.

"And illegal goods. Including . . ."

"Yes?" he said in an exaggerated tone. "Including what?"

"Including . . . the pallisp."

"I see. And does that bother you?"

"Yes, it—"

"You're enjoying the pallisp, aren't you?" he interrupted. "Do you think that just because something is illegal on one world, it is therefore wrong, somehow?"

"You were . . . stealing," Jael stammered. "You were smuggling." Mogurn shrugged, making no effort to deny the charge. And, she noticed, he didn't seem to object to her having seen it. Perhaps he'd even posted it in the expectation that whatever rigger was serving him would see it.

"Actually," Mogurn said finally, turning off his datapad, "all you know is that I was charged with those things. You don't know that I was guilty of any of them." He smiled placidly and stroked his beard, as though tempting her to respond.

"I don't hear you denying it," Jael said hotly.

"True," he admitted. He raised his dark eyebrows. "Would you like me to deny it?"

Jael tried to control her anger. *What happened to your last rigger?* she wanted to ask, but couldn't voice the words. She wanted to rage at him; she was so tightly coiled, so angry that she didn't know how to answer. "I would like to know," she said coldly, giving each word measured emphasis, "where you got the pallisp. And what it is doing to me."

Mogurn smoothed down the front of his navy blue satin shirt and pulled together the front of the violet-trimmed vesta that hung loosely around his shoulders. His eyes came to a focus, and he pressed his palms together in front of his lips to hide a frown. "Of course. What shall I tell you? That it is a medical instrument? That it is utterly safe when used with knowledge and care?" As he gazed at her, his eyes seemed to be intently gauging her response.

"Medical instrument?" she muttered, trusting him less than ever.

"Yes, of course." Mogurn tipped his head to one side. "Well, psych-med, actually. It is said to have certain uses in the treatment of, for example, severe depression."

Then why are you using it on me? she wanted to shout.

"I find, however, that many people enjoy its use." Mogurn steepled his forefingers, interlocking his hands in front of his face. "It must be used with caution, of course. There are those who would tell you it is . . . addictive, who are terrified by that thought, and I . . . well, I do not accept such claims. It is simply a question of using it correctly."

"Addictive?" she whispered, so softly he could not have heard.

"There is no reason to fear it. After all, the pallisp brings pleasure, does it not?" Mogurn's voice softened. "Don't we all enjoy the sensation of pleasure? Pure pleasure, unadulterated by the complications that muddy our lives, the petty jealousies and guilt that rob us of whatever grim joys fate brings into our lives?" His gruff voice became almost delicate. "Isn't that something that all people should have the right to enjoy? Even riggers? Shouldn't riggers have that right, too, Jael?"

Jael swallowed; she had no idea how to answer anymore. Perhaps there was some truth in his words, but she was speechless with anger at the way she'd been manipulated. Speechless with fear. And with, even now, an almost overwhelming desire to go under the pallisp again. To feel the warm caress of its presence within her mind, and the tickling suggestion of love and companionship against her soul. To feel the golden light of that inner sun—

"Is there anything else you wanted to discuss, Jael?"

Startled, she tried to think. *Yes! What about the theft, the smuggling. . . ?* None of the words made it to her lips.

Mogurn had risen to his feet. "We do, after all, have flying to do. A ship to bring into port." His brusque hurry-up tone had returned. "If you've finished with your breakfast . . ." He gestured impatiently as he turned to leave the commons.

Despite the knot in her stomach, Jael swallowed a large piece of syrup-drenched griddlecake and drained her cup of coffee. Sliding her dishes into the disposal unit, she glumly followed Mogurn to the bridge.

"Why don't you want me here while you fly?" Mogurn turned from his instruments and peered at her darkly. In the gloom of the cockpit, his eyes looked angry and threatening.

"It's that—" Jael bit her lip "—it's that it makes me nervous sometimes. It makes it hard for me to keep the flow stable, to keep the impressions clean, and clear." She drew a breath. "I can rig better when I know I'm not being watched. When I can feel alone, and safe."

"Safe?" Mogurn said in a tone of surprise. "Safe? Have I ever threatened you, Jael?"

Jael shook her head. "No, but I . . . well . . . that's all I can

tell you. I feel safer, and I feel better, when I'm alone here."
She pressed her lips together and forced herself to stare back
at Mogurn. She had very few strengths to command against
the ship's owner, but this was one of them: she could make
any reasonable request that bore on the safety of the ship or
her ability to rig, and expect it to be granted. Without her
flying skills, Mogurn would never see planetfall again.

Arms folded across his heavy chest, Mogurn studied her
with his dark, stern gaze, keeping her frozen as she stared
back at him. At last he released her from his gaze. "Very
well," he said. He glanced at the instruments one more time,
then indicated the rigger-station with a tilt of his head. "Go
ahead and take the net. Don't tire yourself." With that, he
turned, his silken robe spinning in folds, and strode from the
bridge. The door darkened to opacity behind him, leaving
Jael alone in the gloomy compartment.

Does he distrust me now? Jael thought, staring after him.
Do I care? She turned and repeated the inspection of the
instruments that Mogurn had just made, and then she
climbed into the rigger-station. She stretched out and gazed
up at the monitors, and closed her eyes and tried to relax,
to forget about Mogurn and the pallisp, to think only of the
ship, and the Flux.

Her senses darkened and sprang outward, into the net.

Chapter 8
THE MOUNTAIN ROUTE

SHE FLEW through a vast and clear purplish sky. She floated like a seed high over a strangely glowing blue- and green-mottled landscape. The net glittered faintly around her, binding her to the invisible ghost of the spaceship. She spread her arms, and in the net they billowed outward as great sail-like wings, filled with a rising updraft of wind. Jael rose, soaring.

The landscape beneath her was an odd matrix of color, reflecting her mood, her uncertainty. It was a phantasmagorical land, bubbling with distant flame red volcanoes, and glinting rivers of silver threading through cyan valleys and shadowy plains. This was not a landscape in which she could imagine anyone living, certainly no one human. It took her a while to calm down from her confrontation with Mogurn; but eventually her feelings quieted, if they did not disappear altogether, and she flew silently through empty skies, lost in the sort of daydream in which no thought lasted for more than a moment or two, and few images lingered.

She felt a sort of wistful melancholy. She did not pursue any of the concerns that had so recently preoccupied her.

Whatever worries she had about Mogurn and the pallisp did not need to reach her here, in this haven from all worries. At least that was her hope. She flew slowly on the wind, not bothering to seek out faster currents. Whether they reached their destination sooner, or later, did not matter to her. Hours went by, and she remained content to float, to drift.

Occasionally, despite her efforts at detachment, the landscape below shimmered and flared in response to tremors that surfaced within her own heart, aches that she was determined to leave unnamed. They were longings and fears that she wanted desperately to leave behind, that she was determined not to allow expression. But she was not always the master of those feelings. Whether she willed it or not, they sometimes erupted into the landscape—sometimes with unfocused phosphorescent fire among the hills, sometimes with tiny billowing bloody plumes, sometimes in the form of shadows dancing over the land like the dark ghosts of aerial acrobats. Those aches were always present within her, and when they found their way out, the landscape always responded.

She began to wish she could change the image, and drift away, leaving this heartache landscape behind. But it was a tenacious image, with a powerful hold on her. However her abilities were growing, whether it was through experience, or through exposure to the pallisp, her imaginative powers remained many-sided. She was not immune to darker visions encroaching upon her freedom.

The com-signal chimed in her consciousness, and Mogurn's voice broke into her solitude. *Jael, what's wrong? The feedback out here looks poor. It looks unstable.*

The landscape turned to brimstone and filled the sky with a rising, burning haze. She tried to control it, to subdue the sudden eruption of anger at the sound of Mogurn's voice. *Nothing's wrong. Everything's fine,* she answered curtly.

Are you sure? Mogurn's voice was a growl in one corner of her mind. She envisioned him on the bridge, squinting anxiously down into the rigger-station, leering at her still form. His voice was bodiless here in the net, but she was sure that physically he must be very near. She had to work hard not to lose her equilibrium. She countered an instinctive urge to avoid him by retreating to the extremities of the net; that wouldn't help.

I'm fine, she insisted. The image was showing signs of disintegration. The outer edges of the landscape looked unfocused, almost frayed. Mogurn's interference was creating a potentially hazardous situation. The ship was beginning to shake in the turbulence. Mogurn might not have been able to feel it inside, but here in the net there was no mistaking it. Jael drew more energy from the flux-pile, trying to stabilize the image.

I'm depending on you, said Mogurn.

I know. Now please leave me alone to do my job!

Very well. I'll be back to check later.

Jael didn't respond. She thought hard, searching her imagination for something that would help her to stabilize this situation. She focused on the angry horizon, aware that her focusing power was indeed stronger. Had the pallisp really aided her? The colors at the horizon bled, and a crimson sunset swelled over the mountains off to what she envisioned as the northwest.

Mountains. She was startled by the realization. The mountains she and Mogurn had talked about: the ones that he wanted her to skirt. She'd felt their presence from afar; it had just been a question of when she would reach them and what form they would take—and how, or whether, she would skirt them. The route through the mountains was the more direct one to their destination, Lexis, and just now she was feeling inclined to bring this flight to an end as quickly as possible; but there were reports, and not just Mogurn's warnings, that the mountain route was more dangerous, with tricky currents. And, of course, dragons.

Jael smiled at the thought. That, of course, was what Mogurn was worried about: the legends in the rigging community—and that's all they were, legends—which held that dragons lived in these mountain routes along the fringes of Aeregian space. They were real dragons, according to the legends, fire-breathing dragons that lived in the Flux as humans lived and breathed in air. There had been some discussion of the subject back in rigger school, where it had been treated about as seriously as the legends of the "ghost rigger ships," the lost "Flying Dutchman" ships of interstellar space. No instructor could swear that the dragons did not exist, objectively speaking, but one knew well enough what they thought. Dragons made for vivid and wonderful stories, but not one teacher or rigger in a hundred believed that they were real.

Still, the rumors persisted as rumors do: riggers in the starports boasting, telling tales of dueling with dragons. And not just dueling, but conversing. Still, Jael gave even less credence to the boasts of riggers than she did to the carefully disclaimed references in school. So far as she knew, there was no real evidence for believing that *anything* actually lived in the mountains—or, for that matter, anywhere else in the Flux. But according to the library hypnos, there did seem to be a special quality to the Flux in this corridor that almost demanded mountain imagery in the minds of passing riggers; and sometimes it evoked dragons, as well, or images of dragons. Maybe some riggers believed the dragons to be actual living inhabitants of the Flux, but Jael had never met anyone with actual firsthand knowledge. The library nav-hypnos described them simply as unusually compelling images. Of course, that didn't mean they were harmless. Even imaginary dragons could threaten a ship, if they were vivid enough in a rigger's mind. Either way, it sounded dangerous to pass that way. It sounded glorious.

And that was why Mogurn had warned her away, she was sure. Still, he had not absolutely forbidden her to fly in the mountains—and after all, she was the rigger, wasn't she? It was she, not Mogurn, who chose the images and the streams of the Flux to ride. He could suggest a route, but the ultimate choice was hers. And what did her senses tell her now?

Stretching the focus of her vision, she tried to spy out the distant range. There was still turbulence from her confused emotions; she could distinguish only the general rise and fall of the mountain peaks. She would have to move in closer to see anything useful. And that might not be such a bad thing to do, despite Mogurn's fears. The greater demands of close-in flying would help her to focus, help her to discipline her imagination.

She banked slightly to angle in that direction. The net sparkled around her as she grew excited—at the thought of quickening the flight, at the thought of danger. Perhaps she shouldn't really do this, not if the danger had become an attraction for her. But there were times when one simply had to take charge, to do things for one's own sake. Mogurn's fears be damned, she thought.

Abruptly she transformed herself into a mountain eagle, and she caught a new current and soared northwest, pulse racing, net glittering like jewels in the Flux.

Ahead was twilight, emerging from sunset. Mountains stood jagged and black against a wine red sky that deepened into evening. The mountains were much closer now, more fully revealed to her awareness. She scanned ahead with just the slightest feeling of unease, using the edges of her mind to explore the approaching shadows. Would there be dragons? She doubted it; still, there was no way to know absolutely. And she had not yet decided whether she would actually violate Mogurn's request.

A sense of quiet anticipation settled in as she flew on eagle wings ever closer to the range of peaks. A part of her almost hoped that dragons would appear—if for no other reason than to ease her loneliness.

The com-signal chimed again, chilling her.

Isn't it time you came out? asked a bodiless Mogurn.

A sudden crosswind made her shiver. *Is it?* she asked, stalling.

You've been in there for hours, Jael. Too long.

Really? It doesn't seem that long.

What's the matter, Jael? Don't you want to come out?

She hesitated, torn by conflicting desires. He would be waiting to give her the pallisp, she knew. But this was not a good place to leave the net unattended, not with the mountains approaching. *It might not be safe to leave right now,* she said finally.

Not safe? Why not?

She spread her wings to catch a warm updraft. *Because . . . there might be dragons.*

His eyes squinted furiously, or so she imagined. *Dragons? Dragons? Jael, have you taken the mountain route?*

Jael beat her eagle wings with sharp strokes. *Yes. That is— no, not exactly. But we're near there.*

Find a stretch of safe passage. And then you come out and see me in my cabin, Jael. His voice touched her like ice, and she stopped pumping her wings. His anger made her tremble. She saw distant lightning among the peaks, reflecting her sudden fear.

All right, she whispered, and the world suddenly seemed even colder and lonelier. She did not want to leave here to face him, of all people. But neither did she want to lose the pallisp tonight.

You should have thought of that before, she thought.

Banking left, she brought the ship into a heading that would take it parallel to the range, if there were no unexpected shifts in the wind. She thought she could probably safely leave the net here. Still, she delayed leaving—gliding in a gentle breeze, watching ominous dark peaks drift past, far off to the starboard. She wished that somehow the fear and the loneliness would subside.

Finally, when she could no longer justify staying, she set the stabilizers and the alarms. Her senses melted back into her body as she withdrew from the net, and she opened her eyes, blinking, half expecting to see Mogurn squinting in at her. But the bridge was deserted, gloomy and lonely. There was nothing here to greet her but the instruments, and for that she was grateful.

She stretched as she stood beside the rigger-station. She realized for the first time that she was hungry. And tired; her limbs were heavy with fatigue. She wasn't sure which she wanted more, sleep or food. But Mogurn had said to come immediately. Sighing, she left the friendly gloom of the bridge and went to Mogurn's door. She pressed the signal. The door paled and she stepped inside.

Mogurn was seated, smoking his long pipe. His eyes betrayed nothing of his thoughts. He rose and silently gestured for her to sit. She slid onto the bench-seat, conscious of the crystal tapestry twinkling over her head, wishing she could spin around and disappear into that miniature world of light and refraction. Mogurn frowned, studying the end of his smoking pipe. The smoke curled toward her, stretching out like a vaporous hand. "Why did you disobey me?" he asked.

Jael shivered, certain now that she would be denied the pallisp. Perhaps that was for the better, but she could not see it that way now; all she could see was the relief and the warmth that the pallisp could bring to her. "I . . . meant no disobedience," she murmured, shamefully aware that it was only half true. Yes, he had not strictly forbidden her to fly that route, but of course she had been aware of his desires and had—yes—rather relished ignoring them. Had quietly relished his fear of the mountains—his fear, she presumed, of dragons that almost certainly were not real.

Mogurn stepped closer, hovering over her, alternately blocking and exposing the light behind him. Jael squinted nervously up at him. "Did I not say that I preferred the longer route, Jael? Was there some special circumstance you haven't told me of, some need to take the more perilous course?"

Was that fear in his voice? No. He was the master. Jael bit her lip. "I . . . was having trouble, the other way. But this way it was . . . clearer. And I wasn't worried. I think, well, the stories about . . . dragons . . . are just stories. I don't consider them real."

"Oh?" Mogurn glared at her with his bloodshot eyes. "Tell me, Jael—what is *real* to a rigger? Can you tell me that? Is it what is in the Flux—or what is in the rigger's mind?" He drew a lungful of smoke and exhaled it as he spoke. "It doesn't matter, Jael—either one can destroy us."

Jael met his stare for a moment, then nodded mutely.

"And, drunken sods though most riggers may be," he added bitterly, "one should never laugh at their reports, should one?"

Her face burned at his sarcasm. "No. But still, it's just legend!"

"Is that it, Jael? Just legend? When riggers report what they have *seen* and *felt*, is that just legend?"

Jael shrugged. How many riggers, she wondered, had actually reported dragons? Not many, she was sure. But she said nothing.

"Now, are we still close enough to our original course to turn back onto it?" He exhaled another cloud of smoke, which drifted past her face before being drawn into the ventilators. Jael opened her mouth to reply in the affirmative, but something made the words stick in her throat. Instead, she shook her head. "We can't avoid the mountains?" he growled. She shook her head again, with greater determination. Mogurn stared at her, drawing smoke from his pipe and exhaling it in repeated large plumes. Finally he turned away in silence.

Jael watched as he laid his pipe on the reading table and returned to her, pallisp in his hand. "All right. It is time." His voice held no kindness, nor did his eyes. But the sight of the pallisp sent a thrill down Jael's spine. Unhappiness and loneliness welled up in her; she hated the realization, but she was shivering in anticipation of the joy that would come from the thing.

At Mogurn's gesture, she bent her head forward and pushed her hair aside. Out of the corner of her eye, she saw Mogurn's arm reach, saw the pallisp gleam . . . and felt the cool touch of the probe. She felt the pallisp's warmth reaching into her with shimmering energy; felt that warmth encircling the ugly, waiting feelings of alienation, fear, anger; felt it closing around those feelings like flowing blood, healing and soothing and transforming the emotions, softening her inner defenses and filling her with the warmth of joy and love . . .

The wave turned icy cold. Jael swayed dizzily as a tide of fear and dread welled up inside her, sweeping away all other feelings. For a moment, she was disoriented as well as frightened. Her thoughts were flooded with pain and confusion. Then she realized—the pallisp was gone. She sat back, blinking wildly, struggling to hold back a rush of tears. As Mogurn spoke, she could hardly see him through blurred eyes; but he had stepped away from her, and she could see the glint of the pallisp in his hand. "That's all for tonight, Jael. You must understand what obedience means, even for a rigger." Jael tried not to tremble under his gaze, but she was desperate with frustration and need, and helplessness. Slowly, and with great effort, she steadied herself, drew herself upright into a semblance of dignity. Mogurn nodded. "Now, Jael, help me with my augmentor. Then you may retire."

Though dying to scream, she obeyed. Mogurn reclined and she fitted the synaptic augmentor to his head and adjusted the controls, and when Mogurn was reduced to a silent figure fluttering his hands and pawing himself with a blind-eyed grin, she backed away and fled to her cabin.

Her thoughts seemed to roam about the cabin like birds on wing against a distant sky. Her cabin was at once a boundless space in which she felt tiny and insignificant, and a grim claustrophobic cell, threatening to crush her. She stalked the little room like a caged animal, brooding.

The question kept coming back at her: why had Mogurn done this to her? Why use a device that would make her addicted? Was there any doubt that he had known what would happen? What had he wanted, a rigger who was so dependent upon him that she would never leave unless dismissed? It seemed likely. She thought of the pictures she had seen in his cabin, the haunting despair in the eyes of those riggers. Am I that far gone? she wondered. Could she leave him now? Would she have the courage, if given the opportunity?

And what about his promise of heightened sensitivity in the net? Was that a lie, too? She had felt *something*, to be sure; but was it truly an improvement in sensitivity, or was it just an altered coloration of perception? It might well have been real; indeed perhaps that was another of his goals—to have, not just a rigger-servant, but one who could sense the realm more keenly, and perhaps fly faster and more stealthily in the service of his smuggling activities. But at what cost to her mind, to her soul?

She peered at her reflection in the mirror and tried to decide if there was anything different in her own face. Did she look thinner, more worn? More experienced, more capable? She pushed her fingers back through her hair, and exhaled deeply. Lord, how she wanted . . . how she *needed* the pallisp! How she wanted it to take this lonely bitterness from her soul and turn it into something warm. She would almost kill for that. But only Mogurn knew precisely how to use the thing, and so she needed Mogurn, too.

Maybe, she thought, a mist-bath would make her feel better. Checking that her door was locked, she shrugged out of her clothes and stepped into the tiny mist cubicle. She elbowed the start button, and closed her eyes as the mist issued from the walls and surrounded her with a warm swirling dampness. Sighing, she allowed the mist to gently scrub her clean, and she blinked as the droplets dispersed, leaving her skin tingling. She tentatively ran her hands down her body. She inhaled the moist ionized air, savoring the physical refreshment. As she stepped out, she grabbed a towel and rubbed herself down. Then she pulled some loose-fitting clothes out of a drawer and slipped into them. Though she intended to sleep, she felt safer dressed.

She sat cross-legged on her bunk, thinking, feeling the weight of her worries pressing down upon her again. She began to think of her father, to wonder if he had done things like this to riggers in his employ. She drew her knees up under her chin, thinking of Dap, whom she had trusted. Sighing, she switched off the light and stretched out, and after a moment turned on the sleep-field to lift her gently, not quite off the surface of the bunk, to help her sleep.

And then she tossed and writhed, unable to rest at all. Unable to stop thinking. To stop her anger at Mogurn. To stop remembering Gaston's Landing, where her unhappiness had been so great that it had driven her to accept this instead. To stop remembering Dap . . . and that night, and the dreamlink . . .

His willful insistence, his gentle but deliberate deception, promising intimacy and understanding; she remembered the offer of friendship, and his eyes dark and earnest, and his vow: "We'll be looking right into each other, and our souls will link . . ."

And the golden glow of the dreamlink, and the warmth and the seduction . . . and the opening up of her heart and memory . . . and the devastating awareness of Dap's reaction to her need; his revulsion and his fleeing . . .

And her own muted cry of pain, which she had wrapped about herself and forced back in, bottled it so that it could no longer hurt her . . .

And going back to the hall, determined to get an assignment . . . and meeting Mogurn, who had offered her the job . . . and the pallisp.

She started out of a brooding daze, in the near-darkness of her cabin. One small light was glowing at its lowest setting. Obviously, sleep was impossible. She could not forget the pallisp, or the cruel way in which Mogurn had torn it from her. But the pallisp was the only thing that could soothe away these anxieties and fears. It was her only release.

Except, of course, for the net.

Sitting up, she thought about that for a long time. She could go to the net now, of course. That was the one place where she could shape her feelings and play them out in images and render them harmless. Letting dark feelings loose there could be perilous, but was it any less perilous to keep them corked inside herself until they exploded? Mogurn had already warned her once; he would be furious if she went to the net again while he was under his bliss-wire. But if she didn't do something, she would go crazy.

She sat for a very long time, weighing the consequences. The longer she thought, the faster her heart beat, the more it cried out with need. *Damn it, you have to do something!* She could not have the pallisp. There was only one other way out of this.

You are the rigger. You have the power and the need.

Swallowing, she rose from her bunk. And she stood there, swaying, trying to find some resolve that would keep her from returning to the net . . . that would allow her to sleep, or if not to sleep, then at least to bear the pain and the need.

She didn't find the resolve. She found only the need.

Chapter 9
HIGHWING

SHE CREPT onto the bridge and slipped silently into the rigger-cell. The neural contacts touched her neck. Her senses, electrified, sprang into the net.

Her imagination at once sparked a new image: the ship was a balloon-borne gondola in a nighttime sky, riding the winds downrange of a long line of mountain peaks. Jael let the breeze soothe her. After a time, she changed altitude, seeking higher crosswinds that would take her closer to the mountains. She wasn't sure why she was doing it. Revenge against Mogurn for the way he had treated her? Or was it that she was already being punished, and what more could happen to her? Or was it that she really was taking charge, and this simply felt like the right direction to fly? She didn't know. The gondola swayed as she passed through an airstream moving the wrong way; then she found another that carried her in the direction she wanted.

She set her sights upon the approaching range. A single full, creamy moon sank slowly toward jagged black peaks, jutting like sullen teeth against the horizon. Backlit by the moon, a blunt-nosed mass of clouds was moving out of the mountains toward her. She liked the effect: the gloom of night and eerily lighted clouds that looked like moving glaciers. Or like bold angry pincers that could reach out to shred her balloon . . .

The balloon disintegrated abruptly. She caught at the air with her hands. For a moment, she and the starship tumbled earthward, her arms flailing and grasping; then she overcame her panic and deliberately remade the image. The ghostly net shimmered and became a varnished wooden glider, whispering in the wind as it sliced downward through the air. She was perched astride its fuselage, and she tugged and pulled at the airfoils until it leveled out in flight. And she thought: Take care! Dangerous thoughts could smash the ship into splinters as well as any physical force, and the pieces would be left to drift forever in the currents of this strange reality, the Flux.

The wind soothed her face, and gradually soothed her mind and her spirit as well. She let her feelings swirl ahead of her in the sky, in the emptiness between her and the clouds far ahead. Her feelings would not hurt her out there. Let them dissipate in the cool emptiness.

Time passed and she drew steadily closer to the mountain range.

The dragons stormed out of the clouds in random formation, like gulls out of a rain squall.

Jael stared out into the moonlit night in astonishment. Dragons! Dreadful winged shapes, they wheeled before the distant clouds. Sparks of red flame flickered about them. Jael could scarcely believe the sight before her. Dragons couldn't be real! They were something from fairy tales and primal dreams, from racial fears and magical desires . . . from lies fabricated by boastful or delirious riggers. But . . . *there were dragons* in the sky right now. And several of them were flying toward her.

Jael searched her thoughts, wondering if she might have provoked this image from her own imagination. She felt nothing, not even the slightest tingle of recognition. Was it possible that the dragons actually were real . . . living creatures, living in the Flux? She controlled the glider with tight movements and watched them come.

The dragons grew in the moonlight. They certainly appeared real enough: rugged, fierce-looking creatures, breathing fire into the air like the dragons of folklore. Most of them banked away to soar and circle far off her wingtips. She felt a moment of relief. But three of the creatures closed to intercept her, circling into a tight orbit around her glider. They maneuvered quickly, banking and veering, their movements hard to follow.

One swooped close, startling her, but giving her a good glimpse of its features. It was solid all right, its scales like polished pewter gleaming in the moonlight, but with subtle colors rippling beneath the surface. The creature's head was rough hewn, as though of living stone. Its nostrils flared coal red as it craned its neck toward her; its eyes shone with ghostly green light. Its wings were broad and serrated, beating the air powerfully. As it circled around behind her, another dragon swept directly across her path, alarmingly close; then all three drew off to a more comfortable distance.

She held her course, thinking frantically. What was one supposed to do when met by dragons? Storytellers in the spacebars spoke of dueling. Could it be that those tales were not just boastful nonsense? These dragons looked real, and fierce, and eager for battle!

This one is mine, she imagined she heard a voice say.

She shivered, wishing she had flown another way.

Are you afraid? she heard, and this time she knew she really had heard it.

She glanced around, frightened, thinking that perhaps Mogurn was on the bridge, taunting her in punishment for her disobedience. But the voice, though it murmured in her head, was not Mogurn's.

You are afraid, said the voice. *Shall we be kind, and kill you quickly?*

It was one of the dragons speaking! She was terrified and astounded. She glanced over her left shoulder and discovered one of them flying close alongside, just a little behind her. Its gleaming eyes and smoldering nostrils were as clear as marker lights. *What do you want?* she asked, her voice trembling.

The dragon exhaled a plume of flame, startling her. It edged closer, its eyes flickering like green lanterns. She banked to the right, thinking, This can't be happening! The dragon drew even closer as she veered, following her movements with ease. Its eyes glowed brightly, emerald green. The turbulence from its wings buffeted her, and she had to fight to control the glider. *What are you doing?* she cried in protest. *Leave me alone!*

The dragon puffed a cloud of sparks. *Does that mean you don't want me to kill you straightaway?* It dropped back . . . and then, with a powerful series of wingstrokes, flew up in a tight loop around her, peering closely at her as it banked and dived. Moments later, it was once more flanking her left side. *Do you prefer to die in battle?*

No! Jael cried. *I want you to leave me alone! Who are you and why are you doing this? What do you want from me?* She hunched low on the glider, drawing the net in close around the edges.

Child! called the dragon. *What a strange one! Do they send child-spirits to duel with us? Such questions! You want to know who I am, and—*

I am not a child!

The dragon's harsh laughter filled the air.

And you haven't answered me! she added fearfully.

Nor shall I, said the dragon. *But so many questions not to answer, all at once! Do you think you're the first outsider to come here, spoiling for a fight?*

Jael gaped at the creature. *Then it's true . . . about the dueling! And you dragons . . . are real!*

The dragon made a noise that might have been a sigh or a snarl. *Of course! Now duel, rigger!* With deft wingstrokes, it climbed high above her; then, dropping one wing, it dived. It bore down upon her in the moonlight, its massive shape growing large, larger—

Jael screamed.

The dragon thundered as it dropped past, raking her with fire. Jael's skin sizzled, and flames crackled along the wings of her glider. Gasping, she changed the image: a sudden flurry of snow cooled her and quenched the flood of energy in the net. She changed the glider from wood to a fireproof alloy.

The dragon approached from the side, flapping its wings slowly. It eyed her with a glowing eye. *Not badly done, for a demon,* it conceded. It banked away and put distance between them.

Jael stared after the dragon, dumbfounded. Before she could gather her thoughts to reply, it turned again and streaked toward her in another attack.

Jael froze, helpless. She tried to make herself small, to protect her flanks. The dragon grew with terrifying speed. *STOP IT!* she screamed.

The dragon broke off its attack, veering away in surprise. *And you wonder what I'm doing?* it murmured. It circled back, warily. *There is something different about you, rigger. What is it?* In the distant moonlit clouds, the dragon's fellows looked like small dots, wheeling and maneuvering in the air. The dragon glanced at the others, with what looked like uncertainty. *If you didn't want to duel, why did you come here?*

Struggling to keep her glider steady, Jael was dizzy with confusion, with fear and anxiety. *Well, I . . . don't know. But I wasn't expecting anyone to try to kill me!*

The dragon banked closer. *And just what did you expect?*

I don't know, she admitted, and wondered why, indeed, she had come into this mountain range. She thought, but didn't say, that she hadn't really been expecting dragons or any other living thing to be here.

The dragon snorted, then spoke in an almost conciliatory tone. *You don't know what you expected, but you didn't expect to duel. What, then? Do you want to talk? Do you want to just fly along and chat lightheartedly? We could do that, I suppose. I could promise not to kill you.*

Jael drew a breath. *Can I believe that?*

Why not?

She eyed the dragon, unable to tell whether it was mocking her or not. *Can we really just talk? No dueling?*

The dragon tipped its head and winked its luminous eye. Jael nodded uneasily. She didn't know what to make of this creature, but she knew she didn't want to fight it. She decided to change her image again: the glider disappeared and she became a winged pony, beating into the wind. *Very nice*, said the dragon, drawing in close alongside her.

She didn't answer. The night was changing, the clouds closing in. She could no longer see the other dragons. A moonbeam broke through the clouds to show a jagged mountain slope, very near, with mist swirling around it. Jael had not realized that they were so close to the mountains. *Do you know where we're going?* she asked.

Yes, said the dragon with a crafty chuckle. Suddenly it sideslipped over her and seized her with its great talons. Jael's breath went out with a gasp. The dragon bent its head down to peer at her between its forelegs. Its jaws gaped, and its hot breath rushed over her. Jael struggled, terrified. She squirmed and twisted and managed to roll forward in the dragon's grip just enough to kick up with her hind pony legs. Her hooves caught the dragon squarely in the stomach and it wheezed, releasing her. Jael tumbled in midair, beating frantically with her wings but losing altitude. She was dropping headfirst through the mists. She glimpsed terrifying sawtoothed slopes rushing upward to meet her. Frantically she transformed herself into a hawk, warped her wings sharply, and pulled herself out of the dive. She climbed again toward a safe altitude, looking around in vain for the dragon.

Well done, it said, right behind her.

Panicked, she looped up and into inverted flight and twisted back down behind the dragon. *You liar!* she shouted. *You promised and you lied!*

The dragon glanced back over its shoulder. *Well, I didn't exactly promise—*

You as good as promised! Is that a dragon's kind of honor?

Well—the dragon said hesitantly—*where demons are concerned—*

You mean you all lie? she screamed.

Only when dueling riggers! the dragon snapped—and what it did next, she could hardly believe. One moment it was in front of her, and the next it was above her, and then behind; and it curled its wing around her like a net and scooped her toward the mountain. Jael trembled and fluttered, a frightened bird, as they plummeted through the darkness. Abruptly the dragon lurched to a landing on a black outcropping of rock. Holding her loosely, it craned its neck to sniff at her with huge smoldering nostrils, to peer at her with its enormous glowing eyes.

Jael fought to control her fear and rage. Shaking, she puffed up her hawk feathers and stared back up at the creature. *You lied, and now you intend to kill me! Is that it?*

The dragon cocked its monstrous head slowly. *I didn't actually lie, you know. I tricked. One is expected to do that with demon-spirits. Didn't they tell you that when they sent you here?*

No one sent me! Jael snapped. *I just came! And not to duel! And I'm not a demon! Why do you keep calling me that?* She choked in the dragon's breath; the air around her was suffocating, trapped by the creature's great wing. *Would you mind letting me breathe?*

Hissing, the dragon opened its wing. *You certainly are different from any rigger I've ever heard of. Not that I've personally met any before, mind you. Until now, I wasn't even sure that your kind really existed. Perhaps you had better show yourself as you really are.*

The world remained wreathed in fog, but the cool night air revived her somewhat. *All right.* Concentrating, she transformed herself back into the image of Jael LeBrae, human woman, in the nexus of a ghostly neural-sensory net. Haloing the net was a shimmering ethereal spaceship.

Impressive, said the dragon. *Is that all you, or are you riding some sort of magical beast? What do you call it? A spaceship?*

She made the spaceship disappear, wondering how many like it the dragons in these mountains had destroyed. She stood on the outcropping of rock, lonely and frightened and cold. *My name is Jael LeBrae*, she said.

She felt a shudder, as though an earthquake were shaking the rock at her feet. The dragon's eyes opened wide. It gazed at her in astonishment, then reared its head back and roared in dismay. Its cry was deafening, reverberating through the mountains and the mist. *I did not ask your name!* it bellowed. *Why have you given me your name!* It blew a searing gout of fire up into the night, and scratched at the rock, its talons grating horribly against the stone.

What's the matter? Jael cried, covering her ears. *Have you gone mad?*

What's the matter? the dragon thundered. *What's the matter? What are you? You're no demon! Demons don't give names! They never give names! Don't you know anything, rigger?*

Of course I'm not a demon! Why did you think I was? What kind of insanity is this? The ground continued to tremble at her feet. What was going on here?

The dragon was clearly disturbed by the vibration, too. It tipped its craggy head this way and that, then angled a troubled gaze at her. *Rigger, this is strange. Most strange, indeed.* It muttered to itself for a moment, as though weighing contradictory thoughts. *It is almost as if you were—but no.* It shook its head. *I'm sure that is impossible. Impossible!* Angrily, as though frustrated, it vented flame and sparks from its nostrils.

What are you talking about? Jael demanded.

Never mind, the dragon snarled. It snorted out another blast of flame. *Tell me, rigger—don't you know the power of names? You act so innocent! Names are everything! I cannot kill you for a demon, knowing your name. You are—*and he growled a guttural word—*garkkondoh—*and fumed, *a person! You are real!* Its throat rumbled like a volcano threatening to explode.

Of course I'm real! Jael shouted. *You're not making any sense at all! What do you mean, names are everything?*

The dragon shook its head unhappily. Finally it settled down enough to speak, its voice quiet in her mind. *Perhaps that was an exaggeration. Nothing is everything. But—*and it fixed her with its glowing, glowering gaze, before continuing grudgingly—*I perceive, I am afraid, that there is more to you than meets the eye. I had not expected such an action from a dem—from a rigger.* It glared in thought for a long moment, then sighed rumblingly, shaking its head. *Perhaps, though . . . I should have. It would seem that I am obliged now by honor—*it sighed again—*or perhaps by more than honor—to give you my name in return. And then I will no longer be able to trick you, or* *to duel without*—and he made another guttural sound—*hakka, cause.*

Jael ground her teeth. *What are you talking about? Never mind! I don't even want to know your name!*

The dragon settled down glumly. *And I shall have to learn more about you. Very well. If it must be. I am Windrush-Wingtouch-Highwing—Terror-of-the-Last-Peak.*

I don't want to know! she snapped.

I suppose you may call me Highwing. You might as well know that my name is of some note in the realm. And I am the sire of the four fastest young dragons in the whole of—

You are a braggart, also, Jael interrupted, startling the dragon into silence. It shifted its position awkwardly; the crag was small, compared to the dragon, and there was hardly any room left over for a frail human. That, Jael thought, was as good a reason as any to take her leave. *Look, I only want to be on with my flight,* she informed him. *You've been . . . most enlightening. But this isn't helping me reach my destination. I'm afraid I must leave now.*

Leave? Highwing rumbled. *That is impossible!*

Why?

Well—that is to say—you must make up your mind! The dragon scrutinized her with large, luminous eyes. *You really didn't come here to duel?*

I told you. No.

Highwing vented smoke, squinting. *In that case, it must be that you have come here for . . . another reason. I am troubled by this, rigger. Jael LeBrae. I am . . . troubled . . . by the meaning of this. And by you.*

By me? she murmured. And she realized, but with only a dizzy half-awareness, that his eyes were shining hypnotically into hers. She wanted to turn away, but could not; there was a terrible magnetism in his gaze. She became aware of a strange sensation in herself, as though she had turned transparent, as though the dragon were seeing much more of her than the surface manifestation she intended to show. *What are you doing to me?* she whispered.

There seemed to be a rush and a hiss around her, a flurry of activity that she could not see.

She may well be the one, said a voice—not the dragon's.

She tried to focus, to see who was speaking. She could not move her gaze.

That is easy for you to say. That was Highwing's voice, barely audible. *Do you know the trouble it would cause? Who am I to make such a claim?*

You must judge that yourself, whispered the other. *But remember the words. Remember Skytouch.*

There was a long pause. Then Highwing: *I remember Skytouch very well.* There was renewed anger in the dragon's voice.

Do you? It would not always seem so, from your actions.

Iffling, speak to me not of things that are not your affair! hissed the dragon. *Begone!* And with those words, he blinked, releasing Jael from his gaze.

She drew a deep breath and shook her head, trying to refocus her eyes. Something small and luminous and ghostly, hardly more than a flicker of light, floated in the air beside the dragon. *As you wish,* spoke the voice that she had heard moments ago. And the flicker of light vanished. Jael stared, dumbfounded, into the dark air where it had been. She looked slowly back at Highwing.

Aaahhhhh . . . the dragon sighed, steam trailing from his nostrils. *There will be unhappiness about this, that is certain. Great unhappiness.* He stared at her for a long moment.

What was that? she asked.

What was what?

That thing I just saw.

Oh. The iffling. The dragon sharpened a foreclaw on the rock. *Meddling creature. Still, I may have erred in sending it away so soon. But its words . . .* Highwing hesitated.

Troubled you, Jael said sarcastically.

Highwing blinked. *Indeed. And you—I must learn now what to make of you.*

You don't have to make anything of me. Just let me go.

The dragon cocked his head. *Oh? And if I did? Do you think you would leave this realm alive? You have already been noticed, you know, and not just by me. Did you not feel that shudder in the underrealm? You have placed yourself in great danger by com-*

ing here. Do you think they would let you leave? His eyes shifted to her left. *You would not be the first outsider to die in their flame . . . if their boasts are to be believed.*

Jael followed the direction of his gaze. The other dragons were still wheeling in the night air against the moon. She had forgotten about them. She could see tiny billows of flame; the dragons were not too close now, yet close enough to attack, if they wished to. *Do you mean . . . that riggers are . . . always killed?* she asked, swallowing.

Highwing answered in a mutter. *Who knows, really? There is little enough that is certain, these days.* He paused in thought. *Though there is one, or I should say, rumor of one who . . . walks in the realm as a free demon. More than that, I don't know. But—*

He was interrupted by voices grumbling in the distance: *Highwing . . . Highwing . . . why do you wait?*

Highwing's voice rumbled to full power. *THIS ONE IS MINE!* he thundered, blasting the air with fire. *YOU MAY LEAVE US ALONE!*

He was answered by distant, haughty laughter. But the other dragons seemed to move farther off. Jael watched them uneasily. She turned to Highwing. *I am yours? Is that what you think?*

Steam curled into the air from the dragon's great nostrils. *Let us say that I fear that you are mine,* the dragon said with evident reluctance. *Something is greatly amiss here, one known as Jael. You have come innocently, it would seem. As the words say.*

The words?

The Words. The speaking. The prophecy. As the iffling has reminded me. If you are the one . . . He sighed again, then raised his head, as though cutting off his train of thought. *I have already done the unthinkable, in sparing you. And yet, it seems I must. To refuse would be to concede to those . . . to allow those who do evil to the realm . . . to prevail.* Jael tried to interrupt; but he continued speaking, as though following disconnected thoughts, his voice growing deeper. *Ahhh, and yet even so, I feel . . . I sense . . . still another force, another evil at work. Something that has nothing to do with me, or this realm.*

Something within . . . you! How strange! His eyelids closed and opened again. He seemed surprised. *Perhaps several somethings. I cannot say precisely.* He drew a long, rumbling breath and seemed to debate something in his thoughts. *I almost fear to ask this, but . . . do you wish to tell me of it?* he said finally.

Jael felt a growing sense of unreality. The dragon was making no sense to her. *Tell you—?*

What is troubling you.

I have nothing to tell you, she said, a little dizzily, *except to mind your own affairs.* His insistence was wearing at her. And every time he looked at her she felt naked, as though he were looking right through her, finding every one of her faults.

I have received your name, and given you mine, the dragon said in an injured tone, as if that explained everything. *You proposed the bonding, and I accepted, in honor. I trust you will not abuse the privilege. You may trust me, as well.*

After you lied and tried to kill me?

That was when we were dueling. And before I knew that you were—or might be— He paused, then grumbled something under his breath which she didn't catch. *Well, in any case, it was expected.*

Not by me, it wasn't.

The dragon stared at her without answering. In the silence, she knew that she should be on her way. But something in her did not quite want to go, something apart from her fear of the other dragons. Something in her wanted to learn more from this Highwing. He spoke of things she did not understand. But he almost sounded as if he had . . . expected her, somehow. The dragon cleared his throat steamily. Some of the clouds broke and stars appeared over the mountains. Jael stared at them longingly, thinking of her dream: flying among the stars. That was what she was doing now. Wasn't she?

A voice broke the silence, neither hers nor Highwing's. *What's going on?*

The dragon peered around in confusion, but Jael recognized the voice with a shiver. *I'm flying, Mogurn,* she answered, her voice tightening.

Jael, come out of the net at once, ordered Mogurn's bodiless, furious voice.

I can't, she said, with a glance at Highwing. *There are dragons close by. Very close. Please don't argue with me,* she thought fervently. *Our lives could depend on it.*

Mogurn's answer was harsh, but tinged with fear. *Can you get us out of it? Out of trouble?*

I'm trying. If you let me.

Do so. When we're out of trouble, you come and see me, Jael. I'm very disappointed in you. Mogurn broke the connection abruptly.

Jael shuddered and gazed off into the night, not meeting the dragon's eyes. Still, she was aware of his eyes glowing at her, through the thin curls of smoke that rose from his snout. *I think I begin to perceive,* Highwing murmured. *You must answer to someone . . . in your realm. Your spaceship. And that disturbs you. Am I right?*

Jael didn't answer, but something made her turn her head and look into those enormous eyes. The intensity of his gaze caused her to shiver. He seemed to be thinking deeply about something. *Without friend will come one,* he murmured to himself. *Giving her name, will come one. Ah, Skytouch!* He shook his great head in dismay. *Jael,* he said finally, and his voice became so soft that it was almost inaudible. *You present me with a dilemma. What I am about to suggest is . . . not done . . . in this realm. And yet, it seems required by honor, by my obligation not to abuse what you have given me—in your name, and your . . . garkkondoh . . . real self.*

She squinted in puzzlement. *What do you mean?*

The dragon cleared his throat, noisily and at length. *Perhaps it would be better if you came with me for a little while. It might be that I can help you.* Almost wistfully, he continued, *A dragon helping a rigger. Imagine! Let us hope that I am right.*

She shook her head. *I don't understand you.*

The dragon's eyes glinted. Then she thought she heard something like a rumble of laughter, or perhaps a darker kind of sound, very soft, very deep in the earth. As the sound died away, Highwing said, *It appears that I am your servant and friend now, Jael—and you mine, if you will. It has been made our duty to help each other if we can. So the Words would seem to say. And so, you really should—must!—come with me.*

But I don't see why, she persisted. *How can you ask me to trust you?*

The dragon answered softly, *Because you have come to me. And because I seem to be all you have at the moment.*

Jael stared at him, wide-eyed with amazement. But for no reason she could understand, she felt her suspicions fading. A host of fears streamed through her mind: about Mogurn, and the pallisp, and the safety of her ship. And then they seemed to drain away. For some reason, a part of her wanted to go with this dragon—where, she didn't know. Never mind that he had tried to kill her. She squinted at his huge steady eyes, set within that great knobbed and finely scaled head. Strange as it seemed, she felt no threat. Certainly the dragon had nothing to fear from her, and if he meant to harm her, there was no need for him to resort to trickery. *I suppose,* she said, *you're going to promise not to hurt me. And you'll expect me to believe that.*

The dragon looked at her thoughtfully. *No one can promise not to hurt another—can one, Jael?*

Jael half closed her eyes, feeling a pain well up inside her. She tried to shut it away, but couldn't.

A moment later Highwing added softly, as though to himself, *There may be great hurt, before it is all over. But perhaps that need not concern us now.*

She scarcely heard him, thinking suddenly of her ship and her flight. Never in her rigging experience had she heard of anything like this. But what were her choices, really? She was in a dragon place now, and subject to attack on sight. It seemed better to be with a dragon who, perhaps, intended no harm to her. *What exactly,* she said finally, *did you have in mind?*

The dragon blinked, dimming his eyes momentarily, like a

ship's signal lights at sea. *Climb onto my back.* He turned around carefully on the crag and crouched low.

After a long hesitation, Jael climbed up and perched astride the base of his neck, just in front of his wing joints. She took a deep breath and clutched his neck.

Hold tight, he said, and sprang into the night air.

Chapter 10
A DRAGON'S TRUTH

THE WIND whispered in her ears, sighed through her hair. She clung, dizzy with confusion, with relief and fear and uncertainty. The power in the dragon's wings was unnerving at first, but after a time the stroking movements began to feel soothing. Instinctively, she stroked his silken-hard scales.

That feels good, right behind the ears, Highwing remarked, as he flew.

Abruptly she stopped. *Too bad,* she muttered.

Highwing chuckled and banked so that she could see the landscape below. They were flying very low over the mountain terrain, dark ravines and jutting rock rushing by, only dimly visible in the scattered moonlight. Highwing suddenly banked the other way and dropped into a plummeting dive. Jael clung breathlessly. Beneath them, a valley stretched open, all shadow and glimmering moonlight. She peered past Highwing's head, straining to pick out detail. *Where are we going?* she shouted. The dragon belched a flame in answer.

A moment later, he slowed his descent. They were approaching what looked like a wide, billowing, diaphanous curtain hung across the air, a sparkling veil of mist. Highwing glided directly into it. Jael felt the cool touch of the mist on her face and smelled a sharp tang in the air. With a dizzying rush, she felt a strange internal sensation, as though time and dimension were twisting around and through her—almost as though they were passing from one level of the Flux into another. That seemed unlikely; but something was happening, and it felt like something peculiar to this place, this realm, this region of the Flux; it was something peculiar to the dragon and his powers.

Even as the mist billowed around her, she caught glimpses of dark stone walls sliding by, almost enclosing her and the dragon. She had no idea how far they had flown, or in what direction, and she was losing track of time, as well. Suddenly the mist vanished and they were flying free again, under a gorgeously clear, starry sky. A mountain slope still sprawled beneath them, and they glided down over it, toward a place that shone golden in the night like a half-concealed valley.

I must be dreaming this, she thought. I must be creating the image. And yet . . . she knew that she was not.

Highwing followed a descending trail of glitter strewn in the air. The sparkling trail descended into an open forest—a most peculiar place, with soft lights hanging in the boughs of the trees. And the trees! They were like nothing she had ever seen before: some had graceful, upward-arching branches and cup-shaped leaves; others had long trailing violet strands that reminded her of terran weeping willows; still others had round silver leaves and small glowing spheres that might have been fruit, or perhaps actual lanterns. There was a remarkable profusion of flowering bushes, with extravagant and luminous blossoms.

It is real, Highwing remarked, perhaps reading her thoughts as he angled low under a glimmering archway that spanned an opening in the trees. Gossamer strands crisscrossed over their heads as they glided through a long pavilion lined by shadowy trees. The dragon barely fluttered his wings; they floated as effortlessly as spirits in the night. *This is a . . . special place for me*, he murmured. *It is a place of power, and a place of memories. No outsider has ever seen it before. Do you like it?*

It's beautiful, Jael whispered. She gazed about in fascination as they emerged from the arching pavilion. Off to the left, she spied a small waterfall spilling into a starlit pool. Several odd-looking creatures with spindly legs stood at the pool's edge, drinking from the water. A sudden waver in the air caught her attention, a quivering light. The creature again—what was it?—the iffling? No. It was another dragon, but it was shimmering and transparent, as though it were only half there. Moonlight seemed to gleam off its scales, though there was no moon in the sky now. Its eyes flickered orange and seemed to focus on them. Jael thought she heard it speak, its voice a muffled grumble in the air. She could not understand any words, but she heard an unmistakable dissatisfaction or anger in its tone, and for some reason it made her shiver.

Highwing's throat began to rumble in answer. She could not understand what he was saying, either; it was like the sound of a distant thunderstorm. But the two voices intersected and seemed to shake the air, and she sensed that some power was being played out between the two dragons—a dangerous power, she thought, a contest of wills. And then the night air grew still, and she blinked, and the other dragon was gone. There was nothing at all to indicate that it had ever been there, except a buzzing dizziness in her thoughts. She drew a breath. *What was that?*

Hm? Highwing inquired.

What was . . . that dragon . . . ?

Nothing. A mere disturbance in the underrealm. It was nothing.

What do you mean, nothing? You and that dragon sounded—

We were having a minor disagreement, is all. The dragon tossed his head like a horse. *It was nothing.* He was silent for a moment. Then: *Jael, take a good look at this place I have brought you to.*

Jael shook her head and focused on the garden and the pool.

This is no mere garden. This is a place where we will begin to learn more of each other.

It is very beautiful, she said softly. *But what does it have to do with me? And I want to know, what did you and that other dragon say to each other?*

Highwing did not answer for a moment. He hovered, motionless and silent, then suddenly craned his neck to peer back over his shoulder with an enormous, faceted green eye. *Little one—such endless questions! I wish I could remember your name. What was it?*

Jael! she said stiffly. Then she saw the fire glittering in his eye and realized that he was teasing her. She flushed with embarrassment.

Little Jael, the dragon said.

Quit calling me little!

The dragon shivered, his scales rippling under her. *But you are—physically, at least. Don't you know that if we are to share a friendship, we must be truthful with each other?*

She bristled, before snapping, *We won't have any friendship if you keep calling me that!*

Highwing cocked his massive head in amusement. *You say that now, large Jael. But you would not duel, as a demon-spirit should. You convinced me that you are no demon. You gave me your name—and commanded my honor.* The twinkle was gone from his eye now. *And so we have come here, to this place where I might weave together certain powers, where we might learn more of the truth of each other.*

Jael hiked herself up to look the dragon squarely in one eye. Hah! she was going to say, but her gaze locked with the dragon's, and the word never came out.

Suddenly she knew what he meant by *power*. She had looked into the dragon's glowing eyes once before, but this was . . . different. His gaze seemed infinitely deep now; it drew her inward, enveloping her. She felt herself falling deeper, deeper, into the luminous abyss of his inner eye, toward a cool faceted fire that burned within that emerald lantern. She fell through one of the dazzling facets and into a stream of upwelling light. It seemed a warming light; and she sank into it as though falling weightless down a twisting spiral pathway, toward the inner fires, and into the light of the dragon's very essence, its consciousness . . . its soul. And she found a mind peering back at her in wonder and curiosity.

Dimly, she recalled something like this in the dreamlink. Then she had been afraid, but now she felt no fear. This being was different from anyone she had ever encountered before, more powerful and curious by far. But beneath the layers of curiosity she glimpsed a deep sorrow, an unexpected kindness, and an interest that was without malice, though overlaid with caution. She caught reflected images of herself and realized that the other was peering deep into her own thoughts, probing her memories and her fears, probing her very being. For an instant, she wanted to resist. But no . . . this was a gentle probing, and she found herself wanting to be open. . . .

A host of memories rose up like silvery bubbles, floating free into the light. She was aware of her feelings drifting by as though they were something separate from herself. She saw herself rigging with schoolmates, and later with Mogurn. She saw herself walking in a meadow with her mother, identifying flowers. It must have been long ago, because they seemed happy. It was before her mother had left her husband, taking Jael with her. It was before her mother had died, in the autumn of Jael's eleventh year. It was before Jael had gone back to live with her father. She saw Dap coming to see her at the rigger school, he the senior, she the novice. That was in happier times, too, sharing hopes and tales. Once, she saw her father actually being tender with her mother, and then she saw him raging, slapping her brutally. She knew he wasn't even angry with her, but with his failing business. The memories came faster . . . the dreamlink, and the pallisp . . . and the rush of bubbles was too fast and too shiny for her to follow, and it made her dizzy to try . . . and a part of her was crying now . . . and that made it all blur. . . .

There were other memories as well, but they weren't all hers. She saw dragons quarreling and contesting for power, and dragon honor darkened by jealousy and distrust. She saw weavings of spells in a place called the underrealm, spells of crafting that created garden-places like this one; and she glimpsed other powers at work, threatening to ruin them.

She heard a name that sounded like *Tar-skel*, a strange name, murmured fearfully in private moments and dismissed in others, and she shivered at the sound of it, feeling unaccountably afraid. She saw someone named Skytouch, a fragile-looking dragon, nearly transparent, with glassy scales and wings, in a place called Dream Mountain. Words she could not quite catch echoed around that memory, and she knew only that they were laden with both uncertainty and expectation, with ancient hopes and fears. A terrible hurt seemed to well up with the memory—an absence, and a deep and bitter longing.

She drew away from the pain with a cry, and the sound resonated down the pathway into the light and reverberated back in a sympathetic chord of dragonly surprise. She felt a great fear and a need being closed off, hidden. The pathway between the minds flickered, and parted. Astonished, Jael pulled free of the dragon's gaze and sat back blinking.

What had just happened?

She wasn't sure. But though her head was ringing like a muffled bell in the aftereffects of the broken linking, one fact echoed with remarkable clarity. She had hardly been aware of it during the linking. But this dragon counted himself as her friend and companion. He truly did.

She wasn't sure why. Was it because they had exchanged names and stopped their dueling? That was part of it, but not all. He had looked deep into her, into her soul; and though he had not understood everything he saw there, he seemed to have understood enough. He counted her as a friend. And he was violating dragon tradition to do so. Because he had somehow, on some level she could not understand, expected her.

She closed her eyes and tried to remember what she had seen. For she had looked into his memories as he had into hers, and she had witnessed something—barely a glimpse, really—of the world that Highwing inhabited. *Dragon honor . . .*

All was not well with dragon honor or with this realm. And Highwing thought it no coincidence that she was here now. But he did not want to speak to her of it, or to frighten her.

But what did any of that have to do with her? Was he, perhaps, mistaking her for someone else? She was supposed to be flying between the stars; that fact had almost escaped her. She stretched her senses back through the rigger-net, testing; she felt the ship, and the flux-pile energizing the net, holding her here in the reality of the Flux. And it was a reality. Should she pull clear now, try to remove herself from danger, if she could? She thought of the pallisp and its blissful release. Should she face Mogurn and explain her folly, suffer his wrath in hopes of forgiveness and a chance to try again . . . in hopes of the pallisp, to warm and fill her heart? Later, she could return and try to modify the image. But to what purpose? This realm seemed unlike other regions of the Flux; it was what it was, and did not seem to care for her attempts to change it. Besides, Mogurn was very angry with her. He would never give her the pallisp now.

And what of Highwing—this dragon who had made her his friend? He suffered his own pain, it seemed. Her heart was pounding, remembering. She opened her eyes again and looked at the dragon. His neck was still craned, and he was gazing at her silently with his huge glowing eyes. It seemed that no time at all had passed while she'd been lost in thought. *Who—?* she began, then shook her head. *What—?* She paused. The dragon's nostrils smoked inquiringly; he averted his head a little to avoid blowing smoke into her face. She sighed. *Highwing,* she asked, one image coming suddenly into focus, *who is Skytouch?*

The dragon's eyes closed. He did not answer.

I'm sorry. I don't . . . mean to pry. But I saw . . . her? And the iffling, the iffling spoke of her. So I . . . wondered . . .

Highwing's breath whistled out in a high-pitched sigh. Jael trembled. Finally he answered, in a whisper so low she could barely hear, *Skytouch was my mate.*

Was . . . ? Jael felt, suddenly, a very large lump in her throat.

She is gone, Highwing murmured. *Gone from this realm. Gone from this life, to the Final Dream Mountain. I miss her . . . the touch of her thought.* His eyes blinked open, then closed to slits. *It was with her help that I created this place . . . this garden. I have not been here often . . . since . . .*

I'm sorry, Jael whispered. She swallowed and sat silent on the dragon's shoulders, unconsciously stroking the dragon's scales. He sighed softly. After a time, she cleared her throat. *Well—* she murmured haltingly, *what was it that you had in mind for . . . us, then?*

The dragon's eyes opened wide, and she sensed a change in his mood. He turned his head to face forward again, and with a wing thrust sent them gliding forward again, and upward, away from the magical pool. He flew with gentle downstrokes of his wings. *Perhaps, diminutive one,* he murmured, *I can help you with some things. Then we will see, perhaps, what is to become of us. From this garden, I can reach out with certain powers, and to certain other places. If you are willing to come with me . . .*

Jael tightened her grip on his neck.

From the forest-garden, they flew up through a barren landscape, a mountain slope with broken, angled rock faces, glistening here and there with ice. It seemed a lifeless place, but in its starkness it was as beautiful as the vale they had just left behind. As they flew, Jael's mind filled with questions—about the other dragon, about what it was that Highwing expected of her and why that troubled him so, about Skytouch, and the iffling, and about what Highwing was planning to do now. But she could not seem to voice any of those questions. Perhaps it was something in Highwing's mood, conveying a reluctance to talk. She rode in silence, mulling the questions in the privacy of her own thoughts.

Suddenly Highwing's massive head lifted. *Look!*

Above them a series of faceted, angular cliff faces gleamed faintly in the night, towering over the dragon and human with an almost glacial presence. Here and there among the broken facets of rock she glimpsed dim openings. An intuition told her that in those alcoves something lurked—dragon powers, dragon magic. She shivered and clung to Highwing in wondering apprehension.

The dragon wheeled slowly through the air, picking his

way upward into a maze of ravines and passageways, all darkly foreboding in the night. Again Jael felt that curious twisting sensation of time shifting in her own mind, as though each turn through the maze moved the dragon and her backward or forward in time, compressing years or stretching seconds to infinity. She quickly became disoriented, and in the gleaming icy rock faces she began to imagine that she saw human faces, or images of worlds she might have seen once, worlds she might have lived in, worlds that might have existed in another time and space. She glimpsed weeks and years of rigging experience compressed into a fantastic array of visions.

Highwing, what are we—? And she could not finish the question. She closed her eyes, trying to shut out the dizzying feeling of déjà vu.

We're here to learn something, Highwing murmured. *I don't know what we'll find, either.*

Even with her eyes closed, she was still aware of the dragon's wings beating slowly, or Highwing banking and turning and climbing ever higher and deeper into the maze. She was aware of a sprinkling of stars overhead, peering down at her; aware of the flat faces of rock passing by—some glistening with a sheen of ice, some dull and dark. And when she opened her eyes, it was all just as she'd been envisioning it.

The dragon approached a sheer cliff face, with a narrow ledge across its middle and the cracked shape of a cave opening. He lighted upon the ledge, at the entrance to the cave. *Shall we?* he inquired.

Jael swallowed. The cave looked black and forbidding. *I don't know,* she managed at last. *I won't try to stop you, I guess.*

Highwing chuckled softly and crept forward into the cave. Jael's fingers whitened as she clutched his neck. A roof of shadow passed over them, and they were suddenly enveloped by darkness. She struggled not to tremble or cry out. He is not doing this to harm you, she thought. Trust him.

Look ahead, Highwing murmured.

She rose up cautiously and peered past his head. A pale glow was visible in the darkness. As Highwing moved forward, she became aware of the stone walls widening outward. They were entering a cavern, and it was filled with a pale silvery light that shone down through the ceiling. Far in the back, an enormous spiderweb shimmered, spanning the width of the cavern. It seemed alive. There was a brief sparkle of light across its strands, then a vertical rippling of cold fire.

Jael watched without understanding, an uneasy feeling growing in the pit of her stomach. *What is this?* she whispered.

A place where we will see . . . whatever we may see. From your thoughts, Jael . . . your deeper awareness . . .

The web danced with ghostly quicksilver, and suddenly stilled. Jael found herself gazing into a living window.

She was gazing into the past. Her past.

Gazing at Mogurn.

It was Mogurn at the spaceport, not on the ship. The background came slowly into focus: the dispatching room at the spaceport, the rigger lounge off to the right, the stewards' offices to the left. But large and clear in the foreground was Mogurn: Mogurn the businessman, the thief. Mogurn the trader in illegal and immoral goods. The image quivered momentarily, and then she saw that he was talking with someone, with the spaceport crew steward. The steward to whom Jael had complained. The steward who was to respond by selling her into bondage.

This was not the scene as she recalled it. Was it possible that some part of her mind had seen this and remembered it without her conscious awareness? Hanging tightly onto Highwing's neck, she strained to hear what the two men were saying. She could hear nothing; they moved their lips in silence. Both men smiled meanly at something Mogurn said, and then the steward turned and pointed. A female rigger sat some distance beyond them, in the rigger lounge. Jael squinted, and trembled, recognizing herself. She was dozing in her seat. She was stunned to see the fright and the loneliness apparent on her own face, perhaps set loose in her sleep.

Mogurn leaned toward the steward, grinning. He withdrew from a hip pouch—just far enough for the steward to see—the pallisp. The steward nodded, winking. The two men touched hands, and something twinkled between their fingers. A bribe. Then the steward called over another young female rigger, Toni Gilen, and whispered something to her. And Toni nodded and went to speak to Jael—who awoke and rose, bewildered.

Jael clutched the dragon's neck in anger, as she watched herself approach the two men, conclude the transaction, and give up the one promise, the one vow she had made to herself—never to accept work from an unregistered shipper. Then she watched herself prepare, unknowing, to surrender to the pallisp.

Her stomach knotted, as for the first time she actually saw the greed and the arrogance in Morgurn's face as he presented her with his proposal. Had she been too blind to notice it before—too desperately wanting to fly? It was so obvious that he had intended, from the very beginning, to enchain her with the pallisp!

The dragon stirred as she struggled with her rising anger, as she admitted to herself the hatred that was growing, like a malignancy in her heart. She felt a profound humiliation welling up, so powerfully, she hardly heard Highwing whisper, *This is how it began, then? May I see more?* Without waiting for an answer, the dragon fell silent, and the image rippled and changed.

It was Mogurn's cabin, and Mogurn was standing above her, smiling as he lowered the pallisp to the back of her neck for the first time—smiling, because despite his protestations of innocence, he knew what he was about to do.

Her humiliation burned, became rage. *You bastard! You lying bastard!* she whispered. *God, how I hate you!*

And beneath her, the dragon stirred and said softly, *I begin to understand. Shall I burn him for you, Jael?*

Yes! she cried, blinking back tears, not even knowing what she was saying or thinking, just hating from the depths of her soul this man who had enslaved her. *Dear God, yes! Burn him, Highwing! Burn him!*

Highwing lifted his head and breathed fire. His breath was a blowtorch, a leaping flame that engulfed the cavern.

Jael drew back from the heat, shielding her eyes. The ghostly Jael in the spiderweb vanished, but the ghostly Mogurn whirled in surprise. He screamed, just once, before he died in the incinerating fury of the dragon's fire. Jael shuddered as the scream died away, shuddered at the sight of this man dying in hellfire at her command. She shook with rage and fear and remorse, but did not take her eyes from the fire, from the blazing tatters of the spiderweb that were all that remained of Mogurn. She thought she smelled burning flesh, and that only made her tremble even harder, choking. She wept, pressing the side of her face against Highwing's neck. *What have I done?* she whispered to herself. *What have I done?* And she felt a great poisonous cloud of hatred churn up out of her heart and leave her, joining the smoke and fury that filled the air.

But when the fires died and the smoke cleared from the gutted cavern, from the place that had held the image of the man who had bought her and used her, she felt something else rise up inside her and release itself—a great breath of cold fresh air in her heart. She felt a cry of freedom bubbling up, rising—a rush of jubilation—and she wept again, but this time with joy instead of sorrow. And when the flood of emotion drained away at last, it was replaced by an enormous backwash of weariness.

Do you feel better now, Jael? Highwing asked, in a whisper so quiet she almost didn't hear him.

Yes, she thought, not answering aloud. Yes, I feel better. And she blinked and looked away as the dragon craned his head and gazed at her. His eyes glowed, and she sensed him peering into her, trying to probe what had just happened. She let him; she was too weary to try to understand it herself.

She scarcely noticed as Highwing took her away. As they flew out of the cave, the cool night air of the mountains flowed past her cheeks, billowing her hair; but her thoughts were blurred, confused, leaden with weariness. Time strained against itself, shifted, and finally seemed to slip by unnoticed.

Eventually her wits began to return to her, and her strength. What was happening in her ship, in the "real" world outside of the Flux, while all of this was going on? she wondered. The real Mogurn had not died just now—at least, she didn't think so—but she knew that something had changed in her as a result of what Highwing had done. She realized she didn't really care what Mogurn was doing, or thinking. Or where his pallisp was.

The dragon was flying her through a steep-walled and heavily misted vale; they were still climbing upward through the mountain maze. She felt a chill on her skin, but didn't feel cold. Absently, she stroked his scales, relishing the physical feeling, the sensation of touching another. She wondered, as they flew, why she should have feared this dragon—indeed, why the two of them should ever have thought themselves enemies. An image flashed in her thoughts, a memory she'd not known she possessed. It must have come from her soul-link with Highwing: a glimpse of a wave of power passing through this world like a seismic tremor from one end of the realm to the other. She had felt it before, but not understood it; she sensed that it had started when a dragon had befriended a rigger. She was puzzled by the image, but was too tired to speak to Highwing of it now.

She rode the dragon in silence, content not to think or to speak.

After a time, Highwing banked suddenly to the right. He dropped through a shallow layer of mist and descended rapidly. He swooped into a bowl-shaped dell, flared his wings, and landed. Jael rose up on his shoulders and looked around wonderingly. The dell was a small, wooded place, a tiny grotto of life in the midst of starkness. The flow of time had indeed shifted during their flight, because twilight was just fading here, the sky a patch of deepening blue. Highwing and Jael sat in silence, watching night settle in around them and among the trees. As the darkness deepened, hundreds of gnat-sized fireflies appeared, darting and corkscrewing through the air like so many fiery atoms. At first, Jael found them amusing. But hundreds more continued to stream in from the surrounding darkness, until a cloud of whirling sparks filled a large open space between two of the largest trees. *What now? What are we going to see?* she asked.

Highwing hesitated, before admitting, *I'm not sure.*

Jael felt a tingling at the edges of her mind. She was about to speak again, when the whirling sparks coalesced into a blurred nimbus of light. And from that pale light stepped a young man. Someone she recognized.

It was Dap.

Jael's breath stopped in mid-exhalation. She tried to suppress a shuddering confusion of anger and happiness. Dap looked exactly as Dap always had, handsome and mild-mannered and gentle. But—in the shimmering light of the dragon magic, she saw something else, something astonishing. Dap was frightened. Not of anything visibly near, and not so frightened that one would see it immediately; but beneath his calm and gentle exterior, illumined somehow by the power that brought this image, there was a simmering anxiety. Dap's brave expression disguised a terrible fear.

He was standing near the dreamlink machine, the sunglow of the dreamlink field warming him. Nearby, she imagined, an invisible Jael was being warmed, as well. She felt her humiliation rising again like bile as she recalled the experience. But as the dreamlink field grew, Dap's anxiety became even stronger, though thinly veiled by his cheerful exterior. How could she have failed to see it before? Had she been so self-absorbed? Images of Dap's flights danced around him like tiny sunbursts: the rigging, the companionship with Deira, the sheer joy of the net. But was it such a single-minded joy as he had portrayed it to Jael? There shone the warmth of his companionship with Deira, and there smoldered his sorrow, his hurt at her leaving again, leaving him behind. How had Jael failed to notice that hurt? Because he had hidden it so well? Or because of her own blindness? *Dap*, she began— and then stopped, because she knew he could not hear her.

And then her own memories sprang to life in the field, crowding out Dap's—her memories dancing and bursting about Dap's head: images of her father opaquing doors behind him, leaving Jael in openmouthed pain as he retired with his women and his boys; and her brother, before the groundcar accident that took his life—bitter with the rejection and disillusionment that he never allowed expression, though it tore him apart; and Jael's frustration at their father's careless neglect, shutting out all of their pain, teaching them how to make walls but never windows.

All this Dap caught—without warning—in a tidal wave among Jael's other memories, or fantasies of memories: flights and friendships and loves that might have been, desperately lonely fantasies, unfulfilled rigger fantasies. They were all suspended in the dreamlink, where Jael had let them free. *Jael, it doesn't have to be that way!* he whispered aloud, frightened by the enormity of her pain. And she remembered her answer, all too well. *Just fantasies,* she'd lied, even as she tried desperately to sweep them away, to hide them where Dap couldn't see them, where no one would see them again. But Dap had known better—the truth could not be hidden from the dreamlink, once it was out—and she saw it now on Dap's face as he drew back from his unseen cousin sharing the field with him. And Jael started to hate him all over again now, as she saw the horror on his face, and she felt again the betrayal and abandonment as Dap shrank away from her.

Why is he drawing back? she heard, and it was the dragon whispering the question.

Why? Because he thinks I'm . . . because he's a lousy . . .

But the expression on Dap's face was not revulsion, she realized suddenly, though it had been staring her in the face all along. It was fear. Fear and shame: fear of his own needs, so terrifyingly like hers, and shame for his utter helplessness in the face of hers. Just as she had tried to hide her terrible desperation from him, so had he hidden his own.

And so afraid of the pure naked hurt was he that even now, in the sight of Jael and Highwing, he fled. And as he ran, back into that nimbus of ethereal light between the trees, Jael heard Highwing's voice, asking softly, *Shall I burn him, like the other?* The dragon drew a deep breath.

No! she cried, startled by her own vehemence. *Don't hurt him! I didn't know—I never realized!* And suddenly she was quaking with shame, shame at her own anger. She should have seen that Dap had abandoned her out of . . . cowardice, perhaps, or inadequacy—but not out of malice, or in judgment. She'd thought him steady as a rock, unshakable, older than she and wiser. But he was not a rock, he was just a rigger, her cousin. No better than she; no worse.

Highwing sighed, and the image of Dap and the pale light vanished in a cloud of sparks. Highwing's nostrils glowed a dull red. *Did you remember it that way?* he asked, rumbling throatily.

No, Jael whispered. *No, I didn't.* And she fell mute, remembering the abandonment she had felt, thinking that Dap loathed her as everyone else did, for things that weren't her fault, and remembering how she had vowed never to let anyone touch her soul that way again.

But that came from your own memory, Highwing murmured. *A part of you knew the truth. You do not always see clearly in your memory, do you?*

Why no, I . . . she began, and hesitated, because she had no idea how to explain.

Well, then, Jael—look up. I see something else happening. The dragon lifted his head and snorted sparks into the air.

Reluctantly she lifted her gaze. For a moment she couldn't see anything except the dark shape of a cliff overlooking the glade. And then, high atop the cliff, in a sheltered aerie, illuminated by she knew not what, she saw the dark figure of another man.

Who is that? she hissed. Highwing didn't answer at once, but a suspicion was already growing in the pit of her stomach. There was something familiar about the shape.

Don't you know? Highwing asked finally. Without waiting for an answer, he sprang aloft and beat into the wind toward the aerie. Rather than flying directly to it, however, he veered to one side and alighted upon a high ledge from which they could look across and see the place clearly.

But Jael already knew. The man was her father. He was a cold-eyed, stiff-limbed man, exactly as she remembered him. He looked perhaps a little older, a little wearier, a little more dour. He was gazing outward from the aerie, as though expecting a caller; but the manner of his stance suggested defensiveness, retreat, as though he feared to leave this shelter. His eyes stared, his mouth curled with distaste, as they had on other occasions, when he'd wondered aloud why he had saddled himself with two former wives, an unhappy son, and a self-pitying daughter. His eyes shifted then, and seemed to light upon Highwing and Jael. Upon Jael. And that gaze was the same look of contempt he'd lavished upon her for as long as she could remember. She remembered her own rage, which had been building for years.

Kill him, she said softly, loathing rising out of the depths of her heart. *Burn him!*

She waited for the explosion of fire from Highwing's throat, the lance of flame that would destroy her father as it had destroyed Mogurn. But the dragon made no move to carry out her command. *Highwing?*

And then she knew why the dragon hesitated. He'd seen the answer in her soul. It was not because he was protecting her father, but because her father was already dead. He'd died three years ago, at the hands of a slighted lover, while Jael was still in rigger school. What point was there in burning him now? Jael cursed futilely, squinting across to the aerie where this man stood, hopelessly cold and desperately alone, this man who had turned his shipping company into a den of thievery and abuse, who had turned two wives against him and taught a son and daughter how not to feel. Jael pressed her forehead against the dragon's scaled neck, weeping inwardly. And then she felt something . . .

She looked up and saw a change in the light that illumined her father's face, a deeper, softer glow. And she realized that *he* had changed, too. She was seeing him at an earlier time, a happier time. Behind him, she glimpsed her mother's face, just for an instant, but it was long enough to see that she was gazing at him with genuine love. Love, but pain too. Was it a happier time? His mouth was tight with indecision. But about what?

Jael drew a breath, and then she knew. She had been young then, too; too young to really understand; but this was the turning point, her father's business fortunes at their lowest ebb, the family-owned shipping firm teetering at the brink of collapse. It wasn't his fault, his mouth seemed to say. The registry had turned against him, and his own colleagues, and now he'd lost the passenger license, and there were incompetent riggers, as well, who had cost him two ships and plunged him into debt. And now he had to make a choice. A shipper on the edge could survive a lot more easily flying unregulated. Hang the registry. The quality of the riggers was a lot more uncertain, but how could it be worse than he'd seen already?

Anger and pain hardened his face. Jael had no idea whether or not his anger was justified; there was so much she didn't know about how it all had happened. But the effect on him was clear, as his face metamorphosed in the dragon light. The anger was sealed up within him, and he closed himself up like a steel wall, hard with bitterness. Behind him, Jael's mother's face grew drawn and terrified. Finally she was gone, and as Jael watched she felt glad that her mother's pain had ended years ago. But her father's pain only grew, and like some tormented, twisting animal he lashed out at those closest to him.

And the family name became a badge of shame. Jael did not even know, really, all that her father did to turn the shipping community against him. She did not want to know. She knew only that his suffering, like her mother's, had ended only with his death. But Jael's hadn't. Damn him, couldn't he at least have given *something* to her, some encouragement to her dream?

Didn't he, Jael? Not ever? whispered Highwing.

What? Jael saw another image beginning to form, and suddenly she knew what it was, it was the rigger school, and she erupted with rage. *Stop it, damn you! No, he didn't—not ever— not except by dying and leaving us for good!* She bent her head to the dragon's neck and wept. For her mother . . . for her brother . . . for herself. What could possibly make it right? Nothing, it seemed. Nothing at all. *Get rid of him, Highwing, get rid of him!* she whispered, rubbing away her tears.

Shall I burn him? Highwing asked softly.

She almost said yes, then sighed, straightening up. *I guess not. What's the point? Maybe he suffered enough, I don't know. But it's over.* She drew a painful breath. *Let's just get the hell out of here.*

The aerie darkened, where her father had stood. Highwing

glanced back at Jael, his eyes glowing. Then he spread his wings and leaped into the air. *I had thought that you might— well—*

What? she asked darkly.

Never mind. The dragon seemed thoughtful. *But I understand now, a little, I think.*

Take me out of this place! Jael snapped, as fresh anger welled up inside her. The dragon vented smoke from his nostrils in sympathy. For some reason that enraged her still further, and she hammered on his hard, resilient scales with her fists. *Take me out of this accursed valley and let me finish my journey in peace!*

A flurry of sparks escaped from Highwing's nostrils. *Do you really mean that?* he asked softly, his powerful voice trembling with dismay.

Yes! Jael cried in a whisper, knowing that it was her pain speaking. *Yes, I want to leave!*

You won't consider . . . you mean you don't intend to—

Highwing! she cried in torment. *Take me away!*

As you will, my friend, Jael, the dragon sighed. He shook his head almost imperceptibly, muttering unhappily. But with mighty wingstrokes he beat higher and faster into the night.

Chapter 11
PARTING

THE DRAGON circled, climbing. The mountain peaks surrounded them like dark towers in the night, sullen shadows against the moonlit clouds. *When I take you out of these mountains,* Highwing said sorrowfully, *we will be near the place where I must leave you, but you will be closer to your destination than you were when we met. I had thought . . . well. Never mind. There is nothing to be done, I suppose—except to say good-bye.*

Jael recognized the sadness in the dragon's voice, but her mind burned with far too many images to respond. Anyway, what did it matter? It was the dragon's fault for bringing her to this place of magic, stirring up memories of pain and sorrow. It had seemed all right until the very end, when there'd been no escaping the pain, not even the satisfaction of seeing the offender's image burned by dragon fire. There was no such solution where her father was concerned. *Why? Why?* she whispered to herself, not meaning to speak it aloud.

Highwing seemed to understand her thought. *I did not know what we would see or how it would feel,* he murmured. *I only showed you what was in your mind.*

She nodded, grunting. She didn't know why she felt angry with him, really, but she did.

Did I do wrong, Jael? If so, I am sorry.

She shook her head and silently clung to him as he beat his wings, carrying them toward the highest reaches of the mountains. Memories continued to flash through her mind: her brother gathering his dignity, unable to share his hurt even with his sister, who loved him; Dap and the other riggers struggling with their own loneliness and fear, and the competition for jobs in which they were all victims; a rigger named Mariel who had once treated her kindly, and Toni Gilen who had innocently come to her with a message from the steward, from Mogurn; and Mogurn himself, in the deathlike oblivion of his synaptic augmentor. And worst of all, memories of a father who in the end had loved no one, least of all himself.

She clung to Highwing because she was trembling so hard, shaking as the feelings followed the images faster than she could respond to them. Memories of pain and anger and loneliness and frustration; they were spawning a cyclone in her soul, a storm that would probably have swept her away in the Flux if Highwing had not been here to protect her. She scarcely saw the mountain peaks passing by on either side, dark and grim in the night, or the clouds that muffled them and then opened to the sky, or the stars that gleamed like diamonds and then stretched peculiarly into spidery lines . . . in response to the sensation of speed . . . to her growing fatigue in the rigger-net.

In the rushing wind, she finally raised her head and hiked herself up on the dragon's neck, realizing with a shock that she was exhausted, that she had been flying in the net for too many hours. *Where are we going?* she whispered, finding herself incapable of speaking any louder.

On the way to where you wanted to go, said the dragon.

If I went away—to sleep—could you stay with my ship until I returned? Even as she spoke, she sensed the net sparkling with distorted colors. She was losing her ability to control her own presence here; she had to get out. She felt an inexplicable jab of pain, of loneliness, at the thought. She didn't quite want to leave Highwing.

I will be here.

Sighing, Jael gathered her senses with an effort of will and altered the image slightly, materialized an image of her ship as it was bound to her through the net—just its ghostly nose protruding out of nothingness into the Flux. She set the stabilizers astraddle Highwing. *This should help keep us together. I'll see you in a while, then.*

A plume of smoke. *Yes.*

Jael withdrew. Her senses darkened, accompanied by a wave of dizziness—and rekindled back in her own body. She climbed out of the rigger-cell and stood, trembling with exhaustion, in the gloom of the starship's bridge. She stretched and felt her joints popping; she had been in the rigger-station, motionless, for a very long time—longer than she would have thought possible. Was that Highwing's work? Or had the pallisp increased her abilities and stamina in the net? She shrugged wearily. What did it matter?

She was ravenously hungry, even hungrier than she was tired. She stole into the galley and quietly wolfed a dinner of tasteless fish and vegetables and bread. At any moment, she expected an angry Mogurn to burst in upon her. But when he had not appeared by the time she was finished, she began to wonder. He had been awfully anxious to see her, to vent his anger. Was it possible that the virtual-Mogurn's death in the net had . . . no, don't be ridiculous. Perhaps she should just go to sleep and worry about it later. But she could not so easily ignore Mogurn's absence, and he had told her to come see him. With a lump of fear in her throat, she disposed of her dishes and tiptoed into the hallway.

She crept to Mogurn's door and, after a long hesitation, pressed the signal. There was no answer. She paled the door, which was unlocked, and peered in. Mogurn was unconscious under his synaptic augmentor, his eyes rolled up into his head, a grimace stretching his mouth. He was so still that for a moment she thought he might indeed be dead; but no, his chest was rising and falling slowly. He hadn't been able to wait for her help, apparently; he was too addicted to his augmentor. Or he'd been too angry.

Jael frowned, thinking involuntarily of the pallisp. She realized that she didn't really need or want it just now. She could live without it while she slept. Good, she thought. Very good. Returning to the commons, she left a brief note for Mogurn, stating that the ship was out of danger. Then she went to her own cabin and fell almost instantly into a deep sleep.

She blinked as her dreams fled, visions of snarling mythical creatures disappearing in plumes of golden radiance. Her eyes focused on the ceiling of her cabin, plain pale green. She tried to focus her thoughts . . .

. . . and suddenly remembered Highwing.

She drew a sharp breath as the memories streamed back into her mind. Highwing! Had that all been a dream? For a moment, she was confused by doubts about the reality of what she remembered—or thought she remembered. Dragons in the Flux? Living creatures who spoke with humans and looked into their souls . . . and called them "friend"? It was surely impossible; it flew in the face of what she knew as reality. And yet, her memory sang with the reality of Highwing.

Mogurn's voice startled her: "Are you being paid to sleep?" The anger in his voice was sharp. Too sharp.

With a shock, she turned her head to look at him standing in her doorway. She saw his drawn-looking eyes glaring at her, and she despised him. She imagined him cremated by dragon fire.

"Make yourself ready and come see me in the galley," he ordered, his voice trembling. Then he vanished.

Scowling, she forced herself to rise. Mogurn's tone worried her. He sounded unwell, perhaps unstable. She wondered if he might have suffered a synaptic overdose on the augmentor; she had not been there to set the level for him, and she had no idea what too high a level might do. She'd have to be careful—best to get back into the net quickly. And besides, Highwing was waiting for her. (Wasn't he? He was . . . if he was real. . . .) A queer ache settled in her chest as she thought of the dragon; it reminded her of the longing she had once felt for the pallisp. But the pallisp held no attraction for her now. She wanted only to be with Highwing.

Dizzy with confused emotions, she showered and changed and crossed the hallway to the commons. Mogurn was already eating. Under his baleful gaze she punched breakfast for herself. She slipped silently into her place across the table from him. She felt the powerful presence of his stare as she lifted a piece of toast to her mouth, but she didn't meet his eyes. She struggled to keep her head steady; she struggled not to show her fear, or to show how badly she wanted to return to the net.

Mogurn spoke as she took her first bite. "Twice now, you've disobeyed and entered the net without permission. And you've put us in danger from . . . dragons." He drew a raspy breath, and his voice shook a little, betraying his own fear. "I take it from your message that we are clear of dragons now?"

Jael swallowed her toast. Highwing, burn him! she thought desperately, wishing that the dragon could be here to obey her, to protect her. She closed her eyes and chose her words with care. "Not entirely. We could still have trouble." She opened her eyes, meeting his glare at last. "But we are nearing the final current to Lexis. It should not be too much longer." She nodded to herself and carefully spread some three-berry preserves over the rest of her toast. "I should return to the net at once," she added, taking a large bite.

The tic had returned to Mogurn's face; the corner of his left eye had a life of its own, twitching and jittering nervously. He squinted, trying unsuccessfully to control it. "You don't like me much, do you, Jael?" he said tightly. He didn't wait for an answer. "You never did. Did you? But you like your pallisp well enough, don't you? Don't you, Jael! Well, there is no one else who can wield the pallisp for you on this ship, Jael—or off the ship, either!"

Jael held her gaze rigid, avoiding his eyes. I do not need a pallisp, she thought. Not any longer. Nevertheless, she trembled under Mogurn's stare. "There will be no more mistakes, Jael. No more disobedience. And no pallisp! Not until you have removed this ship completely from danger." Mogurn smiled queerly, triumphantly, and crossed his arms over his chest.

What a pathetic man, Jael thought—however powerful he might be, however cruel. What weapon did he hold over her now? She might fear him physically, yes, but—"I do not need your pallisp," she said aloud. And her throat constricted as she said it, as she wondered if it really was true. Before he could respond, she hurried to say, "And now I should return to—"

"You stay until I command you to leave!" Mogurn shouted furiously. Jael froze, scarcely breathing.

An alarm from the bridge trilled, signalling changes in the Flux. Mogurn started, his expression changing to fear. He was terrified of what was happening in the net. He jerked his head around. "Go!" he said bitterly.

Jael hurried. If Highwing had left her . . . or if it had all been a dream . . .

When her senses sparked outward into the net, she found herself astride a tremendous dragon, flying in clear bright winds over low mountains. She cried out with relief. Two setting suns, pink and orange, shone in the sky before her. The sky overhead was a sea of liquid crystal, and she knew at once that she was bound upward for that sea. *Greetings, small one*, sighed the dragon, snorting fire into the air.

Jael hugged his neck, wanting to cry. Her anger toward him had evaporated. Now she wanted only to stay with him. *Highwing*, she asked softly, *did you call me?*

The dragon pumped his wings slowly. *I wanted you to return*, he said. *I don't know if I called you or not.*

I knew it was time to come. Jael fell silent, waiting for the lump to disappear from her throat. It didn't. *Are we—almost at the end?*

Of my range, yes, Jael. Dragons do not go beyond these foot-hills. I am zigzagging to go more slowly, but yes—we are almost at the end. Do you wish me to fly straight?

She shuddered at the thought of the dragon leaving her, leaving when she had only just begun to know him. To believe in him. To believe in his world, his reality. *No . . . please. Oh, Highwing, can't you come farther with me? Or can't we go back?*

Even as she spoke, she knew that it was impossible. She had a ship to bring in, and even Mogurn was her responsibility. The currents of the Flux were inexorable; dragons could fly against them, perhaps, but Jael and her ship could not.

Highwing turned his head and regarded her. *I wish it were so, Jael. I had hoped—hoped that you would—* and his voice broke off sorrowfully.

What, Highwing?

The dragon sighed. *It doesn't matter.*

That I would . . . stay? she asked, her eyes stinging.

Yes.

Her heart nearly broke. *I wish . . . but I cannot,* she whispered.

Highwing's throat rumbled. *No . . . no, I see that you must continue, that you have duties to perform.* He turned straight ahead and flew slowly, ponderously.

Before, when I wanted to leave, Jael said, half to herself, *you were only trying to help me, just as you said you were. I didn't believe you then.* She felt a rush of shame, and tears came to wet her cheeks. *Highwing, there's so much I don't understand! So much about your world—and you! Isn't there something I can do to help you, as you helped me? I don't want to part like this, Highwing. What will I do?*

Sometimes friends must part, the dragon said softly. *But as for helping me, I think perhaps you already have.*

Jael stroked his scales sadly, in puzzlement. *How, Highwing?*

The dragon flew in thoughtful silence. *Our worlds are not the same,* he said at last, not answering her question directly. *Each has its own troubles. But you have been my friend. And now you must seek friends in your own world. That is the way of it, I suppose.*

Jael could not speak, could not think how to answer.

But I will still be here, thinking of you. Never has any dragon met such a rigger. And as Highwing said that, his powerful voice seemed to catch and hesitate. *It will be a memory for me to treasure,* he added finally.

Jael wept, and only after a long time did her tears dry. She still had no answer to the terrible question deep in her heart: How could she dispel the awful loneliness that was already closing in around her? The pallisp drifted into her mind, and she pushed it away. No, the price for that comfort was too high. The wisdom that Highwing had shown her was greater than the wisdom of the pallisp. Greater than Mogurn's wisdom, or shelled-in emptiness.

Things will be different for me now, she murmured hopefully, as though to the wind.

Highwing heard her and answered, *It will be different for me, as well, Jael.* He spoke in a voice that sounded glad, and yet troubled, in a way that she did not understand. *Never again could I duel a rigger without thinking of you. You, who have my name—and I yours.*

Will you . . . duel other riggers?

I think not, Jael. I think not. I . . . do not know what will become of me and . . . riggers.

They flew on in silence. He had never told her just what the other dragons would think of his befriending her. And now, somehow, she was afraid to ask. She found herself repeating his full name to herself, in her inner voice: Windrush-Wingtouch-Highwing—Terror-of-the-Last-Peak . . . a name to be remembered and treasured.

The lowest of the mountains drew near. *Highwing, if I fly this way again, will I find you?*

The dragon's breath caught, and he suddenly breathed fire. *Of the other dragons, beware. But believe that I shall be looking for you. Cry, "Friend of Highwing!" and I will hear you, though all the mountains lie between us.*

Jael thought she felt a tremor pass through the earth below, and she wondered at it. Of the other dragons beware. . . . She trembled with emotion. *Then let us fly high now, and part in the sun.*

The dragon complied at once, soaring upward, toward the inverted lake of sunset crystal above their heads. Jael leaned with him into the wind, feeling it sting her cheeks and toss her hair, feeling the glowing radiance of the celestial ocean overhead, filling her eyes and her soul. As the two suns set, their radiance blazed in full color into the sky. Channels opened in the clouds, and light poured through in great rays, washing over Highwing and Jael, and they flew up one of the beams, into the crystal sea, where colors shifted brightly and the currents of the Flux moved in streams and gossamer strands. And here, she knew, Highwing would leave her, for this was not a dragon's realm.

Highwing shivered, and she thought she heard echoes of weeping. The dragon blew a great cloud of smoke and sparks, and a single brilliant, billowing flame. Jael caressed his neck one last time, and then extended her hands into space and turned them into great webs touching the streamers of light. *Farewell, Highwing!* she cried softly, scarcely letting the words pass her lips.

Farewell, Jael! said the dragon, and he wheeled and suddenly Jael was no longer astride him but in flight on her own, flying as a rigger once more. Highwing banked and circled around her, and he issued a long, thin stream of smoke in final farewell. Then he banked sharply away and plummeted.

Jael gazed after him, holding back her tears, as he dwindled toward his own world. *Friend of Highwing!* she cried, and her voice reverberated down the sunbeams, and perhaps she was only imagining, but she thought she heard his laugh echoing in the distance below. And then she set her sights ahead and knew that the tears would flow again for a while, but eventually they would dry; and she looked in the shifting sky for the currents that would carry her to her destination star system, Lexis, to the end of this voyage, to normal-space. And she began to plan how she would tell Mogurn that she was leaving him and his pallisp, and she laughed and cried and turned her thoughts back to the sky.

Until I return, Highwing, she thought. Then she saw the streamer she wanted and caught it in her webbed hand, and with her the ship rose high and fast into the current.

PART TWO

RIGGER FRIEND

Chapter 12
CONFRONTATION

THE MOUNTAINS were well behind her when she at last set the stabilizers and prepared to leave the net. She didn't leave right away, though; in fact, she almost released the stabilizers again and returned to active flying, so reluctant was she to depart. In the end, she knew that she had no choice; she could not stay here forever, and Mogurn had already interrupted her twice, demanding to know the ship's condition. But she couldn't help gazing wistfully astern, where the realm of dragons had long since passed out of sight. Drawing a deep breath, she turned her attention forward, to the clear golden atmospheres ahead and the tiny flecks of distant star systems. At last she withdrew from the net.

Mogurn was in his cabin, smoking. He barely stirred when she entered; his gaze was directed to the wall-holo near the door. Jael was almost afraid to turn her head to see what was on the holo, but when he didn't move, she steeled herself and looked. It was an empty image, a featureless grey-green space like a window into an infinitely deep ocean. She shivered a little and wondered what was making him so still, what he was seeing in that blank holo. Failure? Death? Perhaps she didn't really want to know. Pressing her lips together, she turned to face her captain.

Mogurn gave no sign of noticing her. He puffed, and smoke curled up around his head.

"The ship is clear of danger," Jael said quietly. "We're out of the mountains. We should be entering the final current to the Lexis system in a couple of days, I'd guess. Ahead of schedule."

Still there was no response from Mogurn. Was this the man who had so urgently needed to know what was happening?

"If you have no questions, I request sleep time now." She might as well have been speaking to the wall. With a shrug, she turned to leave.

She was halfway out the door when she heard Mogurn's voice behind her, strained and oddly thin. "There will be no pallisp for you today."

Turning, she gazed at him in cold wonderment. "I do not want the pallisp," she said softly. "Tonight or—" she hesitated—"ever again." If he heard her words, it did not show. Puffs of smoke streamed up past his reddened, unseeing eyes. "Good night," she said, and did not breathe again until his door was opaque and the length of the hallway stood between her and Mogurn's cabin.

Mogurn did not come out again for the better part of a shipday. During that time, Jael flew the ship well along toward Lexis . . . and she struggled not to think about the pallisp.

The latter was more easily intended than done. Her friendship with Highwing may have rendered the pallisp unnecessary while she was in the net, but Highwing was no longer here. The memory of the dragon was strong in her mind—but so too was the memory of the pallisp. More than once in the net she found herself caught between the two memories, longing for both, knowing she could not have the one and dared not have the other. She caught herself gazing backward, behind the ship, unconsciously trying to conjure the image of Highwing. With painful determination, she pulled herself back from that impulse, which was not only futile but dangerous; she had to accept the fact that she was alone. To remember Highwing and his deeds was a very good thing, but to wish for something that was impossible would only draw her back into another form of dependence. And along that road lay the pallisp.

She had made a vow to herself—and to Mogurn—that she would have no more of that instrument. She had broken one vow already, just in coming aboard this ship. She was determined not to break another.

Nevertheless, she found it difficult to concentrate in the net. The second time she caught herself drifting off course, she cut short her flying time. She left the bridge with a great emptiness in her heart—an emptiness that she dared not fill in Mogurn's cabin.

She went to the galley instead. Two sweet muffins and three cups of clove tea later, she felt stuffed, but no less empty. *Highwing, why couldn't you have stayed with me just a little longer?* she thought uselessly, picking at the crumbs on her plate, as though she didn't know the answer.

You will find others, she seemed to hear him say.

It wasn't much consolation.

Cry, "Friend of Highwing!"—and I will hear you, though all the mountains lie between us. . . .

Tears ran silently down her cheeks. Even as she wept, she knew that if she could just keep that one thought clear in her mind, that image of Highwing waiting for her, then perhaps she could resist and defeat the pallisp. She had no choice, really. It was a battle she had to win.

Mogurn glared at her across the table. His eyes were wide, bloodshot, and angry, and his hair was uncombed. He looked as though he had slept in his robe, and probably had. What he had been doing in his cabin, she could not imagine, but it had not calmed his temper. He had emerged for the evening-watch meal, and she had just informed him that she was planning to leave the ship at Lexis starport.

He rose half out of his seat. His voice sounded like an old pipe gurgling. "We have a contract, Jael LeBrae! You are bound to this ship, and to *me*, until that contract is fulfilled! Until you have returned me to Gaston's Landing!"

Jael stared at him, and could not help thinking of the old sea-travel stories of cruel and piratical ship's masters. Mogurn so clearly fit the image now; she didn't know how she could have missed it, when they first met. He was just the sort of captain that her father, her accursed father, might have hired. Ruthless, uncompromising. She was afraid to answer him, but more afraid not to. She struggled to make her voice steady, as the words came out in a rush. "That contract is a fraud. It did not allow you to use an illegal and addicting device on me. You have endangered the safety of your ship and crew—as I expect you probably endangered your last crew!" And when she was finished, she knew she had just indicted him in the worst way possible.

Mogurn's fist slammed down onto the table. Jael jumped involuntarily. "That is a lie, rigger! It is *you* who have endangered this vessel! And now you refuse the one thing that can redeem you, that can make you a rigger worthy of the name!" He waved a finger across the table, his face contorted by rage. "But you *cannot* refuse it!"

Sit steady, Jael thought grimly. Do not move or let him gain an upper hand. You need not give in to him. And she sat and stared back at him—though for a long dreadful moment, her fear was almost greater than her determination. Finally she took a breath and said, with anger in her voice, "What *did* happen to your last rigger, Captain Mogurn?"

Mogurn's eyes bulged, and his gaze broke. He lurched away, while she caught her breath, trembling. For an instant, she thought perhaps she had won. Then Mogurn wheeled back toward her, fire in his eyes. But this time he did not meet her gaze, or even seem to see her. He stalked past her, out of the commons.

Jael peered after him, through the empty doorway. Would he leave her alone now? She hardly dared to hope. Something in his expression had filled her with dread. But perhaps he was going to take refuge in his synaptic augmentor; perhaps he would simply lose himself there, leave her in peace, leave her to finish the flight. She looked down at her dinner.

Her stomach was in knots. But perhaps, she thought, the worst was over.

She heard the footsteps in time to turn her head—but too late to dodge the hand that clamped onto her shoulder. Involuntarily, she let out a cry of pain. She shrank from Mogurn's glaring eyes. In his left hand he held the pallisp. "What are you doing?" she gasped, as he tightened his grip on her shoulder.

"I have brought you what you *need*, Jael!" he crowed, in a voice that quavered between madness and triumph.

"Are you crazy?" She tried to rise, to wrench free of his grip. "Let me go!"

He gazed at her with a queer smile, then released her shoulder. She stumbled out of her seat and backed away, but not fast enough. He struck her in the face with the back of his hand.

The blow sent her reeling across the room. She staggered into the wall and fell to the deck. Stunned, she raised her head as Mogurn strode over to tower above her. "No!" she whispered.

"You'll take your pallisp," he growled. "Whether you want to or not. You will take it."

Jael closed her eyes to slits. For a moment, she felt a cool, calm certainty that Mogurn held no power over her. Not unless she allowed him to.

"Well, Jael?" He bent toward her.

She resisted an urge to spit in his face. "I'll take nothing from you," she murmured. She saw his knuckles whitening around the handle of the pallisp. She tried to scramble away on the deck. But his hands were quicker, and he grabbed her wrist with one hand, while with the other he hooked the pallisp behind her head and jammed it up against the base of her neck.

"I am not threatening you, Jael," he said in a frighteningly controlled voice. "But I have made you a promise. And I always keep my promises." He did something with the pallisp.

Jael shuddered as a wave of stimulation rippled up her spine. "Damn you," she breathed, and then her voice was taken away by a rush of warmth that flooded her body, her mind. The pallisp was reaching deep into her brain, where it could bring comfort or deep shuddering pleasure.

No! she whispered, but the sound never reached her lips.

And then it was stripped away as quickly as it had come—and she gasped and blinked, struggling to focus her eyes. Her hand, under its own control, reached out for the pallisp. She could not help wanting it; she was aware of the folly, but could not stop.

Mogurn's laugh filled her head, and she blinked, realizing what she was doing. She jerked her hand back; she struggled futilely to escape his grip. His breath was hot in her face. "Want it?" he hissed. "Don't want it? Want it? Don't want it?" He twisted her wrist and pressed the pallisp to her neck again . . .

She cried out, shuddering with pleasure and pain. "Damn you! *Damn you—*"

Once more it was yanked away, and she huddled on the floor, panting. Struggling to catch her breath, she glared up at him. She knew that if she were exposed to enough of this, no matter her resolution, she would become addicted beyond hope of recovery.

Mogurn's expression was a hideous mixture of anger and triumph. She blinked and attempted to form words with her mouth. Her lips and tongue would not respond. Leering at her efforts, he brought the pallisp down again. She ducked her head away and managed to hiss, "You will never get to Lexis without me!"

His hand stopped halfway down, the pearl grey ball of the pallisp inches from her face. His eyes glared into hers, and she held that terrifying gaze, wondering if she had finally penetrated his consciousness. He drew the pallisp to his chest and straightened stiffly. "You," he said, "have taken an oath."

Jael snorted contemptuously.

Mogurn's eyes widened with indignation. "You have taken an oath!" he roared. "An oath to bring this ship to port. You will be nothing if you deny that oath. Nothing! Do you hear me?"

Jael began laughing bitterly. An oath? Yes, she had an oath to fulfill, but it did not extend to this, not to suffering this kind of brutality. Perhaps she could do the worlds a favor by losing this ship, and herself and Mogurn with it, in the uncharted currents of the Flux. Which would be the greater evil—to betray her oath, or to bring this man back to civilization?

Mogurn released her—then struck her in the face again. She crouched, guarding her face against another blow. It didn't come. Cursing silently, she raised her hand. But Mogurn was no longer looking at her. He seemed to have forgotten her completely. He was gazing into space; his left hand, still holding the pallisp, was hanging toward the deck.

Jael lunged and snatched the pallisp and scrambled across the floor with it.

"YOU!" he howled, whirling. "Come back here!"

Jael sprang up to a crouch, holding the cold steel of the pallisp close to her breast. "Don't come close to me!" she warned.

"Give me that!" Mogurn advanced, glaring, hand out-stretched.

"Stay away."

"GIVE—IT—"

His hand shot out to grab her left wrist. She twisted away and cocked her right hand back, and without thinking twice, hurled the pallisp with all of her strength.

"NO!" he shrieked.

The pallisp hit the far wall with a thud, and a sharp crackle of broken circuitry. Her breath exploded with a gasp, and she closed her eyes, oblivious to the pain as Mogurn seized her and threw her against the wall. She struggled to stay on her feet, to stay away from him.

Mogurn stalked over to pick up the pallisp. As he rose with it, his eyes were clouded. Jael tensed for another attack. Mogurn's mouth worked to form words. He stared down at the pallisp, the ball of which was now flattened. He sput-tered, struggling to speak, and finally croaked, "Bring . . . this ship in . . . you will bring this ship in . . . you wretched little *bitch!*" And without looking at her again, he strode from the room.

Jael was as astonished as she was terrified. She looked about the galley, where she had been planning to eat her meal. She shook her head and took a few steps toward her cabin. Then she turned and ran instead to the ship's bridge.

For a long time, she sat in the pilot's seat, not entering the net but merely studying the clustered instruments, monitoring the ship's condition and tracking its movements in the immediate surroundings of the Flux. There was little to be done; she felt like an ancient sailor of the seas on night watch in a windless night, keeping her ship on an even keel and monitoring its drift against the current, but doing little that would significantly affect her course or speed.

It gave her a small measure of comfort to sit here, to eye the empty rigger-couch that could take her into another world, when she was ready, a world that was subject to her mood, her whim. Yet, she wasn't ready to go into the net just now. It would only bring back to life her fury at Mogurn, and her longing for Highwing—and the disruption to her flying could be perilous. Dear God, she missed Highwing! She thought, too, of her father—of the man revealed to her by the light of dragon magic. She wondered if she ought to have hated him or pitied him. It all seemed less clear now, without Highwing.

Finally, in the gloom and the quiet, she began to feel calmer and eventually she grew drowsy. She kept at it a while, clicking display knobs and studying the abstract images that conveyed technical information. Eventually, she blinked, realizing that she was nodding off and had not understood a thing she had seen in the past ten minutes, and she rose with a sigh, blinked wistfully at the rigger-station, and retired to her quarters. From Mogurn there had not been a sound.

She pressed the LOCK setting on her door panel, then checked it, and double-checked it. She exhaled and loosened her tunic. She did not remove it, but stretched out in her clothes on her bunk. She reached out to wave the light off, but hesitated, and instead left it on at a low level. Sinking back to rest her head on the pillow, she closed her eyes.

Within moments, she was lost to the cottony realm of sleep.

She dreamed of a spaceport peopled by dragons, of a Gaston's Landing where great lizards strode among the spaceships and guzzled convivially at the bars. A spaceport where she, a dragon like the rest, wove spellbinding tales of her flights, embellishing hardly at all.

Chapter 13
DEADLY FORCE

THE AIR had become dense and suffocating, and she struggled to overcome the resistance in her windpipe. Her dream was turning to nightmare; she flailed with her arms, but they were pinned to her sides. There was a sour, gagging breath in her face. Something was close, too close . . .

Her eyes blinked open and she saw shadow. She tried to sit up in a single convulsive lunge. She grunted, still flat on her back. The shadow moved. As consciousness returned, she realized that someone dark was looming over her, pinning her to her bunk. She struggled—futilely—against the other's much greater strength and weight. She tried to cry out, but the weight was pressing down on her so hard, she couldn't get enough breath.

"If you stay quiet, it won't hurt," Mogurn whispered in a gravelly voice, his face close to hers.

Jael's muscles spasmed at the sound of that voice. Squinting desperately past Mogurn, she saw her door open to the lighted corridor. Her locked door had meant nothing to him. She shook with hatred and fear.

Mogurn's laughter filled her ears. "I just came to see that

you were safe, Jael. You were so . . . distraught." He inhaled raggedly. "I thought perhaps you needed some company."

Jael finally sucked in enough breath to curse, "You *bastard*—"

His hand dropped to the front of her tunic and yanked hard. The fabric tore, exposing her breasts. She gasped and struggled to cover herself; but Mogurn was straddling her, pinning her hips down with his weight, keeping her arms trapped with his knees. Squirming desperately, she jerked her left arm free and struck futilely at him. Mogurn grabbed her arm roughly; she yanked it free again, gasping in pain. "Hold . . . *still!*" he growled—and struck her across the face.

She grunted and twisted away. He was too heavy on top of her. He grabbed her tunic again and ripped it to her navel.

Jael struggled not to cry, not to let him see her terror. Mogurn was grinning at her in the dark. There had to be some way to fight him, to equalize the odds—some weapon. She thought frantically, but there was nothing within reach. Then her free hand, groping at the side of the bunk, found the sleep-field control. She wrenched it.

Mogurn's weight, and her own, lessened abruptly. Mogurn seemed not to notice, as he raised himself up to grab the waistband of her pants. Jael saw his hand tighten on the last vestige of her protection. He was breathing roughly and hoarsely as he fought to hold her, to grip the fabric of her pants. She saw the bulge in his own.

Jael fought for breath against sudden, overwhelming revulsion. She looked up and saw eyes ablaze with mindless determination, a forehead sweating with the effort of controlling her. "*You stinking coward—you bastard—*" she gasped.

His eyes came into focus, and his lips grimaced in triumph. "If you will not have your pallisp, Jael," he said, panting, "you will have—this!" He jerked hard on her waistband.

The seams held.

He cursed and shifted his weight.

Instinctively Jael brought her knees up—and exploded with all of the strength in her body, ramming her knees up into his groin. She twisted, as he bellowed with pain and fell back away from her. His hands clawed at her, trying to stop his own motion in the sleep-field; but he was gasping, stunned with pain. As he tottered at the edge of the sleep-field, she brought her feet up and kicked hard to his chest. Mogurn fell backward out of the sleep-field, dropping with his full weight off the end of the bunk.

Jael half leaped, half fell from the side of the bunk. She hit the floor hard, but scrambled frantically and was out the door and into the hallway before Mogurn could get to his feet. He staggered after her, roaring with anger.

His yell terrified her, but she didn't stop. She ran past the bridge. Her ripped tunic flapped wildly, exposing her; her bare feet slapped the deck. She passed the commons and hurtled around the bend of the passageway, and stopped, panting. There was nowhere to run. But she heard his whistling breath, his footsteps.

She whirled to confront him.

The passageway was empty; she'd heard a hissing ventilator. But the footsteps were real, approaching around the corner. Where could she go? The corridor simply went in a circle, and a small one at that.

"Come here, rigger-bitch!"

The only place to flee was downward, to the other decks. She darted to the access port and hit the OPEN square. "You!" she heard. The hatch slid aside, lights blinked on below, and she leaped for the ladder. She caught the rungs with her hands and banged her toes before catching a foothold. "*Come back here!*" Mogurn appeared, lunging. She hit the CLOSE square from the inside of the shaft and gasped thankfully as it hissed shut, cutting him off. It gave her a few seconds; the compartments were hermetically separated, and the hatch wouldn't reopen until the safeties recycled.

She backed away from the bottom of the ladder and turned warily. She half expected Mogurn to appear from some other direction. Had she escaped, or just trapped herself? There were two power decks; she was on the topmost. There was a soft hum of generators, and a single flickering indicator light. She hunkered down behind the end of the control panel. A ladder to her right would provide a quick drop to the next level, if she needed it—if she were quick enough. She opened the hatch and peered down. Should she keep going now? She had no idea where the safest place would be.

There is no safe place.

Mogurn was insane with rage, insane enough to destroy himself by attacking his rigger. She might have to knock him out, or even kill him. Was it his life or hers now? Had it come to that? If she hadn't been aware before of how much she wanted to live, she was aware of it now.

Highwing, she thought. You didn't save my life—my sanity—just to let me die like this, did you? *Did you?*

But there was no answering thought. Highwing was not here. Highwing was in another space, another reality. Highwing could not help her.

The ceiling hatch hissed open at the other end of the compartment. She peered over the top of the console. One foot appeared on the ladder, then another. Mogurn descended into view. He turned and spied her at once. "Enough, Jael!" he snapped, from the ladder. "I command you not to move!"

Her decision was made instantly, without conscious thought. Her feet took her over the hatch to the next deck, and she was dropping, swinging by her hands from the rungs, feet dangling. Mogurn's bellow echoed after her, before the hatch closed.

She was now on the bottom power deck. It was darker here; the center of the deck was an enormous round chamber, surrounded by a shielding wall. That was the flux-pile, where the energies were harnessed that caught at the fabric of space and drew the ship into the Flux. It seemed to hum, though perhaps that was her imagination.

The absurdity of her situation nearly made her laugh out loud in bitterness. In the emptiness of interstellar space, she was being forced to defend herself against the only other human in light-years, a madman turned rapist. It made no sense.

But rationality was not a factor here.

She had only seconds to hide, before Mogurn would be through that hatch. She circled around the main body of the flux-pile. There were three hatches: to the outer airlock, to the flux-field chamber, and to the cargo hold. She hit the OPEN switches to the airlock and cargo hold, though neither offered much hope. She couldn't go unsuited into the flux-pile, but there was a rack of tools near the maintenance hatch, and a control board to one side. She could threaten sabotage. *But that won't stop him; he's mad.* From the tool selection, she grabbed a large wrench.

Fight, flee, or hide. But decide fast!

She heard the hatch open from the deck above. She ducked into the cargo hold, slapped the hatch closed, and dived to her left down a narrow aisle. It was very gloomy here, with only a single dim safety light near the hatch. It was also very cramped, with solid racks of shipping containers on both sides. The aisle dead-ended; there was nowhere to run.

Jael walked silently back and drew herself up to the near side of the hatch. She took several deep breaths and cocked the arm holding the wrench. She gripped the wrench so tightly her hand hurt. She waited.

Her hand began to sweat, her arm to tremble. *God damn you, Mogurn—come, if you're going to come!* She felt tears welling in the corners of her eyes, and she cursed and blinked them away. No time for that. But how much time did she have? She couldn't hear a sound from the other side of the bulkhead. But he was there. He surely would not stop once he knew she was cornered. But suppose he wanted to frighten her, or make her suffer, waiting. Suppose he—

The hatch hissed open and Mogurn lunged through, panting, a massive form against the portal. *Now—hit him!* She found her arms resisting, as though frozen. Mogurn turned. For an instant she saw nothing but his mad, gleaming eyes—and his mouth open in maniacal delight. He stepped toward her.

She swung the wrench at his head. He grunted, deflecting the blow with his arm. The wrench glanced off his shoulder, and something metal flew from his hand and clattered to the deck. He staggered forward. Jael struck him again on the shoulder, and again. He stumbled against a crate and fell to one knee. She gripped the wrench with both hands and with a groan of rage swung it down again, hitting him at the base of the neck. He went down to both knees. She raised the wrench for a final blow.

Mogurn swung around, roaring, and dived for her legs. She jumped back, but he caught her left ankle, and with a snarl tried to pull her back to him. "Goddamn . . . little bitch!"

Terrified, Jael pulled away and hacked downward at his arm until he let go with a grunt. She leaped through the portal to the power deck. Swinging around, she stabbed desperately at the CLOSE plate. This time she was too late. Mogurn lunged and blocked the hatch from shutting. Jael fled.

The airlock inner hatch was still open. She banged the CLOSE switch and dived into the chamber as the hatch was sliding shut. "Oh, God—please!" she cried, stumbling, almost falling to her knees in the chamber. For a second, she shuddered helplessly, then she looked up, frantic for anything that could save her life. But she had just trapped herself in a place from which there was no escape—except into space. Airless space.

Hanging behind a clear locker door were two spacepacks. She yanked open the locker and pulled one out. "Please work," she prayed, snapping it around her waist. She reached for the activator, then glanced up, and through the airlock window, saw Mogurn staggering toward her. Grabbing the second spacepack, she clutched it to her side and switched on the one she was already wearing. She was instantly surrounded by a gleaming hermetic forcefield. She reached for the control to bleed the airlock—thinking that if she could evacuate it even partially, the safety interlock would prevent Mogurn from opening the hatch. Never mind that she had nowhere to go; at least she'd be safe for the moment.

But Mogurn reached the control panel on the other side first. The hatch slid open, silently it seemed, and he staggered in. She could see him screaming at her, but his voice was a bare mutter through the forcefield. He hit the CLOSE control, then reached for her. His bearded face was purple with rage. She swung again with the wrench, but he stepped past her, evading the blow. She swiveled, her back to the wall near the control panel, and jabbed at him with the wrench. Through the forcefield, she heard the words, *"I'll kill you—!"*

With a grunt, she raised her elbow and hit the EVACU-ATE switch twice and the OUTER OPEN switch twice, the command for emergency fast exit.

Mogurn saw, and understood, what she had done. He gazed at her in wide-eyed astonishment—then fear—and dived for the spacepack locker. It was empty. He stared at her, frozen, his chest heaving as the pressure in the airlock dropped. His eyes narrowed when he saw the bulge of the second spacepack under the glimmering forcefield of her suit. And she knew what he had to be thinking: there was no way to get that pack from her except by turning off her suit first. And he had only seconds before the air would be gone.

There was no sound—just a silent outcry in his expression. Mogurn hurled himself at her, hands groping for her waist and for the control on her pack. She struck at him with the wrench, but he ducked under the blow, and she realized that he was groping not just for the control at her waist, but for the airlock control panel, as well. "Get away!" she screamed, and clung desperately to a handhold on the wall, struggling to keep herself between Mogurn and the controls.

His hands were around her throat now, squeezing, but she couldn't feel any pressure through the suit, she could only see the hands trying to kill her, and the terrible emptiness and horror in his eyes as he fought for his last lungful of air.

The outer hatch slid open, and Jael's breath caught. She'd been expecting, instinctively, to see the cold blackness of space, and the stars—but of course they were not in normal-space, they were in the Flux. And the Flux was not something that the naked eye was meant to behold. There was blackness, yes; but there was also a swirling mélange of color, a light that *tore* at the eye somehow, a dreadful vapor of light that was like nothing she had ever seen, a light that some-how streamed out of and through the blackness and disap-peared back into it. And it poured now into the airlock.

Jael nearly succumbed to vertigo in that instant, but she

kept a desperate grip on the handhold. She was hardly aware of it when Mogurn let go of her. His eyes were bulging, still alive, as he floated away from her—his hands still reaching, still clutching, but clutching now toward emptiness. There was no longer any rage or any plea for life in his gaze; there was no expression that she could understand. It seemed to Jael, as she clung to the wall and watched him float out the hatch, that it was taking Mogurn a very long time to die.

She saw him reach out—hopelessly, she thought—toward the emptiness of this strange kind of infinity. And then he seemed to shimmer and dissolve, stretching out into the distance like a man of multicolored vapor and smoke, hands first, then head and body and feet following.

And then he was gone, and there was only the mad, numbing, eye-rending, stomach-twisting swirl of the Flux.

Several seconds, perhaps several minutes, passed before she managed to turn herself around and touch the control to close the airlock hatch.

It was longer still before she turned off her spacepack and retreated back into the cold, silent emptiness of the ship.

Chapter 14
SAFE HAVEN

FOR THE next forty-eight hours, she scarcely left the net. When she did, it was to face nightmares in her sleep and imagined ghosts in the hallways of the ship. She couldn't eat. Twice, she woke sweating to the vision of Mogurn's face leering at her out of the air. She never turned off the light, but that didn't seem to matter; anytime she allowed her mind to rest, her guard to fall, she was jerked back by visions of Mogurn.

In the net, it wasn't that much better; but the net, at least, was partly under her control. She flew through thundering, menacing skies, flashing with lightning and rain. The ship was buffeted by winds, tossed by unexpected turbulences. Through it all she flew fast and hard, determined to reach Lexis in the shortest possible time. Fatigue meant nothing to her anymore. Once, she thought she saw Mogurn's face rising through the mists of the Flux, rotating to face her, challenging her with a glassy-eyed stare; and for a long, heart-stopping moment, she thought that she had finally met her match. How could she hope to battle a spirit that had no physical reality? And then, as the fear washed through her and ebbed away, she knew that it was her own thoughts that had placed Mogurn there. And if her thoughts could bring him, they could send him away.

Leave me, you wraith . . . you are nothing, she whispered into the mists. And he smiled cruelly and drew closer, or seemed to.

In the end, it was only by darting past him, by outrunning him in the winds of the Flux, that she managed to escape from the ghostly Mogurn. Once he was gone, though, he never returned—not as long as she remained in the net.

Hours passed, two days passed, and the dim flecks in the distance drew steadily nearer.

The mists slowly evaporated around her as the ship rose through the layers of the Flux, surfacing toward normal-space. Moments later, Jael and her ship emerged into star-spiked blackness, into the grand emptiness of ordinary night, the infinity into which women and men had been born. At first she didn't even try to take a navigational mapping; she simply gave a tremendous sigh of relief and luxuriated in the view.

Then she checked, and yes, that yellow star blazing against the night was the sun of Lexis. She had reached her destination star system, or its edge. She called at once to the Lexis spacing authorities and asked for a tow.

It was two days now since Mogurn had attacked her. They had been two of the longest days of her life, and during them she had learned several things. She had learned that she still wanted the pallisp, though it was gone; and she didn't know if she ever would be free of the yearning. And she had learned that she could still combat the desire—as long as the pallisp was broken, and the temptation out of reach. Her determination to be free of it was as undiminished as her desire for it.

She prayed to be freed of the nightmares, too. In some of them, it was she who died, not Mogurn. In others, it was not Mogurn she killed, but her father. And she wondered, had her father been as mad as Mogurn? She remembered times when he had stood before her, ranting incoherently,

"Master your demons, Jael, master your demons or they'll rule you," babbling advice he'd never taken himself. In the ship's log, she had recorded an exact description of Mogurn's attack and her own self-defense—partly for the record, and partly in hopes of purging her mind of the horror. It had helped a little, but not much.

One question still unresolved in her mind was, what were the chances that anyone in the starport would believe her about the dragons—or should she even tell them? She felt somehow that her relationship with Highwing was a private thing, not to be shared with strangers; there was much about it that she didn't understand herself. She might have her hands full convincing the authorities that she was telling the truth about Mogurn's death. Would they be more or less likely to believe her if she added a fantastic-sounding story about dragons in the Flux?

She would just have to wait and see. The planet Lexis was light-hours away, on the far side of its sun.

It was, in fact, more than another full shipday before the tow appeared; and by that time, with nothing to do but worry, she was in a state of almost complete emotional exhaustion. Then the tow appeared, an angelic emissary glowing golden in the night. It locked itself to her ship and sped inward toward Lexis. During the ride in, there were administrative questions to be answered, since the tow service and landing rights were not free. Jael tried for a time to avoid questions about why the ship's master was unavailable to speak for himself. She wasn't sure how her word would stack up against presumptions in favor of a ship owner, and she was fearful that the tow might simply disconnect and leave her here at the edge of interstellar space if its master began to suspect that he might not be paid for his towing services.

Inevitably, though, the questions from Lexis became more pointed, and finally she sent a com-squirt containing the relevant portion of the log. That shocked the spacing authority into near silence until the tow had brought her into orbit around the pretty blue-and-white, but cold-looking, planet; and until they'd descended into the swirling atmosphere and landed, and the tow had detached and moved on to its next fare.

Jael was met at the airlock by police officers and driven to the nearby administration building. She had about a minute to enjoy the view—the spaceport was situated atop a broad plateau, and ringed by beautiful, snow-covered mountains—before she was hustled into the spaceport police station, a small office in one corner of the building.

The feeling of unreality did not go away then; it simply changed. Numerous officers interviewed her, together and in shifts, so that she could hardly keep track of who was who. At least one, she thought, was a mind-prober. She hadn't anticipated that. They questioned her for hours. They asked how Mogurn had died, and repeated the question, again and again. She told them, and retold them, in excruciating detail. They asked how Mogurn had happened to harass her to the point that she'd felt it necessary to kill him. They asked whether she had provoked him. She answered that she had refused his attempt to use an addicting device on her. They pressed, asking whether she had done anything else to anger him. She hesitated, then answered that she and Mogurn had disagreed on some navigational decisions. One officer cocked his head and gazed at her, but the others seemed satisfied by that. For an instant, she was tempted to mention the dragons, but she held her tongue. They asked about Mogurn's criminal record, and about *her* criminal record. She didn't have one, she answered heatedly. She told them to look in Mogurn's cabin for evidence of his. Asked about the ship's cargo, she said she knew nothing about it. Eventually an officer brought her something to eat. A while later, they told her that they'd checked the cargo, and at least a third of it was quasi-med equipment and drugs, all illegal under this jurisdiction, and probably on the planets of origin. They asked her what she thought about that. She didn't know what to think. She wasn't surprised, though. Mogurn, she told them, had been a thief and a madman. But she couldn't tell whether or not they believed her.

Eventually she was installed in a small dormitory room and told she would be staying there until her case was disposed of. The officer who locked her in gave her the closest thing she'd had to reassurance since her arrival. He smiled—just for a second, before the door opaqued—and told her not to worry.

Easy for you to say, she thought, though not without a flicker of appreciation. She collapsed onto the bunk and fell at once into a dreamless sleep.

"Miss LeBrae? Wake up."

"What?" She sat upright with a start, prepared to leap to safety. She blinked, trying to reorient herself to the strange surroundings. A light blue room; someone standing in the doorway. *Mogurn?*

"Take it easy," said the uniformed woman, entering cautiously. "I didn't mean to startle you."

"Oh," sighed Jael, remembering where she was. Her mind was whirling already. She was a prisoner here, and she didn't know when she'd be free again. But it was safe here, at least. Almost certainly it was safe.

"It's time for breakfast, and then they want to talk to you again." The woman's eyebrows arched, but it wasn't clear whether it was a friendly expression or a suspicious one.

"Mind if I shower?"

"Take your time. I'll be back." The woman turned away and the door opaqued.

Jael trudged into the little lavatory. She peered into the mirror. She thought that the eyes that stared back at her looked tired, and not just tired—older. She ran a hand futilely through her hair, and with a shrug, stepped out of her clothes and into the shower.

The woman was waiting for her when she emerged, dressed.

Jael accompanied her down the hall, and down to ground level. "Where are we going?" she wondered aloud. She also wondered what the woman's name was, but she'd probably been told once already, and she didn't want to ask.

"I told you. To eat."

"Yes, but where?"

The woman glanced at her in surprise. "You're a rigger, aren't you? We're going to the rigger dining room."

Jael blinked but didn't answer right away. "As a guest, or as a prisoner?" she asked finally, as they trotted down a flight of stairs to the basement level. There seemed to be nothing but hallways here, no big lobby, as on Gaston's Landing.

"What?"

"Am I a guest or a prisoner?"

The officer shrugged. "Hard to say, I guess. In here." She directed Jael into a small cafeteria, which was nearly deserted, and said, "Just get what you want and give them this chit." She handed Jael a small piece of plastic.

"Aren't you eating?"

"I'll be right here by the door. Only riggers eat here. Take your time."

Jael raised her eyebrows. "Okay," she murmured.

As she ate her breakfast—real eggs and real bread, a hearty stuff with texture and grain nuggets that, thank heaven, she could see and taste and chew—she eyed a rigger sitting in the far corner of the room. She'd noticed him because he had watched her enter, and watched her sit down, and then not looked her way again for several minutes. It took her a little while to realize that he was not entirely human.

What, exactly, he was, took her longer to decide.

His skin had a bluish silver tint to it, and his face was unusually angular—wide at the top, narrower at the bottom—not exactly wedged-shaped, but that was the closest description that came to mind. His eyes seemed odd, but she was too far away to tell why. She wondered, as she chewed her knobby bread, if he might be a Clendornan rigger, from the far side of the known galaxy. He seemed to fit the description, and Clendornan were known as skilled riggers; but of course, there were riggers of all sorts in the starports—human and otherwise—and she would probably be seeing far stranger-looking people before she was through.

When she glanced back at her escort, she saw the woman checking her wristwatch impatiently. She was tempted to prolong her breakfast just to irritate the officer, but better sense prevailed. Finishing quickly, she disposed of her tray and went to rejoin her guard. "Ready."

The woman led her off down the hallway, and eventually back to the police office. Jael didn't ask what the hurry was. Maybe this was just how they operated here. Maybe they hadn't had this much excitement in a while.

The senior officer who had interviewed her yesterday ushered them both into his office. Today he seemed friendlier. "Did you have breakfast?" he inquired, motioning her to a chair. Jael nodded without speaking; she didn't trust anyone whose demeanor changed so easily from suspicious to solicitous. "Good," the officer said, taking a seat behind his desk. He scowled at something on his desktop, then looked up at Jael. He had a freckled and lined face, and thinning, flyaway hair. Commander Gordache, that was his name.

Jael returned a steady gaze. A part of her was afraid that they would lock her up for twenty years; another part of her didn't care. She'd done nothing wrong. She believed that, even if no one else did.

Gordache cleared his throat. "Miss LeBrae, I'm sure you're anxious for this to be over. As we are. First, I should tell you that we've examined the ship's records and found nothing to contradict what you gave us yesterday. Besides the indictments against Captain Mogurn, we found records indicating that several previous riggers left the ship under unfavorable circumstances. One, at least, took a psych-med discharge." Jael's breath caught; she swallowed, and nodded. "Now, the so-called pallisp that you described has been examined, and found to be a patently illegal psych-med tool. Dangerous as hell. And pretty rare. It took our fellows a while to identify it." He frowned, tapping the desktop with one finger. "Also, a hand weapon was found in the cargo hold near the hatch, which would seem to corroborate your account of an assault against you."

Jael blinked, momentarily baffled. Weapon? Then she remembered—when she'd hit Mogurn with the wrench, something had dropped out of his hand as he'd gone down. She nodded, biting her lip. "I see. Yes."

Commander Gordache looked back at his notes. "It was

a narcotic gun, actually, loaded with a rather nasty coercive. You're lucky to have avoided it, I'd say."

Jael's vision darkened as she remembered the struggle. She felt her hands, her fingertips twitching as they began to re-fight the battle with Mogurn. A coercive. *To make me docile for the rape? Damn him forever . . .*

Gordache looked at her oddly. "However, there is something else here, based on our interview yesterday. There is a notation from the mind-probe operator—you knew you were under mind-probe, didn't you?—to the effect that you appeared to be concealing something in the matter of your disagreement with Captain Mogurn over the navigational decisions."

Jael exhaled slowly, fearfully.

"There is no indication of falsehood in your testimony, just that there's something you weren't saying." Gordache's eyebrow went up. "Would you like to tell me what that was?"

Jael closed her eyes, feeling her heart thump. How could she tell him? Would this policeman believe that she'd been befriended by a dragon in the Flux? It would sound preposterous. On the other hand, the legends of dragons were no secret, even if no one believed in them. "It's . . . hard to explain," she muttered.

"Why is that, Ms. LeBrae?"

She took a deep breath, and expelled it forcefully. "Dragons," she said, raising her eyes to meet Gordache's. "We argued over dragons along the route."

The policeman scratched behind one ear. "Dragons?"

"You know the stories, don't you? Everyone does. You know, talk of dragons along the mountain route in that direction, and of riggers dueling with them and all."

"I've heard the stories, yes."

"Well"— Jael took another breath—"the mountain route seemed better to me, as I was rigging, and so I went that way, and . . ."

"And what?"

She glanced for an instant at the female officer, who seemed to be listening with the blankest expression possible. "And, well . . . we encountered dragons."

Gordache's expression narrowed. "You mean that you encountered manifestations in the Flux which seemed, to you, to be images of dragons?"

Jael hesitated. Was it worth arguing to the police that the dragons were real, that they were living creatures? Would the police believe her? Would they care? Did it matter? They weren't riggers. . . . She sighed and nodded slowly. Let him call them manifestations. It was simpler that way.

"I see." Gordache frowned. "And was there dueling?"

Jael shrugged noncommittally.

"Well, did these dragon images endanger your ship, or the safety of your passage?"

"For a time, there was some . . . uncertainty."

"And then?"

Jael cleared her throat. "In the end, no. There was no danger to the ship."

"So you dealt with the images without mishap," Gordache said. Jael nodded. "But what was Captain Mogurn's reaction to this?"

"He was angry. Very angry." Her face grew hot. "And that's when he tried to force me—to take the—pallisp."

"Yes. Your statement on that is clear enough." Gordache's eyebrows formed a furrow in his forehead. He looked at the woman officer for a moment, then sighed. "Well, there's nothing more we need to ask you right now, I guess. Do you understand what the situation is?"

Jael hesitated. "Not really. Will I be allowed to leave? Will my contract be settled?"

Gordache shook his head. "Not quite yet, I'm afraid. You'll have to stay here at the port until the investigation is complete. But it does look as though you ought to be cleared of charges. Your contract might take a little longer to settle."

Jael nodded slowly, keeping her face impassive.

"You don't seem especially overjoyed."

She sighed. "It's . . . been a hard trip. I was sort of hoping that it would all be over."

"Of course. Understandably so." Gordache looked back down at his report. "Well, I think we can let you move over to the riggers' halls. But you must remain within the port area, and keep yourself available for questioning. Fair enough?"

Jael drew herself up straighter in her chair. "What about collecting my pay? I can't very well get it from . . . Captain Mogurn, now. I guess."

"That would be difficult," Gordache agreed. "Actually, you have put your finger on a particular difficulty."

"What do you mean?"

"Just that the disposition of the ship and its cargo could take some time. We have to determine the ownership of the vessel. Eventually, the legal portion of the cargo could be sold, and you—along with the tow company—would be compensated from the proceeds. But until then, I'm afraid there's just no way for you to be paid—even assuming that your contract is ruled valid."

"Ruled valid?" Jael looked from one officer to the other in panic. "What's to be ruled? We had a contract. Even if he went crazy and tried to—" Her voice choked off. "Even if he went crazy," she said carefully, "we still had a contract."

"Of course. From your point of view. But there are legal problems in executing an interrupted contract. Even when the cause of the breach is the death of one party, or"—he shrugged—"alleged felony. It will take time."

"Time? *Time?* And what am *I* supposed to do? I don't have any money!"

He gestured helplessly. "I understand your difficulty. Unfortunately, the law is the law. But it might be that we can make some arrangement for credit to be extended to you at the rigger quarters. Annie, can you look into that for her?"

The woman officer nodded.

"That's it?" Jael asked in disbelief. "That's all you're going to do?"

Gordache rose. "That's all we can do. I'm sorry. Annie, if you could take her now and assist in the arrangements. . . ."

In her new quarters, in the cheapest private room available in the local rigger hall, Jael lay on her bunk in a state of nervous exhaustion and called to Highwing. *Friend of Highwing! I am a friend of Highwing!* In her thoughts, she cried out again and again. But there was no answer, and of course there could be none. Highwing's realm was light-years from here, and who knew when, if ever, she would fly that way again.

Nevertheless, I am a friend of Highwing, she thought, closing her eyes. Perhaps he can't reach me; perhaps he can't help. But if there were a way, he would. I know that. I must remember that.

I must believe it.

In truth, it was becoming harder now to summon, at will, the memory of the dragon, harder to bring his image clearly to mind. The experience was already losing some of its immediacy; it seemed worlds away, like a vivid dream, receding and fading against the curtain of passing time. Had she erred in not telling the police more about Highwing? It seemed clear that she would not have been taken seriously. Even she, before this flight, would not have believed it. And yet . . . it was a story that she needed to tell *someone*—to share the truth, the reality, the vision—if only to make it clearer and more tangible to herself. I won't lose you, Highwing! she vowed.

Reaching into her pocket, she drew out the chain that Dap had given her on the day of her departure. She'd found it in her duffel, where she'd dropped it when she'd packed and then forgotten about it. She held it up to the light and peered at the pastel rays diffusing through the stone pendant. She wondered at Dap's thought in giving it to her, wondered where Dap was now. Flying, perhaps. Or was he still on Gaston's Landing, trying to conquer his own fears, trying to bolster his inner confidence and resolve to match his outward display? *Dap, I'm sorry . . . that I didn't know. That I didn't accept your apology. That you're almost as frightened as I am.* She coiled the chain around her finger, and let it unwind to dangle again. There was no way to tell him, no way to make it up to him, unless he happened this way, or they met again in some other rigger port. But what were the chances of that?

She had to face the fact that she was alone now, more

alone than ever before. If she was to have any companionship here, she would have to find it herself.

You must seek friends in your own world, Highwing had said.

But what did Highwing know of human society, of rigger society?

What do I know of it?

She awoke with a scream caught in her throat, unable to get air. There had been hands around her throat, trying to squeeze the life from her, hands that were torn from her by a light that her eyes could not see, a light that could not exist.

She gasped, trying to push the memory away. She rose up on one elbow, rubbing her eyes, reassured by the dull yellowish glow of the room light; reassured by the solidity of the bunk. She sank back, trembling. How much longer? she thought with despair. How much longer would she keep reliving the horror?

Finally she rose and went into the shower—a real water shower, not a swirl-mist—and she stood with steaming water pouring onto her head and running down her neck and shoulders, and she finally felt her tension release enough to let her tears flow and mix with the shower water, until the fear was washed away at last.

Chapter 15
ENVIRONMENT ALPHA

In the morning Jael was surprised to discover that she had slept through the night without awakening again. She stood in the center of her room, stretching and bending until she felt limber; then she dressed in her last clean change of clothes and ventured out.

The rigger halls were situated at the edge of the spaceport complex. They were divided into sections for male and female humans, couples, and nonhumans, but the sections all joined in the basement level where the dining and entertainment facilities were located. The dining hall was uncrowded. She overheard, standing in line for breakfast, that traffic in the port was slow this time of year, due to seasonal fluctuations in agricultural exports. She was a little dismayed to learn that, as she'd thought of Lexis as a busy trading port compared to the backwater of Gaston's Landing. It was discouraging to think that work might be scarce here, as well. Of course, she was here to stay until the police were through with her, anyway. And she wasn't sure how ready she was to take to the Flux with the memory of Mogurn so vivid in her mind.

Eating among the other riggers, she felt self-conscious, wondering if anyone had yet heard of the circumstances of her arrival . . . wondering if people were talking behind her back. If so, they were doing it discreetly. She tried not to imagine what they might be saying.

Breakfast was a sort of fried bread made from the folded leaves of a native plant, with a side dish of *hili*, a local fruit. A sign was posted warning of possible allergic reactions to the fruit. Great, she thought. She eyed a small orangish red segment and broke its skin carefully with one tine of her fork. Frowning, she brought the fork to her mouth and took a single drop of juice onto her tongue. It had a faintly limy, sour-sweet taste. A moment later, the roof of her mouth began to itch. Cursing, she drank some tea. That only made the itching worse. She sucked and scratched at the roof of her mouth with her tongue; then her eyes began to tear up. As she got up in hopes of finding a glass of water to drink, the itching suddenly stopped.

Sighing, she sat again and dabbed her eyes dry, glancing around self-consciously to see if anyone else was having the same trouble. Apparently, no one was. She pushed the fruit away, wiped her fork, and cautiously finished her bread dish, which was filling, if a bit greasy. She drained her cup of tea, dumped her tray, and went out for a walk.

There were a couple of lounges and a library in the basement level, all depressingly similar to their counterparts on Gaston's Landing. Somehow she'd hoped for something more exotic. She walked upstairs to the first floor and ventured outside—into an icy blast of wind. She jumped back inside, shivering and hugging herself. The air outside had been shirtsleeve temperature yesterday!

Shaking off the chill, she found a first-floor sitting room with windows that overlooked the spaceport. She paced from window to window, peering out at the snow-covered mountains and wondering why it was so cold here, near the Lexis equator. It seemed a strange climate; she wondered if there were unusual atmospheric patterns or ocean currents on this world. She thought of how much there was to learn of all the individual worlds she might visit in a lifetime of rigging.

She wondered if she would have time to get to know this world at all—or if she would ever get to leave it.

The mountains looked like dragon country. Dragons . . . She shivered, thinking of Highwing. Was it possible that anyone here, where the source of the "myth" was close to home, actually believed in dragons? Or were they relegated to the status of notations on ancient seafaring charts: *HERE BE DRAGONS!* She wished she could ask around, among the riggers in the port. *"Excuse me, but have you ever seen dragons on the mountain approach—real dragons, I mean?"* No, that wouldn't do. But possibly the library would offer some answers.

She went back downstairs to the library and found herself a nav-source terminal. Keying in a query for the galactic-southern approach to Lexis, she found a description not greatly different from the one she'd studied back on Gaston's Landing:

> Flux imagery tending toward mountain landscapes. Occasional anecdotal references to encounters with dragon-like images probably indicates more about associational patterns in the referent riggers' imaginations than about actual features in the Flux. Pattern-cues may exist in the Flux currents to trigger such images. For this reason, many shippers prefer to avoid that portion of the route identified with mountain imagery. However, folktales of riggers dueling with actual creatures in the Flux are no more than that: folktales. No evidence exists to confirm such reports.

It went on for a while about other navigational features. At the end of the entry, she found a cross-reference sidebar.

> Dragonlike images: For further detail on the phenomenon of dragons as perceived living features in the Flux, key to entry: FLUX: ILLUSIONS: EXTANT LIFE: DRAGONS.

Jael frowned, then touched the reference. What she found was a discussion of dragons, whales, ghost ships, and other manifestations of imagination in the Flux which riggers, at one time or another, had attributed to objectively real entities. The conclusion was firm:

> Scientific data does not support the assertion that anything—except a rigger's thoughts, projected through a sensory net—can live in the Flux. Beliefs to the contrary probably derive from tales gathered during the confusing times of transition between *foreshortening* star travel and starship rigging. During that period, stories abounded of visions and "curious folk" emerging from the spatial discontinuities that provided the first window into the Flux continuum. (See FLUX: DISCOVERY OF: PANGLOR BALEF.) However, historical evidence fails to support such reports.

Jael blanked the screen and sat back. There was nothing unexpected in what she'd just read. But the experience of real riggers mattered more to her than anything written in the library. In any case, the question remained: How could she share her experience with someone who might listen? Maybe she couldn't, and shouldn't. She certainly had enough troubles already without drawing that kind of attention to herself. Maybe the best thing to do was just to forget about it for a while.

She thought of Highwing, and a deep ache arose in her heart. Forget that? Forget Highwing and what he had shown her? She couldn't, even if she wanted to—not with the painful, knotted memories he had begun unraveling in her mind. Too much was churning inside her to pretend it hadn't happened. And yet, even so, the memory of her encounter with Highwing was starting to, not exactly fade, but to lose some of its power. She was terrified at the thought of losing that memory; she was determined to keep it strong.

Finally, restless and unsatisfied, she left the library. At least there were people in the lounges, and activity. Though she didn't really feel like talking to anyone, there was a certain comfort in the presence of other human beings, none of whom were being actively hostile to her. There was a certain pleasure in knowing that she had no prior history here; her father's name was much less likely to be known, or if it was known, it was probably remembered as just one more marginal, unregistered shipper among many. Lexis, presumably, had its own roster of most-unfavored shippers. There was no guarantee, of course—riggers traveled to many worlds—but at least she no longer automatically bore the curse of being her father's daughter in a place where her father was hated.

She sighed bitterly, thinking of him, and of what Highwing seemed to have wanted her to do—to let go. To forgive. But it was her father who was responsible for the discrimination she'd suffered back on Gaston's Landing. Was it possible that some of that had existed only in her mind? Had she assumed that people wouldn't like her before they had a chance to decide for themselves? Possibly. But she remembered, too, the jobs for which the stewards had passed her over. That hadn't just been in her mind.

Taking a seat in the darkest of the lounges, she tried to think it through. Her hands began to tremble, and she realized, as she sat in the darkness, that she was nervous because there was something else she wanted right now, and it had nothing to do with her home planet, or her father. And it had nothing to do with dragons. That something was the pallisp . . .

. . . which you are not going to think about anymore!

Not think about it? Not think about the incredible warmth, the soothing energy, the rush of sensory pleasure, the . . . STOP IT! That was about as likely as not thinking about Mogurn again: his hands on her throat, the coiling mists of the Flux tearing him away . . .

Shuddering, she rose and began pacing. There had to be some way to stop the endless thought. She paced out in the hallway, heedless of the occasional puzzled glance; and she paced back into the lounge and frowned over the various holotronic and psychetronic diversions. She'd never paid too much attention to this stuff even on Gaston's Landing. She paced from I/O station to I/O station, squinting at the consoles. Some consisted merely of a headset and a few controls, and some were full-screen displays for gaming and educational resources. She watched one incredibly tall, willowy, young man with the whitest skin she had ever seen, poring over a game board. For a moment she considered speaking to him to ask what he was doing; but when he looked up at her, she blushed at the sight of his eyes, which were masked like a raccoon's, but with large purple stars. She turned away.

In the gloomiest corner of the room (Why did so many riggers like dark rooms? she wondered), there was an I/O mounted on a reclining chair. She slipped into the chair and pulled the I/O closer for a look. It was labeled *Environment Alpha* and consisted of a blinded helmet with temple-contacts and a simple handheld squeeze control. As she fiddled with the devices, she noticed someone watching her from several seats away. It was the same young man—or rather, if she had guessed correctly, Clendornan—whom she had seen in the dining hall yesterday. She recognized the almost wedge-shaped head, flat on top, and the angular brow turned toward her in the gloom. His presence, watching her, was unsettling.

You will find others, she remembered Highwing saying. That seemed a very long time ago now.

The Clendornan's eyes shifted, seemed to sparkle almost luminously, as though he were sensing her attention and returning it. She flushed with embarrassment. She glanced down at the I/O with its controls and helmet. Impulsively she placed the helmet over her head and adjusted its contacts against her temples. She took a deep breath and squeezed the hand control.

Her external vision was gone, but against the blackness she saw a glimmer of blue radiance, which warmed and became an enveloping mauve. She felt a gentle sense, not exactly a sound, of lapping waves. Even in her present state, she found it soothing, calming. As her mind relaxed, something became visible in the distance, slowly drawing into focus. Shapes. Words. She somehow realized that she needed to breathe slowly, to deepen her state of relaxation, to bring them into focus. As she did so, they became clear, floating in holo-space before her, a series of French-curved solids which framed the three-dimensional words:

ENVIRONMENTS ALPHA
1. BURNISHED MESAS
2. MOUNTAIN VISTAS
3. TROPICAL RAINFOREST
4. GLACIER BAY

A moment later, a line of instructions appeared:

TO EXPERIENCE AN ENVIRONMENT, FOCUS ON ITS NAME AND SQUEEZE. SQUEEZE AGAIN TO EXIT.

Ah. But what was her mood? She wanted stimulation as well as comfort. Perhaps the rainforest: greenery and creatures. She focused on selection 3 and squeezed the controller.

The menu image faded, leaving a cyan afterglow. She waited. Then she realized that she was hearing something. Or feeling it. It was the sound, or the sensation anyway, of falling rain, gently drumming rain. There was no wetness, but a softly rhythmic concussion surrounding her, as though rain were beating on a roof while she sat snugly inside, listening.

Almost, she could imagine a tropical forest outside, soaking up the rain. . . .

Soft and shadowy shapes were beginning to emerge from the blue-green glow. As though a fine mist were clearing around her, she began to see first the outlines, then the full forms of trees and shrubs. The mist disappeared altogether. She was standing in a place of shelter, looking out at a riot of greenery, the lush fullness of a rainforest, completely surrounding her. The gentle drumming of rain continued a little longer; then even that subsided and a glow of sunshine swelled down from the sky to take its place. The invisible shelter seemed to open and set her free, and a breeze full of chlorophyll and earth caressed her face.

She wondered if she could walk here. As the thought crossed her mind, she found herself gliding across the tiny clearing, floating like a spirit. As she passed a tree, she saw rainwater streaming off the ends of its broad green leaves. Perched on the upper part of a large leaf was a small orange-toed, red-eyed, iridescent-green froglike creature. It watched her without moving, except for its throat fluttering in and out. Overhead, a group of birds screeched and flapped their multihued wings against the sky. Jael squinted at them for a moment, then moved on. In front of her, two large blue-and-white-checked butterflies pirouetted around each other in midair. She reached out to touch them. They giggled in tinkling voices, then fluttered away. Jael chuckled.

She thought she heard another chuckle, then sensed a movement, in a nearby tree. She turned. A large bird with blazing scarlet and green wings, an enormous golden beak, and bright emerald eyes tilted its head to peer at her. It followed her movement as she approached, then hopped to a lower branch and squawked a welcoming cry. She extended a hand, knuckles up, and the bird gently mouthed her fingers with its open beak. "Aren't you a pretty thing?" she said, thinking that there was something familiar about this bird. It took a moment to make the connection. It reminded her of a bird she had often seen as a child, in a petting zoo near her home. It had been a favorite animal of hers, in a happier time.

"Awwk—yawss," answered the bird brightly.

Startled, Jael cried, "Oh, you talk, do you?"

"Tawwk—tawwk," the bird croaked, winking.

"Ho." Jael grinned and tickled its throat, pleased to be able to touch it. Its throat feathers were silky smooth. "Do you have a name?"

The bird winked again. "No name! Nope—awwk!"

Jael studied the bird, tilting her head one way and then the other. The bird mimicked her movements. "I wish I had something to give you, but"—Jael opened her empty hands—"sorry."

"Rawwk! Pocket-t-t—pocket-t-t!"

"What?" Jael reached into her right-hand coat pocket (Since when was she wearing a coat?) and felt her hand close on something. She drew it out. It was a cluster of bright purple berries on a stem. "Why, what's this?"

"B-b-berries!" shrieked the bird. It cocked its head back and gave an open-beaked cry: *"Scraw-w-w!"* It edged along the branch, closer to Jael. "B-b-berries?" it asked, eyeing her hopefully.

"Would you like these?" Jael asked, holding the cluster up for inspection. The berries looked ripe and full.

"P-pleeez!"

Jael smiled and held them out toward the bird. "Here you go."

The creature bent forward and, with surprising delicacy, nibbled a berry loose from the bunch. Jael glimpsed the berry rolling onto its tongue; its beak clacked once, and the berry was gone. "Whaww!" the bird exclaimed joyously, then bent for another.

"Take all you want," Jael offered. She needn't have spoken. Once the creature had started, it made short work of the bunch. Jael tossed the bare stem away and held her hand out again. The bird rubbed against her knuckles, wiping berry juice off its beak. "I'm afraid that's all I have," she said consolingly.

"Arrk—plenty—thankew pleez!" The bird perked its head up suddenly and looked around. "Whooz that?"

Jael turned. "What do you mean?"

"Sorry," she heard, from behind one of the trees. Someone stepped out, raising his hands in apology. It was the Clendornan she had seen in the lounge. "I don't mean to intrude," he called.

Jael stared at him. "Excuse me, but—what are you doing here?"

"Well, I . . ." He approached cautiously. "We chose the same environment, it looks like. And"—he looked at the ground, then up again—"the system put me in here with you."

"Is it supposed to do that?" Jael asked, squinting.

The Clendornan tilted his head, turning his silver-blue skinned face; the movement reminded her of the bird's. "That's a little hard to say, actually. It's supposed to be able to tell if both parties want privacy or not." He made a noise reminiscent of throat clearing, except that it overlapped with his next words. "Do you object to my being here? I'll gladly leave. I've no wish to intrude." He made a sighing sound. "It is very peaceful here, isn't it?" His mouth formed into a zigzag shape; she wondered if that was supposed to be a smile.

Jael felt a scowl coming on—and remembered Highwing's parting advice. She was aware of tension growing in the back of her neck. She *had* wanted to be alone, she'd thought. And yet, now, she didn't quite want to send him away. She could always leave herself, she supposed, if it got to bother her. She resisted the frown and shrugged. "It's okay. I don't mind."

"Thanks." As the Clendornan glanced around, Jael tried to get a better look at his eyes. They seemed clear and oddly luminous. "My name is Ar," he said, not quite facing her. "What's yours?"

Her breath caught, as she remembered another time when names had been exchanged. She had been the one to speak first. "I—that is, *Jael*," she stammered. "Jael LeBrae." She froze with embarrassment, then said, "I'm sorry . . . you said your name was—"

"Ar." His mouth zigzagged again. "That's A-r, usually, though it actually just means the letter R, which is short for Rarberticandornan, which is my legal Clendornan name. Most people don't even try, they just call me Ar."

"Ar, then." Jael nodded tentatively. "I'd introduce you to my friend here"—she gestured at the bird, which had been quietly hopping about while they'd talked—"except that he doesn't seem to have a—"

"*Jayl!*" the bird shrieked. It cocked its head, peering at her with a wide-eyed expression. "Jayl!"

"That's right," she answered, then glanced back at Ar. "He's very friendly, but he says he doesn't have a—"

"Arr! Arr!"

"Right. Ar." Jael squinted at the bird, wondering suddenly if it were having fun at her expense. "You said you don't have a name, right?"

"No name! No—AWWK!" The bird fluttered its bright

wings as Ar shook a finger in its direction. Suddenly it screamed, "*Name Ed! Name Ed!*"

Jael's mouth opened slightly. "Oh! I see."

"Thank you, Ed. Honesty is a more appropriate quality," said Ar, coming to stand alongside Jael. He frowned up at the bird, then muttered in an aside, "He's quite an exuberant bird, Ed is."

"I can see that. You two know each other, then?" Jael tried not to show her disappointment. She had rather liked the notion that this bird was her own personal discovery.

Ar turned to face her directly, giving her a first clear look at his eyes. She was stunned speechless. Deepset in his almost triangular face, they looked like clear crystal orbs, shining with a pale inner light. He seemed to have no irises, whites, or pupils. But as she gazed, half-aware of her rudeness, she realized that his retinas—or whatever took the place of retinas—were visible. They looked like tiny purplish puffs of steel wool, or glitter, nested at the backs of his eyes. She was suddenly aware of his amusement, and she blushed. "I'm sorry, I didn't mean to—"

"Don't mention it. Everyone does it." Ar's lips straightened, then crinkled. "Actually, I'm considered to have quite lovely eyes on my own world."

She couldn't tell if he was being serious or teasing. "Oh. Yes, well I . . ." And she realized that she had no idea what they had been talking about, before she'd glimpsed his eyes.

Ar turned toward the bird. "I'm sorry if I sounded as though I have some special intimacy with Ed, here. I've only met him twice before, and I've been in this environment quite a few times." He extended a long-fingered hand toward the bird. Ed prodded at his finger with his golden beak.

"He doesn't show up every time, then?"

Ar rocked his head from side to side. "No, I think the environment senses when he might be good medicine for whoever has come in." He was silent a moment. "After all, this is a generated environment. Even though it doesn't feel that way."

"Yes," Jael said. She had almost forgotten. That meant, of

course, that Ed was a construct, as well. Somehow she found that thought disappointing.

"Ed feels real to me, though," Ar continued. "I think he's a copy of an actual bird mated to an evolving intelligence program. It looks as if he's taken something of a shine to you. That's probably why he was teasing you about his name. Isn't that right, Ed?"

The bird drew his head back and snapped his beak at the air, as though trying to catch invisible insects. He gave no sign that he had heard.

"Come on, Ed," said the Clendornan. "You like Jael, don't you?"

The bird bit at the air with finality, then cocked his head and squawked wordlessly. Jael frowned. He hopped closer to her. "Jayl?" he murmured. He opened his beak and closed it gently around her wrist. "Gwawk."

Jael was moved by the gesture; she regretted that he was only a machine thing. "I wish you were a real bird," she murmured wistfully.

Ed squawked and fluttered his wings violently. He launched himself into hovering flight and banged among the branches, screeching, "*Awwk—reeel—REEEL—awwwwk!*" He lighted on a higher branch and glowered down. "Hurrrrt—hurrt feeeling! Ed reeel! Rarrk!" He fell silent and gazed mournfully down at them.

"I'm sorry, Ed!" Jael said in surprise. "I didn't mean to hurt your feelings! I didn't know you were real. Can I make it up to you?"

The bird hopped back down, with a flutter, to his previous perch. "Okk-kay," he squawked. "Okk-kay! Made up-p. Like Jayl—like Jayl."

"Does that mean you'll come see me again—next time I'm here?"

Ed dipped his beak. "Be here. Ed be here. Bye, Jayl! Bye, Ar!" And with a flutter of color, he was gone.

Jael blinked in amazement. Hesitantly, she raised a hand as if to wave farewell. She looked at Ar, suddenly embarrassed by her gesture.

"Sensitive guy, I guess," he said. "Would you like to see

some of the other environments? They can be pretty interesting, too."

Jael considered the offer dazedly. The artificiality of this setting came home to her suddenly, along with a feeling of restlessness. She shook her head. "I don't think so. Not right now." She hesitated, not knowing what to say, just knowing that she suddenly felt uncomfortable being around this stranger, and she wanted to leave. "Um . . . bye, I guess." She squeezed the controller in her right hand.

The rainforest dissolved in a grey fog.

Chapter 16
AR

REMOVING THE helmet, she rubbed her eyes. The gloom of the lounge seemed unreal to her now, after the environment. But one thing that brought her back, with a jolt, was the sight of the Clendornan removing a helmet from his head and looking awkwardly in her direction. Of course. *He's still here.*

For a moment, she didn't move a muscle. She'd left the environment because she had wanted to get away from him. *Or did you just panic because you didn't know what to say?*

Ar rose and walked toward her. He paused, resting a hand on the back of the second seat over from hers. His gaze, clear and luminous even in the gloom, met hers. "I'm sorry if I upset you. I didn't mean to. But I wasn't sure . . . how else to . . ." He hesitated, a strange, soft gargling sound coming from his throat.

"I beg your pardon?" she murmured, puzzled.

He seemed embarrassed. His voice sounded as if he were underwater. "How to introduce myself. Since you're new here, I mean. And since, when I followed you into the sys-. tem, it didn't keep me out—"

"You figured you were invited in?" Jael asked in sudden irritation.

"Yes, well, I . . ." His breath went out with an animal-like sigh. "The system is supposed to know . . ."

Jael frowned; she wondered why she had felt that moment of annoyance. She tried to think of another reply.

Ar's head was tipped, his mouth flattened. "Well, as I said, I'm sorry. I won't do it again." His eyes dimmed. "I just wanted to apologize. I'll be going now." He started to walk away.

She drew a breath. "Wait."

He stopped, turned.

Jael felt dizzy, her head full of uncertainty. "I'm . . . sorry, too. It's okay, really. I guess if the system thought I didn't want privacy, then . . . it wasn't your fault . . ."

When she couldn't finish her thought, he said in a steadier tone, his voice like smoothly sanded wood, "I understand you've had—ah, a difficult beginning here."

She shook her head. "Come again?" Suddenly she understood, and as the full realization unfolded, she stared at him in horror. *The entire spaceport knows about me, that I killed Mogurn! Everyone knows.*

"Well, I . . ." he murmured apologetically, as though he'd read her mind. "The authorities are not always as discreet as one might wish. Yes, if that's what you're thinking, most of us know that you brought your ship in after . . . defending yourself . . . against your captain." He took a long, whispering breath. "It is, if I may say so, both an alarming and an inspiring story."

Jael could not answer. Her worst possible fears were confirmed. Everyone knew. Everyone was watching her.

"And I sense your unease with this subject," he murmured. "Again, I am sorry."

She looked away and spoke hoarsely. "If you know all about it . . . then there's no need . . ."

Ar's voice quavered again, drawing her attention back. "Please—I do not know all about it. Nor can I read your thoughts, as perhaps you fear." Jael tensed, as he voiced precisely her fear. The Clendornan shook his head slowly. "I can sense emotions only, and that I cannot help doing. But

I do so—I suppose you would say, analytically. I perceive that there is pain, for example. But in merely knowing that, I can neither peer into your soul to know your secrets, nor can I, unfortunately, do much that might alleviate the pain."

Jael felt a thickness in her throat. "Yes? Well, I'm not looking for a counselor, anyway."

"No no no, I did not mean that." Ar's breath came in a long sigh. "I am sorry, I should not have said—"

"Well, you did say it!"

Ar drew himself up; his angular head seemed slightly off balance atop his shoulders. "Let me put it differently, if I may," he whispered. He hesitated for several long moments, then said, "I . . . do not fly solo. I must find a rigging partner before I can fly again. And therefore . . ."

Jael held her breath, frowning.

"Well—I do not seek a partner only. I am in need of a friend, as well. And I thought . . . I sensed a . . . *resonance*, if you will." And his breath sighed out, and he stood very still, looking down at her with his luminous, liquid eyes.

"Well . . ." Jael cleared her throat. She didn't know what to say to that. Didn't this, this Clendornan, know what an emotional wreck she was? She felt a flush of weakness; she thought of the pallisp, and how much she had wanted that thing, *did* want it, even now; and she thought of Mogurn, and just the memory of the man made her sick, but the main thing she remembered was, I killed him, I killed a man. She rested her head back in her chair, fighting a wave of nausea.

Ar was watching her expectantly, waiting for her to finish her reply. There seemed so much to say, so much to get straight in her mind. "I—I guess I could use someone to talk to, if that's what you mean," she murmured at last.

The zigzag in his lips deepened.

She rose, unsteadily, and stuck out a hand. "Glad to meet you—Ar." The Clendornan gripped her hand gently; his fingers wrapped nearly all the way around hers. She forced a smile. "So, did you have anything special in mind? Can we maybe get out of this dungeon for a while?"

* * *

Ar did have an idea, but he was hesitant about launching straight into it before they had time to get to know each other a little better. Jael assured him that the last thing she wanted to do was sit around making small talk, if there was any chance of getting out of the rigger hall for a while. Ar thought a moment, then agreed. His idea required permission from the police—but when he accompanied Jael to the station and explained, Commander Gordache granted the okay with a bored wave of his hand.

"You'll need a warmer-vest," Ar said, leading her to the other end of the spaceport building, through yet another underground tunnel. "It can get pretty cold outside. But we'll be in a transport bubble, so it's really just for safety."

A half hour later, they'd checked out the necessary equipment and started across the open spaceport in a transport bubble. It was an aircar, but so tiny and light that it felt like little more than a floating air pocket; the canopy was just a transparent forcefield that enclosed them like a soap bubble. Despite the icy winds gusting across the field, Jael felt toasty. "Where exactly are we going?" she asked, peering around at the ramps filled with parked spacecraft. She could not see *Cassandra*, which was probably just as well.

Ar pointed into the distance, far beyond the field. "See the second peak to the right of that tracking tower? That's it. It'll only take a few minutes to get there."

"You've been there before?"

Ar's eyes shone. "Oh, yes. It's my favorite spot on Lexis. I've been waiting for an excuse to see it again."

Jael took a good look back at the mesa-top spaceport. As the bubble accelerated out beyond the edge of the mesa, she glimpsed a hoverrail train climbing the side of the cliffs from a spur line far below, disappearing into a tunnel near the top. The ground transport facilities were all embedded in the upper part of the mesa. Lexis was a world of substantial wealth, but from this vantage point, the outlying land looked like a wild frontier.

The bubble sped away from the mesa, and she sat back and enjoyed the view. Ar's hands were in constant motion, pointing out sights to her. The transport bubble knew where it was going and didn't need their help getting there. Jael felt her stomach drop as they began rising toward the distant peak. She gasped, looking down. "It's beautiful!" A ruggedly contoured valley was visible far below, half blanketed with snow. From a settlement nestled in the valley, whiskers of smoke curled into the air.

"It gets better," Ar said.

They flew on, steadily gaining speed.

The peak seemed to rotate in space as they approached it in a curving sweep from the southeast. It was a tremendous work of stone and wind, sculpted by the ageless forces of nature with a seeming indifference to gravity. Like an up-stretched arm, it seemed to speak of the earth's own primitive desire to reach to the sky. As they circled its cliffs, Jael clung to her seat, peering breathlessly down over the tumbled slopes. It was impossible not to feel that at any moment the bubble of their transport might burst and dump them, like seeds from a pod, onto the rocks far below. She was embarrassed by her nervousness. After all, there was nothing here that she could not envision in a rigger-net, and she was a skilled and fearless rigger, wasn't she?

The bubble zoomed closer to the ice-sheeted rocks, creating a dizzying illusion of imminent impact. The bubble cut to the left and slowed dramatically; then it shot upward, as if making for the summit, and suddenly shifted again into forward motion and glided terrifyingly close to a sheer red-stone cliff. It hugged the tortuous contours for twenty seconds, before rising to meet a ledge near the top of the cliff. Seemingly abruptly, the bubble came to rest, perched upon the ledge. Jael's breath caught in her throat. They were practically among the clouds, perched in an aerie where birds would scarcely dare to fly.

For the first few moments, she was terrified. They seemed so precariously perched that the slightest puff of wind could send them tumbling. "Really, we're quite well secured," she heard someone saying, as though in a fog, and eventually she focused on Ar's words, something about "gravity anchors." She nodded to show that she believed him, even as she struggled to make her eyes and her mind absorb the reality. Finally she drew a slow, deep breath and began to enjoy herself.

The view was astounding: mountain peaks contesting for dominance against the sky, ravines and wilderness valleys etched with barren rocks and snow, with ridges and tufts of winter trees. There was no sign of civilized life. The inhabited valley was out of sight behind the peak. They might have been thousands of kilometers from the nearest intrusion of society. Graceful arcs of cirrous clouds drifted high over the peaks. One towering summit was shrouded by a white mist that seemed to have gathered at that peak and nowhere else. In the other direction the sky was an astonishing cerulean blue.

"It makes me feel like an angel," Ar said softly, his breath whispering in and out beside her.

Jael's eyes widened at the image, but she didn't speak; she was too moved by the grandeur. She suddenly was conscious of being alone here with a man, an alien man whom she hardly knew, experiencing such an unexpected depth of wonder. It seemed . . . odd. She thought wistfully of Highwing. This was a place he would enjoy, would know how to love properly with dragon dignity and magical wonderment. She sighed silently. It was no good wishing for a friend who would never, could never, be here with her.

"Jael, would you like to *really* see it?"

She turned her head slowly, reacting to Ar's words.

Ar was gazing at her, his clear eyes almost ethereal with a luminous presence that seemed somehow to reach out to her across an enormous gulf. She shivered; and he smiled, in his cracked and crinkled way, and she realized that he was waiting for her to respond. "If you think it's beautiful now," he murmured, "it's possible to make it come even more alive in your mind. It can give you visions to rig by, visions you'll never forget. Would you like to try?"

The meaning of his words was slow in penetrating. "Well, I . . . don't know . . ." she murmured, as she felt the first tug of apprehension.

The Clendornan gazed back out over the mountains. "It's breathtaking just as it is, isn't it?" he said softly. "There's no need to do anything differently, if you don't want to. Look down in that valley." He pointed. Sunlight had just broken through a cloud to blaze into a series of ravines where snow seemed to be glittering in the air. "See those puffs of snow? We just missed seeing a slide, I think. I'll bet no one has ever been down there on foot, at least no one of your race or mine. It's pure wilderness, and so close to the spaceport."

Jael peered in the direction he was pointing and felt a tug of regret, wondering, despite her instinctive fear, what he'd been planning to offer. She was astonished at the trust she already felt toward him. He seemed to have no intention of forcing anything upon her, and she found that greatly reassuring.

Ar's eyes sparkled as he scanned up and to the right, where something—a dark speck—was moving along the face of an impossibly steep slope. "Let's see if we can get the magnifier on that," he said, touching one of the controls. There was a sudden distortion in the bubble as the forcefield produced two circular lens effects, one in front of each of them. Moving her head, Jael could see the magnified image of the mountainside swimming beyond the lens. After a moment, she located the dark speck, enlarged. It was a four-legged animal, perhaps a kind of mountain goat. But this high? It was impossible. Surely there was nothing for it to graze on at this altitude.

"I think it's a marten's centaur," Ar said.

"A flier? It looks like a goat to me. And a pretty brave one at th—" She interrupted herself, as something began to unfold on the animal's back. She gaped in astonishment as the animal stepped off the side of the mountain, wings spread wide. It began a graceful looping flight high over the rocky slopes. Jael lost it in the magnifier, but she could still see it unmagnified as a tiny black speck in the air. "What's it doing all the way up here?" she murmured in amazement.

"Prowling for hawklyn eggs, probably," Ar said, flicking off the magnifier. "They're superb hunters."

Jael nodded, astonished. She looked back at her new friend. "Ar? What was it you were going to suggest?"

Ar drew something from his jacket pocket and placed it on the narrow console between them. It was a small polyhedron of some sort, made of a glass or crystal as clear as his eyes. It was mounted on a base, with tiny controls.

Oh no . . .

Ar touched one of the controls. "It's just an enhancement device, to let the emotional effect accumulate. I'll set it at a low—" His expression changed, his mouth flattened as he noticed Jael's reaction. "Do you not want me to do this?"

"I just . . ." Jael drew a deep breath, struggling to push down memories of the pallisp, and the fear. But surely this was nothing so powerful as the pallisp. Probably more like . . . "Ar, is this—is this a dreamlink device?"

"A dreamlink—?"

"A synaptic . . . augmentor?"

His head tilted slightly. "In a manner of speaking. But it's an extremely gentle device. You will retain full control of your . . . thoughts."

Jael closed her eyes, trying to focus on reason. Was it so wrong? Was there any harm? For a moment she felt a terrible rush of anxiety. She thought of the time with Dap, and how she had allowed her fears to ruin an innocent and beautiful experience. Would this be the same? Perhaps—but could she continue to be ruled by her fears? She swallowed. "Okay," she said huskily. "But put it on the lowest setting—and turn it off, if I yell." She opened her eyes. "All right?"

"Of course," Ar whispered. His fingers hesitated over the controls. "We don't need to do this, you know."

She weighed her fears. "We'll try . . . just a little."

"Okay." Ar touched the switch and sat back.

Jael felt her breath go out in a long sigh. She felt an inward melting sensation. A feeling of relaxation and well-being filled her. It was indeed gentle, unthreatening. She imagined the wind outside the bubble, caressing them and floating them away into this scene of staggering beauty, this land of majesty and grace. She imagined herself floating on that wind like the marten's centaur. As she gazed into the distance, the peaks and valleys, the contours of rock and ice and sky, seemed to merge into her own being. She felt that the world out there was alive, that they were sharing in one life energy that flowed around and through this place high in the mountains.

And beside her, she was aware of Ar. Clendornan, new-found friend. She was aware of his companionship, of his feelings for this land, this place of ancient geologic violence and astonishing peace. She felt herself drawn toward him, sensing that here indeed was someone she could trust, some-one who could give her warmth . . . warmth and compan-ionship . . .

Like the pallisp . . .

"Turn it off, please," she whispered. She was not even aware of the desperation in her voice until Ar's hand darted out to flick off the device, and the feelings of wariness that had so quickly grown in her began to fade. She was aware of Ar looking at her in puzzlement, and perhaps hurt. Her own eyes were focused on the opposite peak, on infinity, on the spaces that were slowly growing cold and vast again, magnificent but distant. Distant and safe.

After a minute, she looked at Ar. His clear, purple-retinaed eyes were watching hers. She didn't know what to say, ex-cept . . . "I'm sorry." But what she was sorry for, Ar could not know, could not understand. How could he?

"I perceive your feelings," Ar said finally, his voice a lonely sigh of wind. "I have unwittingly stirred sorrow. I am sorry, Jael."

It's not your fault. You can't know. No one can know.

"Is there anything I can do?" he asked, gesturing helplessly to the mountains and valleys, as if they somehow possessed the powers of comfort that his instrument had not.

Can you take away the past? she thought hopelessly. Can you take away the pallisp and what it has done to me? "Per-haps," she whispered very softly, "we should return now."

"From this beauty?" he said, his voice a lament.

She nodded. Yes. From this beauty. From this awesome, terrifying beauty. She closed her eyes and nodded again.

She heard and felt nothing, but when she opened her eyes, the bubble was in flight, arcing through a windswept pass between two peaks, speeding back toward the spaceport.

Chapter 17
REMEMBRANCE

SHE SPENT what remained of the afternoon alone, scowling in thought and wishing for things that could not be—wishing for a captain she'd not have had to kill, for a father she did not have to forgive, for a dragon who could make it all happen by magic. By evening, she'd been alone with her thoughts long enough. Vowing that this time she would be honest and open with him, she sought out Ar.

She found him in the rigger hall dining room, picking at a cakelike substance that had been provided for dessert. His eyes followed her as she approached his table. Neither of them spoke, but his mouth formed a tentative crinkled shape as she paused; she set her tray down and took a seat across from him. She didn't know what to say, or how to start, so she simply nodded self-consciously and began to eat. Ar remained silent, poking at his dessert.

"It seems," Ar said suddenly, as she was halfway through her rice with beancurd sauce, "that there is a problem when you are confronted by something that makes you feel emotionally warm in a certain way, or perhaps too close to something."

She paused in her chewing, nodded, and continued eating. Ar watched her, glancing down at his hands once in a while, perhaps so as not to stare at her. He seemed ill at ease, making a soft muttering sound. Probably he thought he'd stepped over some human boundary again. Nevertheless, he tried again. "Is there a chance that you might want to air the problem, or perhaps use another person for feedback, or as a source of context?"

She was just starting her dessert at this point. She frowned, considering his question—which she understood to mean, Do you want to talk about it? She nodded. Before Ar could say anything else, she took a bite of the cake. It tasted like moldy bread. "Aack," she said, spitting it out onto her plate and hurriedly covering it with her napkin. "Is this a bad joke?"

For an instant, Ar seemed puzzled. He rubbed the left ridge of his skull, where his hair was thinnest, with his fingertips. His eyes seemed to darken flickeringly. Finally, after swallowing some water to get rid of the cake taste, Jael laughed at his expression. "I didn't mean you," she said. "The cake. I meant the cake."

"Ah."

"And yes, I would like to talk to you. But you must be— that is—well, patient. It's not easy, everything that I . . . might want to say. I want you to know that beforehand."

"I understand."

"Well, I'm not sure that you do, really. When we were up on the mountain today, there were some rather strange things going on in my mind." Her face grew hot. "Well . . . I don't actually know how to explain it. I'm not sure I understand it either, you see." She looked down at her plate, and pushed at the repulsive dessert with her fork. "But I think I . . . want to."

"Good."

She laughed uneasily. "You might not say that once you've heard it all."

The Clendornan carefully brought his fingertips together. "I guess that's what we'll have to find out. Isn't it?" And he echoed her laugh, but his laugh was a hiccupping sound, from deep in his throat. It sounded odd, coming from someone who seemed so solid and strong and . . . if he were Human, she would have thought him quite masculine. She didn't know what he was as a Clendornan.

With a shrug, she said, "You know someplace we can talk?"

The place they found was a suite near Ar's room, in the nonhuman rigger dorm. As they walked over, Ar explained the housing policy here, noting that Clendornan were housed separately from humans, despite the similarity of their physiological needs. He thought it a little silly, if not outright discriminatory, but there were advantages to the arrangement, as well. The nonhuman section was greatly underused at present, which meant that more spacious quarters were available. He didn't know why the nonhuman population was down; it might just have been part of some natural cycle of interstellar commerce. It did, however, make things lonely sometimes.

"I had a friend here who was a Pendansk," he said. "You know the Pendansk?" Jael shook her head. "Very tall, spindly fellows, with narrow faces. Low-oxygen breathers. We weren't really suited for rigging together, but I enjoyed his company until he rigged out with another Pendansk, a few weeks ago. Here we are."

They entered a small sitting room, musty with the smell of some prior inhabitant. It was quiet and secluded, and that was all Jael cared about. Ar fussed, making two cups of Clendornan tea. Jael sipped the sharply aromatic blend. To her surprise, the flavor was quite delicate, reminiscent of lemongrass. She waited a few moments after swallowing—mindful of allergic reactions—and when she felt nothing, went ahead and took another sip. The gesture, the ritual of drinking the tea, was soothing.

Ar asked if a log fire would be all right, and a fireplace and crackling fire appeared in the center of one wall, between the stuffed chairs. Jael could feel the heat from the holo, and could have sworn that she smelled burning wood. "Ah, that's good," Ar said. "We don't have fireplaces on my world. But they are a wonderful invention, one of humanity's true gifts to civilization. I try to enjoy them whenever I'm on a human world." He tilted his angular, top-heavy head and gazed into the flames. The flickering light danced within his eyes.

Jael nodded. She felt the same way, though she would have preferred the real thing. Still, the movement of the flames calmed her spirit. As she stared into the heart of the fire, she began to think again about what it was she wanted to tell Ar. Somehow, gazing into the fire, the prospect of sharing her feelings no longer seemed so frightening.

She began to talk. It was hard at first, partly because she didn't know where to start. "I flew with Mogurn because he was the only one who would give me work," she explained. But that wasn't what she wanted to say, really. Now that she'd brought it up, however, she felt she had to explain about her father's reputation on Gaston's Landing and how it was a truly parochial colony where more than one person's career had been ruined by rumor. Ar listened silently, apparently following the thread, as she digressed even further. "I had one good friend there, my cousin Dap, who was a rigger too. Is a rigger. Except that we had a problem just before I left with Mogurn. And that's why . . . well, when we were on the mountain, and you turned on that enhancer, I had such a reaction. . . ."

She became breathless talking about Dap and the dreamlink, partly because the memory still disturbed her, and partly because she was avoiding other things that she needed to talk about—Mogurn, for instance, and his attempt to enslave her with the pallisp. And his more direct attempt at domination, when the pallisp had failed.

But Ar was a patient and gentle listener, and in time she got around to describing Mogurn. What she didn't get around to was something that she was afraid even Ar wouldn't believe. But it was never far from her thoughts.

The fire was crackling low, as the holo-logs burned. Ar touched the switch to put on another log. As the flames climbed higher again, he peered at her with his liquid eyes. "Is there something missing from this story?" he asked softly, giving no sign that he was tiring of listening to her. She looked at him as though she didn't understand what he meant. "Perhaps I have listened carelessly. But I still do not understand why this Mogurn was so angry with you. Was it only because you rejected his pallisp?"

"He was furious when I said I didn't want it anymore," she insisted, though she knew perfectly well what Ar was driving at, even if Ar didn't.

"Well, what was it that enabled you to break free of the pallisp? You said that you were becoming addicted to it. It sounds like a truly frightening instrument—and I do understand now why you were so cautious up on the mountain, although the enhancer we were using was entirely different from what you have described."

Jael blinked, gazing into the fire. In the dancing flames, in the glowing coals at the heart of that fire, she could almost swear that she saw the stirrings of . . . dragon magic. She sighed, nodding. She knew that now was the time, if ever there was a time, to tell him about Highwing. But she had trouble starting again, because this was so much more difficult to explain. Ar waited, silently. Eventually the silence itself seemed to prod at her until the story she'd been longing to tell began to rise up, to bubble up, in her heart. "Ar," she asked softly, "do you know of the legends of dragons that live in space, in the Flux, along the mountain route to the southwest of Lexis?" As she spoke, she felt the memories stirring to life.

In Ar's silence, she sensed his puzzlement. "Well, the legends are true," she whispered, and she didn't stop until she had told him the entire story of her encounter with Highwing: how he had saved her from the other dragons; how he had looked into her soul, and their spirits had become entwined in friendship; how the dragon, through his gifts of sight, had helped her to begin to break free of some of her inner demons. By the time she was finished, her voice was strained and cracking, her eyes brimming with tears.

Neither of them spoke for a while after that. She dabbed at her eyes, feeling embarrassed—until she remembered that Ar wasn't human, and somehow that reassured her. Somehow, she didn't mind making a fool of herself in front of a nonHuman, as she would have with one of her own kind. She didn't know if that made any sense, but it was how she felt.

At last she looked up into Ar's gentle, curious gaze and wondered if he believed her, or *could* believe her. She wondered if anyone at this starport could believe her. She had burdened Ar with a great deal this evening. But . . . he was her test case in this, as well as being a new friend. His gaze was luminous with empathy, but there was a certain reserve. "Well?" she murmured at last.

Ar stroked the upper ridge of his skull for a moment. "That," he said finally, "is a very moving story. I am awed by the imagery—by the vividness of your emotional awakening—by the changes you began to experience within yourself. It was splendid, *is* splendid. A truly inspiring example of rigging."

"Well—thank you. But, Ar . . ." she began, and stopped, suddenly uncertain.

"It must have seemed very real to you, Jael. As real as if literally true." Ar closed his liquid eyes and reopened them.

He didn't understand, then. Didn't believe her. "Ar," she said softly, trying to make her voice strong and steady. "It was real. Those things happened to me. I'm not making it up."

The Clendornan eased his head to one side. "I'm sure it was extremely real to you, Jael. And that is the mark of a powerful rigger."

She felt a pressure in her forehead. Was this how everyone would react? She was grateful that she had not risked trying to convince the police. Bad enough with a friend. "No, Ar, you're not getting the point."

"But I do understand the phenomenon."

"No, you don't."

He gazed at her. "Please . . . what don't I understand?"

Jael felt terribly inarticulate. After all she had just told him . . .

"The images you cast were extremely vivid, as you—"

"Ar, it was not just images. That's the whole point!"

"Jael, wait." There was a groan of distress in Ar's voice.

"Please. We must take care to distinguish myth from reality. Now, I hold myth and imagination in the highest esteem. They help us to deal with our reality, to understand it in ways that may sometimes be clearer than literal definition."

"Ar, I'm not talking about that."

He continued without hearing her. "But you must know which is which. Of what benefit is the symbol if we confuse it with the object? What is the use of a map if we confuse it with the territory it represents? But isn't that the challenge of rigging—to map the territory imaginatively, and to know the territory *by* the map—because we can never really know it directly? That's why an experience like yours is so moving, because it pushes to the very edge, until the two become nearly inseparable."

Ar's words were so earnest, and his insistent redefining of her words so acute, that she found herself thinking, Why am I so sure? But she *was* sure; she knew what had happened to her. Didn't she?

The Clendornan paused, staring at her. His voice lost its steadiness. "Do I need to apologize again? I sense that I'm causing you confusion. I'm not reacting the way you'd expected, or hoped."

"Well—*no*."

"But you wouldn't want me to speak dishonestly."

"Of course not." Jael groaned, wondering how this had all become such a confusing jumble. Why wasn't it clear? Why couldn't he believe her?

Ar stroked the ridge of his head, considering. "You wish me to accept the literal reality of what you experienced on that flight?"

"Yes! That's what I've been telling you!"

He was silent a moment longer. "I have never heard anyone speak of such a thing, Jael. Not seriously, soberly, I mean. It is . . . difficult."

"I know!" She sighed. "That's what the library says, too. But the library's wrong! Damn it, Ar, do you think I would have let Mogurn get that mad at me for something that was just imaginary, for something that I could have turned on or off at will?"

Ar rocked back. "I wouldn't assume that you could turn any image on or off at will, under any circumstances. If the image is powerful enough, if it is convincing enough—"

"That's not it, Ar!"

The Clendornan fell silent. "Well, then, there is really no way to know, is there?"

"If you'd just believe me—"

"Objectively, I mean. For someone who wasn't there when it happened, there's no objective test to separate imagination from reality."

Jael shrugged unhappily. "I guess not. I guess there isn't." She sat back and stared at the fire, at the flickering, unreal burning of the holo-flame, and thought, *I know the difference. Don't I?* She looked at Ar again. "Don't you think it's possible that I could make that distinction?"

Ar's lips slowly formed into a half crinkle. "Of course, Jael. But this is my nature—analytic. Please forgive me. I cannot help being who I am." Jael started to answer, but Ar waved her to silence. "Still, I perceive that you believe very strongly. And though I know you but little, I respect you. I will consider, Jael. I will consider as best I can."

Jael nodded into the flame. That was about all she could ask, wasn't it? *Wasn't it?*

Chapter 18

ED

THOUGHTS OF Highwing were driven from her mind the next morning by a call from the spaceport police, followed by a meeting with one of the investigating officers and a representative of the spaceport shipping commission. At issue was the disposition of Mogurn's starship. There was no way for Jael to collect her pay until the cargo and ship were disposed of; and that couldn't be done until the ship's title was assigned—either to Mogurn's company, or his heirs, if any, or to the government of Lexis.

What the officials wanted from Jael was more information about Mogurn. She had little to offer beyond what had been found in Mogurn's cabin, and none at all about the legal status of Mogurn's ship. Her own contract was of little help. There was no indication that he'd had a company or partnership other than his private ownership of *Cassandra*. Nevertheless, the officials kept her for the better part of the day questioning her about the contract, as well as pursuing further details of Mogurn's death. She bore it all with stoic patience. What choice did she have?

By the end of the day, however, she learned that no action

was contemplated against her for Mogurn's death. This came as a considerable relief, even if she'd seen no reason for them to question her actions in the first place. But it was clear that she had no chance of receiving her flight pay anytime soon. And that meant that she was going to have to try to find work, which meant a rigging assignment. When she saw Commander Gordache and asked if she would be allowed to fly, he shrugged and said, "You have to eat, don't you?"

She sighed, glad that if nothing else, they recognized that fact. But how she was going to get work, and with whom, she didn't know. She thought about what Ar had told her, that he was looking for rigging partners. She liked Ar, certainly, despite his frustrating obtuseness last night. But would she be able to rig with someone, knowing that such a gulf in understanding existed between them? Would anyone else be more likely to believe her? Ar, at least, didn't question her sanity; she wasn't sure if the same would be true of others.

She returned to her quarters, weary and discouraged. There was a message from Ar, asking if they might meet later. She didn't bother to reply, assuming that she would find him at dinner. He wasn't there, however, and she ate her evening meal in lonely solitude, staring at some of the other riggers and thinking, Would you believe me if I told you about dragons on the mountain route—real dragons? When they looked at her, she wondered, did they see anything but a renegade, a captain-killer? Thoughts of the pallisp drifted into her mind, and she chased them away angrily. She was starting to feel the old despair creep back into her thoughts.

After dinner, she paced through the lounges, looking for Ar. When she didn't find him she decided to pay a visit to Ed the cyber-parrot. She found a vacant Environment Alpha I/O, donned the helmet, and entered the psychetronic space of the system.

She was horrified to find that the environment selection menu had changed: the desert-mesa scenario was gone, supplanted by a methane tide-pool, and the rainforest had been replaced by an ocean sunset. *Ed!* she shrieked silently to the holographic image. *What have you done with Ed!* Trembling, she tore off the helmet and sat upright in her seat, enraged, glaring around the gloomy lounge. "You bastards—how could you change it?" she whispered. How could they? She stalked out of the lounge, looking for someone in charge.

It took a while, but eventually she found a red-eyed young man working in a back office who considered her question with some puzzlement and said that, yes, the scenarios in Environment Alpha were replaced periodically for variety. It was just a matter of swapping data grains in and out of the control console. He wasn't really supposed to, he said, scratching at the scrawniest beard Jael had ever seen, but he guessed it would be all right to put the rainforest back in as long as no one else complained. "Thank you," Jael breathed, surprised by the intensity of her own feelings. She realized now that her reaction had been a little extreme.

"The thing is, though—they're getting ready to take those machines out and replace them with new hardware, and all new data grains," the young man remarked, as he rummaged through a drawer, looking for the rainforest element. "So enjoy it while you can, because in a few days it really will be gone. Here it is." He grinned and held up a small nodule between thumb and forefinger. "I'll stick it in. By the time you're back in the system, it'll be up and running."

Jael hurried back to the lounge and donned the I/O helmet again. As promised, the rainforest selection was once more on the menu. This time she materialized walking, or floating, along a footpath under a canopy of dense greenery. There were blossoms everywhere: in purples, oranges, yellows, whites, and pinks. She glimpsed, darting through the tree branches, several birds and one snake. She didn't see Ed.

Gliding along the path, she spotted a pair of monkeylike creatures swinging from branch to branch, speeding through the forest. A long, bushy-tailed rodent peeked out of the underbrush and chittered up at her. It scratched at the ground, insistently, peering up hungrily. Peanuts or death! she imagined it threatening. With a frown, she checked her pockets and found an assortment of nuts. She tossed them toward the animal, which scrabbled about, gathering them up. Three more of the rodents dived out of adjoining bushes, and they began quarreling over the nuts. Jael walked on.

The ground underfoot was springy. She stooped for a closer look and discovered that the path was carpeted by a thick, spongy moss. As she pressed her fingers into it, a small purple-blossomed plant near her hand drew away, leaves rustling nervously. "What's the matter?" she asked, instinctively reaching out to touch it. She stopped herself when the plant rustled again, and with a shrug she stood up. As she walked away, she heard a tiny sigh. Behind her, the plant was tiptoeing across the path. Noticing her glance, it scuttled quickly into the brush. There were some awfully curious beasts here, she decided.

Moving on, she noticed a large cluster of leaves nestled in the center of a short broad-leafed plant. The cluster was shaped like a large blossom, the color of dark cinnamon. At her approach, it broke apart into a dozen fluttering insects. Startled, she stepped back. The insects took wing straight toward her, then swerved away. Flashing apart, they flew to a nearby tree and converged on a branch like a reversed holo of an explosion. Rising onto her tiptoes, Jael peered up at them. They looked just as they had before: like a dark, heavy flower.

"Rawk! Bugs! Bugs!"

Jael spun, looking for the source of the voice. She couldn't see him. "Ed! Is that you?"

"Yawp!"

"Where are you?"

"Up here! Up here!"

She craned her neck, twisting around. She saw a tree with slender branches minus leaves, but with a skirt of hairlike tendrils that looked like fine rootlets. The parrot was perched near the top of the tree, peering down at her. He fluttered his green and scarlet wings in greeting. "Ed! I was looking for you!"

"Always here! Always here!" The bird cocked his head, surveying the land.

"Come on down?"

"Aarrrwwk! Sure." Ed swooped. He landed with a dazzling flutter on a branch near Jael's hand. "Hi, Jayl!" he squawked.

"What have you been up to?" She held out her hand to let him rub the side of his beak against her knuckles.

"Rawk. Who, me?" He turned his head to look around.

"No—your cousin Ned. Of course I mean you!"

Ed opened his beak, as though considering what to say. His tongue twitched. He made a stuttering hiss, which might have been laughter. "But Ed not reel! You say Ed not reel! How can poor, not-reel Ed be up to any—"

"*Ed, stop that!*" she scolded.

He clacked his beak shut and gazed at her silently. "S-sorry."

"Good." She took a breath. "Hey, let's be friends, okay? No smart remarks about what's real or not, at least between you and me. Okay? We're both real. Right?"

Ed sneezed. "Arr-right!"

"Good." She frowned, remembering suddenly what the attendant had told her—that Ed might not be around much longer. She shivered, trying to put the thought out of her mind. She'd just made a friend; she didn't want to think about losing him. "Ed," she sighed, "half the time I don't even know what's real anymore. You know, with all of these worlds, and this stuff in here"—she waved a hand around the landscape, which was difficult to think of as an artifice—"sometimes it's hard to keep track."

"Yawp. Ed knows."

"Do you?" She squinted at the brilliantly colored bird, who was now preening himself. "Do you, Ed? Tell me something. Do you know about riggers?"

Ed stopped preening. "You rigger," he stated.

"Right. But do you know what we do? When we're working, I mean?"

The bird seemed to squint at her, considering. "F-fly," he said hesitantly. "You fly. Yawp?"

"That's right, we fly. But it's a little different from the way you, well . . ." She paused, trying to think how to explain it to Ed, who lived in a world that in certain ways resembled the Flux. He probably had no understanding of the difference between his reality and hers. But she could think of no way to explain it, so she changed the subject. "Anyway, I was talking to Ar yesterday—you remember Ar, don't you?"

"Ar. Sure."

"Well, we were talking about someone I met a while back, someone who was a terribly good friend to me while I was with him—"

"Awk? Parrot?" Ed interrupted, stretching his neck.

Jael laughed. "No—no, he wasn't a parrot. Actually he was a dragon."

Ed cocked his head. "Graggon?"

"*Dragon.* Sort of a great giant lizard, except that he flies, like you."

"Arrwwk. Glizzard—yokk." Ed tilted his head this way and that, as though trying to picture it.

Jael continued impatiently. "Yes, well anyway, the point is that I was telling Ar about this dragon, and Ar couldn't believe me when I told him that the dragon was real. It was as though *I* couldn't believe it when you told me that you were real."

The parrot flexed his wings vigorously. "Ed reel!"

"Yes, I know. I made a mistake before, when I said that you weren't. And that's what I'm trying to tell you. I'm sorry and I wish I hadn't said it. I understand now how you feel, because of the way Ar reacted when I told him about my dragon friend."

Ed pushed his beak toward her and nuzzled it into the crook of her elbow. She murmured and gently stroked the top of his head. He suddenly hopped up onto her shoulder and began to nibble at her hair.

Jael laughed self-consciously. She hadn't meant to bare her soul to the parrot. And now that she thought about it, was it even true, what she had said? She'd implied that Ed was real in the same way that Highwing was, and vice versa. But Highwing lived and breathed, in the world of the Flux. He was not a construct; he was objectively real. That was what she had struggled to convince Ar of. But what about Ed? He lived—and breathed, she supposed—here in this cyber-reality.

He learned and changed—and thought, apparently. And hadn't Ar said that he was based on a real parrot?

Ed stopped nuzzling her hair and announced, "Glizzards."

Jael's heart almost stopped, as an image of flying dragons crossed her mind. An instant later, she realized that Ed wasn't talking about dragons. Perched on a boulder nearby, half shrouded by overhanging branches, were three bright green, ruby-throated lizards, each the size of her forearm. They appeared to be doing pushups, rising and sinking on their front legs as they breathed. "They're very pretty," she murmured. "A bit different from what I was talking about, though—different from the dragons."

"Aww?" Ed rustled on her shoulder. "Ed would like— awwk!"

"What, Ed?"

"Like see graggons—dragons!"

Jael turned her head until she was practically eyeball to eyeball with the parrot on her shoulder. "What's that?" She laughed. "*You'd* like to see dragons?"

Ed squawked, deafening her. "Yep. Ed like see dragons." He twisted his head one way and then the other. "You take Ed? Go see dragons?"

"Ah—" Her voice caught as she remembered what the young attendant had said.

"Yes? Awww." He nuzzled his beak in her hair. "Ed like Jayl."

"Well, I wish I could, Ed. I'd like to."

"Yes? Yes?" The bird hopped about excitedly on her shoulder, then jumped to the nearest branch and began prancing in front of her. "Good! Good! Ed happy! Rawwwk!"

"Ed, wait a minute!" She thought furiously, heart pounding. How could she explain her way out of this? "Ed, stop that a minute. Please!" The parrot became still, except for his darting eyes. Jael drew a breath and exhaled noisily. "Look, Ed. I said I'd *like* to take you with me to see the dragons. I didn't say I could do it."

"What? No?" Ed's feathers ruffled, a blaze of scarlet and green, and slowly drooped. His eyes turned down.

"I just don't know how, Ed. I don't even know if *I* can

ever see the dragons again." Her throat tightened as she said that, as she thought of Highwing. She kept talking, more rapidly. "Even if I could—the thing is, Ed, I wouldn't know any way to take you along with me. You live here, in this world. And I can't take it with me." But even as she said that, she realized that, in principle, at least, what she'd said was untrue. This was a cyber-world and Ed a cyber-bird, and in theory there was no reason why it couldn't all be carried in a tiny software nodule that could be tied into the rigger-net. But she had no idea how, in practice, she could obtain a nodule containing Ed.

She gazed at the parrot. With head bent and neck feathers askew, he looked about as dejected as a parrot could look. Her heart sank for him, and for herself. She'd certainly miss him. "Maybe there's a way," she murmured. "Maybe. I'm not sure. I'm not even sure when or if I'll be flying again. But if there's a way . . . *if* there's a way . . ."

Ed's head came up a fraction of an inch.

She sighed. "I'll see what I can do, okay? That's the best I can offer. Will you accept that?"

Ed hopped back onto her shoulder and pecked affectionately at her hair. "Ed happy. Happy as can be," he said—not quite with the same joy as before, but with hope, at least, in his voice.

"Good." She stroked the side of his head with a finger. "And now, old friend, I think perhaps I should see if I can find my other friend, Ar. Be here when I come back?"

"R-r-right here! Right here! B-bye!" With a flash of color, Ed launched himself up into the thick tree cover.

Jael waved, and then the rainforest dissolved around her.

She didn't have to look far to find Ar. He was sitting at a nearby station, playing with a screen-display game that flickered shifting colors onto his face. He looked up, crinkle-mouthed, as she approached. "Jael," he said.

"Am I interrupting you?"

He passed a hand over the display screen and it went dark. "I was just waiting for you. I thought you were probably—

well, that maybe you'd rather not be interrupted." His luminous eyes met hers.

She blinked. "It would have been okay. Actually I was looking for you earlier."

"Oh? Do you have news?"

"Me? No, not particularly. I just thought maybe—"

"I have news," Ar said brightly. He gestured to the seat beside his.

Startled, she sat. "What is it?"

"That depends somewhat on whether you are free to take a rigging job. And whether you want to."

Jael opened her mouth, dumbfounded.

One corner of Ar's mouth went up; the other corner went down. "Does that mean that you are? That you do?"

"Well, I—yes—I mean, of course, I'd have to apply for clearance." She stammered, only half sure of what she was saying, because she was trying to absorb all of the possible implications of his question. "There's that whole legal thing." Still, she remembered, Commander Gordache had implied that they'd allow her to work.

"I understand," Ar said. "But if they're willing to let you go, there's an opening on a flight coming up, for a two-crew." He hesitated. "I know this is awfully quick. But would you be interested in rigging with me?"

The rush of thoughts made her dizzy. "Yes—that is, I think so. Yes. But . . . Ar? There's one other thing I have to ask you." This was going to sound ridiculous, but she had to say it. "Do you remember Ed, the parrot? In the rainforest environment?" Ar's eyes glimmered as he nodded. "Well . . . Ed sort of asked to come along with me the next time I flew."

Something funny happened in Ar's eyes. They brightened, then darkened. "He *what*?" The left corner of Ar's mouth formed a zigzag.

"He, uh—he wants to see dragons, he said."

"Dragons!"

She raised a hand hastily. "Okay, okay, don't say it! I know. I told him I didn't know any way to do it. But I . . . well, I promised to try to find a way. And—I just found out that they're taking him out of the system soon. The whole rainforest. He's going to be"—she swallowed—"terminated."

Ar made a soft wheezing sound, which might have been a laugh, or a sign of distress. "Ed? Dragons?"

"I know. I know. I told him I might never get to fly that way again, anyway. But he wants to come along. In theory it ought to be possible, right? It's just a technical question, isn't it?"

"Well—I don't know, really." Ar's eyebrows flexed, dusty silver against his bluish forehead.

"It must be. Okay, so you don't believe in the dragons. I suppose you'll say that Ed isn't real, either." Jael looked down at her clenched hands. She could hardly blame him. Certainly she had given him enough impossible things to believe already.

Stroking the ridge of his head, Ar answered, "I wouldn't say that exactly. Ed is a cyber-parrot, yes, so in one respect he is an artifact. But if he's based upon a real parrot, and if his personality has been allowed to evolve naturally, then I would have to say that he is real. Even if he doesn't exist outside of the psychetronic environment."

Jael felt an impulse to ask how, then, he would distinguish Ed from the dragons he thought unreal, but she thought better of it. Time enough to argue about that later. Instead, she asked, "If I can get clearance, and we rig together, will you help me try to get a copy of Ed onto our ship?"

Ar stared at her for a long time. His eyes seemed to flicker, as though very fine lines of fire were dancing upon the violet wool in their clear depths. Then his face broke into a broad, cracked zigzag. "You have made yourself," he said, "a deal."

Chapter 19
CYBER-RESCUE

GETTING CLEARANCE from the police took just one visit with Commander Gordache. The police were no longer interested in restricting her movements, and Gordache encouraged her to find work so that she would not have to continue drawing housing credit from the spaceport administration. It seemed likely that her claim for flight pay against the Mogurn estate would be held up in the legal process for weeks or months.

With Ar, she went to the rigger offices and applied for the posted two-crew position. They were hardly the only riggers looking for work, but the situation was far less grim than it had been on Gaston's Landing. As it happened, most of the present competition was vying either for larger ships or solos. However, since she and Ar had never crewed together, they were required to take a simulator test to demonstrate compatibility. They did that in the afternoon, in the basement of the rigger hall.

They were installed in linked rigger-stations, where they rehearsed all normal checkout procedures for flight. Computer-generated Flux simulations were fed into the sensory net, along with randomly selected flight problems. It was strongly reminiscent of her training simulations, and Jael felt in the groove almost from the beginning. She and Ar developed a quick rapport, trading images back and forth as they zipped through the synthetic landscapes. With surprising ease, she put her fears aside, closing off those areas that she wished to keep private, and testing only the imaging powers that she needed in the net with Ar. But then, of course it was easy: she knew it was only a test. That was both the beauty and the weakness of tests of this sort; they were useful enough as a gross measure of competence, but they could not really show how a team would function in the actual tricks and twists of the Flux. Only starflight itself would reveal that.

With their partnership rating in hand, they were left to await word on the position itself, which could easily take days. That gave them time to think about other matters—among them, Ed.

Rescuing the parrot was not going to be easy. She knew, even as she planned to do it, that her desire was not entirely rational. But the parrot had somehow found a place in her heart—quite unexpectedly—a place of warmth that in a strange way reminded her of Highwing. Could a cyber-parrot give the same kind of friendship as a person—or a dragon? She supposed he would be closer to a pet. But she didn't care; she just knew she didn't want to lose Ed, not now, not without giving it her best try to rescue him.

Unfortunately, she could not locate the young man who had helped her last night, and the people who worked in the back rooms today either couldn't or wouldn't tell her exactly when the Environment Alpha system would be removed, or even whether the rainforest element would be left intact until then. She did learn that the data grains were all imported from off planet and allowed to grow and mature in place. The Ed that she knew was a unique denizen of this particular artificial intelligence "data garden." If she couldn't save him before he was removed, there was virtually no hope of recovering him. There also seemed little hope of her obtaining a data readout of his personality in any straightforward manner. Her spirits were low as she reported back to Ar.

Ar told her that he had an idea or two. The rest of the afternoon, while Jael worried, Ar did some asking around the spaceport. That evening he met her in the dining hall. "I might have a method," he reported. "It's not foolproof. But it's the only thing I could come up with." With a surreptitious glance each way, he held up a small black case. He opened it carefully. Cushioned on red velvet was a pair of thin cerametallic disks, each about a centimeter in diameter. "These could be Ed's ticket out," he murmured.

Jael peered at them curiously. "What are they?"

"System probes. They have data grains sufficient to hold Ed's identity matrix, plus the AI growth medium, plus at least some of the ambient data that convey the rainforest environment." Ar's voice was a husky whisper. He seemed actually to be enjoying this. "You'll wear these on your temples when you go into the environment. They'll take control of the input/output circuits in the helmet. Once you're in the environment, they'll send probing commands back into the AI system itself." His voice dropped lower. "They're actually security-breaking probes, which makes them . . . well . . . don't ask me where I got them, okay?" He hiccupped and continued, "I don't expect that this system was designed with extensive security, so the penetrating AI modules in here should be able to get in and set up the readout without too much trouble. I hope so, anyway."

Jael cleared her throat. "We're going to hijack him right out of the system?"

Ar smiled in his peculiar way. "We're saving his life, yes? Anyway, his existence in the system will continue, until they pull his plug—but we'll have him, too, and we should be able to load him into a nodule that you can connect with the rigger-net systems."

Jael nodded hesitantly. She hadn't expected quite such a clandestine operation.

"Are you ready to give it a try, then?"

Her breath eased out in a sigh. They rose and walked to the rigger lounge.

Both Environment Alpha I/Os were occupied. Jael shot Ar an uneasy glance. He shrugged and gestured to the nearby seats. They would have to wait. Jael tried to relax, staring alternately at the ceiling and at her fingernails. Don't worry, she thought. Ed's still there; he's safe. But she might as well have been trying to hold back an avalanche. What if they pull the rainforest again before I get in there? What if they already pulled it? What if they turn off the whole system? By the time one of the riggers in the Environment Alpha seats stirred and lifted the I/O helmet from her head, Jael's nerves were a wreck. She tried not to stare as the other rigger rubbed her eyes and readjusted to the outer reality. Finally, an eternity later, the woman rose and vacated the seat.

Jael hurried to take her place. Ar caught her arm as she was about to set the helmet on her head. He held out the open case containing the probe disks. Right. Don't forget your tools. She sat quietly while Ar fitted one disk to each of her temples, then checked, as she lowered the helmet, to ensure that its probes rested on the disks. She took a deep breath, aware of the lingering smell of the woman who had just worn the helmet. She felt like a criminal. Remember, she thought, you're trying to save his life.

"Go on," Ar murmured in her ear.

She squeezed the trigger.

The rainforest, blessedly, was still in the system. But Ed was nowhere to be found. The forest was damp and misty, and strangely quiet. The light seemed odd, grey and flat somehow. Apparently it was early in the morning in this place, this world.

She wondered if the AI things in the probes were already in the system, recording. She didn't want them to fill up on the wrong things. *Leave room for Ed*, she thought hopefully. *If I can find him.*

Scanning and recording ambient data. Please state when primary data matrix has appeared.

The instructions appeared in her mind, rather like a voice in the net. Good, she could deal with that. *It has not yet appeared. Searching for it now*, she answered.

Did Ed have some way of knowing when she had entered his world? she wondered. She could only hope so. She walked toward a break in the underbrush. It seemed to be the beginning of a path. There was a patch of dense mist hugging the ground in the break, but she didn't think much of it as she stepped through—until something grabbed at her ankle, and a spike of pain shot up her leg. "*Ow!*" she cried, jumping back, rubbing her ankle. She glared down at the little bank of fog and kicked at it.

A small bush ran out of the fog, screeching nastily. It swiped at her leg again with a thorny branch, but she jumped clear and watched warily as it retreated across the open ground. Before it had gone far, it plopped down with an indignant *whuff.* "Fine. Now stay out of my way," Jael snapped. The plant gave no response, but a moment later, began issuing fog from its thorns. Within seconds, it was completely hidden by a new bank of vapor.

Jael curled her lip at it. Suddenly it occurred to her that the thing was probably being recorded. Great, she thought. All I need is something like that popping out in the net. *If you can understand me,* she thought to the system probes, *don't keep that plant!*

Deleted.

Relieved, she stepped onto the path from which the plant had emerged. More wisps of mist rose from the branches, curling about her face. Fearful of meeting more hostile life, she moved with extra care. What was going on here? she wondered. Why was it so foggy, anyway? She walked for some time, encountering only mist-shrouded trees and occasional scuttling creatures—heard, but not seen. "Ed?" she sang softly. "Are you here?" As the minutes passed, she began to worry that something might have happened to him. Was it possible that a part of the environment had been removed, and Ed with it? What hope would that leave her? She searched the mist with growing anxiety.

A branch brushed her neck, startling her, and something

red fluttered with a shriek in her face. "*Gah!*" she cried, jumping, as it flew up out of sight.

"Yawk!" cried the red thing, fluttering down again.

"Ed!" she shouted, hope and fear pounding in her heart.

A patch of mist cleared. Ed was flapping his wings on a perch less than an arm's length in front of her face. The path, hidden by the fog, had taken a sharp left turn. She had nearly walked into a thicket of branches. "Jayl!" Ed squawked, hopping up and down on one of the branches.

"Ed—thank God! I was beginning to think you were gone."

"Nope. Ed here. Right here." His wings folded closed.

"Didn't you hear me calling?"

"Yawp! Woke Ed. Early—it's early!"

"Early! Is that where you were—asleep?" The parrot nodded and let his eyelids fall shut for a moment; then they sprang open again. She laughed. "Well, good. Don't move. Don't go anywhere. There's something we have to do." Ed cocked his head and at once began to pace nervously side to side on the branch. "I mean it," she said. "Don't move at all."

"Urkk." The parrot became still. He blinked once.

"Great. Stay right there." *This is it. This is Ed,* she thought to the system probe. *Primary data matrix. Can you find all of him, or do we have to do anything?*

Probing now. Recording. Please do nothing.

She nodded again, almost imperceptibly. "Ed, this has to do with your coming with me when I leave. Do you still want to come?"

"Awwrrrk. Yes! *Yes!*"

"Good. Then please stay very still. Don't talk."

The parrot obeyed so completely that he looked dead. His eyes grew wide and dark, and remained unblinking. He appeared to have fallen into a trance. Jael waited. She wasn't sure what she expected, perhaps that he would simply sit there while his memory was drained, or copied. But she wasn't prepared for what happened next.

Ed's eyes seemed to grow larger. His dark pupils appeared to expand in his head, at first looking a little odd, then grotesque, as they grew out of proportion to the rest of him. Soon his pupils threatened to swallow his entire head in darkness. The final expansion happened very quickly, a great circle of blackness ballooning out to absorb not just Ed, but the entire forest. Jael was uncertain whether the darkness had actually expanded, or her own viewpoint had zoomed into the pupil of Ed's eye. She wasn't sure if it mattered.

In the darkness, she began to glimpse images of a brightly colored, fluttering parrot winging through a forest; of the same bird, smaller, pecking its way out of a shell; of it eating seeds and berries in the wild, and flocking with others of its kind. And more confusingly and fuzzily, images of being enveloped in a net, and captured; of being confined and wired at the head; of being drained off, poured off, and let loose in another and altogether different place, which at first seemed to have little reality or substance. But eventually that world became clearer and more solid, until it resembled the original. It was a world of curious inhabitants, where people appeared and disappeared, where the bird could speak articulately, where it could learn, where it could converse and get to know these people called riggers. A world where, in time, it met someone named Ar and someone named Jayl.

The images became a blur, past and present merging. Eventually Jael could see nothing but a grey fog. Then the fog cleared, and she was staring at Ed, seated on his branch. The bird cocked his head, one way and then another, looking puzzled. "R-r-r-k-k-k," Ed sputtered.

"You okay?" Jael asked.

"Ukk." Ed stretched his wings. "What—awwk—happened?"

"I'm not sure," Jael admitted. *Did you get him? Were those his memories?*

Ed's primary memories and physical characteristics have been merged into our system. We require additional time to collect further ambient environmental data, plus redefining adjustments on Ed.

Jael looked around cautiously. *What do you want me to do?*

She felt an odd whirring sensation that seemed to surround her hearing and vision, before she heard,

Insufficient capacity for all aspects of the environment. Explore elements of this environment that you would most like recorded, taking Ed with you, if possible, for contextual fit.

Jael blinked, absorbing the instruction. She looked at Ed. "Well, Ed . . . what happened, I think, is that you're now living two lives. One of them is in my head."

"Hawwwww-k-k-k?" He peered at her.

"Yes. Well, it's a little hard to explain, really. But a part of you is living with me now . . . and it will go with me when I leave. Along with a memory of this place." She gulped, wondering if Ed could possibly understand what she was saying.

Ed hopped closer. "I come with you? K-k-k-k?"

"In a manner of speaking, yes. You've been split. You'll be here. But you'll also be with me."

"*Rawwwkk! Not want stay! Want go! Want go! Not split!*" Ed fluttered his wings in distress.

"But, Ed—"

"No no no no no!" Ed hopped furiously, tossing his head. "Want go with you! Only!" He cawed raucously, then peered into her eyes. "Jayl take? Not leave here? Pleez, Jayl? *Pleeez?*"

Jael's breath came with great difficulty. She should have thought of this before. Ed wasn't going to be happy just being told that a part of him was with Jael. But she hadn't planned on actually removing him from the system. She didn't even know if it was possible. *Is it?* she asked the probe. *Can you take him, and not leave a copy behind?*

Do you wish total transfer and removal?

She hesitated. *Yes, I think so,* she thought nervously.

Wait.

She waited. Ed looked at her nervously. He seemed to loom closer. His eyes expanded again, his dark pupil swallowing the entire vision. And then it turned transparent, and the forest was visible again. But Ed wasn't. The branch upon which he had been perched was empty now. There was no evidence that Ed had even existed. "Ed?" she asked cautiously.

"Y-k-k-k," she heard. But the sound was from inside her mind. Looking around, she still saw no sign of the bird.

"Ed, where are you?"

"Gokk. Don't know. Here with you. Somewhere. Think. Awwrk."

Jael nodded to herself. She had done it now. There was no turning back. She took a deep breath and began walking along the path again. *Probe, no more removal. Copy only.* "Okay, Ed—I want you to watch what's happening if you can. Tell me if you see anything you want to take along with you. This will be your last chance."

Feeling more like a thief than a liberator, she moved through the forest, noting the most beautiful elements and tucking the images silently into her invisible pack.

Chapter 20
RETURN TO SPACE

IT TOOK less than three hours from the time Ar received a call, for them to meet and reach agreement with the master of the two-rigger ship. The ship was corporately owned, fully registered, and under the command of one Mariella Flaire, an affable businesswoman whose homeport was the same as the ship's next destination, a world named Vela Oasis. Flaire was a tall woman with rosy skin and silver-streaked reddish hair drawn back into a tight coif. She spoke with Ar and Jael for almost two hours, showing them the pertinent logs and reviewing their rigging performance records. Flaire seemed favorably impressed. Jael felt a passing urge to ask why she was even being considered for the job—she had, after all, killed her last captain—but Flaire addressed the question without being asked. Looking straight at Jael, she said, "You come well recommended by the police investigation team. They said that you know how to take care of yourself, and your psych-profile is good. I guess you had a tough flight last time."

Jael opened her mouth and closed it, staring at the woman. She seemed to be waiting for a reaction. Jael didn't know what to say, so she just swallowed and nodded. Flaire's eyebrows went up a fraction of an inch. "Is it safe to say that if I don't give you a hard time, you won't give me a hard time? Can we work together?"

For a moment, Jael felt her voice frozen in her throat. The last time she'd trusted a ship's captain . . .

But this isn't Mogurn. Ar trusts her, and Ar can read emotions better than I can. Something loosened in her voice then, and she heard herself saying, "Yes, ma'am. I'd like that a lot—to be able to work together. To cooperate." The words, in her mouth, sounded empty; but in truth, she meant them.

Flaire cracked a smile and turned her attention back to the records, nodding in apparent satisfaction. Jael remained silent after that, her heart thumping.

A short time later, Flaire granted them their commission, and they shook hands all around. They would be lifting off the next morning.

Starship *Seneca* was a tall, shiny craft, no larger then Jael's last ship, but with a steely, needlelike appearance that contrasted with *Cassandra*'s teardrop shape. Jael hoped, gazing up at it, that it would contrast in other ways, as well.

"It looks well kept," Ar remarked, standing with her on the ramp. "The maintenance log was quite complete."

Jael nodded. Her thoughts were scattered. She was thinking about the world they were setting sail for, and wondering how they would fare on it; she was thinking about rigging with Ar, and wondering what it would be like to have a partner in the net, after flying alone with Mogurn; she was thinking about Dap, whose gold chain she still carried. She was thinking about a bird whose personality and memories she carried in tiny data grains in her pocket; and she was thinking about Highwing. "Shall we board?" she murmured.

Ar hefted his bag, and together they strode up the ramp. A lift took them to the entry point, high on the ship's gleaming silver flank. Stepping aboard, they found the flight deck, bridge, and living quarters. The accommodations were arrayed along the ship's long axis, flanking a central hallway, with the bridge at one end and the commons at the other.

They went to the bridge first, to acquaint themselves with the layout.

They were not long on board before Mariella Flaire arrived to join them. She invited them to take their pick of the empty cabins, of which there were several, and disappeared after saying that she was ready for departure whenever they were.

It took them very little time to settle in, and by the time Flaire reappeared, they were completing the final checkout on the bridge. Jael was in the number two rigger-station, testing the Burnhardt neural network, while Ar monitored the systems from the external control. "Does the ship meet with your approval, riggers?" Flaire asked, standing at the rear of the bridge.

"Everything seems in order, Captain," answered Ar. "Jael, are we ready?"

Jael was half in and half out of the net. "Anytime," she answered, her voice coming out in a dreamy drawl. She withdrew from the net and lifted her head to peer at Flaire. "Do you have any special . . . requests . . . about the route?" she asked, remembering Mogurn and the mountains.

Flaire raised her eyebrows. "Just get me there safely. Do you have all the information you need?"

Ar responded from the forward end of the bridge. "We have everything provided by the library, Ma'am. And I myself have passed along this stretch more than once. I anticipate no problems."

Flaire nodded. "Make ready for the tow, then." She stepped to the com and called the spaceport dispatcher.

Hours later, when the tow released them to the darkness of space, Jael and Ar were waiting, poised to take the ship down into the currents of the Flux, visible from within the net as a soft layer of clouds beneath them. They grinned at each other across the winking traceries of the net, and when Flaire gave the okay, they reached out together and seized the cottony stuff of the Flux and drew the ship down into it.

The wispy clouds caressed them as the ship sank, and then

the Flux turned clear as a glassy sea. Jael and Ar became swimmers, stroking side by side through the water, dipping their arms in rhythm. After a time Ar dropped back a little, bringing up the rear with a smooth backstroke, while Jael took the lead. They had to cross a few shifting currents before they found one coursing in the desired direction, but from that point on, they made smooth and steady headway toward the distant shore of Vela Oasis.

Time passed quickly in the net, as did the leagues, miles, and kilometers of the Flux—all of those units of measure being equally irrelevant to the light-years of normal-space. They made good progress in their first hours, and in the sessions that followed, and they found that they were indeed well suited to working together. Ar had a deft touch in the net, and a good sense of stability, while Jael excelled in glimpsing changes in the stream and crafting new images to help them move smoothly through the changes. Jael adjusted quickly to sharing the net. If she occasionally missed her solitude, she felt more than compensated by the joys of mutual aid and challenge, of trading and sharing images with another.

The sea became a dancing stream, and they, fish darting in it. Later, the stream of water became a jet of golden oil coursing through a clear-walled pipeline, and they, a pair of bubbles joined at the waist to a larger billowing bubble sailing down the stream of oil. *Take care that we don't burst!* Ar laughed, as they quivered and stretched in the stream. And she answered, poking and testing at the limits of her bubble, *If we do, we'll just make ourselves over!* There was no real danger as long as the flow remained stable; the only thing they really had to watch for was a divergence or turbulence in the stream, which could indicate dangerous conditions developing along their course. So far, the way was smooth.

Out of the net, in the ship's commons, they talked of the route ahead and of the future. Jael felt a curious contentment in working with Ar, a kind of happiness she'd not felt in a long time. She was amazed to discover that they were growing steadily closer in friendship, and she wondered, had her life before this been so lonely that it could shock her to sense a true friendship developing? Did she dare trust what was happening? It was a disorienting prospect, growing close to this Clendornan; yet it was easier in a way than it might have been if he'd been human, and therefore more threatening.

Still, for all that they were comfortable together, she felt an awkwardness in discussing certain subjects with him . . . such as Highwing. She suspected that Ar simply did not like the thought of dragons. Several times he skillfully deflected their conversation away from the subject, or simply drifted off into a reverie, humming Clendornan chants. It was clear that he did not believe in the reality of her experience, though he soberly respected the effect that her *perceived* experience could have on her life. Eventually she gave up trying, and as the trip went on, her memory of the dragon realm blurred a little more around the edges, seeming ever less real, even to her. Alone in her cabin, she thought often of Highwing, but her memories had an increasingly dreamlike quality.

One worry she didn't have, and for which she was grateful, was whether her friendship with Ar would turn into something sexual, real or potential. While there was, physically speaking, nothing to prevent intimacy between a human woman and a Clendornan male, the urges didn't seem to arise, at least not as they did between the human sexes. Perhaps the reasons were biochemical, perhaps something else. It was a concern that she was relieved to be free of; she wasn't even of a mind for that sort of thing with a human male, had there been a suitable candidate around. She was content to spend long hours close to Ar, knowing that the bond growing between them was of the mind and the spirit, rather than of the body.

It wasn't until they were well into the flight that she seriously entertained the idea of releasing Ed from his cybernetic containment. Since she was a little uncertain how Ed would work out in the net, she'd held off until she and Ar had worked out their own rhythm of flying together, smoothing out minor differences in style, and until they had earned Flaire's confidence in their rigging. But by the fourth shipday of the journey, she felt ready to try.

It's okay with me, Ar said. *But will he know what to make of this landscape?* They had taken the form of great-winged birds, soaring over a softly rolling plain marked with patches of scrub.

Why don't you change it to something he might like, while I step outside and hook him in.

Ar agreed, and she left him flying while she withdrew from the net. She paused a moment, relaxing with deep breathing. They were already accustomed to working in overlapping shifts—sometimes rigging together, sometimes not—so there was no need to hurry. Once she felt back in her own body, she climbed out of the rigger-station and went to her cabin. She retrieved the data interface device containing Ed and brought it back to the bridge. Reclining on her couch, she peered overhead for an input socket to the rigger-net computer. After examining the clear plastic connector on her storage device, she plugged it in, then tested the connection. But she hesitated before returning to the net. She was eager to see Ed, yes . . . but a little nervous, as well. What if something had gone wrong in the capture process? Or what if it went wrong here? She wondered if she could accidentally terminate Ed by hooking him up incorrectly.

Quit worrying, she thought. *The ship could spring a leak, too, but you're not worried about that, are you?*

She closed her eyes and sank back into an awareness of the Flux. The landscape was changed, startlingly so. The scrub and the plains were gone. The currents of the Flux were flowing by in great literal streams, colored in gorgeous sunset hues of oranges and reds and golds. The ship itself was a small oasis floating in a sea of color: a tree anchored on an uprooted, flat-topped clump of earth, just large enough for the riggers to walk around on. Tree and ground, the entire oasis was gliding majestically through space. Ar was sitting cross-legged under the tree, seemingly lost in meditation. Both hands were pressed to the ridges high on the sides of his head; his luminous eyes were fixed straight ahead. He was humming soft, strange syllables, through pursed lips. He was humming several pitches simultaneously, with a result that could not be called harmonic.

Jael stepped carefully around the tree. *Let me know when I can talk*, she said softly.

Ar nodded almost imperceptibly; he was steering the ship from within his meditation. Jael sat beside him and enjoyed the view. After a time, the humming stopped, and she sensed him emerging from his solitude. He turned his head and smiled in crinkling fashion. *We're stabilized. Do you have him ready?*

I think so. Jael gestured at their surroundings. *What's all this?*

Do you like it? I thought we'd give him a tree, for starters, and keep everything else spare. We'll fill in as we need to.

Jael nodded. *Shall we let him out now?* She tried to keep the worry out of her voice and failed.

Ar tipped his head slightly. *Are you having second thoughts?*

Just afraid it won't work, that's all.

The Clendornan's eyes widened, luminous and expectant. He nodded slowly.

Jael worried her lips together. *Well, here goes then.* She closed her eyes and reached back into the system, nudging the controls with her thoughts. Opening her eyes, she extended a hand and gestured upward into the tree.

There was a shimmer in the lowest branch, and a flicker of emerald green, then a squawk—but no parrot. *Ed?* she called.

Yawk! said the branch.

I can't see you. Do you see us?

The branch rustled, and the parrot's head appeared, disembodied. *Jayl? Jayl? Brawwww!* it shrieked, turning to and fro, trying to locate her. Jael started to call out again, when the parrot-head finally tilted down and spied her. *Yawk! Jayl!* The head hopped forward, and as it did so, the rest of the body emerged, apparently from thin air. Ed stretched his wings and tail-feathers wide. Trilling in wonder, he peered around. *DID IT! Yawk! You did it! Did you do it?*

Jael grinned up at him. *Looks like I did, Ed. I wasn't sure until now.* She beamed at Ar. *Thanks, Ar.*

Yow! Where—b-b-rawk—where are we?

How do I explain that to a parrot? she wondered.

She didn't have to. Ar replied, *We're about halfway between where we were when we met you, and where we're going to be.* When that elicited only a puzzled craning of the neck from the bird, he added, *You're a rigger now, Ed. We're between the stars, but what you're seeing is something that only we riggers see.*

Ed made a creaking noise deep in his throat and hopped down from the branch with a flutter of scarlet on green. He paced up and down the strip of ground between Jael and Ar, and looked from one to the other? *Rigger?* he crowed. *Rigger?*

That's right, Ed. Be prepared to see a lot of things you would never have imagined, Ar said.

Rigger! Braaw-w-k! No kidding!

No kidding, said Jael.

The parrot cocked his head and peered up at her with a glistening dark eye. He made a swallowing movement, seemingly speechless. He peered at Ar. He hopped forward to the edge of the flying wafer of earth they were riding on, and peered over the edge, at the streaming currents of space. With a shiver, he stepped back. He flapped his wings and hopped up onto Jael's knee. *Long way down,* he said, clacking his beak.

Long way, Jael agreed.

Ar, crinkling a smile, extended a hand toward their direction of flight. He closed his eyes and did something. The earth, the tree, and the riggers came gently to a new heading and picked up speed.

Chapter 21
PARROT RIGGER

MARIELLA FLAIRE joined them in the commons that evening. They had seen little of her since the trip had begun; she seemed to have had her own work to do, which kept her in her cabin much of the time. But now she wanted to know how her riggers were faring in the journey.

Ar and Jael glanced at each other over their dinner plates. Jael wondered, should she tell the captain that they had loosed a parrot in the rigger-net? There was nothing unusual about riggers bringing helpful data-additions into the net, but most riggers didn't bring in *live* additions. Flaire seemed to sense their unspoken communication. "You both look pretty happy with yourselves," she observed. "Does that mean it's going well?"

Ar and Jael nodded together. "Progress is fine. We're right on schedule," Ar said, sparing Jael the need to decide how to answer.

"That's encouraging. So you haven't had any problems? You will let me know if you do?" Flaire looked from one to the other, with a bemused smile. "Is it my imagination, or are you both being awfully quiet?"

Jael stirred self-consciously. It was a good-humored query, and yet she found the unwelcome memory of Mogurn and his suspicions crowding into her thoughts. For an instant, her head was filled with her past warring with her present. Ar, however, was already answering Flaire's question. "I think we're both remembering some of the imagery from the net," he said. "Sometimes it stays with us afterwards. Ordinarily we don't discuss it on the outside. But we can, if you wish—"

Flaire raised a hand to stop him. "Not necessary. I don't believe in interfering with the work of my crew, beyond expecting an honest accounting of progress, or of problems, if you're having any." Her gaze shifted to Jael. "And you're not having any. Is that correct?"

Jael nodded emphatically, forcing a smile onto her face. "Yes," she said, clearing her throat. "We're working together quite well. And the route so far has been smoother than we could have hoped for."

"Good. Then I'll leave you to it." Flaire rose from the table, disposed of her own dishes and, wishing them a good evening, retired to her cabin.

Jael sighed, glancing at Ar. He grinned, in his crinkle-faced way, and after a time, she felt her tension melt away like snow on a sunny day.

The next morning, back in the net, they woke Ed from the storage device to join them in flight. Jael instructed him to stay clear of their manipulations of the Flux, but the warning seemed unnecessary. Ed appeared content to perch and watch, perhaps rustling around from time to time, but generally staying out of the way.

At least, that was how the day started.

The first difficulty came when Jael tried to bring a piece of Ed's rainforest into the net. They were only a few shipdays shy of Vela Oasis, and their path was laid out before them in a glorious spangle of celestial highways and galactic whirlpools, a romantic's vision of the universe, a grand vista of exploding light that took Jael's breath away. They moved through the vision in a stately waltz, their ship a small garden in a bubble gliding upward along a luminous milky path. Their movement, and the image of the garden, seemed stable enough to risk letting a few elements of Ed's original environment into the net.

Try just a little at a time, and we'll smooth out the wrinkles while we fly, Ar suggested, taking up a position in front.

Rrrick-k-k! Yes!

Jael quickly discovered, however, that there was no simple way to introduce the rainforest gradually. Ed himself was a special case; he had been partitioned by the storage device as the "primary matrix." But bringing in something like a single tree was not so simple. The ambient environment was stored ingeniously and compactly, but not conveniently for limited retrieval. As she probed the storage medium, she felt like a child groping blindly in a magician's bag, wondering what her fingers were touching. After a minute, she decided she might as well create the image and put it to use. A black satin bag materialized in front of her.

Yawk! Good, good, Ed chortled, hopping down to a low, surrealistic-looking bush so that he could peer at whatever was coming out.

Stay back, now, Jael warned. She glanced around. Ar was seated on a large rock, steering their course by shifting his body weight from side to side. He was humming, as usual, a raspy, vaguely dissonant tune. A flurry of sparkling things flew by, carried on the gentle breeze made by their headway. The objects were probably Flux analogs of accreting heavenly bodies in formation—planets or asteroids, perhaps. *Seneca* was bypassing a region of space that was heavy with star and planetary formation. Flux abscess—a dangerous distortion of the continuum—could occasionally be a concern in such regions, but all the indications looked safe. *Okay?* she called.

Yes, we're in the clear, Ar said, barely interrupting his humming. *See that cluster up ahead?* He pointed to a distant patch of light at the end of a long, twisty pathway. *That's Vela Oasis. We're already homing in.*

Jael nodded. She reached into the magician's bag. Ed clucked and craned his neck, bobbing his head like a pigeon, trying to see. *Here goes*, she murmured, feeling something on her fingertips. She drew it forth; with a glint of light, something unfolded into three-dimensionality—then seemed to vanish. An instant later, there was a great fluttering around her head, and she ducked down, startled. The air overhead was filled with leaves, all suspended in midair, and clustered in the shape of a tree. *Good grief*, she muttered, as Ed squawked in delight and puzzlement. Where was the rest of the tree—the branches and trunk? She probed in the bag again. Something large and cold unfolded into the net.

Hrrawwk! Ed cried.

Jael scowled. It was a damp stone face, with four sticky lizard's feet, without the lizard, walking up its side. This was not helping. She felt a breeze on her face and glanced up just in time to see the suspended leaves blow away on the wind.

Tree gone, Ed announced.

So I noticed, she sighed. Now what? She reached into the bag once more and drew out a long tree branch. There was a small cluster of leaves at its tip, and a pair of bright red lionflies stretching their wings.

Ed leaped from his perch and dived toward the insects. *Hawwwwwk! Eat!*

Ed, wait! Her cry came too late. The parrot shot past the lionflies as they fluttered up into the air, over her head. *Ed!* The parrot banked and circled, pursuing the two bright morsels. They dodged nimbly through the air, fleeing higher and higher, and Ed pursued energetically, seemingly undaunted by the panoply of galaxies reigning overhead.

Jael watched anxiously. How far could they range out of the center of the net without upsetting Ar's stable flight? *Ed, come back!* she pleaded.

Ar stopped humming and turned his head. *Is anything wrong? We're coming up on a divide, and we'll need to keep it steady.*

Uh-oh, Jael breathed. Ed was now almost to the edge of the bubble that surrounded them in their idyllic garden. If he went much higher . . .

She felt a shudder as the parrot rebounded, squawking,

from the bubble's edge. That answered one question; he was as "real" in this net as the riggers, and despite his small size, he could rock the net with surprising leverage. *Ed, get back down here!* she shouted. But the parrot was too preoccupied to pay attention.

Jael, I need help, Ar murmured, his voice hardening with greater urgency. *We've got to get past this divide, and we're veering.*

Jael felt a moment of faintness. Veering off course, because of Ed? *Is it that bad? He didn't hit us that hard, did he?* She reached out to assist Ar, but not before another jolt rocked the net. They were losing their fine control. Terrific, she thought—and we told Mariella we were doing so well. Foolishly, for an instant, she allowed her thoughts to dwell, not on how to deal with the problem but on having to report it to her captain. The memory of Mogurn rose in her thoughts, looking angry and spiteful. Damn you—get out! she thought. You are no longer my captain! Mariella Flaire is my captain now!

She reached out, fusing her strength with Ar's.

Ar was busy trying to untangle the forces in the splitting stream of milky light. They were on the wrong side, in the left-hand stream; the one to the right was already curving away, and diverging fast. *If we can just slip across—*

Ar's words were interrupted by a metamorphosis in the starscape in front of them, an enormous face materializing in the sky, looking sideways but turning to face them as it became three-dimensional and solid. It was the face of Mogurn, raging. His eyes were mad with hatred. *My God*—Jael whispered. She tried to choke off her own breath, but it was out already—her terror was out in the net. Could Mogurn have survived somehow and returned to seek his revenge?

No, surely it's impossible . . .

Mogurn loomed closer. The ship, the garden, the bubble began to turn and list. Jael knew that her fear was the worst thing to allow in the net right now, but she couldn't stop her terror as Mogurn leered and drew close enough to reach . . .

Jael, get rid of that—!

Ar's call was drowned out by Ed's: *Y-y-aaaarrr-w-w-k-k!*

The parrot came plummeting down, landing on Jael's shoulder with a mad flutter of wings. His claws gripped her like iron, but his wings flapped in panic. *Arr-arr-arr-arr-arrkkk!*

Ed, stop it! she hissed. But she knew the reason for his terror. It was her own, radiating, distorting the energy balance of the net. *Ed, it's just . . . it can't be . . .* But she really wasn't sure anymore. Could he have survived, somehow, with his hatred and his lust for domination? Who knew what was possible in the Flux?

Jael, it's not real! Ar shouted, as he struggled to keep the ship under control. Angry tremors were shaking the net; the heavens were swarming threateningly around them. They were beginning to spin.

Not real, Jael forced herself to think. Not real. She drew in a great breath and rose up suddenly to confront the face of Mogurn. Her breath escaped in an angry exhalation, and the face slowly became . . . transparent . . . then vanished. The tremors began to die away at once. *He's gone,* she reported, ashamed of having endangered the ship by allowing a careless memory-image into the net. Mogurn was not here threatening vengeance, and never had been.

She closed her eyes and whispered, *Ed—shhhhh. It's all right, calm down.* She was talking to herself as much as to the parrot, but she felt his nails easing their grip on her shoulder.

Rarrk, Ed murmured, kneading her shoulder gently. *What . . . Jayl . . . what happened?*

She gasped as her heartbeat finally slowed. *It was something . . . that once terrified me. I don't know if I can explain it. But there's no need to be afraid now. Ar . . . I'm really sorry.* Unhappily, she squinted to focus on the stars. *How do we stand?*

Regaining control, Ar replied. The rotation of the sky was stopping as he stabilized the net. *I'm afraid that we are now off course. And I'm not, immediately, quite sure how to get us back on.*

The wind blowing through the garden seemed cooler and damper now. Jael shivered, looking off and down to starboard. The current that they had lost was still visible as a streamer curving off into the distance. *It's a bad break,* Ar said. *If it hadn't all come just as we were hitting that divergence, we could have taken it in stride.* He was clearly unhappy, but wasn't laying blame. He didn't have to.

Ed twisted his neck, looking anxiously from one to the other. *We do wrong?* he croaked in a thin, frightened rasp. *Ed do wrong?*

Jael closed her eyes. *No, Ed. I mean . . . that is, we both did something wrong. It's not your fault. But . . . in the future . . . we can't have you flying around wildly like you were a minute ago. That makes it harder for us to keep control.*

Ruk-k-k. Didn't mean to, the parrot said mournfully.

I know. You didn't. She glanced at Ar, who was righting them on the stream and examining various alternatives for getting them back over to the correct current. *It was more my doing. My carelessness. When I got scared by that face, you did, too.*

K-k-k-scared. Not now.

Jael nodded, dismissing the subject. She needed to help Ar with the navigation. Without speaking, she gazed out into the spangled light against the dark, trying to spy out a route that might take them toward the hazy patch that was their destination. It was visibly receding from them now, or seemed to be. *There must be some way to get back over there.*

Ar crooned a stuttering tune to himself. *We might have to take a long way around.*

While Jael was thinking about that, a shudder passed through the net and something flashed over their heads like a meteor. She ducked instinctively. It was a good reminder: they were passing close to some disturbances in the nearby layers of normal-space. There was no cause for panic, but one thing was certain: they should try to move clear, to avoid the risk of more serious trouble. *Ar, maybe we'd better change this for a fresh perspective.*

Ar's luminous eyes looked to her, awaiting suggestions.

Her mind went blank for a moment, then she drew a deep breath and took control of the net from him. The night sky full of wonders disappeared, and a tremendous crystal of frozen water appeared in its place. They were surrounded by clear ice, stretching to infinity. It was shot through with hairline cracks, white and silver traceries that meandered through the icy realm, betraying flaws and boundary layers and points of stress. They were moving through one such flaw in the ice, like a microscopic creature floating through a fine sievework of melted ice in the heart of a glacier. Off to their left, a cluster of dirty spots in the ice betrayed the locations of nearby gravitational disturbances. Tiny cracks emanating from that region crossed their own pathway, especially ahead, where the cracks became dangerously dense. They could steer clear of the hazard by sinking deeper. As one, they stretched out the net and angled the ship gently downward.

Jael peered off to the starboard, toward their original route. If only they could move backward, against the current, to rejoin it . . . but that was impossible. Farther ahead, the correct path branched with fine traceries like the fernlike shape of ice crystals forming out of liquid water. It seemed so close to them, and yet so far out of reach. She couldn't quite tell where it led, or visualize their ultimate destination through the ice. *Ar, can you see anything?*

The Clendornan was shaking his head, as another voice broke in: *Excuse me for interrupting. May I speak without disturbing you?*

Ms. Flaire? Ar asked.

Yes. I felt dizzy, several times—and thought I felt the ship shaking. Is there any trouble?

Ar's luminous eyes met Jael's, before he answered, *We had some difficulty, yes. But we are out of immediate danger.*

The answering voice carried a distinct note of worry. *Out of immediate danger? Does that mean there is still a problem?*

Jael felt a flash of annoyance, and an unreasoning urge to tell Flaire that they could straighten it out faster without her interference. Didn't she know that they were the riggers— not her? Jael struggled to control the thought; she knew it to be irrational, an echo of Mogurn.

Yes, Ar said, seeing that Jael was keeping her silence. *There is a problem, still. But not a serious one, we hope. We are having to choose a somewhat different course. We experienced turbulence and momentary loss of control. But we've stabilized the situation.*

Rawk, Ed interjected. *Right.*

What was that?

Ar met Jael's glance of alarm and said, *That was Ed. He's an enhancement we're using. We'll . . . be able to tell you more, a little later.*

There was a pause, before Flaire answered, *Very well. You are the riggers, and I'll leave you to your work. Enhancements and all. But please remember—I'll want a full accounting.*

Of course, Ar replied. *But just now we need to focus on correcting our course.*

With what seemed to Jael a grudging acknowledgment, Flaire terminated contact with the net. Jael looked at Ar and said, *What do we do now?* then she thought bitterly, *Why are you asking him? Aren't you a rigger, too?*

Ar's clear eyes seemed to track over her face, evaluating what he saw there. *Jael, you can't rig properly if you're feeling angry. Or guilty.*

Damn it—I know that! she snapped, her frustration finally erupting into the net. *I can't help it. That's just the way Mogurn was, watching over every little move I made.* She felt herself flushing; she was being unreasonable, and knew it. But she couldn't help resenting Flaire's intrusion.

Ar hummed dissonantly for a moment. He reached out a long-fingered hand and tickled Ed's neck. The parrot stirred, opening one eye at the Clendornan. *If you're feeling guilty because of letting Ed in, don't.*

Arkk. Right.

Jael fumed. *That's not it!* But wasn't it? she thought. If not, why was she reacting so strongly?

Jael, she was within her rights to inquire. I thought she was actually quite restrained about it, considering that she felt the whole ship shaking.

Taking a breath, Jael tried to voice her agreement, and couldn't. Once more she found Mogurn returning to her thoughts; she forced the memory away with an extreme effort of will.

Ar touched her arm with his long, delicate fingers. *Jael, do you trust me?*

She was startled. *Yes. Of course I do.*

Then trust me now. His luminous purple eyes focused on hers. *I am no expert in Human relations, but one thing I am sure* of. *You have to decide whether to trust people and work with them, or not. And if disturbing memories linger from someone you've trusted mistakenly, then you just have to let go of them.*

She closed her eyes. *I can't just make my feelings go away.*

No. Perhaps you cannot erase them, but you can learn to manage them. You can decide not to let them interfere with your work, or with the way that you react to people who are innocent.

She gazed at him for what seemed a very long time. It was probably only a few seconds. Then she felt something pushing at her hand. It was Ed, nuzzling her knuckles. She laughed, despite herself, and stroked his back. She felt her tension slowly easing. *Okay,* she said, with a sigh. *I would have gotten over it anyway, you know. But thanks, I guess.* She looked beyond Ar, to the realm of their flight. Ice, in infinite dimensions of distance. *Now, hadn't we better decide what we're going to do?*

Ar nodded, turning. He gazed into the ice for some time without speaking. Jael tried to visually trace out the distant pathways, but it was difficult to determine where they ultimately led. Ed tiptoed around, peering hopefully.

It appears to me that there's a large body of water between us and where we want to go, Ar reported. Jael saw what he was pointing at: an area of blurriness, or refraction, which upon closer scrutiny seemed to be an enormous pocket of water in the heart of the ice. At least, it was a boundary layer of some sort, and their destination was on the far side of it.

Can we pass through it, do you think?

The question is whether we can get to it. Ar traced out the melt-flaw they were moving in now, and while it seemed to meander in the general direction of the water boundary, it was impossible to tell whether it actually came into contact with it.

Jael immersed her hands in the current of icy cold water. *There's only one way to tell, isn't there?*

Ar agreed, and together they bent the ship's course, seeking a downward flow into the fracture.

The curvature of the flaw was clearly visible now, and it was evident that it turned away from the water boundary.

They were so close to the boundary that the feeling of frustration was almost palpable in the net. An apparently impenetrable layer of ice separated them from the liquid sea that might otherwise carry them toward Vela Oasis. Vela itself was visible as a shimmering mirage-like goal on the far side of the watery deep.

What if we change the image? Ar suggested.

The structure is there in the Flux, Jael said doubtfully. *We can try, but I don't know what good it can really do.* Still, they were now drifting past what seemed the closest approach they would make to the water layer. If there was anything they couldn't see because of the peculiarities of the image, now might be the time to try something new.

Yawk, yawk! Ed sputtered, hopping in front of her. *Go now! Go now!*

Jael frowned at him. *What are you talking about?*

Now! Now! Let me! Cawww! Go for break! For broke!

Ed don't—Jael began, then paused. The bird was really quite agitated. He was stalking to and fro, peering down in the direction that they wanted to go. *Do you see something we don't?* Was it possible that the bird's eyes and instincts could show them a way that they might miss themselves?

Ar rubbed the ridge on the side of his head, looking thoughtfully at the bird. *Ed? What do you mean?*

The parrot beat his scarlet-feathered wings, launching himself up over their heads. He was a brilliant flash of emerald and red, darting back and forth. *Brawwwwk-k-k! Ed can get you there! Let Ed do it! Now! Now!*

Ar's luminous eyes showed no more certainty than Jael felt, but if there was any way . . .

Okay, Ed, she said nervously. *I don't know what you have in mind, but you can try it. But be careful!*

YAWWWWWWK-K-K! The parrot flashed upward, spiraling high above them. *Yes, I do it,* came his voice, thin with distance.

But what is he doing? Ar asked.

Jael didn't answer. She watched Ed reach the peak of his upward arc, watched him flip over into a dive. *My God,* she thought. The parrot was hurtling downward like a rocket, toward them . . . toward the bottom of the net . . .

Toward the layer of ice.

Did Ed know what he was doing? He couldn't possibly understand . . . could the net withstand the stress he was about to put on it?

She started to scream to Ed, to tell him to pull out—then changed her mind and shouted to Ar to let go of the tension, to allow as much slack in the net as they possibly could. She felt the net loosen and slip—

SCREEE-AAIIIEEEE-E-E-E-E . . . !

Ed flashed down past them, down. The net stretched. Jael had an afterimage in her mind of Ed's beak outthrust like a battering ram. Ed and the ice layer converged, and he hit the ice with a concussion like a thunderclap—and the ice shattered, a heavy pane of crystal breaking into fragments that tumbled away from the impact point. A hole appeared behind him as he dived deep into the water below.

Jael gazed down in astonishment and heard the parrot's voice distantly calling, *Jayl . . . Ar . . . follow . . . follow. . . .* The parrot turned, circling at the utter extremity of the net.

For the barest fraction of a second, Jael and Ar exchanged glances of disbelief; then, combining their powers, they re-shaped the net and pitched the ship downward on the path blazed by Ed. The Flux itself had been altered, as water from their channel flowed slowly into the opening Ed had created. The ship moved sluggishly, at the best speed they could coax from it. *Hold on!* she called to Ed. *Don't tear the net!*

Hurry . . . hurry . . . came the distant reply.

Ice was already beginning to form again, to close off the opening. They reached the hole just as it contracted to the ship's size, or perhaps a little smaller. *Gather it in!* Ar shouted, drawing the net in close on the sides. It helped, but they were still too large; and they hit the opening with a CRUNNNCH, and a grating sound, as they slowed. Jael kicked out to the side, hard, and something gave way—and they slid free.

They were through, gliding downward into the icy clear waters.

Ed spiraled up, swimming gracefully. With a shriek, he popped up into the bubble and perched between them, neck twisting this way and that, as though he were trying to look everywhere at once. *Yawk, yawk! We did it? We did it?*

We did it, Ed! You did it! Jael hooted.

The parrot clucked, clacking his beak. *Good! Good! Yuck-yuck! Yup!* And with a great happy sigh, he fell silent and watched as Jael and Ar turned their full attention to rerigging the ship.

Slowly they oriented themselves and spied the distant hazy form of their destination. Now they had only to locate the best current in these waters, but already they were moving in the right direction. Behind them, the realm of ice was receding into memory, and the way ahead appeared clear and true.

Chapter 22
VELA OASIS

"I'M HAPPY to report that we should be arriving ahead of schedule," Ar announced, as Ms. Flaire joined them in the commons. Jael had already eaten half her dinner; she was starving, after what they had been through today.

Flaire lifted a decanter to pour herself a glass of wine. She paused in the middle of the motion. "Ahead of schedule? I thought we were in trouble. In fact, since I spoke with you earlier, I thought I felt another—"

Ar's nod cut off her words. His voice rumbled deep in his throat, and Jael recognized a tone of humor. "What you felt was us making a readjustment in the options that were available to us." Flaire frowned in puzzlement, and Ar explained, "We passed through a boundary layer—truthfully, with more success than we expected—and we located quite a strong and steady current toward Vela Oasis. Our destination is now well in sight."

Flaire's eyebrows went up as she tipped the decanter and poured a small glass of ruby-colored wine. "Just like that?" With a gesture, she inquired if either of them would like a glass. Jael blinked, and nodded emphatically.

"Well, it wasn't quite that simple," Ar conceded.

Flaire poured for Jael. "I imagine not. Are you certain you don't want any?"

"No, thank you. One of us needs to stay clear."

Flaire nodded and held her glass to the light, rotating it by its stem. "So. Are you going to tell me about Ed?" She smiled wryly. "I thought you might fill me in on the nature of the problem that you had?" Her gaze shifted from one to the other.

Ar glanced at Jael and said, a trifle less confidently, "Yes . . . Ed. Well—"

Jael cleared her throat. "Never mind, Ar. I'll explain it." She felt her voice tighten, and she took a small sip of wine, determined to tell the story without regret or self-consciousness. Ed, after all, had proved himself quite a rigger in the clutch. "Ed," Jael said finally, "is a parrot . . ."

Ms. Flaire's eyebrows rose again, higher than before.

The Vela Oasis starport loomed before them like a great golden-spired city on the horizon. Starship *Seneca* was a raft on a fast-flowing river flanked by gently rolling green hills. They all clung to the raft as they were swept along by the current, Ed perched firmly on Jael's shoulder.

The trip was nearly over.

Only a few hours later, they brought the ship spiraling out of the Flux, into the starry night. Floating in interplanetary space, they put in a call for a tow. Then they had some time to rest and plan what they wanted to do after planetfall.

Ar was in favor of getting back into space again as soon as possible. "After having a look around Vela Oasis, of course," he said, as they relaxed in his cabin. He was fiddling with a small music synth, producing an appalling series of arhythmic sounds, pulsing with strong, semiharmonic beats. Jael had come to realize that Ar's ideas about music were considerably different from her own; it was something she was going to have to learn to put up with. Oblivious to her occasional winces, Ar continued, "Once you're doing well, it's best to keep working if you can, I think. At least until you've established a good record." He added sheepishly, "I've never managed to get more than two flights in a row, myself. But with any luck, Ms. Flaire may ask us to keep rigging for her." He silenced his synth and peered at her, his eyes sparkling with hints of gold in the purple webbing of his retinas. He stroked his head-ridges with his fingertips. "Of course, you might feel differently. Maybe you don't want to."

Jael laughed. "Is that your way of asking if I'd like to keep rigging with you? The answer is yes." As Ar's lips crinkled, her thoughts turned inward again. She wasn't really thinking of the immediate future so much as the long term. Aware of Ar's curious stare, she sighed and murmured, "I was just thinking about . . . Highwing. And wishing I could fly that way again some time." Her lips twitched with a wistful smile. Truthfully, though, it was not just Highwing but also the pallisp that had been fluttering through her mind. Nearly this entire flight has passed without her thinking of the pallisp, and even when she had thought of it, she'd only felt vague flutterings of desire. That was a comforting realization.

"Highwing," Ar echoed. The room light angled into his face as he tilted his head, and reflected brightly from the violet filaments deep in his eyes. His mood seemed to turn pensive. "Highwing is still very real to you, isn't he?"

"Yes, Ar, of course he is. You still don't believe—"

"I was surprised," Ar said, interrupting, "by what Ed was able to do today. Cracking the ice like that. I was surprised that such a thing, such a change to the Flux, was possible."

Jael sighed in exasperation. "What's that got to do with—"

"I'm trying to say that I'm not sure anymore what is possible and what isn't," Ar said. A faraway look came into his eyes. "I'm not saying that I'm convinced, and I don't think one should go flying into dangerous places without good reason. But"—his gaze flickered back to Jael—"I appreciate your feelings. Your desires."

"Ah."

"Even if I don't . . . share them, exactly."

Jael nodded, gratified to have achieved that much progress, at least. "Right. I know. Still . . ." She let the thought go, with a shrug. "Mariella hasn't hinted to you whether she wants us to stay on, has she?"

Ar shook his head. "She seems happy with us. But no, not yet."

And that, Jael reflected, was the bottom line. They couldn't choose their future when they didn't know what their choices were. For now, it was just a matter of waiting. Of flying into a new port, and waiting.

But that, she thought, was the life of a rigger. The life that riggers everywhere accepted as normal . . . even if it felt anything but normal to her.

Mariella Flaire was little in evidence during the rest of the flight into Vela Oasis. Jael noted from the bridge, though, that there was a good deal of communications activity between Flaire's cabin on *Seneca* and the planetside network. Business activity, she presumed, though they knew little of the nature of Flaire's business. During the tow, she and Ar contented themselves with watching the growing ball of the approaching world, an ocher-and-green planet with thin, wispy clouds. They passed some of the time trying to devise a method for letting Ed out into the spaceship proper, so that he wouldn't be confined to the net. But once it became clear that the required holotronic circuitry wasn't on board, they postponed the effort.

It was only as they were on final approach orbit that Flaire appeared on the bridge. "I apologize for the long silence," she announced, "but I've been tied up with some rather difficult negotiations planetside." She rubbed her fingers together uneasily. "I'd hoped to be able to continue on directly from here, with you two as my crew—if you were willing—on a series of rather tightly scheduled stops. But . . ."

Jael's heart sank.

". . . I'm afraid I'm going to be held up here for a while with some bureaucratic problems. Nothing to do with you, or this ship and its cargo, but it could wreak havoc with my schedule. However," she looked up suddenly, intently, "I've been quite favorably impressed with your handling of this ship, and with your forthrightness and dependability."

So you'll give us a good recommendation? Jael almost said aloud.

"So with that in mind, I have a proposal for the two of you."

"Yes?" Ar murmured.

"I'd like to retain you to rig a four-system circuit, following my original schedule. You would be flying alone, while I stayed on Oasis. Your last stop would be back here. At that time we could discuss future arrangements, if everything in the meantime has worked out satisfactorily." She paused, looking uneasy. She seemed to feel out of place on the bridge, as though uncomfortable with the trappings of star piloting.

Jael noticed this in a disconnected sort of way, because her own thoughts were spinning in astonishment. Had Flaire just asked them to take charge of her ship and rig with it, just the two of them, for an entire series of flights? She looked at Ar. His gaze was unperturbed, as though he had been expecting this all along, but she knew he'd expected no such thing. It was not unheard of for riggers to be put in sole charge of the ships they flew, but it was uncommon. Usually, it happened to riggers with considerably more experience.

"You can take some time to decide," Flaire said. "I realize that this may put more of a burden of responsibility on you than you would care to take on. But it's important to me that these flights be made on schedule. I trust the two of you, and I don't have anyone on Oasis whom I would care to put in command over you."

"Thank you," Ar murmured.

"Do you need some time alone to discuss it?"

Ar and Jael glanced at each other and nodded. Flaire, looking vaguely relieved, left them on the bridge.

"She seems preoccupied by this corporate problem," Ar said.

Jael nodded. "But what an offer!"

"Yes." Ar's eyes rotated to look at her. "It sounds attractive. But two cautions come to mind. We don't know the situation; but suppose that, by the time we return to pick her up, her business turns out to have fallen on hard times."

"We might not get paid. Is that what you're saying?"

"Just that it's a possibility. Personally, I believe that she is an honest woman, and that it's a risk worth taking. What do you think?"

"I think so, too. But you said two cautions."

"Oh, yes. Well, just that . . . we have never flown together without a captain to provide backup stability, and to take ultimate responsibility for the ship, which is no small thing."

Certainly, that was true, Jael thought. And they were not without their own weaknesses as riggers, as they had learned on this flight. But, remembering the kinds of captains they *could* find themselves serving under, she was inclined to take on the responsibility, if their employer found them worthy of it. "I don't think we should turn down an opportunity like this," she said finally. "It might never come again."

Ar studied her for a moment, considering.

"Although," she added, as an afterthought, "I guess I would want to know what we'd be carrying." She thought Flaire was honest, too, but she remembered Mogurn and his illegal cargoes.

"Agreed. But if the cargo's satisfactory. . . ?"

Jael smiled. "Let's give her a call, shall we? I want to fly."

By the time they landed on Vela Oasis, they had a new contract with Flaire and a tentative flight schedule. Their ground time on Oasis would be short—just a day and a half, enough time to service the ship and to offload their cargo of commercial data grains and semiprecious crystalloids, and to reload with a manifest of local art and light-tech products. Soon they would be on their way again. That suited Jael. She was curious enough about the world before them, but more than that, she was eager to be on to her next rigging challenge.

The city of Carnelius on Vela Oasis was a noisy and exotic place, one that reminded Jael of the lore of the ancient Middle East on Homeworld Earth, long before Humankind had first set out for the stars. There were outdoor bazaars, jewelry merchants, and street after street of brightly bannered buildings crowded with shops and trading malls selling textiles, carpets, fine stones, holo-art and hard-art, and goods of every sort. Everyone seemed to be selling, but Jael couldn't quite figure out where all of the buyers came from. Offworlders, probably. Bargaining and bartering seemed to be the norm here.

Jael had real spending money now, for the first time since she'd left Gaston's Landing, but she felt reluctant to spend much of it on goods and fineries. With Ar, however, she searched the holotronic supply houses for devices to enable them to project Ed into the ship. They found that and more. Entering one shop specializing in environment enhancements, they found themselves in a grove of exotic plants and sculptures, ranging from solid "smellies" to sparkling translucent "impressions" that glowed and twisted in the air. Jael was enchanted by a holographic aviary, in which breathtakingly colored birds flitted in and out of nothingness and swooped over their heads or perched and sang out their courting songs. "Ar—" she whispered, "do you think Ed might like some birds for company?" Even as she said it, she wondered if they could possibly afford something like that, anyway.

Ar, studying one of the birds, bent to murmur something to it. The bird squawked and flew away. Ar straightened. "I don't think they're smart enough," he said. "They don't seem to be talkers."

Probably just as well, Jael thought. Ed might feel territorial about his position aboard the ship. And the ship's owner might feel strange about having her ship overrun by holographic birds. Jael turned to leave the store, but paused when she glimpsed an unusual tree in a corner of the grove. It was small and delicately shaped, like a bonsai; its branches were dusted with gold, and its leaves shone with a pale inner glow that seemed to brighten as she approached. She gazed at it with delight. "How much?" she asked the shopkeeper.

He was a tiny man, just like the tree. "It is a rare one, no?" he beamed. "It is a limited edition, a *stondai*. I sold one only slightly less beautiful last week for three hundred cassaccas. But I can see that you appreciate it for more than its outward novelty. I would only ask from you"—he made a small supplicating gesture with his fingers—"two hundred fifty. For the chippette. Have you a projector?"

"We do," Ar said, indicating the parcel under his arm. Jael leaned close to Ar and asked how much two hundred fifty cassaccas was. He closed his eyes, calculating, and told her. She blanched. "Bargain him down," Ar suggested.

Jael sighed. What did she know about bargaining? She was innocent of such skills. Well . . . She took a breath and said to the shopkeeper, "Yes. Well . . . I like it very much, yes. But I do think, ah . . . that it's . . . ah, a trifle too much, really. Would you consider, maybe"—she coughed delicately—"*less*?"

The man studied her gravely. He seemed frozen in place. Suddenly he flashed a smile and nodded, with the barest movement of his head. "You are indeed a careful shopper," he murmured. "I suppose I could let you have it for—oh, dear—perhaps for two twenty-five. That would be—well, the best I can do, really." His face tightened as though he were reconsidering. "I . . . yes." He sighed. "I think I could let it go for two twenty-five. Yes."

Jael gazed at the tree, agonizing. Ar's hand, inconspicuous at his side, was making a pushing-down motion. She swallowed, and her voice seemed to freeze in her throat. "I, um—" She coughed again. "Two fifteen?" she squawked, her voice cracking like Ed's.

"Oh!" The shopkeeper's face looked pained. "Oh—my—" He didn't move for a very long time; he just stared at the tree. Then he sighed deeply. "Yes," he whispered. "Yes, we do need the business." He looked up and smiled faintly.

Jael felt a pang. Was she being unfair? But it was still a lot of money, for a data grain. She glanced at Ar; he shrugged. "Okay," she said. Ed, I sure hope you like it.

Jael was quiet as they left the store, the small case in her pocket. Ar finally broke the silence. "What's the matter? It's a very beautiful tree. It will look fine on the ship."

She nodded, striding through the mall. "I got taken, didn't I?" she said at last, stopping to face him. Suddenly she felt very young, foolish, and incompetent.

Ar's lips crinkled. "Do you like it? Was it worth it to you?"

She laughed and didn't answer, except to herself. *Oh, I hope so. . . .*

On the way back to the ship, Ar stopped at a booth and purchased a new music synth; one that apparently made *only* discordant sounds. Jael stood by, trying to be encouraging, trying not to wince as he sounded a few bars for her. "I will play it only in private," Ar promised with a chuckle, putting it in his pocket.

Before they reached the spaceport, she found her interest in buying had fully awakened, and she returned to the ship carrying two beautifully dyed blouses. Undoubtedly, she'd paid more for them than she might have if she'd bargained more skillfully, but she no longer cared.

Later, Ar talked her into returning to the city for an evening balloon ride. They watched the sun set over the dusty plains surrounding Carnelius, and over the spaceport far out on the plain. They saw the spires and towers of the city glinting crimson and gold below them, and the street lights, many of them oil or gas lamps, coming on as twilight settled in. The balloon pilot provided a running commentary on the sights, but Jael paid little attention, her thoughts were turning to the sun and the sky. The city seemed a beautiful place to touch down in, and to spring away from, as though on a magic carpet.

By the next afternoon, they were indeed ready to spring away. *Seneca* was loaded and cleared for departure, their flight plan filed and approved. They said farewell to Mariella Flaire at the spaceport and took their final orders. Soon afterward, a tow was lifting them into orbit around the planet, and then out of orbit, into deep space, away from this world of exotic beauty.

In the shipdays following, they rigged down a long channel in the Flux, following a heavily trafficked pathway among the several worlds of the Vela cluster. It was one of the ironies of starfaring—that the known Flux pathways among these relatively close-together (in stellar terms) worlds, were comparatively long. Flux distances were always many orders of magnitude shorter than normal-space distances, but not always in direct proportion. And so they had a voyage some seventeen days long crossing the few light-years that spanned the Vela cluster.

They grew steadily more proficient in their teamwork in the net, and even began to introduce Ed to some of the rudiments of their work. Jael still marveled at the parrot's actions that had brought them to Vela Oasis, but she suspected that it had been largely luck that the parrot's instincts in breaking through the ice had been the right ones for the particular situation—though she couldn't discount the possibility that Ed had actually perceived something that they'd missed. While she didn't propose to make a full-fledged rigger out of the parrot, she hoped that he could learn to sense when he should stay out of their way, and when he could be free to join in with their actions.

During rest hours, they began assembling the holotronics to allow Ed freedom to rove the ship, or at least the commons and their quarters. They were four days into the flight when Ed first materialized in the commons, and they celebrated by toasting one another with carbonated fruit drink. Ed dipped his ghostly beak into Jael's glass and came up sputtering. Since his beak was only a holo-projection, the drink remained undisturbed; but Ed squawked happily and burbled at how wonderful and strange, terribly strange, this spaceship was. Jael's stondai tree sparkled in the corner of the commons, surrounded by a soft-focus holo-garden, and Ed promptly adopted the stondai as his favorite perch.

After that, the parrot was awake most of the time that they were, either in the net if one of them was there, or flying about the ship. They set up the last remaining projector in one of the empty cabins, and after some experimentation succeeded in projecting part of the rainforest there, so that Ed could have a place to retreat to if he felt homesick. It wasn't quite as real to Jael and Ar as the Environment Alpha system had been, but Ed seemed to enjoy it.

The time passed, and before they knew it, they had already made their call at Vela Delta Prime, where Ar looked up a Clendornan friend from his pre-rigging days and Jael spent a day sunning herself on the sandy shore of a warm, hissing ocean. Soon after, they were in space again, bound south and clockwise-inward on the galactic spiral for Seraph's Heaven, a collection of worlds where they were scheduled to make three stops. That was a journey of thirteen days, to be followed by a flight northward again, back toward the Aeregian worlds.

The flight to Seraph's Heaven went flawlessly, and it was a lively collection of worlds that they visited. But on the return northward they ran into trouble again—and this time it wasn't something that Ed could help them with.

PART THREE

DRAGON

Chapter 23
ACCIDENT IN THE FLUX

JAEL HAD just joined Ar in the net. It was a strange new image that he was rigging through: a vast network of what looked like the needles and branches of a fantastic evergreen tree, illumined by various colored, eerily reflected light sources. None of the landscape was quite in focus, so that the needles formed crisscrossing patterns that evoked a sense of form and shape without actually defining it. The ship was a silent, dark raft gliding among the needles. Ar was perched astride its nose, and Ed was on his shoulder, muttering softly. *How do you like it?* Ar asked, without turning to look at her. His voice was a murmur; he seemed not quite in a trance, but close.

It's very pretty. What is it?

Ah, I'd hoped you would recognize it. Ar looked back. He seemed disappointed. *Don't you know the tradition of Kristostime, the festival they celebrate on, I don't know how many worlds—*

Kristostime? Yes, of course I know it. Jael created a perch for herself beside him. *But what made you think of that? And what does it have to do with this?* She waved her hand at the scenery.

Ar hummed to himself. *When I was young, I once visited a human family during that festival. They had a tree of needles that was decorated with lights and shiny colored ornaments. It was very beautiful.* He glanced at Jael. *One of the human children and I spent hours lying under that tree in a darkened room, peering up through the branches and needles at the colored lights, and imagining entire universes in what we saw. And those images have lingered in my memory ever since.*

Jael stroked the neck of the parrot, marveling. She had no such memories from any festivals, but this landscape made her wish that she had.

It's an image from an ancient human tradition, you know, Ar continued. *It was our stop at Seraph's Heaven that made me think of it. That name comes from the same tradition, I believe. Though I don't understand the tradition itself very well, I find it a source of many vivid images. Do you like this one?*

Jael nodded. She relaxed and followed his instructions. She gazed without trying to focus her eyes on any one thing. The lights became blurry reflections of ruby and emerald and gold, lending quiet energy to the landscape, while the angled branches, with their dark needles, suggested form and boundary. She smelled balsam and spruce, and imagined exotic scents from other worlds. And as she let herself merge with the image, she knew that Ar had chosen well.

Floating dreamily, like thought itself, they wended their way through the intricate spaces evoked by the tree. The actual way was clear to her by intuition, if not by eye. It was as though they were being led by one light among all of those here, and though its identity seemed to flicker and change, they always recognized it: sometimes as a glow of ruby, or of deepest cerulean, or of amethyst purple. Always there was a gentle incandescence leading them in the direction they needed to go. She grew to feel content with that, as both Ar and Ed seemed content with it, as they wound silently around and through, like spirits moving in a world where no mortal being could live or breathe.

And so they traveled for a long and satisfying time . . .

Until a blinding light burst off to their left, as one of the colored globes exploded. For an instant, it seemed to be only a flash of light. But Jael had scarcely turned to look before the concussion hit. The first shock was mild, hardly more than a rumbling in the net. But something felt wrong, frighteningly wrong. An instant later, a second concussion hit, with a tremendous BOOOOM-M-M-M . . .

Ar—

A blast of ice-laden air slammed through the tree like a tidal wave, exploding needles and knocking aside branches like feathers; and in the wrenching blur, she felt the ship veering to one side, as a mighty force lifted and turned them. There was nothing to do but hold on.

Swinging branches swept into Jael's face, and lights flashed in her eyes, and she smelled something burning. At first she thought it was the net on fire, and she had to suppress her own panic, quenching an image of a sheet of flame flashing through the net. Then she realized that it was coming from the outside. She heard Ar shouting, and he sounded miles away, but she heard . . . *check the net configuration . . . tell if we're* . . . then his voice was momentarily lost in the hiss. But she knew that he was contending with the ship's movements so that she could deal with the net itself. She scanned backward and discovered that it was indeed unraveling. The power balances in the flux-field were flickering like candles in a stiff breeze. She would have to correct it fast . . .

Jael, can we move out of this—Ed, calm down!—can you tell if it's safe to leave the Flux?

Ar's call stopped her in mid-effort, because she was getting nowhere stabilizing the net. Perhaps he was right, they should surface and reestablish themselves in normal-space. *Take us up SLOWLY!* she answered. *We don't know what we're going to find!*

Ar was already doing just that, and she extended all of her senses to detect what they might be emerging into. They should be escaping from the worst of the storm as they surfaced . . . except that the storm was growing steadily more furious as they rose through the layers. Soon the entire Flux was glowing brightly with energy. The remaining tree branches were burning around them.

Jael, can you tell what we're getting into?

The sky was not darkening as they spiraled toward normal-space—it was brightening. There was a terrible glare in the sensors, and little detail; but the energy flux was incredible. *Ar, take us back down! GET US THE HELL OUT OF HERE!* They were surfacing in a tornado of cosmic activity—a nova, or a black hole, or who the hell knew what. They had to get out of there, and fast.

Jael, I need help! Ar shouted. *We've got to ride it through!*

Without answering, she worked furiously to strengthen the flux-field, to give Ar the power and leverage he needed. When she shifted her attention back to the outer net and the Flux, she found a winter avalanche carrying them thundering down a mountainside, great blasts of snow erupting on all sides. Ar had produced an image that he understood, but he could not change the forces that were there. Wherever and however they were being taken, they had no choice now but to ride it out, to try to keep from being buried or destroyed. It took the full power of the flux-field, and all of their strength to keep any control at all over their fall. And not only theirs: she also glimpsed Ed bent in flight, head down, all of his effort focused on flying straight and true in the midst of a terrible tempest.

She saw blurring snow, flashing white, and felt the ship rumbling and skidding and threatening to tumble end over end, and all she could do was brace herself behind Ar and join in his efforts. Time itself seemed stretched and distorted, affecting her perceptions. But as they clung and shouted encouragement to one another, the intensity of the avalanche gradually began to diminish. Eventually they were able to steady the ship in its downward plunge, and to keep it on the surface of the sliding snow, skiing it down the slope that was ever so slowly flattening out before them.

And finally, with her own heart pounding and all three of them gasping, they shuddered and bucked and came to a creeping halt. The sudden stillness was eerie, almost frightening in itself. Ed came to huddle, shivering, under her arm.

Only the slow sifting of snow beneath the ship reminded her of the fury they had just been through. They looked at each other in silence, and they looked around them at a landscape full of mountains, a tremendous range of mountains—all still, and white with snow. It all looked a little dark, and that was because some of the power from the flux-pile was leaking away, instead of going into the net. Jael wondered, and knew Ar was wondering, what had gone wrong.

And she wondered as well: Where are we now?

It took a good deal of time on the bridge, studying the net-memory analysis, to piece together what had most likely happened. Apparently they had passed close to a Flux-abscess of some sort, a knot or distortion in the continuum that could easily have destroyed them. In this case, it seemed to have been a linkage to some sort of cosmic-scale disturbance in normal-space—perhaps a powerful jet erupting from some sort of highly energetic stellar object, or even a black hole system. They had not gathered enough information to be certain. But one thing she did know was that they were lucky to be alive. Whatever the object had been, there must have been an unusual degree of penetration into the Flux continuum. And to have struck with so little warning—was it simple misfortune? Or had they made a fundamental error in their navigation? It was a sobering reminder of the need for constant vigilance.

Unfortunately, the analysis of the ship's systems revealed something even more sobering. The flux-pile had been damaged, either by the storm itself, or by the stresses put on it in riding out the storm. They were going to be hard put to reach their destination, or any starport at all.

Jael and Ar faced each other across the instrument panels of the bridge, where the data showed all too clearly on the screens. "Well—" Ar said, and gestured silently.

"We can't repair it, can we?"

"I don't think so. But we're not crippled altogether; we do have the power to continue. The question is how much leverage we'll have in the net—how responsive she'll be."

"And how long it will last." Jael tapped the display. "The power drain was pretty severe."

"So we have to choose a heading according to how difficult the rigging will be, and how quickly we can make the passage. Those two factors are not necessarily compatible."

Jael thought about that. They didn't know yet where they were, or how far off course they had been knocked. It was hard to guess what their choices would be. They would have to spend some time in the navigation library.

Ar rose unsteadily. "Jael, we both need to rest before we do much else. But I think it would be wise to go in shifts, and not leave the ship untended. You can sleep first, if you like, while I go through the library."

Jael snorted. "You think I'm going to be able to sleep after this? You were in the net longer than I was. Why don't you sleep? I'll see what the library has on this." She was a nervous wreck; she might as well try to unwind by doing something useful.

Ar agreed, and with a comforting touch on her shoulder, left her to monitor the bridge—left her to look for clues, if there were any to be found.

By the time Ar reappeared, she had spent hours in the rigger library computer and twice dipped into the net to make observations, and she'd made an astonishing discovery. She could scarcely believe it herself, and wasn't quite sure how to tell Ar. "It's no coincidence," she said, feeling more than a little giddy.

"What isn't? Who said anything about a coincidence? Are you feeling all right?"

She nodded, in profound weariness. "I'm fine. But the mountains. It's not a coincidence about the mountains."

Ar had brought her a mug of cocoa. He set it down beside her, then sat and studied her face. He looked more alien than ever at this moment, no doubt a trick of the lighting. His head seemed so top-heavy, she thought it would tip off his neck. His mouth opened and moved. "Jael. What mountains?"

She blinked. Words came with difficulty. "The image we

finished with . . . the avalanche. When we hit bottom, we were at the base of a mountain. A range of mountains. Don't you remember?"

"Yes, of course I do." Ar's eyes seemed to glow at her. "What about them?"

"I know those mountains. I've been here before, but farther up the range." She paused, wondering if she sounded crazy. "I felt sure we were too far away, even though we're en route to Aeregian space. But Ar, we went *way* off course—carried by the shockwaves, I guess. Anyway, I'm almost certain that we're near the same mountains . . . where I met . . . where I met . . ." Her mouth resisted forming the words. "Where . . . Highwing . . . lives." Her voice sounded like a sigh, or an appeal.

Ar was silent for a long time, not looking at her. She took a series of slow, deep breaths, waiting for him to answer. He murmured something to himself and studied the instrument readings for a while. Finally he said, "If that's true, then we'll have to be extra careful, won't we?"

"Careful? Yes, but—" *Highwing!*

"Dragons, Jael. Remember? If it's true, what you say, then they're dangerous. Dueling, and so on. Correct? You can vouch for that."

"Yes, but Highwing won't do anything to us—"

Ar's cautioning hand stopped her. "Perhaps not. Perhaps not. But Highwing is just one dragon. What about the others? If your memories and the legends are literally true, as you say, then we could be facing any number of unknown dragons, besides the one you know." Ar's voice was steady, sober. He sounded worried; she'd hoped he'd be reassured.

"I suppose that's true," she whispered, remembering suddenly that Highwing himself had said that not all dragons would be as welcoming to her as he had been. "But if we are anywhere near Highwing, if he can help us . . ." And her voice failed, but she remembered clearly Highwing's parting words to her: *I will hear you, though all the mountains lie between us.* And she knew that even if Ar did not take those words seriously, she did. She must.

"Jael," Ar said gently. "What else have you learned about

our course? What's the shortest route to a starport where we can put in?"

She sighed, and her head seemed to hurt as she spoke, though it was really not so much a pain as a blurring of her thoughts. "I don't know yet. I just . . . don't know . . ." And her voice failed again, because the truth was that she had her suspicions that they would have to cross the dragon realm in any case, but she didn't want to say that, didn't think Ar would believe her . . .

She started, as Ar caught her. She'd been falling over, falling asleep.

"Time for you to get some rest," Ar murmured as he guided her toward her cabin. "Time enough for all of this later. . . ."

When next she spoke with Ar, it was in the net, after she'd awakened from a long, deep sleep filled with dreams. She could not remember the content of the dreams, but the intense fear and longing in them lingered for hours after awakening. She found Ar assessing the region they had left the ship in; he had not changed the image significantly, nor released the stabilizers. He seemed in a pensive mood.

Have you determined the nearest port? Jael asked softly. She looked around for Ed, but didn't see him.

Ar nodded. Raising his eyes, he noted the way she was looking around and said, *Ed went to sleep. I think I was making him depressed.*

Jael's mouth opened. She didn't know what to say. Until now, Ar had been her best defense against depression. Finally she murmured, *What did you find?*

The Clendornan chuckled somberly, his great, wide-topped head tipping from side to side. *That apparently you were right.*

She shook her head, confused. *What do you mean?*

These indeed seem to be the same mountains as those of the "dreaded mountain route" to Lexis. I found the three closest starports, but every possible course to them entails traveling through, over, or around these mountains. Ar's voice was flat, and that, more than anything else, revealed how disturbed he was.

Jael stared at him, trying to draw a breath. Conflicting

emotions were rising in her; and she knew that she had better sort them out quickly, because one thing she had not counted on was that Ar might be afraid. Afraid of what could lie within those mountains. Afraid of what she had told him, what she knew to be true; afraid he would learn that she had been right all along. His fear was not visible, but she sensed it—she knew.

Ar surveyed the mountains that rose from the horizon, above the dunes of snow cradling their ship. *It's going to be a hard way to go,* he murmured finally, making an obvious effort to be optimistic.

Yes. It probably will be. She too was aware of the limitations of their ship, with its impaired flux-pile. But she could not keep away other thoughts, nor could she keep the beginning of a smile from her lips. *But there might be a way that's not visible to us yet. A way that we won't find until we've really looked.*

With Highwing's help, she added in the silence of her thoughts. But meeting Ar's sad, frightened eyes, she found she could think of nothing more to say.

Chapter 24
A REALM CHANGED

FRIEND OF HIGHWING. . . !

Her voice reverberated from the mountain cliffs as they glided closer, ever closer to the foreboding-looking peaks. It seemed a harsh land, grimmer and somehow less alive than she'd remembered. They were in a different part of the range now, and perhaps this region has always had a different character. But her intuition, her rigger instinct, told her that something had changed, and she had an uneasy feeling that it was more than just the outward appearance.

For hours now they had been rigging closer to the mountains; for hours she had been calling out to Highwing—hoping that he would remember his promise to her, hoping that he would hear her voice. Hoping that her memory was true, and that everything she had been claiming to Ar would be proved now, when it mattered. There had been no response of any kind to her calls. But of course, Highwing could be far away; he could be at the other end of the range. And while he had shown her powers that seemed magical, he was not omnipotent. She could only keep calling, hoping, and trusting.

At her back, Ar was maintaining the fine-tuning of the flux-pile and the stability of the ship. Ed was perched nearby, watching eagerly for signs of giant lizards. *It's a long mountain range,* Ar remarked. *The topography could be deceptive. Are you sure that we're downrange of the area you flew through before?*

She shook her head. *I can't really be sure of anything.* Except that there is someone who will hear me, and answer. But was she even sure of that? Who knew what length of time had passed here in the Flux, while she had carried on her life on the outside? Suppose Highwing had grown old and died . . .

She deflected the thought. *Can we angle off to the starboard, toward that pass we saw earlier? It looked like an easier way through.* Unfortunately, the winds were unfavorable for moving in that direction. But no matter which way they flew there would be difficulties and hazards.

Ar agreed, and the ship turned, coming to the new heading like a sailing ship beating into the wind. They continued moving steadily, if more slowly. As the peaks drew closer, she shouted again: *THIS IS JAEL, FRIEND OF HIGHWING!* and again her voice echoed back to her, attenuated by the distance.

Rrrrraww. Smell glizzards there, Ed muttered. He had his head craned to the starboard, toward the north of the pass, as they'd denoted the directions here. Jael watched him uneasily, wondering if his observation was serious, or just wishful.

There was a late afternoon haze in the air, obscuring distant details. Perhaps that was why she didn't see them until they were startlingly large against the slopes: dragons, at least half a dozen, wheeling and banking to close on the intruder, the spaceship. Jael's heart almost stopped as she focused on the living shapes. *Ar—!*

A tongue of flame billowed in their path. A great-winged reptile swept past in front of them. A dark-jeweled eye rotated to peer in their direction, glinting with unreadable intent.

As the creature veered away, Jael cried out frantically: *I'm seeking Highwing! Where is Windrush-Wingtouch-Highwing—Terror-of-the-Last-Peak?*

The air erupted with a thunderous commotion as the dragons reacted to her cry. They flew one way and another around the riggers, rumbling and billowing fire. Jael sensed Ar's alarm. Ed was beside himself, squawking, *Graggons, graggons!* Jael was speechless; this was hardly what she'd been expecting. The dragons, too many and too fast to follow, swarmed closer and closer, filling the air with smoke and fire. She remembered now that this was how it had happened the first time, until she'd made peace with Highwing. Perhaps she could make peace again.

Please! she shouted. *We want to talk to you!*

A gnarled-faced dragon wheeled around from the front. Jael started to speak—but a billow of flame and sparks erupted in her face and a voice rumbled in her mind, *DO YOU THINK TO MEDDLE AGAIN IN THIS PLACE, RIGGER?* The dragon sheared away, rocking the net with turbulence. Jael gasped, struggling to maintain control.

No! she yelled. *Ar, be ready for a fight! Fireproof us! Ed, stay behind me and be still!*

As he assisted Jael in strengthening the bubble of the net that surrounded them, Ar asked worriedly, *Jael, what's going on? Are these real, or are they from your memory?*

Were they real? she thought in anguish. Of course they were! And yet—she remembered her false image of Mogurn, and just for an instant, doubted. Could this all be a manifestation of her own fears? *Highwing!* she cried out desperately, hoping to drive fear from her thoughts.

Another blast of flame splashed over the net, and a great dark shape rocked them as it flew past. *Begone!* it snorted contemptuously.

Or do you think yourself a guest here? laughed another, passing just as close.

Fear began to give way to anger. *We are here to see Highwing!* she shouted, as Ar strained to hold the net firm. She was well aware of their reduced strength in the net and had no idea how long they could survive a real attack.

A new voice seemed to echo from the cliffs. *IF YOU HAVE*

COME TO SPEAK THAT ACCURSED NAME, THEN YOU TOO WILL DIE!

Jael shivered, and following Ar's push on the stern-position, helped him veer away from two dragons that were rising from below. The creatures shot upward, past them, as *Seneca* rolled into a dive. Flames blossomed around them, but only for an instant. *Jael, we have to know!* Ar shouted. *Is this real or isn't it?*

REEEL! IT'S REEEL! Ed shrieked, taking flight over their heads. *TERRIBLE! TERRIBLE! FLY AWAY! FLY AWAY!*

Ed, stay down, damn it! Jael shouted. *Yes, it's real! I don't know what's wrong!* She did not dare cry out for Highwing again. The best thing she could do was to get them out of here. But how? Above them soared a sky full of dragons. The horizon offered only barren peaks where they would be as vulnerable as lambs. Below them loomed cliffs and jagged slopes, and they were moving too fast to spy a hiding place, even if one existed.

I'm changing the image, Ar said, and Jael offered no objection. She felt a moment of lightheadedness, and her vision blurred perilously—they were too damned close to those rocks now!

She heard a squawk. *That way! That way! Hrawwwk!*

Ed flew down toward the rocks, and the landscape shimmered and became solid again, unaltered. *It won't change,* Ar said, and his voice was calm, but tinged with fear.

No, Jael whispered. *This is the landscape that is. But if we can't change it, we can change ourselves instead!* She swallowed and looked up, where the dragons were circling—and saw them peeling off one by one to dive for the attack. *We've got to make ourselves smaller, and find a place to hide.*

This way! Ed screamed, batting back up toward them and spinning in midair to dive again.

Jael didn't hesitate, and Ar was right behind her. They wrapped the net tightly around themselves; the three of them and *Seneca* became as one—a hawk speeding toward a crevice in the nearby cliff. The parrot led the way flawlessly; he was terrified, but his keen eyes brought them directly into the narrow opening. The cliff seemed to swallow them, as a splash of flame seared their tail.

An angry dragon raked at the outside of the crevice with its claws. *IF YOU WOULD BE OUR GUEST, THEN COME WITH US!* it bellowed raucously, its voice reverberating through the stone. But they were out of reach now, in a narrow cave that seemed to extend far back into the mountain.

They sped onward, transforming themselves into a bat, seeking the deepest recesses of the cavern. Was there an end to this cave, this fracture in the mountain? Jael couldn't tell. Ed urged them onward into the darkness. A stream of dank air flowed past, chilling Jael to the bone.

Eventually they slowed, to rest and gather their wits. Jael, trembling, whispered silently to herself: *Highwing are you here? Are you anywhere?* And to Ar: *Maybe we can go all the way through to the other side of the mountain, and then we can . . .* and she ran out of words, because in fact she had absolutely no idea what they could do, even if they succeeded in passing through the mountain.

Ar was very close to her in the net, his voice calming. *They knew Highwing's name, Jael! They knew it. But they hated it. Why?*

Yes—why? she thought. She had reacted with such alarm to the immediate peril that she had not focused on what the dragons had said: *You too will die. . . .*

My God, she whispered. Had Highwing died, then—killed by his own kind? Or were they threatening to kill him? *Ar, if those were enemies of Highwing . . . if it was something that I did . . .*

She hesitated, feeling a terrible dread. She remembered suddenly the moment in which she had given Highwing her name, and the tremors that had shaken the mountains in response. She felt as though those tremors were echoing inside her right now. She remembered that Highwing had said there would be trouble because of what he had done, in befriending her. If he was in danger now because of her . . . *Ar, is it possible—do you think there is any way that we could—?* Her voice caught, and she couldn't finish the question. But she knew this: if Highwing was in danger, she could not just leave and pretend she hadn't known.

It was obvious that Ar understood her intent. *Jael, what could we possibly do to help your friend? We're in terrible danger ourselves. And we don't even know where he is.*

Their eyes met in the gloom of the net. Jael wished she could somehow will him to understand how deeply her heart went out to Highwing, and how much she would risk for the friend who had helped her so. But she could find no words.

They were gliding slowly through the darkness, twisting and turning to follow the narrow passage. She could sense the stone passing close by on either side of them, and was grateful for Ed's sharp eyes and instincts. The parrot was completely absorbed in finding a way through this labyrinth of darkness. They passed a patch of wall that glowed dimly, perhaps from phosphorescent lichen or moss. It was an eerie sight, and she shivered as she turned to watch the ghostly light disappearing behind them. *I know we're in danger,* she said finally, her voice echoing softly. *But I owe him, Ar. More than I can say. If there's any way I can help him, I have to try.*

When Ar didn't answer immediately, she took his silence as deliberation. There was a change in him, and she thought she knew what it was. It was that he believed her now. He had seen the dragons, seen their fury—not as a tale, but as reality. And he wanted to get away from it; he didn't like the dragon reality, didn't like it at all. But now, it seemed, they would have to make some choices. And her choices might not be the same as his.

She had no idea how far they had traveled through the body of the mountain, when Ed squawked, fluttering his wings, *Aarrk. Coming out, coming out.*

Jael peered ahead, and indeed there was a vague lessening of the darkness, and a fresher smell to the air. But would dragons be waiting for them on the outside? *We must be very careful coming out. I suggest we stay small, until we know we are in the clear.* Ar didn't answer, and she assumed control as they neared the exit point. The rocks widened, became a gloomy cave, slowly brightening. They were still in the form of a bat, quick and maneuverable in flight.

They emerged from the mountain, gulping in the fresh air, then began a slow, zigzagging flight. They searched the sky in all directions; there were no dragons visible, or anything else living. A smoky red sun was going down behind a line of mountains to their left. They had emerged, apparently, deep within the range. Which way should they go? Toward the sun? That might take them out of the range, Jael thought, out of the dragon realm altogether. She wasn't sure. She hesitated, thinking of Highwing. Peering to the right, she saw nothing in particular, but felt something, a small familiar twinge. She turned that way, on a heading that would take them even deeper into the mountains. Ar followed silently.

I wish I knew what was happening here, Jael muttered, as they sailed slowly through an evening gathering into night, guided only by starlight and by intuition. *I wish I knew what was wrong.*

Ar's voice betrayed his tension. *One thing I know is that we don't belong in this place. It's not our territory, Jael. And what about our ship? We're responsible for the vessel, you know.*

She nodded, but had no answer. She knew that Ar's fear was intensified by his newly shaken assumptions about reality. At least that was what she told herself. Maybe she was endangering her crewmates and ship by proceeding on this heading, but she didn't know that for sure, and she didn't want to think about it. Her concern now was for Highwing. She felt certain that he must be in some terrible danger, that nothing else would have kept him from coming to her. She refused to consider the possibility that he might be dead. And if he was alive, she was determined to find him.

But how? She was afraid to call out again. Something about this place felt fundamentally wrong; she could not tell exactly what, but something in her heart, some intuition told her that this place had somehow been twisted and *made* wrong. It was not just the behavior of the dragons. She felt it in the air, in the darkness, even in the starlight reflecting off the mountains, and in the clouds scooting overhead; something was not right here. Ed seemed to sense it as well; he seemed quiet but skittish, as though he were expecting sudden disaster. She remembered the dragon magic that Highwing had once shared with her. Now, she thought she sensed another magic, similar in its power maybe, but dark and brooding, a power that did not approve of her presence here. She felt that they were being watched as they flew through these night-shrouded mountains, and she did not like her feeling of what might be watching them.

Highwing would know what to make of it, if he were here. If he could hear her call. *Highwing*, she whispered, almost silently. *Friend of Highwing.* And she swallowed, afraid that even that soft murmur would attract the wrong sort of attention.

A massive peak loomed off to the left. Ahead and to starboard, a ridge of peaks seemed to stretch out forever. Ar was humming softly as he steered, wielding the tiller of a sailing ship at sea—a sea of air—riding what breeze there was, as Jael smelled and evaluated the air. Ed was perched beside her, turning his head alertly. *Smell something, Ed?*

The parrot made a guttural sound, then said distinctly but softly, *Lizards. Graggons. Nearby.*

Jael felt a chill of fear . . . and hope. *Do you know . . . can you sense . . . whether they are friendly or not?*

Hraww. Nope. The parrot lifted his beak. *Smell them. Close.*

Jael sensed Ar taking a deep breath, then settling back. He was no longer humming. He was afraid, she knew—terribly afraid of what she was getting them into. Nevertheless, he was willing to follow. Whatever she did now . . . she was responsible for his life and Ed's, as well as her own. She drew a breath and said, raising her voice just above a whisper, *I am Jael, friend of Highwing. Who knows where is Highwing?*

The night answered with utter silence.

The dragons came in silence, as well. Ed make a choking sound, and an instant later, Jael saw starlight reflected in the eyes of a great winged serpent as it swept across their bow, shaking them violently. Jael helped Ar to steady the ship, and as she did so, she heard a voice like thunder, calling, *DI-I-I-I-E-E-E . . . LIKE HIM-M-M . . .*

She could not see their foe, or foes, in the night. But she heard a scream of rage—and she and Ar, terrified, drew the net in tight—as a blast of fire lifted them and hurled them downwind. *Ar, hold on! I AM A FRIEND OF HIGHWING!* she bellowed, knowing that it was stupid and futile.

A dragon shot past, its wingtip catching them and flipping them into a dive, its own body illuminated by a glow of dragon fire. *AWAY, BROTHER!* Jael heard, as another dragon thundered past, raking the first with flame. She and Ar struggled to pull out of the dive, cursing the sluggishness of the damaged net; and only after they were level again did it register in her mind that she had seen one dragon attacking another!

She turned to look. A pair of gleaming dragon eyes was bearing down on them from above and behind. *What do you want?* she screamed, ashamed of the fear in her voice, but unable to keep it out.

There was no answer; there was only a dark, reeking wing blotting out the night and enveloping them, with a control so total that there was no hope of escape. Then a voice roared, *I CLAIM THESE RIGGERS AS MINE!* And in reply, there were loud blasts of fury; but Jael, barely able to see beyond the dragon's wing, thought that she sensed the other creatures veering away, leaving them uncontested to their captor.

She and Ar struggled to free themselves. She felt a flash of hope as the wing opened and the night air washed over them, but the hope vanished again as the dragon caught them with its powerful talons. Jael grunted as the net absorbed the force, and she felt a woolly darkness growing around her as the dragon did something to the space surrounding her.

As she lost sight of the mountains and the night, she heard a dragon's throaty voice murmur, *Why do you call out to my father, you foolish riggers?*

Chapter 25
WINDRUSH

THEY FLEW on in silence for a time, until Jael recovered her senses. *What did you say? Are you . . . is Highwing your father?* She felt Ar close to her and Ed trembling nervously under her arm, and the air rushing past, but she could not see where they were going. She was trying hard not to be afraid.

The dragon's voice answered throatily, *That depends, I would say.*

Depends? On what? she whispered.

On who and what you really are, rigger-demon. I am not so eager to give even my father's name without knowing—

Jael interrupted the dragon, her voice almost failing. *I am Jael, friend of Highwing!*

The air trembled suddenly, and the curious darkness that had enveloped them fell away. Once more the mountains were visible in the night, beyond the great set of claws that imprisoned them high in the air. Overhead, the dragon's wings beat steadily. The dragon bent its head down to angle a look at them with one green eye. *I see.* It raised its head again and snorted sparks into the air. *Then, Jael,* it rumbled softly, *I am Windrush, Son of Highwing, and I am grieved and honored to meet you. I shall allow you to see where we are bound.*

Windrush! Jael cried, recognizing a part of Highwing's own name.

Quiet! Do not shout my name, or my father's name, again! Nor, if you are wise, your own name.

Jael drew a breath and asked softly, *Why? What is happening? Where is your father?*

In answer, she heard a soft murmur that was almost like a chuckle, but it seemed to carry no amusement, only sadness. Finally the dragon answered, *In time, rigger. In due time, we may speak of that. But first we must reach a place of safety.*

We can fly, Jael said.

No. I will bear you. It is safer that way. And I sense, rigger, that you are hampered. Your strength is not all that it might be. The dragon beat his wings harder, gaining altitude. *Rest and conserve yourself, and later we will talk about what will become of us.* He was silent again for a moment, before adding, *And perhaps, in time, I will learn the names of your companions, as well. But until then—*

My name is Ar, the Clendornan interrupted, in a low voice. *And this is our parrot—*

Rawk! Ed! My name Ed!

The dragon peered back down in surprise, losing some altitude as he craned his neck. His eyes glowed briefly. *So,* he said finally, working to regain the lost altitude. *You are indeed a strange and impulsive breed, you riggers. So quickly you decide. So quickly. Do you not know that the giving of your name can open you to your enemies as well as to your friends?* He flew in silence for a few moments. *I suppose I must follow in my father's error. I am Windrush. Honored and grieved. I had hoped—frankly—that you would not return to this realm, rigger-called-Jael. Why are you here?*

We arrived by accident, as a matter of fact, Ar answered.

Accident! the dragon exclaimed, snorting sparks. *It must have been some accident to bring you here at such a time as this. Some accident, indeed!*

Why? Jael asked softly. *What danger is your father in? Everything seems different to me here. What is happening?*

The dragon's wings beat the air, making a sound like a sail flapping in a changing breeze. *These are dark times, riggers,* he said, after a pause. *You come here at great peril to yourselves.*

I can see that. But I had thought, as Highwing's friend, that I would receive a better welcome.

The dragon snorted. *Did you now? I trust that you have come to understand otherwise.* Jael swallowed and nodded. *Still,* the dragon sighed, *I must recognize your friendship with my father.*

We, too, recognize her commitment to Highwing, Ar said. His voice trembled only a little as he addressed the dragon.

I see. Admirable of you. I know of Jael's vow—but not of yours, however. I think for now I must blind you to our course. Perhaps all will be made clear later.

Before any of them could reply, an airborne darkness curled in like streaming ink and surrounded Ar and Ed. And Jael, discomfited, was left alone with the dragon—alone, except for the faint rustling of the parrot's wings in the region of darkness.

The aerie was high in the mountains, well hidden within a labyrinth of ridges and outcroppings. Jael had stayed in the net with Windrush, rather than withdrawing into the ship where she might speak to her rigger companions. She had thought it best to watch the route that Windrush was flying, in the event that she had to retrace it without the dragon's help. However, she'd long since lost track of the twists and turns.

They did not speak again until the dragon came to a landing. Wings flapping vigorously, he first released Jael and the inky cloud containing her friends onto a narrow outcropping. Then he himself alighted, gripping the rock with his talons. The dragon was enormous, perched beside Jael. *Can you continue on foot?* he asked, peering down at her. *Will your ship—is that what you call it?—allow that?* His gaze shifted to the ghostly shadow of the ship that trailed behind her, only dimly perceptible in the night.

Jael nodded and made the ship disappear. *What about Ar and Ed?*

The dragon made a *tsking* sound as he peered at the cliff

face above them. Smoke issued from his nostrils, and a rumble from his throat. Jael started. There was now a large opening in the rock wall, where before there had been none. The night air shimmered, and Ar stood beside her while Ed fluttered in the air. The parrot made a grab for her shoulder. *Glizzard!* he scolded. *Graggon tricks! Yaww!*

Dragon, Jael corrected gently. *Hush now, Ed. We're entering the dragon's lair, and you must be respectful of his ways. And of his magic.* She turned to Windrush, who issued a thin stream of smoke into the cave, as though to usher them in. Jael drew an uneasy breath and walked into the side of the mountain.

The stone passageway that she had somehow been expecting wasn't there. Instead, they stepped directly into a mammoth cavern, which was dimly illumined by the glow of burning embers. Drawn instinctively toward the fire, they approached a stone hearth at the end of the cavern, followed by the hissing dragon. Their footsteps echoed hollowly. Jael stood before the hearth, marveling at the firelight that seemed to issue from a silently burning bush. She tipped her head back, peering upward. The shifting fireglow was so dim, and the cavern vault so high, that the ceiling was impossible to see clearly. Ar, beside her, gazed around with eyes that sparkled purplish red. She touched his arm, wanting to say something encouraging, but not sure just what. She let her hand drop and turned to Windrush.

The dragon, more in the manner of an enormous dog than of a serpent, had curled up to make himself comfortable on the floor of the cavern. He gazed at them with eyes that, like Ar's, caught the glow of the hearth; but the dragon's eyes were far larger and more luminous, a deep emerald green like Highwing's. Jael approached the dragon to speak, but found herself captivated by something that seemed to dance within those eyes. There was an entrancing play of light within them, a cool, faceted fire that was more than just light. It occurred to her how much like Highwing's eyes they were—powerful and spellbinding. She had intended to ask again what had happened to Highwing, but it was too late to speak now, too late to stop whatever Windrush was doing to her with his eyes. *You fool,* she thought. *You should have expected it.*

The dragon's gaze was a bottomless well. She was already submerged in it, sinking deeper into the faceted fire, losing her awareness of self, drawn into the abyss of light by a consciousness that was reaching out to touch hers . . . and now it was drawing her into itself, as irresistibly as another dragon had, once before . . . and now it was studying her, observing what it was she wanted so deeply, why she was here, and showing her why that could not be, could never be. . . .

When Jael jerked herself back to a confused awareness, she stepped back involuntarily on the cold stone floor and stared at the dragon in disbelief. Her mind was full of images she did not understand: visions of a dark enchantment across the land; of a great mountain that could not be found, and of the shimmering crystalline beings who lived in it; visions of warfare and strife among dragons; and of one particular dragon persecuted above all, one dragon held prisoner by an angry army of his own kind. She had not been shown that dragon's face, but a tight knot in her chest suggested who it was.

She shuddered, twisting away from the luminous eyes, from the smoldering nostrils. *You did not know of these things,* Windrush hissed, sounding surprised.

Oh, Highwing! Jael whispered to herself. And to Windrush, *How could I have known?* She turned to Ar, who was watching their exchange in bewilderment. She wanted to explain, but her thoughts were churning, so confused that she didn't know what to say. Finally she turned back to the dragon. *Is all this . . . all that you've shown me . . .* and her voice stumbled, because there was so much that she didn't understand, *. . . is all this true? Has it really happened?*

The dragon's voice rumbled, not just with sorrow, but with anger. *Do you think I create such images in my imagination? I am no rigger to create demon visions!* His nostrils steamed as he turned his gaze away. *Forgive me. I should not have used that word, "demon." I have known of you, rigger Jael!* His gaze turned back, and it was full of fire. *I have known of you! My father made known to me his friendship with you. And I have wondered ever since whether to hate you for my father's suffering!*

But why? she cried. *Why has he suffered because of me?* She could still see the image that Windrush had put into her mind moments ago: an image of a lone dragon imprisoned by sorcery in a chamber of stone, imprisoned with no appeal, no mercy, no hope of escape. The image tore at her heart.

Ahh! Windrush sighed despairingly. *Did he tell you nothing of what he was doing? Nothing of the price he was paying? Nothing of the prophecy?*

What? Jael whispered. And she remembered that, yes, Highwing had seemed troubled once or twice. He'd spoken of a prophecy; he'd told her that he was doing something . . . *not done*, whatever that meant. His words had been disturbing to her, but she had been preoccupied and had not understood, and then had forgotten . . . as she had forgotten his warning, too late remembered, to beware of other dragons. She remembered Highwing's brief quarrel with another dragon in his garden; and she remembered a creature called "iffling," whose words concerning Jael had seemed to trouble Highwing, as well.

Windrush's gaze had flashed to Ar, who was gesturing for someone to explain. *Would you know, too? Would you see?*

Ar's breath whistled out. *I would.*

Then, the dragon cautioned, *if you would see, you must be prepared to show me the nature of your own soul, in return. You must allow me to judge your heart.* Windrush paused. *I, too, am now doing what is forbidden.* His eyes flashed deep sparks of fire. *But my father discovered a truth in this matter that I cannot ignore. If you say that you recognize Jael's commitment—*

Look, and judge, Ar said impatiently.

Windrush fell silent. Ar stepped forward to meet the dragon's eyes, and at once stiffened into a trance. Jael, bursting with questions, could only watch. After a hundred agonizingly long heartbeats, she saw Ar break his gaze from Windrush's. He seemed deeply troubled as he turned away. He didn't speak, but sat near the hearth, pondering.

Tell me, please, Jael begged the dragon. *What has happened to your father? Is he alive?*

He is imprisoned, as I showed you.

But why? she whispered. *What did he do that was so terrible?*

The dragon vented steam. *How can I explain, if you have not already seen it? How can I explain the terrible darkness that has fallen over these mountains?* The dragon groaned deep in his throat, a rumble that could be felt through the stone floor. *How can I describe a curse that has . . . so poisoned the minds of my own kind*—and his voice rose in pain—*that I myself have become an outcast, even among my brothers? How can I explain my father's kindness to a human rigger, which I must now honor, because he asked it? I scarcely understand it myself!* He sighed deeply, a great mournful breath of wind. *Do the ancient words hold so much power?*

Jael shook her head. The dragon's voice seemed to have spun cobwebs between her ears. *Ancient words?* Although Highwing had spoken of such things, he had never explained them. *And a curse, you say?*

A cloud of sparks flew up into her face, and for an instant she thought that the dragon meant to attack her. *Curse—yes! What else could we call it? It is not just a great power, it is a blight that has overwhelmed our land since your departure!*

But it didn't come from me! Jael cried, her head buzzing with anger and confusion. She felt grief-stricken, and guilty, though she didn't know what she'd done wrong.

The dragon rasped his talons noisily on the stone floor. *True enough. It didn't come from you. I know that . . . now. But most in the realm blame you, even though they should not.* He turned his head to stare into the hearth. His scales rippled and glimmered with the movement. *Rigger Jael, it would seem that your passage through this realm somehow awakened this . . . power. Or perhaps it was there all along, but your actions caused it to reveal itself.*

She gestured helplessly. *But how?*

Windrush gazed at her with eyes that were deep and sad beneath his massive brow. *There is no simple answer to that question. But your appearance, young rigger, was long ago foretold. Or so I have heard, and so my father believed. The dragon's* left eye opened wider, peering at her. *I know little of such things, myself. It is the draconae, the dreaming ones, who hold such matters in memory for my race. But still, by such Words were we warned. I remember a few of them, correctly I hope.* He spoke softly, reciting:

> *From beyond life will come one*
> *From beyond hope will come one*
> *Without friend will come one*
> *And the realm shall tremble.*
>
> *Challenging darkness will come one*
> *Speaking her name will come one*
> *Innocent of our ways will come one*
> *And the realm shall tremble.*

His voice rose, grumbling. *The Words are thought to say that the appearance of one from the outside will cause a confrontation between, well . . . dragon, true dragon . . . and darkness . . . such as the realm has never seen.* His eyes glowed at her. *Others have come from the outside, and sometimes dueled, and sometimes died, and sometimes escaped without consequence. What they really wanted, we never knew. But you were different. My father believed you to be the One of the prophecy, the One who would lead us out of a darkness that we didn't even know we were in.*

Jael was dumbfounded. She gestured futilely. *But I don't know anything about any of this,* she managed to say at last.

Isn't that what I just said? "Innocent of our ways . . ."

Jael closed her mouth, speechless.

When you first came, and then left without incident, my father thought that he must have been mistaken, that he had somehow misread the signs. But he was not, had not. Windrush paused, staring angrily into the fire. *No, rigger Jael, this curse has not come from you. But you have helped to reveal its presence, and its power. It has, I believe, lived in this realm all along, quietly biding its time while clouding our thoughts, influencing us without our being aware of it. It has lived among us, but we have not seen it, nor wished to see it.*

The dragon snorted, chuckling bitterly. *Oh, even the draconi have always known that there are powers in the world that do not love light, or mercy, or acts of sacrifice and kindness and compassion. But we have hidden from such truths and called them legend. And yet . . . even legend tells us that such powers may lie in hiding, quietly working their mischief, until the times permit their reappearance.*

He grumbled and smoke billowed from his nostrils. *But they must reveal themselves, sooner or later. It was our good fortune to live in quiet times, free of care—for a while. But no longer! We did not listen to the draconae's teachings, or seek them out, until it was too late. Perhaps it was the Enemy's work, muddling our spirit and our thoughts. We did not even realize that we had forgotten our way to the Dream Mountain until it was already too late, and it was gone, and the draconae gone with it!*

And our world—if you could see it now! Friendships and clans lie in ruins. War and madness abound. Dragon honor, true garkondoh, is condemned as unworthy. And our magic! He rumbled, deep in his throat, a rumble of dismay. *Ahh . . . even our powers to create and cherish places and spells of beauty have betrayed us. Our weavings have become fickle and difficult. Many of those who have the skills of the underrealm have been ensnared by the Enemy's promises of power, and turned their skills to his service.* Windrush's voice grew despairing. *My father's garden—his lovely place of sanctuary—has been destroyed. Even this place of safety—it is all I can do to keep it concealed.*

Jael struggled to absorb what Windrush was saying. Highwing's beautiful garden, destroyed? What a terrible crime! She wanted to ask more and to learn about this thing, the Dream Mountain. But even more urgently, she needed to know—and she asked in a whisper—*What exactly has happened to Highwing?*

Windrush's voice rumbled louder. *My father has stood trial before a dragon assembly, on charges of treason to the realm. And a bitter and vindictive assembly it was.* Windrush's voice hardened. *Highwing stands condemned to die.*

Jael's breath exploded from her. She reached out, her hands clenched helplessly in rage. *Why?* she whispered. *Why?*

The dragon considered her with his gaze of shimmering emerald. *For an act of foolish kindness to a stranger, perhaps.*

An act of friendship to a demon-spirit. They hold you, and my father, responsible for the madness that has overcome them all.

Jael was silent.

But they are wrong. I see that, as my father saw it. Nevertheless, your visit and my father's unveiling of our world to you—that perhaps above all!—his revealing of secrets of our realm to one who is not of us—has opened the door to much grief, and the promise of untold grief to come.

Jael turned away, numb with disbelief. How could such a thing be possible? How could she, merely by entering this land, have sentenced the dragons to a world of madness, and her friend Highwing to death? She turned back to the younger dragon. *This . . . darkness,* she said slowly. *This influence. What is its source? Does it have a name?* Something was jangling at the back of her mind, a name she thought she had heard from Highwing, a name that at the time had provoked a feeling of dread.

Windrush fumed, clenching his talons. He didn't seem to want to answer.

Caww! Ed fluttered back to Jael's shoulder from the hearthside, where he had been sitting quietly. *Not fair! Not her fault! Not Jayl's fault!*

The dragon's eyelids blinked ponderously, as Jael hushed the bird. *You may speak rightly, parrot,* Windrush answered. *But the truth is that evil cannot abide the presence of good—and when it is brought to light, it lashes out. My father realized that his actions had fulfilled a dangerous prophecy. He had been told, and he believed, at least in part, and he feared the consequences as much as any. But he knew that there was no turning back. And he exacted a promise from me—a rush of smoke went toward the ceiling—that I would honor his pledge of friendship to you as though I had made it myself.*

Despite her heartache, Jael could not help but be moved by Highwing's determination. *And was it just you? What of your brothers?*

They refused. The dragon's voice sharpened with anger. *Turned against him. Called him a betrayer of the realm, and a sower of trouble. It was two of my brothers who were attacking you when I arrived to bear you away.*

Jael blanched.

My own clan, Windrush muttered, as though he himself could not believe it.

A loud crackle came from the fire behind Jael, and she started, as a flame sputtered up from the embers. She glanced at Ar, his eyes wide and sober. A lump grew in her throat as she turned back to Windrush. *Then . . . he must hate me,* she whispered. *For what he did for me, all of this has happened? His own sons turning against him?*

Never! Windrush thundered. *My father never regretted what he did for you. He would do it all again—and I half wonder myself if he isn't mad. I believed in him. But how long can I believe?* Windrush raised his head and loosed a tongue of flame that blasted the ceiling, and a wail that shook the cavern.

Jael trembled. An image rose in her memory, from the mindlink with Windrush, an image she only now understood: three of the four sons betraying their father—two flying away in open rebellion, while a third was already lost, seduced by the enchantments of a power that would not even reveal itself to the realm. Only Windrush had stood firm, and Windrush was devoured by grief and by fear.

And following that image, another rose: a carbon black peak thrust tall against the sky, the tallest peak in the realm. Gathered near its summit were hundreds of dragons. She hadn't understood that image, either, when she had glimpsed it in Windrush's mind. But now she did. A lone dragon awaited a sentence of death on that peak. And nothing could stop it from happening. Nothing human, and nothing dragon.

It was too much for her to bear. *Take me to him! Please!* she cried out to Windrush, falling trembling to her knees beside the great dragon. *I can't just let him die—not because of me! Not like this!*

And what will you do to prevent it? Windrush rumbled, his voice a confused echo in her mind. *No, there is nothing you can do, and there is no point in all of us dying together. But I promise you this: My father will die proud.*

Jael wept helplessly, leaning against the dragon's forelimb. *Die proud?* What good was dying proud? It was too much;

she could not even think or reason or speak anymore. It was all turning to a blur in her mind. Highwing, no . . . no . . . no . . . !

Someone was speaking to her.

She blinked away her tears and realized that the face swimming in front of her was not the dragon's but Ar's, and the voice rasping in her ear was Ed's, crying her name over and over. And then Ar folded her into his arms, and the tears welled out of her eyes again as she wept with great, quaking sobs.

The cavern was cold, and no amount of pacing before the fire could warm Jael against the chill in her bones, and in her heart. Ar sat and watched her as she paced. He had tried once to coax her into withdrawing from the net for a time, to rest, to sleep. She'd refused, unwilling to leave this realm for even an instant, fearful that she would somehow lose even this last tenuous link with her old friend.

Windrush was lost now in what seemed a strange and tormented sleep. His eyes were half-closed, rolling in their great sockets. From time to time a rush of smoke and sparks issued from his nostrils. It seemed as though he had fled away in spirit, as though his thoughts were somehow abroad in the land, listening for rumor or news, seeking word of hope or peace in a realm that had forgotten those qualities.

Jael had no choice but to accept Windrush's answer about trying to reach Highwing. If Highwing was being held by spells of confinement inside the black peak, there was probably no hope of reaching him—not tonight, at least. But when morning came, she would ask again. The morning light could bring new answers.

Right now, she wished desperately to learn more about the events in the dragon realm since her first visit. She stared at the sleeping Windrush, not daring to wake him, but wanting to question him while there was still time. How much longer could she and her shipmates remain in this realm? Would the currents of the Flux remain still for them, or did those currents hold any force here, in this peculiar pocket of reality? She didn't know. Despite her wariness of the sleeping behemoth, she could not resist tiptoeing close to the dragon's head, studying the rotating, half-closed eyes. Ocean green, even in sleep, the left eye seemed to focus upon her as the faceted fire inside shifted, moving into view between the half-open lids. She hesitated, then found herself stepping closer, gazing into the living light. And before she knew what was happening, she was drawn in again, into the bottomless well. . . .

What do you want to know now? she sensed a preoccupied voice saying, and she felt her own mind answering, *Everything . . . everything about your world, about what has been happening.* . . . And she felt sad laughter echoing around her in answer, as the owner of the voice opened its consciousness to her, or a part of it, even as another part of its mind was occupied in searching out pathways and powers that lay far beyond her comprehension.

Visions seemed to unfold all around her, and the voice spoke as if continuing a story that had been interrupted: . . . *at first there seemed no cause . . . malice and confused desires growing among dragons who had once dwelt together in peace. There have been times in our history when such things have happened before, but we do not remember those times well. Only the crystal ones remember, the females, the draconae. But stories began to emerge of outsiders appearing in the realm—some being chased away, others captured and transformed. No one seemed to know the truth, and many discounted the stories altogether, but the stories themselves came to be a source of discord and strife. What were these demons, these riggers? Were they intruders, to be killed or enslaved. Were they innocent wanderers? Were they a prelude to events foretold by the Words? Rumors abounded, but where was the truth? The strife finally erupted with accusations against my father, and quarreling over who would exact punishment for his actions.*

Images unfolded of dragons feuding, coveting one another's lairs and secret entrances, and breaking the binding spells that held such places of wonder as Highwing's garden. That garden, and others like it, were now destroyed. Images unfolded of jealous contests for power among dragons to whom honor meant nothing. Images of dragons being killed in duels. Of a great mountain disappearing. Of fledglings vanishing from the few remaining places where they had been sheltered. Of the same brothers who had once joined Windrush in flying the length and breadth of the realm, now forcing him into hiding, fearing for his own life.

But this could not have happened for no reason, Jael thought, unable to fully comprehend what she was seeing.

No. It only seemed so, whispered Windrush. *But too many dragons were changing, as though they themselves had fallen under a spell—one that rules not just the air and the rock and water, but the mind, and the spirit itself. It is something that flows deep in the underweb of the realm. It is beyond my understanding, but I know I must resist it. I must believe that others, like me, are living in seclusion, awaiting a sign of hope. But while we hide, the spell continues to work its will over this land.*

And . . . she hesitated, remembering that she had asked this question once already . . . *does it have a name, this spell? Or its maker?*

Well . . . The dragon's thoughts seemed ashamed. *We did not know, or perhaps did not want to know . . . its name. To truly know its name is to admit its presence, to be linked to it forever, for good or ill. But Highwing knew, or at least suspected. And I came to suspect. And lately, I have even heard the name whispered abroad—*

Yes?

The dragon hesitated. His thoughts seemed to uncoil, reluctantly, from around a great knot of fear. *The name is . . . Tar-skel. "Nail of Strength." It is the name of one who would take the realm by fear, and bind it with its power.*

Tar-skel, Jael whispered, shivering, remembering now. She had heard that name only once before, muttered by Highwing, and fearfully.

It is a name known to us through . . . legend. And through . . . prophecy. The dragon's thoughts seemed to stammer. *Through stories whispered by the draconae. By those who dwelled in Dream Mountain, nurturing the dragonlings, when they were not on wing themselves, singing to us words of history, and tradition, and prophecy. They, and the ifflings as well, have spoken this name, Tar-skel, warned us of its threat. We have long known it as a name to frighten dragonlings, a name to inspire fear. But it comes from legend, you see, as well as from prophecy. And we have not really believed the legend or the prophecy. And now both have become real. Tar-skel.* Windrush's thoughts trembled with shame and with fear.

Jael felt a stirring of fear in her own heart each time the name was spoken. She glimpsed images—scattered and fragmentary—of the dragon realm in an age past, when terror and discord were sown through the realm like wind-borne seeds. Sown by one named Tar-skel. Felt, named, but never seen. Not, anyway, for many, many generations.

In the time of my foredragons, long ago—if the legend is true—this one disappeared from the realm, driven from our midst after a reign of turmoil and terror such as we can scarcely imagine.

Driven out? How?

I cannot say. Perhaps the draconae remember, if they still live. The rest of us have forgotten. Oh, we draconi know songs and tales of battle, of heroism and tragedy, and sacrifice, embellished over and over through the generations. The dragon's thoughts paused, reflecting. *But I no longer believe that that is the important or the true part of the story. We draconi, we males, never knew or understood, I think, what sort of one the Nail of Strength was. Or even if "Tar-skel" was its true name. Or even if—as one legend had it—it was an astoundingly ancient being, but one never actually seen by any living dragon. Even after its defeat long ago, legend claimed that it lived on, hiding and sleeping, waiting to return another time.* He sighed. *Would that the realm were done with its evil forever!*

Windrush's thoughts were silent for a time, before whispering, *Our draconi memory is long, in clans and contests and spells; in mountains conquered. But in this, our memory fails us. It is as though my ancestors did not want to remember—as though the memory itself were the evil, to be avoided. And so we believed, or chose to believe, that Tar-skel was nothing more than a tale told to frighten the young ones in their lairs.*

Listening in dismay, Jael heard herself asking, as she floated in the dragon's thoughts, how it was that they had come to believe in Tar-skel now. Had some dragons spoken to the draconae?

Windrush answered mournfully. *We have only their teachings to guide us now, such as we remember them. The Dream Mountain eludes us, in a manner we cannot understand, perhaps kept from us by the power of the Enemy. And without the draconae, without the Dream Mountain, our race cannot continue. There will be no memories or wisdom, no powers of creation . . . and no more young dragons.*

He sighed deeply. *We should have listened better to the draconae when we could. They understood so much better than we. But even without them, in whispers I hear the name Tar-skel. Not openly, but in whispers of thought through the underweb of the world. Even among the draconi—yes, among my own, I have glimpsed thoughts, and a spirit blacker than night, darker than the very roots of the mountains. And corrupt. Yes. And in whispers and rumors among them I have heard the name Tar-skel spoken—not with dread—but with awe and with respect.*

And now the dragon's deepest fears came rising to the surface of its soul. *Behind my father's capture can be found Tar-skel. Behind his trial. And his sentence. And his death that will come. And behind the rage—and the madness—lies the name Tar-skel. The madness that I fear will destroy everything I have ever known . . .*

The dragon's mind-voice was quiet, as an ocean lies quiet between changes of the tides, quiet but with surges and ripples of expectancy beneath the stillness.

After a time, Jael asked what Windrush could tell her about Highwing since she had last seen him.

Little enough, murmured the dragon. *I saw him rarely, though I knew that his once mighty reputation lay in ruins. He came to me toward the end, pursued by scorn. I feared for him, but there was little I could do or say. I was kept from his trial. I only learned the details of that through rumor . . . and through the ifflings.*

The ifflings, Jael thought. She had seen one once, with Highwing. She didn't know what they were, but she sensed that at least they were not on the side of the darkness. She sensed that they bore knowledge. *Can the ifflings help you . . . us? Help us to learn more about . . . Tar-skel? And Highwing?*

There was a long, resonating silence. She sensed a great frustration in the dragon's thoughts, ranging outward through the realm. Finally returning close to her, he whispered, *Perhaps they could. Perhaps. But where are they? Where are the ifflings . . . ?*

And then a new silence closed in, a sad and final silence, shutting her thoughts away from the dragon's altogether.

Jael blinked and stepped back. The connection with the sleeping dragon had been broken. There was so much more she wanted to ask him. Why hadn't Highwing told her, warned her of the danger? Or had he tried? Her thoughts and memories seemed cold and unfamiliar now, as though she were staring at them through a grimy lens. She gazed at the slumbering Windrush, whose eyelids were now closed entirely, and wished that she could somehow open his mind again and ask all of her unanswered questions.

Jael, no. She felt Ar's hand on her shoulder and turned unwillingly. *You must stop this. If you hope to do anything at all, even to find us a safe way out of here, you must rest.* Ar's eyes were filled with sympathy and worry. She wondered if he had felt, or heard, any of what she had just learned from Windrush.

He will wake when he wakes, Ar said. *In the meantime, you, too, must rest.*

I cannot, she insisted. She appreciated his concern. But what good could Ar's sympathy do in the face of the imminent death of a friend and perhaps the destruction of an entire realm?

You must. For the sake of what hope you have left.

Jael stared at him, then walked back to where they had been sitting earlier, beside the hearth and the embers. Resting her head against the stone, she tried to clear her mind, to rest her thoughts. But she kept thinking of Ar's words. Hope. When had she last known true hope? She'd felt it reawakened for a time, with Highwing. But really, when had she lost it? Years ago, in childhood, when her father had succumbed to his dark and brooding depression, when the dreams of the LeBrae business had turned to ashes? Or later, when her mother had died, forcing her to return to live with her father, whose depression had turned to bitterness and cynicism?

She felt a rush of anger at the memory, at the taste of dust that it left in her mouth. Why were these thoughts coming to her now, of all times? She had other worries, far more urgent than some lost memories of her family. She blinked, suddenly aware of her desperate weariness. *Will you stand watch?* she whispered to Ar. *Wake me if anything happens . . . if there is any sign of . . . if Windrush awakens . . . ?*

I will, Ar promised. *Why don't you withdraw just halfway? You can rest without fully leaving the net. I've already rested so, while you've been waiting for the dragon to wake. I found it restoring.*

Undoubtedly he was right. Beside her, the parrot was asleep on a stone perch, apparently doing exactly what Ar had suggested. She would rest, then. And with waking, surely, would come new hope. She prayed that it would. Because right now she had no hope at all.

Chapter 26
FRIEND OF HIGHWING

SHE THOUGHT, in her dream, that she glimpsed a strange, delicate creature that whispered to her of Highwing in his dungeon—of Highwing hearing her call and dying many times over because he had no way to answer her, no way to let her know that he believed in her still, that he remained faithful in his friendship. She thought, in her dream, that the creature entered the dragon's cavern like a spirit-being, emerging from the burning embers of the fire, and disappearing again the way that it had come. She thought that the creature was a fire elemental, and then she thought that it was not that, after all, but instead a slim lemurlike thing covered with silken fur, and that it slipped across the stone hearth with the stealth of a cat. Its appearance made her afraid at first, and then her fears were stilled.

Jael!

She felt a hand touch her, and heard a rumbling snort. She opened her eyes, and saw the rigger-station controls as a ghostly presence over her. She had nearly dropped all the way out of the net. But the sounds she had heard were from the other side, from the world of the Flux. Dazed, she sank back into the net and found herself in the gloom of the dragon's cavern, by the hearth. It seemed unreal, impossible; but she knew that it wasn't. It was as real as her spaceship, as real as her own hands pressed to the cold stone. Ar was shaking her gently. Ed was fluttering his wings, making a gargling sound.

And the dragon, Windrush, had raised his head and was looking around the cavern. *Who is here?*

We are, Jael mumbled. *We never left.*

Not you. Something else. The dragon cocked his head, snorting sparks. *An iffling. While I slept, an iffling was here.* His eyes rotated to gaze at his guests. *Did you see it?*

Ar looked puzzled. *An iffling? There was a moment . . . when I thought I felt, or saw . . . something. But I don't know what it was, and it passed quickly.*

Jael remembered the images in her dream. *I may have seen it*, she murmured. She described the creature that she had seen, or imagined, in her sleep. Was it like the being she had glimpsed once talking to Highwing? She wasn't sure; she hadn't seen either one very clearly.

But Windrush was nodding gravely, his eyes glowing with a smoky inner fire. He seemed perturbed by her report, particularly the mention of Highwing's awareness of her presence. He lifted his head and sniffed the air and shot a frustrated flame toward the ceiling.

Then it was true, Jael thought. The dream-visit had been real. And Highwing was alive, and knew she was in the realm. How could she not do everything in her power to reach him?

The dragon was watching her now, his eyes darkening. *I sense your thoughts*, he observed. *You do not know what you ask of yourself. There is nothing that you can do. Nothing that any of us can do.*

Jael rose and strode to face the dragon at close range. Though his head rested on his forefeet, she had to look up into his eye. He seemed more massive than ever before. The scales that covered his head shone dimly in the cold light of the dying hearth fire. *I must try. And if that means trying alone, I will do that*, she said flatly.

Smoke billowed from the reptile's nostrils. *Are you so certain of what you wish to do?*

I know what I must do.

May I point out, at least, that your strength is limited here? You would not last. It would be best if you let me fly you to the edge of our world, so that you could leave all of this safely behind you. His gaze narrowed. *In truth, you know, our troubles are not your concern.*

Ar made a clearing-of-the-throat sound. *He has a point, Jael. Our ship is damaged. We limped into these mountains. I don't know how we can expect to—*

But Windrush could help us, Jael interrupted. *Couldn't you?*

The dragon gave her a measured look. *I confess that I do not understand your powers, or your role in our world—if you still have a role to play.* He hesitated. *The Words of prophecy, I admit, seem to suggest that you might. But I perceive that your strength has been weakened by the . . . mishap . . . that brought you here.*

Jael could not dispute the point. She scuffed at the stone floor of the cavern with her booted foot. The floor was solid, cold, hard. A part of her wanted to believe that this was all a rigger-illusion, but she knew that it wasn't. Her debts, and her honor, were as real here as they were back in that world of space and stars and planets. Turning to Ar, she said, *I know you don't think we should do this. I wish there were some way that we could split up, so that you could take the ship to safety, and I could go on with this alone.*

Ar reached out with both hands. *Jael, please!*

But there isn't, is there? she continued, not responding to his gesture. *Ar, I have to do this—to try, anyway. At least, that's the way I feel.* She swallowed, knowing that she couldn't make the decision alone. Not only would that be unfair, it would be impossible, if Ar opposed her.

Awk! The parrot flapped his wings violently. *Try! We Try! Yes, Jayl?*

Ar looked askance at the bird before addressing Jael again. *What do you think you . . . or we . . . can do?*

Jael had no plan, and she feared that there was little time left before Highwing's execution. She wished she could remember more clearly what the iffling had tried to tell her in the dream. What would Highwing say to her if he could speak? *Windrush,* she said suddenly, *can you reach out to your father with your thoughts?*

The dragon's breath hissed out unhappily. *I have tried. But there is a barrier preventing me—a sorcery. I cannot break through.*

Was that what he was doing when he was ranging outward with his thoughts in his sleep? Jael wondered. She nodded in disappointment. *What about the ifflings, then?*

A raised eye ridge conveyed the dragon's puzzlement.

Couldn't you contact the ifflings and ask them to help us? If they have touched Highwing's thoughts in prison, then they must know how to reach him!

The dragon shifted position suddenly. He raised a talon, dangerously close to Jael, and scratched at the knobby bumps on the back of his head. *A good idea, perhaps. But I do not know how to reach the ifflings, either. They come to me when they will, not when I will. I wish I could call them to me.*

Jael squinted at him, then paced. There had to be a way. *Do you know how to get to where he is being held?* she asked.

The dragon's eyes glowed dully. *To the Black Peak? Of course. But that won't necessarily help us find him.*

Why not? Don't you know where he is imprisoned?

That, I fear, is a closely guarded secret, Windrush murmured. *He is somewhere deep within the mountain, in a dungeon protected by tightly woven spells that alter the very shape and substance of the world. That is all I know. I do not know the way, nor can I penetrate those spells.*

Jael remembered the magical entrance that had brought them into this cavern. She believed Windrush when he said that such knowledge of Highwing's prison would be kept from him. But there had to be a way!

There was a sudden rasping sound behind her, and then a fluttering of wings, as Ed flew to her shoulder. *Rawk. Coming. Something coming,* the bird muttered in her ear.

Windrush must have sensed the approach at the same time. The dragon's eyes brightened, and he raised his head, sniffing. *It comes!* he hissed in astonishment.

Jael turned to look and her heart nearly stopped. The creature from her dreams was crossing the cavern floor, walking toward them. It moved with four-footed grace, and its head was raised, eyeing them each in turn as it approached. It looked, as she'd remembered, like a sleek, huge-eyed lemur. *Hello,* Jael whispered, scarcely knowing how to begin, knowing only that she had a thousand urgent questions.

You must go to Highwing now, if you would go at all, the creature said, its voice a willowy sigh in her head. Its eyes shone dark and glistening; but the real contact, Jael sensed, was not through the eyes but directly through the mind.

You know how to reach him? Jael whispered. *Can you take a message to him?*

There is no time. Highwing rises to the peak now, and if you would speak to him in this lifetime . . .

Jael felt an electric shock go through her. *You mean . . . he is being taken to his—?* Her voice caught; she could not speak the words.

You must not delay, urged the iffling. *For the draconae, if you will not do it for Highwing. For the memory of Skytouch!*

Jael did fully understand the iffling's words. Nevertheless, she pleaded with it. *Will you come with us?*

I cannot, it whispered. *But you know the way.*

I don't. But one of us does! Jael spun, crying to Windrush. *Do you hear that? You are the only one who knows the way! Will you take us or not? I must know now!* Her breath ran out with a great cry. She gazed at the dragon, then turned back to the iffling.

But it was gone.

Where—? she choked, her breath a cry of pain. But she knew that the creature had delivered its message and departed.

The dragon's breath rumbled indecisively in the back of his throat. Suddenly his eyes glowed with anger and determination. *Climb onto my back,* he said. *The time has come.*

Yawwwwk! Now! shrieked the parrot.

Jael looked at Ar, a growing lump in her throat—and through her own welling tears she saw him nod. Together, they scrambled up onto the dragon's shoulders and clung to his scales.

She never even saw the mountain open up around them as the dragon leaped with full fury into the air.

A predawn wind blew damp and chilly around them as Windrush beat his way uprange, northward and westward. Jael was astonished at the dragon's speed. She glanced back at the barely perceptible ghost of their spaceship riding on the dragon's back, and thought that this was probably the fastest she had ever moved through the Flux—under control, anyway. She and Ar huddled close behind the dragon's head, but even so, the powerful movement of Windrush's wings threatening to hurl them off. Ed was hunkered down in the shelter of her body.

Do you have any idea what we'll do when we get there? Ar asked, his voice barely audible over the wind, as the land-scape spun by.

She shook her head, blinked tears from her eyes. Even as they flew, memories of her father were rising to the surface. She remembered accompanying him into space as a young child, standing with him at the portals as he showed her the hypnotic beauty of the stars of deep space, and shared with her the joy and the desire to cross the gulfs between the stars. This was a long time before the failure, the bitterness, before the hatred. She shivered. Why was she remembering this now? Was it because she was getting closer to Highwing? She remembered the dragon's magic, and thought that it was almost as though it were at work again now, finishing a task that had been left undone, stirring up memories that had been buried for good reason, memories she wanted left hidden. As if to torment her, one more image rose to her thoughts, an early memory of sitting and watching him frown in concentration over his work, of admiring him as she watched the smoke curl up from his pipe, of loving him. Loving him?

She blinked the thought away, determinedly shaking her head. Ar had asked her a question. . . . What would they do when they reached the Black Peak? She had no idea. She knew only that she had to be there. If there was any way to save Highwing's life . . . but what could she possibly hope to accomplish against dragons massed and bent upon murder? And what about Tar-skel? Now that she knew its name, did that mean that she was tied to it forever, always to be its foe? She shivered, and felt a tremor pass through Windrush's massive body.

The mountains changed slowly as they flowed past. The peaks were becoming bolder, more pronounced against the sky, black against grey. The frail light of dawn only hinted at the sunrise that was surely to come. In the air, Jael noticed tiny flecks of light drifting toward them, like windborne sparks in the night. Windrush veered slightly to intercept them. They flashed and twinkled for an instant, as he snapped them out of the air with his great jaws. His wing-strokes seemed to grow stronger, as though he had gained sustenance from the sparks. *Lumenis wind-dust*, he remarked, but didn't explain further.

Jael didn't ask; she had more urgent things on her mind.

There, Windrush said a few minutes later, indicating a dark, massive peak directly ahead. *There you will soon see dragons . . . more than you can imagine. And you will see one dragon worth more than all of the others together.* Sparks from his exhalation flew back past his head, past Jael and Ar.

The sunrise came quickly, a sudden blaze of maroon and gold from the range off to their right. In the glory of the new day, Jael suddenly descried what Windrush had promised: dragons—dozens, or perhaps hundreds, of them—a vast ring of dragons circling the summit of the peak ahead. She recognized it from the images Windrush had shared with her: the Black Peak, highest peak in the realm. It loomed, a great and terrible turret against the sky. The dragons were still far away; they looked more like a thick flock of blackbirds. If only they were mere birds! Somewhere among them should be the one dragon who mattered to Jael. Somewhere among them should be Highwing.

She realized that she was having trouble breathing, and she forced herself to take slow, deliberate breaths, and to relax slightly the grip of her whitened knuckles on Wind-rush's knobs. She glanced at Ar, and saw in his eyes a sober acceptance of what was to come. *If*—she began, and stopped.

If we don't . . . Her voice hurt; she swallowed and shook her head. What was there to say that he didn't already know? Ar smiled, his lips a forced crinkle pattern, and he peered straight ahead, not meeting her eyes. She thought she heard him humming. She nodded and focused on calming herself, trying to gather her strength.

She felt a wave of dizziness and, just for an instant, felt thoughts that were not her own. It was a familiar touch, but it was gone already, and she cried out silently, trying in vain to recapture it. But it had triggered something else in her mind. Another memory rose up hauntingly, infuriatingly, into her thoughts. *Not now!* she cried silently. *Please not now!* It was her father again, scowling, signing the permissions that would send her to rigger school. She wanted to scream her plea—*Not now!*—but she was helpless to speak as the memory flushed through her. Whatever else her father had done, he had allowed her to become a rigger, had left her the money that let her finish the training that took her to the stars, that kept her alive and brought her here. That was what Highwing had seen, and had tried to show her, so long ago.

She felt that distant other's presence again now, but only for an instant, a tickle in her awareness. She recognized the touch of Highwing's magic—still at work, even in the face of his impending death.

Then she saw him. Her breath went out in a frightened gasp.

He was a distant, still tiny figure, perched on the very summit of that black mountain. The other dragons were circling around him like buzzards. Jael could not have said how she recognized Highwing from such a distance, or how she knew precisely what the other dragons were doing—that they were executioners awaiting their moment of triumph. But those facts were as stark in her mind as the newborn daylight, and as hurtful as a searing sun. *They're going to throw him down!* she whispered, scarcely able to voice the words.

No, Windrush answered. *Far worse than that.* And his wings beat with even greater urgency, carrying them ever more swiftly toward the peak. *Butchers! Devils!* he cried out in anguish.

Jael struggled to draw breath into her lungs, but she felt as though a giant fist were crushing her chest. Gasping, she fought to speak. *Closer, Windrush! Closer! Faster!*

The dragon did not answer, but his wings furiously drummed the air. Jael squinted through tears, trying to focus on the peak. *Highwing!* she thought. *Damn them all—I'm here, Highwing!*

They soared so fast and high that the peak mushroomed in size before them. The dragons circling the peak were now just ahead of them, and to the sides. But Jael scarcely noticed; she saw only the lone dragon atop the peak, turning his head to and fro, flapping his wings wide, but not flying. The air around the peak shimmered as though with heat, and it reverberated with the sound of chanting, and that was when she realized, when she *felt* with a shivering certainty, that more than just a multitude of dragons opposed Highwing. There was a powerful sorcery at work, altering the very nature of the Flux, and it was that power which held him prisoner. She heard a thin *Rrrrrr . . . graggons . . .* and realized that Ed was smelling the executioners. He was hunched as low as he could get in front of her, and was trembling with fear.

Highwing's head was turned away from them now. She urged Windrush onward. *Closer.* Suddenly, a hot, reeking blast rocked them, and two black dragons swooped in from either side, nearly colliding with Windrush. *DO YOU WISH TO JOIN HIM, BROTHER?* they bellowed, in voices that seemed to erupt from the bowels of the earth. *WATCH, RIGGER-DEMONS! WATCH! AND YOU TOO MAY JOIN HIM!* The chanting swelled in the air, in a terrifying tongue that tore incomprehensibly at her ears and her mind and her heart.

Clinging to Windrush as he veered from the other dragons, she drew a desperate lungful of air, and the cry exploded from her, full of rage: *FRIEND OF HIGHWING! I AM JAEL, FRIEND OF HIGHWING! HIGHWING, I AM HERE!* And she froze, thrilled and terrified by her own words.

For an instant, all motion in the sky seemed to cease. She saw Highwing turn his head, and across the emptiness of space between them she glimpsed the fire in his emerald eyes, and she felt his mind brush against hers one more time. *Windrush, turn back to him!* she pleaded, and the dragon wheeled around and arrowed toward his father. *AWAY FROM ME, BROTHERS!* Windrush bellowed. And Jael cried, *HIGHWING!*

The chant rose louder and faster, and the air was dark with dragons swarming, and alight with dragon-fire. And through the fire and smoke, she saw Highwing spread his wings wide and full, and leap from the mountain peak. *Yes!* she cried silently. *You can escape!*

But Highwing banked and flew straight toward her, straight into the swarm of his captors. A thundering outcry arose. The air was torn apart like a curtain, and there was a dazzling flash where Highwing had been, and through the din she heard the cry: *You came, Jael! You came!* But when the light faded, Highwing was gone. A chorus of triumph from the executioners was cut short by a tremendous concussion, which lifted Windrush and his passengers and hurled them back from the peak.

Highwing—! Jael screamed.

But he was gone. Only the other dragons remained, and they were already turning to attack their new foes.

Windrush, where did they send him? she cried, her voice cracking with grief.

For a prolonged breath, she heard nothing but the sound of rushing air, and then the dragon saying, *To the static realm . . . to die alone, separated from this world forever . . .* in a voice so dulled by grief and despair that his words seemed to make no sense at all. Jael rose high on the dragon's shoulder and leaned forward over his forehead ridges to gaze into the corner of his left eye. As she linked for just an instant with the dragon's mind, the image came clear in her own . . . *to the static realm . . .*

And she knew what realm that was, a realm that dragons feared as deeply as any human feared the fires of Hades . . .

And in the space of one breath, with no time at all to

think about it, she drew all of her strength around her, drew
Ar and Ed close, and let the full gleaming shape of her starship billow out behind her. Ignoring the screams of rage from
the other dragons, and Windrush crying to her to wait, she
leaped away from Windrush's shoulders with a shout of farewell. And she hooked her fingers into the stuff of the Flux,
and heedless of the babble of voices around her, clawed a
rent in the continuum and wrenched the ship upward, spiraling upward, out of the Flux.

Chapter 27
THE STATIC REALM

THEY EMERGED nearly inside a billowing red sun. The star loomed enormous before them, filling half the sky with its crimson photosphere. Seemingly dark granules and spots swam across its massive face, livid in the sensory-net image. The star poured out a ferocious radiation that was already threatening to overwhelm *Seneca*'s shielding.

Jael, what are you doing? Ar shouted. *Get us out of here!* He was already retuning the flux-pile, preparing to take them back into the Flux.

Ar, no! He's here somewhere! They threw him out of the Flux, into our space!

Ar was stunned silent for a moment. *Jael, it's too late! There's nothing we can do for him!*

Jael worked frantically to engage the ship's normal-space controls through the net. *We don't know it's too late! Ar, help me! We've got to scan for him!* As she spoke, she turned on all of the normal-space sensors, setting them to search for anything solid.

Yawww! Ed took wing in the net. *Find him! Find him!*

Yes—help us! Jael was fumbling with the controls. It was

awkward piloting the ship in normal-space from within the rigger-net. *Ar—can you pull out of the net and handle the ship from the bridge?*

The Clendornan's face loomed large before her. *All right, Jael—but I'm not giving you much time. We can't last long this close to a star, and I'm not going to kill us trying!*

Just do it! He must be close. We left the Flux almost together.

Ar's face vanished, and a moment later, she felt the normal-space controls slipping out of her grasp. She waited, nearly frantic, as the sudden silence seemed to stretch forever. She found herself shaking with fear, and under the terrible strain she felt something shake loose from her subconscious mind. Space itself seemed to quiver as a face rose up and floated before her, in her mind, exactly as Mogurn had appeared in the Flux after she'd killed him. She panted, struggling not to scream. It was her father's face, and she recognized the memory at once. It was her father in his final, tormented year, babbling, "Master your demons, Jael, master your demons!" He had never made peace with his own failures, yet still he haunted her with his failed advice. And yet . . . without him, she realized, she would not even be here . . .

The face disappeared as Ar's voice reverberated into the net: *Incredible, Jael—there's a small asteroid nearby. Its orbit is taking it into the sun's photosphere.*

Her heart jumped. *Is there anything on it?*

Checking now. The imaging is very difficult . . .

Jael's heart pounded as she waited for his report. Then she heard: *There is something on it. I can't tell what. We'd have to shift our orbit inward to approach, and we don't have much maneuverability.*

Do it! she shouted. *Don't waste time talking!*

She felt a shudder and knew that Ar had activated the maneuvering drive. Focusing from within the net, she located the asteroid, almost lost in the glare of the sun. She brought to bear all of the computer-imaging powers she had available . . .

And she saw something knobby on the asteroid's surface. As they closed on it, the asteroid swelled in her view: a gnarled, airless rock, burning up in the glare and heat of the sun. Closer . . . larger . . .

Do you see it, Jael? We've got to make our identification and get out!

She strained, and saw that the object on the asteroid was . . . moving. Or was it her imagination?

Closer . . .

As the image grew, the knob began to look like something flapping in a breeze, an old bag, or a wounded animal struggling pathetically. It looked like nothing resembling a dragon, certainly not Highwing. And yet . . . she felt a tickling at the edge of her thoughts, the presence of something or someone familiar.

Highwing! she whispered in agony.

Jael, you don't know it's Highwing! she heard Ar protesting; or perhaps it was her own inner voice, trying to keep her from doing something insane. But she felt no doubt, she *knew* that her friend was out there, burning up in the sun. She had no idea what physical manifestation a dragon from the Flux would have in normal-space, in the "static realm," but she knew she had to get to him fast. *Ar, get us closer!*

Jael, we can't help him! We can't land, and we can't go outside for him in this!

She could imagine his consternation as she asked the impossible. But she didn't care about that; she didn't care about possible or impossible. *If you won't do it, I will!* But even as she spoke, she realized that Ar was already trying to do what she'd asked. The asteroid was looming very close now, but its rotation was carrying the thing on its surface from sight. *Can you match its rotation, just for a minute? Can you get me close, Ar? Get me close, and I can reach him!*

Her friend was doing just that, and better than she could have done it, even as he protested, *You can't reach anything, Jael! Don't you understand?* But they were close enough now for a clear image, even in the terrible blood-glare of the sun. Ar was bringing them around in a loop to catch up with the rock's motion, and what they saw struggling at the edge of their view, foundering on the surface of that asteroid, was clearly a living being . . .

A dying being.

Dying. Even here, even now, the dragon's spell was at work. She remembered her father dying, a broken man . . . and knew that she could no longer hate him. Pity him, yes, but not hate him.

Highwing was dying . . .

My sacred word, Ar whispered, in disbelief.

Though the creature in the image was little more than a pathetic bag of bones, it nevertheless had a head, and something like wings crumpled at its sides; and it had eyes full of pain, eyes that peered vacantly, searching the sky as though it knew something was close but couldn't quite see it. *Here, Highwing!* she cried softly.

The creature moved its head suddenly, as though it had heard her. And she could have sworn that she heard its voice in her own head, groaning, *You can do nothing . . . don't die for nothing!* And she felt its pain, in a tremendous wave that surged through the net, shaking her. Ed flapped violently, in terror.

Her father had once loved her, had made it possible for her to be here. Would it all be for nothing? Yes, if she could not save Highwing, if she could not give even that in return. . . .

She drew a breath, struggling not to cry out—and suddenly shouted, *I need to be just a little closer, Ar!*

No, Jael . . . we can't . . . the screens are overloaded! We've got to drop back into the Flux—NOW! Do it, Jael!

No more than a hundred or a thousand meters from her, the creature that was Highwing sank helplessly back as the asteroid's rotation brought him back into the full hellish daylight of that swollen sun. The voice that reached her was weak, whispering: *No, Jael—*

Ar, get in here and HELP ME! she screamed. *Ed, help me!*

Whatever they answered, she didn't hear. She only knew what she had to do. She stretched the net to its limit, drawing on all of the reserve power—and it wasn't enough. The instant she sensed Ar entering the net, she seized the normal-space controls and contorted space with the maneuvering drive, dropping the ship toward the asteroid's surface—

dropping in a suicidal dive toward the rock, toward Highwing.

Tears burned her eyes as she thought, Not for nothing! It will not be for nothing!

Jael, no! Ar shouted, as he saw what she was doing.

Be ready to take us down! she commanded, her voice cold and furious. *When I say to.*

Ed must have sensed her immediate intention, because he streaked to the forward end of the net, stretching it . . . and Jael's arms lengthened and reached out for Highwing . . . and the burning rock rose, slanting and rotating, to collide with them . . .

Highwing! she cried. She felt the net brush over him, over the rock; and she molded the net to include the dragon but not the rock, and she screamed: *NOW, AR—NOW!*

Ar's strength in the net joined hers, and over the groaning protest of the flux-pile, they reached into the Flux and pulled the ship down . . .

The asteroid loomed like a massive wall, and they were careening toward it—

—and it shimmered and became transparent—

—and the fearful blazing sun became transparent—

—and both were gone, and the clouds of the Flux materialized in their place.

The net nearly disintegrated from the effort of containing Highwing within it, but somehow it held. As the universe around them changed, as they sank deeper into the ocean of the Flux, passing through layers of change, the creature they were holding began to change, as well.

No longer a bag of bones, he was growing in mass and size. His shape was returning, becoming a dragon shape again, a dragon struggling to spread his wings. *Highwing!* she shouted, her heart breaking with hope and fear. He was struggling, in agony. And the net that supported him was beginning to tear.

Jael, let him go, Ar urged, and his voice, though calm, reverberated in the center of her consciousness, a command that she could not ignore. *Now, Jael—or we'll lose the net for good.*

Yes . . . she whispered. She forced herself to open her arms and release the dragon.

He fell away from them, and before she could do anything more, Ar had already drawn in the net, cutting the drain on the ship's power. She knew he'd done the right thing—they'd nearly lost the flux-pile, and that would have been the end for them—but she could not keep from crying out as she saw Highwing dropping through the air. She shouted to him, and dimly sensed his awareness.

Jael . . . the voice barely whispered over the wind. For an instant it sounded like her father's voice. But it wasn't; it was Highwing's.

Below them now, she saw mountains, and they were descending fast from a great height, through a sky wracked by crosswinds. There was one enormous peak that might have been the Black Peak, and she wondered whether the dragons were still there, and scarcely knew whether to hope yes or no. Then she heard Ed crying, *Graggons near!* and *Fly, Highwing—CAW!—must fly!*

But Highwing was falling, not flying. He was struggling to open his wings against the rushing air. One wing opened a little, then the other, and then he was tumbling out of control. His strength was gone. He was falling, almost certainly, to his death. Jael warped their net into a delta-winged glider, and they dived to follow the dragon as he fell. *Highwing, please pull out of it!* she pleaded, and knew it was futile, crying for what could not be.

Graggon!

The movement was so fast, she scarcely saw the dragon flash up and around them and around Highwing. And she heard the voice before she focused on the form. *You have the power to bring him back!* Windrush shouted, his voice so full of astonishment that his wonder echoed across the mountains.

Windrush, can you help—?

But her words were unnecessary, because Windrush was already beneath his father. She shuddered as the two dragons came together in midair, fearing for an instant that she would watch them both die; but Windrush's strength was sufficient. He caught Highwing on his back, roaring under the sudden, tremendous weight. He couldn't stop the descent, but he slowed it. Highwing, agonizingly, succeeded at last in stretching his wings enough to help support himself. Something of his old glory was at last visible in his form. *Windrush-sh-sh*, he sighed, his voice quaking as he spoke the other dragon's name.

Jael flew closer.

You can fly . . . proudly . . . your last . . . flight . . . Windrush said, his words labored.

Yes. And Highwing's nostrils smoked, though the smoke was carried away in an instant by the wind. As Jael approached, her heart stopping because of what she had just heard, Highwing's eyes turned to focus on her. They descended together, the dragon's gaze flickering with a remnant of its old fire. And for an instant, she felt Highwing's presence in her thoughts.

Jael . . .

Highwing, can you make it? Can you fly? she whispered.

She heard something like laughter, but it was so full of pain and sorrow and joy and inexpressible dragon feelings that she could not really have called it laughter. And she heard, *Little Jael . . . once more only . . . will I fly . . .* and his words ended with a sound that reminded her of chimes ringing across an expanse of water. In that instant, her mind filled with memories of their first moments together, and she knew that she was seeing what he was remembering. Her mind filled, as well, with other images of the dragon realm: Skytouch dying, friends gone and sons departed, imprisonment and terror, and blazing alien heat; and images of triumph and the promise of victory and vindication. And she knew, too, what he saw in her mind: memories of her father, and acceptance and forgiveness. And she heard the dragon's voice again, saying, *You have . . . saved me . . . saved us both . . . so that I may . . . pass from this life with dignity . . . little Jael.* And again she heard the laughter that was not laughter, and she felt something change in the way that the dragons were flying.

Look, Ar murmured in wonderment.

Highwing was spreading his wings over Windrush's. She

could feel the effort, the terrible pain that it was costing him. The dragon's wings caught the wind smartly as they stretched out, shining silver and iridescent in the sun. A jet of fire blossomed from his throat, and he lifted away from Windrush's back. For an instant, Jael feared that he would tumble again; but he drew his strength from somewhere, and though he swayed perilously, he fought his way into a climb. As Jael strained desperately to follow, he turned his head, and his eyes glowed and joined with hers, and he called, his voice clear even through the final pain: *Well met and farewell . . . Windrush . . . riggers . . . Jael!* His breath flared and smoked, and he thundered, *Call, "FRIEND OF HIGHWING" . . . and I will hear you . . .* And before he could complete his words, he began to change, to become transparent.

The sunlight caught him, dazzling, and for an instant he was a dragon of living crystal glass. Living light. Then he was no more.

Farewell, Highwing . . . Jael whispered, choking. She wept helplessly for a moment, before she caught her breath and bellowed raggedly to the empty wind: *FRIEND OF HIGHWING!* And from the wind she thought she heard laughter, chimelike, full of sorrow and joy. Or perhaps she only wished to hear it, his laughter echoing on the wind.

And then they were falling, the net fraying around them. And Ar fought for control, but she could do nothing to help him; her heart was too heavy with grief.

Chapter 28
A FINAL PARTING

WINDRUSH CAUGHT them far more easily than he had caught his father. Jael gasped and clung to his neck. They huddled atop the dragon, Jael pressing her forehead to his rippling scales as she wept. For a long time, she was aware of nothing that was happening, except her grief. *Highwing . . . oh, Highwing . . . !*

She heard a quiet voice in the back of her mind, saying, *You have done well against the darkness, O Friend of Highwing.* At first she tried to ignore it; she was confused not only by the words, but by the voice. It did not seem to be Windrush's, or Ar's. It said again, *You have done well against the darkness. . . .*

She opened her eyes, brushing away her tears. For an instant, she thought she saw a creature glimmering in the air just off Windrush's left shoulder. Perhaps it was her imagination, but what she saw was the iffling, floating half in and half out of this realm. *What do you mean?* she whispered. *I've accomplished nothing.* Even saying it, her pain seemed to grow.

But you have, rigger Jael, answered the quiet voice in her mind. *More than you know.*

She tried to focus her gaze on the iffling, still not sure if it was there. And now it wasn't; perhaps it had just been a strange reflection from the sun. *Ar,* she croaked, *did you just see something? Or hear a voice?*

But it was the dragon and not Ar who answered. *Indeed you have done well,* he said, echoing the iffling's words. *And not just for my father. Look ahead!* And with a jet of smoke, he pointed.

The dragon seemed to be indicating the great peak ahead of them—the Black Peak. Something about the mountain was changing, though she couldn't tell at once what it was. A swarm of dragons was fleeing the area, as though frightened. Frightened? By what? Peering past Windrush's great head, Jael saw that the left side of the summit was shrouded in a strange, silvery mist. It remained so for only a few seconds, as the mountain went through a startling metamorphosis: a portion of the peak seemed to dissolve in the mist, to turn glassy and clear. And within the glass there appeared a sullen red light, like the coals of a tremendous fire, pulsing and flickering. Jael looked away, not believing her eyes; but when she looked back, there was still a piece of the mountain missing, and in its place was . . . fire. Fire? In the heart of the mountain? *Windrush, what's happening?*

To her astonishment, the dragon laughed for joy.

Why are you laughing? she cried.

A change in the spell-weaving, Jael! A change in the underrealm! You have done what the rest of us feared to do! He beat the air, winging toward the peak. *You saved my father's life— and far more than that!*

What do you mean? What are you talking about? We failed! We were too late! As she leaned forward to shout at the dragon, the wind stung her eyes, drawing fresh tears. The sensation was welcome; it numbed the pain within.

No, Jael, you didn't fail at all! The dragon's voice resounded with both joy and sorrow. *Highwing passed in this world—his spirit has passed into the world. You saved him from the final exile. I don't know how you were able, or how you knew. But he is safe from Tar-skel now, and his strength will become ours.* The wind seemed to roar through his words. *Look at the Black*

Peak! It is plain for all to see: you have broken the sorcery that held this mountain!

Jael drew back, no less confused than before. She looked to Ar for help, but he had his eyes shut, as though he could not bear to listen. Finally she realized that he was busy trying to draw together the threads of their rigger-net, which she had nearly destroyed. Jael peered back at the mountain, trying to think clearly through her grief. Most of the other dragons had scattered. The mountain looked now as though a great glass lens near its summit were focusing the rays of a blazing red sun, as though a star had come to life in the peak itself. What was happening to the powers of this world? Don't go too close, she wanted to beg Windrush, but the words froze in her throat.

A terrible spell was woven here, the dragon said, as though in answer to her thoughts. *By Tar-skel, and by dragons who were once called my brothers, before they became his followers.* His voice rang with anger. *Where you see that fire is surely where they imprisoned Highwing—where they gathered their power to twist open the seams of the world, and to hurl him out of the realm. It would have been a terrifying display of power—and they wanted you here to witness it! They wanted to bray at you in their triumph. But they underestimated you! They were too proud, too sure, too eager to show their strength.*

Jael shuddered, and yet could not help marveling. The mountain continued to metamorphose as they soared toward it, until it looked like a window into another universe, a window ablaze with the fire of an alien sun, where a dragon had been sent to die. *Is that fire the remains of their magic? It looks like the sun in our realm, where we found Highwing.*

Windrush glanced back at her in surprise. *Is that true? Perhaps it is the same. You brought him back before the underrealm could be twisted closed again to seal his exile. Perhaps, indeed, a window remains open!* Windrush rumbled approvingly. *Those who labored in that cruel effort must be very angry now.* Suddenly he thundered: *LET THIS PEAK REMAIN AS A TESTAMENT TO THE CONCEIT OF TAR-SKEL! LET HIS DEFEAT HERE TODAY—!*

A crackling flame shot past them, cutting off his exclamation. Jael felt the hot blast on her left cheek, and turned to see a large, black dragon hurtling downward toward Windrush's left flank. *DIE WITH YOUR RIGGER FRIENDS, WINDRUSH!* it bellowed. Flashing low across them, it nearly collided with Windrush, flattening Jael and her friends to the dragon's back. Clutching Windrush's scaly hide, Jael raised her head again. A second dragon loomed on the right, raking them with fire as it too crossed over them.

Apparently their victory had been short-lived.

The two dragons banked into fast orbits around Windrush, snarling in a tongue Jael could not understand. Windrush answered their challenge with a blast of fire, and a roar that seemed to shake the earth and echo back from the mountains. The two dragons veered away, but only for a few seconds. Jael scanned the air to see if others were coming. Windrush might be able to stand off two, but if there were more . . .

Hrrraaawwww! Show them! Ed screamed.

Ed, shut up! she snapped. *Ar, do we have any power left in the net?*

Ar opened his eyes, his lips pressed in a straight line. *Not much, I'm afraid.*

Windrush, what can we do?

Hawww! Show them! Show them!

Jael made a furious grab for the bird—then realized that perhaps Ed was smarter than they were. She gestured to Ar, and together they allowed the starship to billow out behind them, making it as large and imposing as possible. The two dragons, startled, retreated angrily to a more respectful distance. But Jael doubted that they would stay away long. *What next?* she murmured.

The dragon answered, *We must not let them—*

He was interrupted by another blast.

Two new dragons streaked in out of the smoke-filled air. Jael and Ar flattened themselves. The dragons shot past, over their heads, and raked the first two attackers with withering fire. Pivoting in the air, seemingly on their wingtips, they came back around for another pass. A dragon voice filled the air: *LEAVE WINDRUSH AND THE RIGGERS TO US!*

THEY ARE OURS! The first pair of dragons wheeled around, beating their wings angrily, but the new pair were far more determined. They laced the air with acrid fire, until Jael began to choke, clinging to Windrush. The original two finally veered away, snarling, and fled downrange to the left, hugging close to the lower mountain slopes.

Windrush climbed energetically, but the new pair of dragons crisscrossed beneath him until they rose on either side, fuming smoke and fire. They thundered out words Jael could not understand. *Who is this?* Jael whispered, fearing that they had traded bad enemies for worse.

Windrush answered this new challenge with a roar and a tremendous flame, and the others replied in kind. Back and forth they bellowed, fire crackling. Jael clung to Windrush's back. Ed crouched close to her breast, his head in constant motion, peering at one dragon, then another.

Suddenly Windrush cried joyously, *WELCOME BACK, BROTHERS! BROTHERS AGAIN!* And he sent a triumphant tongue of fire into the air.

Jael's breath went out in a gasp.

Rrawwwwwk! Ed shouted.

The two dragons dropped into tight formation on either side of Windrush. Their eyes glowed wonderingly as they studied the riggers and their spaceship. One of them spoke, before Jael could ask Windrush for an explanation. *We felt his passing,* the left-hand dragon murmured, and his voice seemed filled with sorrow, but also with a breath of gladness. *And in that moment, we glimpsed . . . his triumph . . . and our own terrible foolishness.*

When you broke the spell of exile, you released us from a sorcery, as well, said the other dragon, and Jael thought that she heard shame in his voice. *Something changed around us, or maybe inside us. It was as though we had been blinded before, and suddenly we saw—and it was only a glimpse, but it was enough—how we had been fooled, seduced by the power of Tarskel, by our own arrogance in wanting to share in it.* The dragon's voice grew softer. *In that one instant, you freed us . . . to make a . . . wiser choice. We have much to be sorrowful for. We have wronged our father, and Windrush, and you. We would . . . wish to make right what we have done.*

We felt many breaking free as we did, said the dragon on the left. *But . . . many others remain in service to the Enemy. Among them, I fear, is our fourth brother. If indeed he still lives at all.*

Jael was stunned, unable to answer.

Windrush nodded somberly at that last statement. *The confrontation has only begun, then.* He angled his head to glance back at the riggers. *But at least I will no longer stand alone among dragons. Riggers—my brothers! Wingtouch and Farsight, sons of Highwing. My brothers once more!*

The two dragons looked across at Jael, and she thought they seemed nervous. She wondered why, and then realized that they were waiting for something. *Honored to meet you,* she said, nodding to each in turn. *I am Jael. And my companions—*

Ed! squawked the parrot, before she could gesture.

She looked at Ar. His eyes were dim with tiredness, and his lips were thin and straight. Nevertheless, he nodded gravely. *Honored,* he said. *I am Ar.*

The two dragons expelled steam from their nostrils and muttered wonderingly. *Honored,* they replied. *Wingtouch,* said one. *Farsight,* said the other.

Jael nodded and sat back with a sigh. As the three dragons flew in a slow curve around the fiery mountain, she leaned to peer at the landscape below. Was it her imagination, or was there more color in the land than there had been before? It no longer seemed the same stark desolation of black and grey, and it didn't seem to her that the difference was entirely due to the glass-encapsulated glow of the red sun. She spoke to Windrush, and he dipped lower for a better view. The ground slipped silently beneath them. She glimpsed a scattering of green buds, and a few pink and lavender blossoms. The scent of the blossoms rose to her nostrils. *Life is returning here,* Windrush said approvingly.

It was Ar who voiced surprise. *So soon?*

I suspect it never really was gone, Windrush said. *It was sup-*

pressed by the spell-making, by the twisting and straining of the underweb of our world. I guess in time it truly would have died.

Will this happen all over the realm? Jael asked.

Windrush rumbled. *Would that it were so, but how can we know? We have gained one victory against the powers of Tar-skel. But I doubt he will concede the realm so easily. There will be other battles, perhaps many others. But you have won us a beginning, a new hope at last.* He beat his wings harder, as though stirred by the thought of struggles to come. *I am determined, as my brothers now are determined—and the spirit of my father is strong with us. There will be others, as well. As the iffling said, we have a great deal to do. And yet now, perhaps, we will find . . . a way to the Dream Mountain, wherever it has gone, and seek the counsel and the strength of the draconae.*

Jael nodded. She found herself thinking again of her own father, and realized that for the first time in many years, she was able to think of him with a profound sadness, but without anger. She caught Ar's gaze, but could not read his expression. Leaning closer to the dragon's head, she asked, *Is there anything more that we can do?*

Windrush laughed, and his laughter was as deep as an ocean and as full of pain and joy as his father's had been. *We would always welcome your help, Jael! But I think that this battle is not yours now, but ours. You have your own safety, your own duties, to think of.*

Jael felt her gaze again drawn to Ar's. His lips were crinkled in a weary smile. She had almost forgotten their ship, and their damaged flux-pile, and their cargo that had to be delivered. But Ar had not forgotten.

Windrush seemed to read her thoughts. *We will help you if we can. We will bear you to the edge of the realm and leave you on a path that will carry you back to your own worlds.*

Thank you, Ar murmured, as Jael nodded.

The dragon chuckled. *In your thoughts, long ago, you showed me your intended pathway. We can make the remainder of your journey light, and your way easier. But we must not delay. This land will soon be in turmoil, and it will be no place for riggers.*

As he spoke, Jael wondered, How long had they been in the net without a break, anyway? She didn't know if they could make it to the edge of the realm without resting. She recalled one other time, when a dragon had borne her to the edge of the realm while she'd slept, and she wondered aloud if Windrush would do the same for them.

Indeed. Go and take your resting spell, the dragon answered. *We will do the flying.*

Jael nodded in gratitude. As she turned to speak to Ar, he wavered and disappeared. She looked at Ed. The parrot was sound asleep, cradled against her. Sighing, she reached into the net controls and folded Ed into safe storage. Then, with a farewell wave to the dragons, she, too, withdrew from the net.

Ar was standing at the nose of the bridge, staring at the instruments in the gloom. Jael swung out of her rigger-couch and stood beside him, wondering what he saw in the read-outs. Ar looked at her without speaking; his eyes seemed unfocused, the sparkle that usually graced them, gone. She thought she had never seen him look so tired. "I'm sorry," she said finally. "About all of that."

"Sorry?" Ar murmured.

"I didn't mean for you to have to go through it. I—"

Ar sighed and turned away, leaving her in midsentence. He stopped, looked back, and said, "You were right, Jael. About all of it. Now get some sleep."

Then he walked from the bridge.

Jael stared blankly after him, then wearily followed.

She was awakened from a dead sleep by the trilling of the stabilizer alarm. She met Ar in the hallway, coming from the commons. He was chewing, and he handed her a piece of thick dark bread as he passed on his way to the bridge. He looked remarkably refreshed. "I'll check on it," he said. "Take your time."

She hurried into the lavatory and splashed cold water on her face; then she rushed after Ar.

The net was sparkling with a golden sunrise glow. She found Ar astride Windrush, and Ed perched on Ar's shoulder. The dragon, still flanked by his brothers, was soaring in leisurely circles on an updraft. *I was beginning to think that you would rest forever,* Windrush remarked.

Jael yawned, relieved that there was apparently no emergency. *How did you get through to us? You must have upset our net somehow.*

The dragon answered casually. *I sent my thoughts in search of you. And before long, you were here.*

Ar gestured to the land far below. For the first time, Jael realized that they were at the edge of the mountain range. A vast, verdant plain stretched out before them, and a silvery thread—a winding river—meandered in the direction they were now flying. *They have found a route that'll take us to Eri Nine, where we can put in for repairs,* Ar said.

Rawk! said Ed, flapping his wings. *Fix it! Ed want to fly!*

Jael nodded.

It should be an easy flight for you, Windrush offered.

A lump came to her throat then, and she turned to look behind them. The mountain range of the dragons stretched out in a long grey line across the horizon, beneath a powder blue sky. She thought she saw a glint of red fire in the mountains, perhaps from what had once been the Black Peak, but was now something altogether different. Would it stay that way, as Windrush had wished?

The events of the last shipday spun dizzyingly through her mind.

Windrush, she said, recalling a question that had been troubling her. *You told us that the dragons . . . or at least Tarskel . . .* and her voice quavered a little as she spoke that name . . . *had been expecting us to come see Highwing die. What did you mean by that?* The three dragons looked back and forth at each other, puffing steam. Thinking that they had not understood her question, she continued, *It's just that it amazes me—that we should have come along at just this time, by accident, when we were needed.*

By accident? Wingtouch asked.

Why—yes, Jael said, puzzled. She tried to explain to the dragons how they had happened to come to the mountain range, from an unlikely distance, as a result of the Flux disturbance.

Well, Windrush said. *I cannot say that you are wrong. You might have happened to come at just this crucial moment. But . . .*

Jael looked at Ar, who had a pained-looking expression, though his eyes remained closed. The parrot sitting on his shoulder was turning his head suspiciously one way, then the other. *But what?*

Windrush seemed reluctant to say more, and Wingtouch was silent. It was Farsight who finally spoke. *It was likely no accident. I believe that Tar-skel put a great deal of strength into a spell to twist the underrealm outward in hopes of bringing you here.*

Jael was stunned. *But why?* she whispered. *Why did he care about me?*

He hated you! Wingtouch explained, from the other side. Then he corrected himself with a sigh, *WE hated you. You, most of all—you who entered this realm and drew kindness from a dragon's heart. You who answered the ancient Words. You who challenged the darkness, the darkness he—we!—were quietly drawing over the land. How better to punish you both than to bring you here to stand powerless in witness of Highwing's death?* He snorted a small, unhappy gout of fire.

Indeed they punished me, Jael thought. She missed Highwing sorely, and grieved for him. But what she said was, *It's still hard for me to believe . . . that you could reach into our world, and bring us here from such a distance!* And then she recalled that they had not been in normal-space at the time of the accident; they had been in the Flux. Was such a thing possible, after all? There had been some sort of cataclysm in nearby normal-space. Hadn't there? Glancing at Ar, she could almost hear him wondering, too, if they had analyzed their mishap correctly.

Windrush puffed a diplomatic puff of steam. *In any event, you came. And you broke their spell, when we were afraid to try. You have made the realm tremble, as the Words promised. Whatever might happen to us, the dragons will not soon forget you.*

Jael sighed and looked back again at the mountain range dwindling behind them. Her heart ached with sadness, but also with a surprising feeling of fulfillment. She realized that the dragons were watching her. *I'm afraid that the time has come,* Windrush said, angling his head to peer back at her.

So soon? she whispered, though she knew that it was well past time for them to be completing their own voyage. She saw in Ar's eyes that the urgency of their journey was very much on his mind.

Farsight believes that, very soon, there will be a gathering of those who would oppose us, those who might prefer that we didn't remain in the realm, Windrush said. *We must send you off and return to our haven, until we can locate others who will join with us. We must gather our strength until we can find our way to the draconae, to Dream Mountain.*

Jael leaned forward to gaze into Windrush's luminous green eye. The faceted fire there shone back at her. *Will you be in very great danger because of what we did?* she asked softly.

Windrush answered with low laughter. *No more than we have been in all along. But now we see the danger clearly, and we are stronger than we were. What will happen, we do not know. But you have given us hope. You have shaken the realm and given us our new beginning. Think of us, Jael, but do not fear for us.*

Jael nodded, accepting that.

And now, Jael—and Ar, and Ed—I remind you of my father's vow, which is now my own. Rigger friends . . .

We will return, Jael promised, not glancing at Ar until she realized that, simultaneously, he had spoken the same words.

And you will call, "Friend of Highwing"—?

And Windrush, Jael said.

There was a rumble of smoke from the two other dragons, and the names *Wingtouch* and *Farsight* echoed in the air.

The parrot stirred. *Ed! And Ed!*

Indeed. And we will hear you, and join you if we can, vowed Windrush. *And now, let us carry you high and fast.* And the dragon's powerful wings smote the air, gaining altitude above the plain. Jael and Ar carefully drew the net into the shape of a long-distance glider. And just when it seemed that Windrush would carry them to the uttermost limits of the sky, the dragon loosed a tremendous tongue of fire and thundered, *FAREWELL-L-L-L, RIGGER-R-R-R-S-S!* And the earth below trembled with his cry, and it seemed to go on forever.

As one, Jael and Ar shouted in return and warped the wings of their glider. They lifted smoothly off the dragon's back and reached out to seek the air currents that would take them on a long glidepath toward the Eri Nine starport. Jael looked back to see the dragons circling majestically, watching them depart.

Bye, glizzards—graggons! Ed wailed.

Jael heard laughter on the wind; then the three great dragons turned and flew high and fast back toward the mountain range.

Chapter 29
DRAGON FRIENDS

THEY RIGGED in silence for a long time. Eventually, Ar began humming a dissonant Clendornan tune, while Jael fiddled with the adjustment of the flux-pile. They were operating at about half efficiency, but Windrush had perceived their needs well and set them on a strong, steady course. Judging from the navigational library, they should easily make it to Eri Nine, perhaps within a few shipdays.

In time, Ar stopped humming and turned to Jael. He looked calmer and more relaxed than she had seen him in a long while—or what seemed to her a long while. In fact, it had only been a couple of shipdays since their unwitting entry into dragon space. *I just wanted to tell you that I'm glad,* he said, and there was a glimmer deep in his eyes that seemed almost sorrowful.

Glad it's over? Glad we're still in one piece?

He shook his head and looked out at the valley that stretched before them. They were making a gentle right turn past a white, billowy cloud. *No,* he said. *Glad that it happened. Glad that we went in. I may have spoken hastily when I promised to return. But I'm glad we were there. And glad that you were right.*

Right?

About Highwing. And the others. I apologize, Jael, for not believing you. I hope you'll forgive me.

Yawk. To give. I will. Rark. Ed hopped onto Ar's shoulder and nuzzled his ear.

Jael smiled. *Of course I will. Is that why you're being so quiet?*

Ar stroked the ridge over his left temple, then gently touched the parrot's neck. *Actually . . . I was wondering how we could tell anyone else about this. And my conclusion is, we probably shouldn't.*

Startled, Jael thought about that for a while. *I think . . . I agree,* she said. *I don't see what good it would do for the whole spacing community to know about them.* She imagined the chaos that could result from the dragon realm being invaded by curious riggers. The thought made her shudder.

Actually, it's more that I don't think anyone would believe us, Ar said wryly. *I don't want to be laughed at, any more than you did.*

Chuckling, Jael banked to follow the course of the river below. It didn't matter to her if anyone would believe them—as long as Ar believed. Maybe one day, if she ever saw him again, she would tell Dap. Maybe. In the meantime, they had a lot of flying ahead of them, if they were to carry out their commission for Mariella Flaire.

One day we really ought to talk, you know, Ar said, after a long while.

Jael looked at him curiously. He was starting to look almost melancholy. She wondered if he was feeling a letdown. *Talk? About what?*

About humans. About friendships. About trusting.

She furrowed her brow in uncertainty. *I don't follow.*

Ar hummed a few almost-harmonious bars while he tended to the flying for a moment. *Well . . . just that it seems to me that . . . some things have changed around here. In your thinking, I mean. Am I right? Am I wrong?*

Jael frowned and took a long time in answering. Trusting . . . yes. She'd hardly noticed. The dragons. The ifflings. Ar.

Ed. And even, in a way, her father. *Maybe*, she said finally. *You could be right.* She shrugged. *Give me some time to think about it, okay?*

Okay, Ar murmured. He pressed his mouth into a straight line, staring without moving. Finally she touched him on the arm to make sure he was still conscious. His mouth slowly formed a zigzag.

Jael tickled the parrot's bright green throat and rubbed his beak with her knuckles. Ed made a gurgling sound. *Someday we can talk to your heart's content. But just now, can we do some flying?*

Ar's eyes sparkled a luminous purple. With a decisive nod, he took up his half of the net again, and matched Jael's efforts move for move—and together they reached out for the current that wound, silvery and long, before them.

Afterword

I'd like to thank the people whose assistance and encouragement helped me down the long road that this novel has taken. It began as a novelette, "Though All the Mountains Lie Between," written for the anthology DRAGONS OF DARKNESS, edited by Orson Scott Card. I must thank Jane Yolen for nudging me into writing the story in the first place, and Scott for his enthusiastic reception of it—as well as the editors of *The Science Fiction Times* for showing it first print.

Once published, the story wouldn't let me go. It tugged at me, whispering that it was not yet finished; it was a novel that demanded to be written. Meanwhile, I was preoccupied with another very long novel that took five and a half years to write, followed by several other books. But my editor, Jim Frenkel, had read my dragon story, too—and when I presented him with an outline for a novel, he seized upon it at once. And so began a journey of writing and rewriting (woven chronologically around the writing of several other novels), editing and rewriting, and further polishing, that took five more years before the book was finished. But now you have it in your hands, and much gratitude is due Jim Frenkel for his endless probing of the foundations of the story and offering of suggestions. My agent Richard Curtis had his doubts, but he trusted me when I said it had to be done, and for that I thank him.

I also thank the cover artist, Jael (no relation to the protagonist), who, through a chance meeting at a convention, came to produce the painting that graces the front of this book. I offer, as well, a grateful tip of the hat to Janny Wurts, the illustrator of the original story.

As always, thanks are due to the writing group: Mary Aldridge, Victoria Bolles, Richard Bowker, and Craig Gardner, for encouragement and countless helpful criticisms. And finally, to my wife Allysen, best reader and best friend, who always believed I could do it, even when my own confidence failed. I love you guys, and I couldn't have done it without you.

About the Author

Jeffrey A. Carver is the author of a number of thought-provoking, popular science fiction novels, including *The Infinity Link* and *The Rapture Effect*. His books combine hard-SF concepts, deeply humanistic concerns, and a sense of humor, making them both compellingly suspenseful and emotionally satisfying.

Carver first wrote in his "star-rigger" universe that is the setting for *Dragons in the Stars* in the novel, *Star Rigger's Way*, which was first published in 1978. He currently lives with his family in the Boston area.